W9-CDB-003

F MCGARRITY
McGarrity, Michael.
Residue.

2018
on1035315529   **11/01/2018**

482233678   50793050394153   COM9093859
RESIDUE   CODE39
0022144409   003000   214561L4351795000000

RESIDUE

OTHER BOOKS BY MICHAEL McGARRITY

The Kevin Kerney Novels

Tularosa

Mexican Hat

Serpent Gate

Hermit's Peak

The Judas Judge

Under the Color of Law

The Big Gamble

Everyone Dies

Slow Kill

Nothing but Trouble

Death Song

Dead or Alive

The American West Trilogy

Hard Country

Backlands

The Last Ranch

RESIDUE

MICHAEL McGARRITY

W. W. NORTON & COMPANY

INDEPENDENT PUBLISHERS SINCE 1923

NEW YORK   LONDON

Copyright © 2018 by Michael McGarrity

For information about permission to reproduce selections from this book, write to Permissions, W. W. Norton & Company, Inc., 500 Fifth Avenue, New York, NY 10110

For information about special discounts for bulk purchases, please contact W. W. Norton Special Sales at specialsales@wwnorton.com or 800-233-4830

Manufacturing by Quad Graphics Fairfield
Book design by Daniel Lagin
Production manager: Lauren Abbate

Library of Congress Cataloging-in-Publication Data

Names: McGarrity, Michael, author.
Title: Residue / Michael McGarrity.
Description: First edition. | New York : W. W. Norton & Company, [2018]
Identifiers: LCCN 2018019194 | ISBN 9780393634358 (hardcover)
Subjects: LCSH: Kerney, Kevin (Fictitious character)—Fiction. | Murder—Investigation—Fiction. | GSAFD: Mystery fiction. | Suspense fiction.
Classification: LCC PS3563.C36359 R47 2018 | DDC 813/.54—dc23
LC record available at https://lccn.loc.gov/2018019194

W. W. Norton & Company, Inc., 500 Fifth Avenue, New York, N.Y. 10110
www.wwnorton.com

W. W. Norton & Company Ltd., 15 Carlisle Street, London W1D 3BS

1 2 3 4 5 6 7 8 9 0

For my sister and brother, Joanne Burke and Crockett McGarrity

RESIDUE

It had been a week crammed full of military pomp, award ceremonies, celebrations, informal cocktail parties, and casual get-togethers, all in honor of Brigadier General Sara Brannon, retiring commandant of the U.S. Army Military Police School and commander of the MP regiment. Tonight, the ballyhoo would end with a formal dinner in Sara's honor at the home of the Fort Leonard Wood commanding officer, Major General Thomas Christian Benson, and his wife, Margaret. Then, at the stroke of midnight, she would end her twenty-eight-year career of active service, and Kevin Kerney would finally be able to take her home to Santa Fe without worrying about where her next permanent duty station would be, her next rotation into a combat zone, or a peace-shattering crisis that wiped out family plans.

Ten days ago, Kerney had left their son Patrick at home with his maternal grandparents to help move Sara out of her quarters and get everything packed to ship home, thus allowing the new commandant to move into freshly painted, updated housing. With the moving van on a slow, circuitous route to Santa Fe, making stops for other relocating families along the way, they were living out of suitcases in a modest, unadorned hotel room on the post.

Earlier in the week, Patrick had flown in with Sara's parents on a quick trip to attend the change-of-command ceremony, witness the parade in honor of her retirement, and see her receive the Distinguished Service Medal for exceptional meritorious service as commandant of the army's military police school. It was her second DSM.

Patrick was puffed up with pride about his mom during the various events, shooting pictures and video on his smartphone, which was constantly in need of recharging. When he wasn't roaming the post headquarters areas, he was consuming prodigious amounts of food to fuel his growing five-eight frame.

Sara's parents had taken Patrick to Tucson, where they now lived after selling the family's Montana ranch to Sara's brother. Patrick would stay there during part of his spring vacation until Kerney and Sara came to fetch him. Already an academic year ahead of his fourteen-year-old peers, and showing signs of adolescent rebellion, he had strict orders to mind his manners, follow the rules of the house, and complete all his homework assignments due when classes resumed. Sara figured the boy would be totally spoiled by the time they got him back home.

Her husband lounged in the small armchair jammed into a corner of the less-than-spacious hotel room, chatting about how glad he was they'd finally have one address and Patrick could spend more time with her. About to turn fifty, Sara had more endurance, greater discipline, and better smarts than most, if not all, of the soldiers under her command. She had excelled at all her staff and command postings, and the ribbons for combat deployments on her uniform jacket spoke to her courage under fire. The Silver Star, the third highest military award for heroism, testified to her bravery. Next to it, she wore the Purple Heart for a combat wound sustained in Iraq. In army parlance, she was a warfighter. But above all that, she was the most stunning woman Kerney had ever known.

Keeping up with her had kept him fit. But not fit enough to squeeze into the army uniforms issued to him decades ago during Vietnam. Instead, he wore a new dark blue suit, with a pair of highly polished black cowboy boots and a starched white shirt offset by a black necktie adorned with the Military Police Corps insignia he'd bought at the post exchange. At Sara's request, above his jacket pocket he wore a row of the five miniature medals he'd received for serving in 'Nam, anchored by the Silver Star.

Over the years, Sara had worked hard to convince him to be proud of his military service. He had succumbed to her arguments to the point that his pickup truck now sported a New Mexico veteran's license plate.

She slipped into her jacket, buttoned it, took a last look in the mirror, and turned to face him. "Do I pass muster?"

"You're the baddest, best-looking warfighting general in the whole damn army," he answered.

Sara blew him a kiss. "You're such a romantic. Are you going to behave yourself tonight?"

"I promise not to voice my concern about the top-heavy bureaucracy of generals in the post–draft professional army, present company excluded."

"Thank you."

Her deep green eyes still captivated him, her long, sexy neck showed no sign of aging, and there was only a hint of gray in her strawberry-blond hair. She'd turned down a promotion to major general and a prestigious posting at NATO headquarters in Brussels to return to the ranch and, as she put it, "learn how to cowboy all over again."

He never thought she'd really do it, but now that she had, he couldn't wait to have her home on their spread outside of Santa Fe. But first there was the road trip they had planned through the southern states to New Orleans for a few days before driving back to New Mexico by way of Tucson to pick up Patrick.

It was to be a shortened version of a second honeymoon without the encumbrance of an occasionally lurking and sometimes defiant teenager. They'd been looking forward to it for the past several months.

"Why don't we just leave right after the dinner party?" she suggested. "Tom Benson is an early riser and would be glad to see us out the front door before nine. We can drive all night and find a twenty-four-hour diner for a plate of eggs and bacon in the morning, and get a room to crash in for a few hours if we need to. It won't take us more than ten minutes to change, pack, and go."

Kerney loved the idea. "You just want me to stay sober and not talk about how fewer generals would make a better world."

She stuck out her tongue. "I'm serious, wise guy."

"I'm game," he said, standing up. "Let's blow this dump and hang out with some red-blooded American civilians who have no interest in the complexities of modern warfare."

His phone rang before she had a chance to reply. It was an incoming call from Isabel Istee, who almost never contacted him. It had to be important. He hoped nothing serious had happened.

"It's Clayton's mother." He swiped the phone icon and said, "Isabel, how are you?"

"Clayton told me not to call you, but I had to."

"What's wrong? Is someone sick or hurt?"

"No, it's you. The police are coming for you."

Kerney stiffened. "What? Why?"

"They found Kim Ward's remains on the grounds of Erma Ferguson's old home and think you may have killed her. But I don't believe it."

"Jesus." Kerney sank down on the edge of the bed. "Are you certain of this?"

"Clayton told me about it."

"What else do you know?"

"It's all over the Internet. It's being made a big deal that a retired police chief has been accused of murdering someone long before he became a cop."

Kerney shook his head in disbelief. "I don't know what to say. It's crazy."

"Defend yourself, Kerney," Isabel said. "And your family."

"I will." He knew she meant more than Sara and Patrick. "I promise."

He waited for a reply, but the phone went dead. He opened the highlighted message icon on the phone. The text message from Clayton read: *If my mother calls, don't answer.* It had been sent hours earlier. "Crazy," he repeated, staring at the phone.

Sara knelt in front of him. "What is it?"

"I'm about to be arrested for a homicide." He searched for his name under news, and a headline came up: "Retired New Mexico Police Chief Accused of Decades-Old Murder." He gave her the phone.

She read the item and stared intensely at him, her eyes questioning. "Tell me," she demanded.

Without hesitation, he told her about the night Kim Ward disappeared from Erma's home, why she left, and his search to find her. Sara didn't flinch, ask why he hadn't told her about Kim before, or question his innocence.

"What do we do?" she asked.

"I'll go to the local sheriff's office and turn myself in, before deputies and the MPs knock at the door," Kerney said. "You go to dinner with the general and make my excuses."

Sara shook her head. "There is no way I can pull off a charade like that. Any minute, this is going to blow up in our faces. We'll deal with this together. I'll call Tom Benson and explain."

She took the phone from his hand just as flashing emergency lights penetrated the slight opening of the hotel room curtain.

Kerney stood and peeked out. A sheriff's unit and an MP vehicle slowed to a stop at the hotel entrance. "Here they come. What a mess."

Sara shook her head in disagreement as she dialed. "You've always made life interesting, Kerney."

"If you're going to give our regrets, do it quick."

"Tom?" Sara said. "I'm afraid we won't be able to make it."

She listened for a few seconds, thanked him, hung up, and turned to Kerney with worried eyes.

"That was fast."

"He said he understood, and told me to turn on cable news."

"We don't have time for that now," Kerney replied as the sound of hurried footsteps echoed down the tile hallway floor. "Stay where you are."

Heavy pounding at the door ended any further conversation. He opened it and stepped back, arms raised, as two deputies burst into the room, nine-millimeters aimed at his chest. Two embarrassed MPs blocking the doorway looked away from Sara, who stood motionless, hands visible and empty, her face a mask of composure.

The lead deputy holstered his weapon and said, "Kevin Kerney, you're under arrest for the murder of Kimberly Ann Ward."

Kerney was devastated. One of the most important days in Sara's life had turned to shit.

EIGHT
DAYS
EARLIER

CHAPTER I

In a sour mood, Lieutenant Clayton Istee, deputy commander of the New Mexico State Police Southern Zone Investigation Unit, slipped behind the wheel of his unmarked unit, cranked the engine, keyed the radio, and reported on duty to dispatch. On an early April morning, he'd been called into work just as he and his wife, Grace, were about to start a three-day getaway to celebrate their twentieth wedding anniversary. The trip was now delayed, if not ruined, because the Spanish ambassador to the United States was visiting Santa Fe on holiday, and Governor Javier Alejandro Vigil had impulsively invited the diplomat to accompany him to a groundbreaking ceremony for New Mexico State University's Erma Fergurson Artist-in-Residence Center.

The governor, the ambassador, Lieutenant Joe Castellano, the state police supervisor in charge of the governor's security, and Castellano's team would fly down to Las Cruces later in the day to attend the early evening gala event.

The governor's off-the-cuff invitation to the Spanish diplomat had started a chain reaction that quickly rippled down from the governor's chief of staff to the chief of the state police, a descending series of senior headquarters officers, and finally landing in Clayton's lap, with orders to provide additional security for the ambassador.

There was no compelling reason Clayton knew of that Ambassador Ramon Francisco de Cardenas needed to be protected. If there was a credible threat to a foreign diplomat on U.S. soil, the FBI would be fully mobilized and shouldering everybody out of the way long before they'd invite the state police to participate—as little more than observers.

Still, Clayton took his orders seriously. By radio, he called two agents with dignitary protection experience to assist him. Together they'd conduct a security inspection of the center and immediate grounds, coordinate with campus police to make sure everyone entering the event was screened, and protect the ambassador from the time he arrived until his departure.

Paul Avery and James Garcia were experienced agents who worked directly under his command. Total professionals, neither groused about the callout. On a back channel, he gave them a brief rundown on the assignment and told them to meet him at district headquarters ASAP.

Avery wanted to know if it was the real deal or some sort of training exercise. Clayton said he didn't have a clue, but would find out.

With unhappy Grace standing at the front door, Clayton waved and beeped his horn as he backed out of the driveway of his Las Cruces home. He shared her disappointment. With their two kids, Wendell and Hannah, living at home while attending college at NMSU, there was little privacy in their busy lives, and they'd been eagerly looking forward to some time alone together.

Clayton had read about the gala in the Sunday paper. Erma Fergurson had been an NMSU art professor and nationally acclaimed landscape artist. Prior to her death, she donated her home and its extensive grounds to the university, along with a substantial endowment to turn the property into a visiting artists' residence and fund a lecture series, seminars, and workshops on the nearby campus.

From its inception, the Erma Fergurson Artist-in-Residence Program had brought a succession of distinguished artists to NMSU for an academic year, attracted by the beauty of the house, a generous financial stipend, and the steady growth in Fergurson's posthumous reputation as an artist. No artist invited to participate had ever turned down the honor, or complained about its rather modest teaching duties, which included an undergraduate seminar and one free special event for the public.

The NMSU administration had recently decided to leverage the Erma Fergurson Center into a small artists-in-residence colony that could be a hub for high-profile seminars at the School of Fine and Applied Arts. With the successful completion of a fund-raising effort, the university was about to break ground on three new studio residences for visiting artists. University and community officials quoted in the *Las Cruces Sun-News* predicted that the expanded center would attract world-class artists, writers, philosophers, and thinkers, and put Las Cruces on the map as a vibrant travel destination. Additionally, it would boost NMSU's appeal to out-of-state and foreign students, who paid more in tuition and fees than in-state residents.

While Clayton liked the sound of it, he wasn't quite ready to believe that an intellectual and artistic renaissance in Las Cruces would replace the boot-scootin' country mentality of the average citizen.

He'd never visited the center. But he knew that as an undergraduate his father, Kevin Kerney, had rented a small apartment from Professor Fergurson. And it was at NMSU where he'd met Clayton's mother, Isabel, one of the first Apache women to enroll at New Mexico State.

If not for a long-ago fluke encounter on the Mescalero Reservation in the Sacramento Mountains east of Las Cruces, Clayton wouldn't have known anything at all about Erma Fergurson or Kevin Kerney, because his mother had never told him who his father was.

A tribal conservation police officer at the time, living on the rez with Grace and their two young children, he'd cited two Anglos for trespassing. Kerney, the deputy chief of the state police, had flashed his credentials, hoping to avoid the citation. Clayton wrote him up anyway and thought nothing of it until a few days later, when Kerney confronted Clayton's mother and forced her to reluctantly admit that he was Clayton's father.

When Clayton learned the truth, he wasn't at all pleased. The whole sticky mess of having a father he didn't need or want in his life, and a mother who'd lied to him for years about some Anglo college boy knocking her up and disappearing, unsettled him. In fact, it pissed him off.

In quiet moments of reflection, it still did at times. But not today. Today, he was curious to see the place where he'd most likely been conceived. Most people wouldn't give it a second thought, but as an Apache, a member of a nomadic nation of people defined by the very ground that they walked, it was part of Clayton's tradition.

He wondered why he'd never thought to visit the place before. Perhaps he'd let himself slide too far into the White Eyes' world.

Over the years, he'd heard bits and pieces of the story. How Isabel, pregnant and about to graduate as a nurse with a bachelor's degree, had been forced by her Apache parents to dump Kerney. And how Kerney, not knowing she was pregnant and eager to get his ROTC commission and fight in Vietnam before the war ended, had given up trying to win her back.

In Clayton's mind, both parties were guilty of poor judgment, although he still vacillated about who pissed him off more, his mom for not telling Kerney the truth, or Kerney for not being sharp enough to figure out why she'd abruptly rejected him.

It was certainly a different take on the old "love is blind" cliché. He figured they were two people who had simply baffled each other.

Most of the time it was ancient history and didn't matter. Life, his job, and his family intervened big-time. He rarely saw Kerney, who lived with his family on a ranch up in Santa Fe, and his visits home to the rez to see his mother, now retired and busy traveling the world, were becoming more and more infrequent.

Clayton shook off the memories as he pulled into the district office parking lot. Only Captain Luis Mondragon's marked unit was outside the front of the building. If there was a serious, imminent threat to the safety of Ambassador Ramon Francisco de Cardenas, every sworn officer on duty would have been assembled.

In his office, Mondragon leaned back in his desk chair, with his trophy wall behind him, and shook his head in response to Clayton's question. "There's no known threat to the ambassador. And it's not a training exercise, it's politics."

Divorced, with his ex-wife remarried and living in Albuquerque, Mondragon had three passions: his job, weight lifting, and riding his Harley. When he got suited up to ride, he easily passed for a biker. All he lacked were club colors.

"What politics?" Clayton asked. "The governor's supposed to be a shoe-in for reelection."

"The Spanish ambassador's visit is a great opportunity to show off Vigil's statesmanlike potential," Mondragon said, sounding more like a political analyst than a cop. "The protection detail gives the event today some additional media razzamatazz, and will help put him in the national spotlight. Besides it's good, free publicity before the primary."

Mondragon wasn't engaging in idle speculation. He had a direct pipeline to his brother-in-law, a former sports reporter for an Albuquerque television station who was currently serving as Governor Vigil's press secretary.

"You almost sound like you know what you're talking about, Cap," Clayton joked.

Mondragon ran a hand over his almost totally bald head and grinned. "You didn't hear it from me."

The handheld radio sitting on Mondragon's desk announced the arrival of Agents Avery and Garcia. He pointed at his office door. "Your team is here. Go forth and protect the honorable Spaniard. And when you get home, tell Grace I'm sorry your wedding anniversary trip got loused up."

"She holds you personally responsible."

"Ouch," Mondragon said with a fake grimace.

———

Paul Avery and James Garcia were complete opposites in appearance. Garcia, short, stocky, barrel-chested, with a dark complexion, was Mexican-American, but looked more Apache than Clayton. Avery, as lanky and lean as a long-distance runner, had movie-star good looks, with high cheekbones and deep-set brown eyes. Appearances aside, both men shared a real love for their jobs. Nothing was more satisfying to them than getting the bad guys off the streets. They were exactly the kind of cops Clayton wanted working for him.

He intercepted Avery and Garcia in the reception area of the district office, ran down the assignment, and gave them the skinny on why the Spanish ambassador suddenly needed dignitary protection.

As they walked to their units, Avery laughed. "Politics. Now it makes sense. I Googled the guy looking to see if he was involved in some kind of political controversy, or was a member of the royal family or something, but found nothing."

Clayton shrugged. "Let's keep him safe anyway."

"Do you think we can?" Garcia deadpanned.

With Avery and Garcia following, Clayton led the way on the

drive through the foothills, soon leaving the pavement and following a bumpy, dusty county road to the turnoff to the center, a gently winding, freshly graveled lane bordered by mature desert willow and New Mexico locust trees swaying in the slight April morning breeze.

A quarter of a mile in, the center came into view. The adobe house had sharp, clean lines and a typical flat pueblo-style roof with a low parapet that anchored it to the land. The tan stucco blended with the scrubby, rock-strewn foothills. The needle-like spires of the Organ Mountains towered behind on the eastern horizon.

A row of tall, southwest-facing windows looked out on the sprawling city of Las Cruces. Ever-expanding subdivisions peppered the foothills, and the city now crowded the green ribbon of the Rio Grande Valley. A good distance away on the northeast side of the house, a pine tree windbreak protected a fenced, fallow garden accessed by a pea-gravel walkway.

Large boulders and extensive rockwork accented a circular driveway in front of the house. Stands of bear grass, Apache plume, and three-leaf sumac, artfully placed among the boulders, splashed a soft green against the hardscape. Interspersed were beds of pale yellow ground cover that nestled up against the rocks.

All in all, it was a spectacular place, in its day probably one of the most expensive houses in the entire county.

Kerney had once spoken to Clayton of Fergurson as his mother's best friend and his surrogate aunt. Never married, she'd amassed a fortune thanks to the increasing prices her paintings commanded, and her astute investments. Kerney had inherited a northern New Mexico ranch from Fergurson, which had ultimately made him financially well off.

Clayton had never given any of it serious thought. Seeing the house, he realized that Erma had made herself one very rich lady.

Two vehicles were parked outside, a landscaper's pickup truck with a magnetic sign on the driver-side door, and a commercial van with a broom, mop, and bucket painted on both side panels. A man at the corner of the house worked at smoothing out a gravel pathway with a rake, while a woman on a stepladder busily washed the southwest-facing windows.

Clayton called in their arrival to dispatch, and as they approached the front door an older woman in her fifties stepped outside to greet him. Wearing jeans and a long-sleeved pullover, she stood framed in the open doorway, looking somewhat testy.

No more than five-three, she had short brown hair, an oval face, and carried a few extra pounds around the waist.

"I was called and told you were coming," she said with a frown. "Is this absolutely necessary?"

"I'm Lieutenant Istee," Clayton replied with a smile, ignoring her question and displaying his credentials. "Agents Avery and Garcia will be assisting me. Are you Cynthia Davenport?"

In the face of Clayton's civility, Davenport's expression softened slightly. "Yes, I'm the director of the center, but really I don't see the need for all of this."

Clayton nodded sympathetically. "I understand, but the ambassador's attendance at the event requires more security than usual. We'll try not to be too intrusive."

Davenport's expression lightened a bit more. She stepped aside and gestured for the officers to enter. "I'd appreciate that. What do you need to do?"

Clayton didn't immediately respond. On a table inside the foyer sat a model of what the center would look like upon completion. The hideaway estate in the foothills was about to be transformed into a compound with a sunken amphitheater separating the new studios from the original residence, all echoing the mid-1950s feel of the place.

He told Davenport he liked the look of it, which earned him a small smile, and asked for a copy of the evening's program, the guest list, and the names of the vendors hired for the event. He explained they would first do a thorough visual inspection of the house and immediate grounds, to be followed by a wider perimeter search.

"We'll need access to every room," Clayton added.

Davenport's sour look returned. "How long will it take? I have people coming to set up for the ceremony, caterers arriving later—there's so much to do."

Clayton glanced into the long living room, empty of any furnishings, with a wide tile floor. Opposite the windows overlooking the city, a low rectangular fireplace without a mantelpiece or a visible chimney was nestled in the wall. On a sidewall that led to the kitchen, linen cloth covered what Clayton assumed to be either a framed picture or a plaque.

"We'll work as quickly as we can," he replied.

With a curt nod, Davenport disappeared into the kitchen and quickly returned with a key ring and some papers, which she handed to Clayton before excusing herself to make some phone calls.

Clayton divided up the tasks. He would do a walk-through of the premises, Avery got the grounds, and Garcia would start checking the guests and vendors.

Garcia frowned as he paged through the guest list. "Besides the governor and ambassador, there are two hundred names on this list, including most of the local politicians, university big shots, government officials, and even the commanding general of White Sands Missile Range. Maybe you should call out more troops."

Clayton shook his head. "We're not here to protect two hundred people, just the ambassador."

"I was only trying to make things more interesting," Garcia said with a smile.

"What else have you got?" Clayton asked, shaking his head in mock dismay.

Garcia scanned the vendor, media, and caterer list. "Three TV stations are sending remote satellite broadcast trucks, cameramen, and reporters," he said. "Also, reporters from the Las Cruces, Albuquerque, and El Paso newspapers will be here. Then there's the caterers, servers, cleaners, setup crew, representatives from the construction company, the architectural firm, and so on and so on." He waved the papers at Clayton. "That's a *chinga* lot of folks to run through the system."

Avery gave Garcia a look of feigned disgust and left through the front door.

"Most of the people coming to this party are the elite of Las Cruces," Clayton replied. "Cross out those you know by sight or reputation, and get started on the rest."

"Think I'll find any assassins or domestic terrorists?"

"You never know what will turn up," Clayton replied, as he turned away to track down Cynthia Davenport, who'd failed to provide him with a copy of the program for the groundbreaking ceremony.

He found her standing on the rear portal of the house, talking on her cell phone while gazing across an open swath of cleared ground at a shiny-clean yellow backhoe loader sitting behind an orange mesh construction fence that stretched in a circle for a good fifty yards, completely enclosing it.

A medium-sized piece of heavy equipment, it had a shovel in front to move dirt and backfill, and a bucket in back for digging and trenching. In front of the fence, facing the portal, were six gold-painted garden shovels on a portable rack.

"Is the backhoe out there for show?" Clayton asked, after Davenport took the phone away from her ear.

Davenport gave him a real smile. "Yes and no. After the governor and the other dignitaries dig their symbolic spadeful of dirt, the machine will roar into action for a few minutes, signaling the start of real construction."

"That should be very dramatic," Clayton noted.

Davenport's smile broadened. "That's the whole idea. I had the contractor fence the approximate site of the future amphitheater to keep the guests and media from getting too close. We don't want any accidents or injuries."

"Very smart." Beyond the fencing, a good hundred yards from the house, Clayton could see three sets of survey stakes with pink ribbons fluttering in a light, intermittent breeze, likely designating the placement of the planned studios.

"We'll get great television coverage out of it," Davenport replied, sounding pleased with herself.

"I bet you will. Do you have a copy of the program?"

Davenport nodded. "Yes, in my office. I was about to get one for you. You can start your search, or whatever you call it, there."

He followed Davenport around the side of the house to the attached garage, where an exterior staircase led to her office above. As they climbed the stairs he asked her how much land the center owned and learned it was a hundred and sixty acres, all bought by Fergurson over the course of many years.

Davenport ushered him into the front room, a small rectangular space furnished with a desk, chair, and a side table parked next to the front door piled high with copies of the program. A partial wall with a built-in bookcase separated the room from a narrow galley kitchen. The door on the back wall probably led to a bedroom and bath.

This had to be Kerney's apartment, Clayton thought as he tried to envision Isabel and Kerney snuggling on a couch, or sharing a meal in the breakfast nook at the back of the tiny kitchen. Nothing came to him.

Davenport handed him a program. "Do you need to see the rest of the office?"

"Yes, I do." Without waiting for permission, Clayton checked the bedroom, which had been turned into a cramped conference room with a table, chairs, and a fax machine in a corner. The closet was filled with office supplies. The out-of-date bathroom had pale green tile, matching floor linoleum, and a recessed medicine chest behind a mirror above the sink containing some over-the-counter remedies, lipstick, and makeup. The windowsill above the claw-foot bathtub had bottles of shampoo, conditioner, and body lotion. On the shower curtain hung a sleeveless black and ivory dress with a slightly flared skirt. Davenport's outfit for the ceremony, Clayton guessed.

Before returning to the front room, Clayton looked over the program. The governor would arrive at four p.m., and after some face time with the guests he'd unveil a plaque honoring Erma Fergurson and make a few remarks to the assembled guests. The entire party would then move outside to the construction site for the groundbreaking ceremony. Joining the governor would be the president of the university, the president of the NMSU Foundation, the mayor of Las Cruces, the dean of the College of Arts and Sciences, and the local state senator.

Back in the front room, Davenport stood next to her desk talking on the phone. Clayton slipped two copies of the program into the jacket of his sport coat for Avery and Garcia. When she hung up, he asked where the living room furniture had been stored.

"Below my office in the garage," she answered.

He held up the key ring with four keys. "What do these open?"

She explained one was for a shed behind the house that held yard and garden tools, one for a locked kitchen pantry that contained fine china, crystal stemware, and silverware used for special events, one was for the closet in Erma's studio that held her work that wasn't on display, and one was for the garage.

"Please don't disturb the studio in the house," she asked. "I've had it carefully staged to look just the way it did when Professor Fergurson lived here."

"I'll be careful," Clayton promised as he left.

———

After five minutes of squeezing around looking under the Danish modern living room furniture stacked in the garage and examining the half-full cans of paint and boxes of screws and nails on the built-in shelves along the back wall, Clayton locked the door and went looking for Garcia, who was sitting in his unit busily entering names in the computer.

"No hits on dangerous people yet," he commented with a bored sigh.

Clayton handed him a program through the open unit window. "Keep trying. There has got to be at least one lawbreaker on those lists we can arrest."

"Jesus, I hope so," Garcia called out as Clayton turned away.

In the living room, Clayton discovered portable rectangular tables had been set up in front of the bank of windows, along with a podium positioned by the fireplace. On the walls were four of Erma Fergurson's oil paintings, each one with a typed label next to it describing the scene and year it was painted.

Fergurson used heavy, repetitive brushstrokes in her work, and Clayton had to stand back from the landscapes to see them clearly. They had a vibrancy that drew him in. The one of Hermit's Peak up by Las Vegas in northeastern New Mexico appealed to him the most. He'd hiked to the top of it with Grace and the kids back when Wendell and Hannah were still young enough to enjoy doing things with their parents.

Clayton peeked behind the linen veil on the sidewall that separated the living room from the kitchen. The bronze plaque honoring Fergurson consisted of a relief profile of her as a mature woman. Inscribed on it were the years of her tenure at the university, the distinctive signature she used to sign her paintings, and a brief statement honoring her talent and generosity.

Fergurson's studio was down a short passageway off the living room. Soft light poured in from two large windows that framed the tall spires of the Organ Mountains. An unfinished watercolor sat on an easel, pencil drawings were haphazardly arranged on top of a large print table, art books were stacked on an old Spanish Colonial writing desk, and a paint-splattered artist's smock was draped over the arms of a tattered upholstered easy chair. There were tubes of paint on a small side table next to the easel, along with several wadded-up rags.

Clayton gave Davenport credit for a good staging job. The studio looked like Fergurson would appear at any moment.

He unlocked the closet, which held two dozen or more large framed Fergurson landscapes. He'd seen no evidence of an alarm or security system in the building and wondered what kind of insurance the center carried. Any wannabe criminal who knew what he was looking for could easily break open the closet door and make off with valuable paintings, many worth six figures each.

He finished his sweep with a plain-view inspection of the two bedrooms and the adjoining bathrooms, stepped onto the rear portal, and called Grace to tell her he'd be home in plenty of time to take her to dinner at her favorite restaurant.

"The governor and the ambassador are due to leave here at five," he added. "We can still celebrate our anniversary. Go ahead and make reservations for us."

"Are you sure?"

"Yeah, this is all political theater."

"The bed-and-breakfast in Santa Fe is holding our room."

"We'll leave early in the morning."

"I was hoping you'd say that. I love you."

Clayton smiled at the thought of being alone with Grace. "Me, too. I'll be home after five."

He disconnected just as Paul Avery came around the corner of the building.

Avery pointed over his shoulder with a thumb. "There's a locked shed back there."

Clayton tossed him the key ring. "Did you check the backhoe?"

"It's clean, no bomb or explosives. In fact, everything appears perfectly normal. I don't think the ambassador has anything to worry about."

"Finish up, return the keys to Davenport, and meet me at your unit."

"What's next?"

"We'll take a ride together around the property. You drive. I'll ride shotgun."

Avery twirled the key ring on his index finger. "Ten-four."

———

There were several old jeep trails on the land that put the suspension on Avery's unmarked unit to the test.

"We should have taken *your* vehicle," he grumbled as the right front tire bounced in and out of a gully that cut across the rutted trail.

Too busy looking for signs of human activity, Clayton didn't respond. Considered the best tracker in the department, he conducted an annual training session at the law enforcement academy in Santa Fe to teach the basics of reading sign and tracking fugitives.

So far, all he'd spotted were one rusted can and the stump of a juniper tree cut down years ago with a hand ax. Several times he had Avery stop so he could get out and look around. He found an abandoned coyote den on a slope under a rock ledge and a shredded truck tire partially covered by dirt, home to an active ant nest.

It was time-consuming, but Clayton knew better than to let down and lose concentration. That's when bad things could happen, especially to cops.

After two hours, he decided he'd seen enough of nothing and ended the sweep. They left the property through an old ranch gate that accessed a county road, drove to town, stopped at a burger joint near the university, ordered takeout, and took it back to the center, where they corralled Garcia, who'd just finished clearing all the vendors' employees. With Davenport's permission, they ate lunch in her office.

Clayton didn't mention it was the very place where his mother and father had hooked up decades ago. Besides, Garcia and Avery were too busy eating their burgers and arguing about which baseball teams would make it to the World Series in the fall.

He put his half-eaten burger away and called Liz Waterman, chief of the NMSU Police Department. She said her officers would direct traffic to the entrance of the center, staff a control point there, verify the occupants of cars, visually screen all vehicles before allowing entry, and manage parking on the grounds. Six campus officers would be on scene two hours before the event began. Clayton thought the plan more than adequate, and was pleased he didn't have to ask Luis Mondragon to send uniforms to help.

He left Avery and Garcia debating a World Series yet to happen, sidestepped caterers unloading vans, and walked to the fenced garden, which badly needed weeding and tilling. At the far end stood an old gray wooden bench, with sturdy arms and a spindle back. A carved inscription on the top rail read IN MEMORY OF MATTHEW & MARY KERNEY—Clayton's paternal grandparents. He wondered if Kerney had made it.

He sat on the bench and gazed at the house and the southerly hills beyond, the angle of the sun low in the cloudless sky, heating up the day. It was clear and calm enough to see a trace of distant farmland that bordered the Rio Grande and dwindled away to nothing north of El Paso.

Clayton glanced at his wristwatch. Two hours to go before the guests, governor, and ambassador arrived. It was that in-between time when not much happened. As he started back to the center, he cautioned himself to stay alert.

———

Half an hour before the start of the festivities, all was in order and ready to go. Long tables draped in white linen positioned in front of the living room windows held covered trays of finger food, disposable plates and utensils, bottles of wine, plastic glasses, and elaborately decorated confections. Next to the fireplace stood a portable podium complete with a built-in speaker and microphone.

Outside, three TV satellite trucks were parked on the south side of the house, where Avery and Garcia had conducted inspections of the vehicles, mostly to amuse themselves.

By four o'clock, virtually all two hundred well-dressed guests had arrived and gathered in clusters inside and outside the center, chatting, strolling, drinking, and nibbling.

Clayton studied faces, looking for people who seemed nervous or distracted, a stray loner on the fringe of the crowd, or someone loitering where the VIP cars would arrive. He didn't count on appearances to trigger suspicion; perps came in all varieties. Today, there wasn't a person in sight who set off warning bells.

When Davenport, dressed in her black-and-ivory sleeveless dress, announced the governor and the ambassador would be twenty minutes late, it didn't dampen anyone's spirits.

Twenty minutes later as promised, Governor Vigil and Ambassador Francisco de Cardenas arrived, causing a stir of excitement as folks surged toward the car. They came out of the backseat smiling, the ambassador first, tanned and sporting a neatly trimmed mustache and a full head of salt-and-pepper hair, followed by the governor, tall in his mid-fifties with brown hair, broad shoulders, and the athletic build of a former college running back.

Avery and Garcia quickly formed up and moved within arm's reach of the ambassador, while Joe Castellano and his team forged a path for the governor, who paused here and there, shaking hands and chatting his way toward the front door. Ambassador Cardenas kept pace, greeting guests with smiles and handshakes. Video cameras recorded, smartphone cameras flashed, shutters clicked, and TV reporters talked into their microphones as the two men inched their way inside.

In the living room, Clayton stayed near the front door. Joe Castellano soon joined him. A little over six feet, Joe was taller than Clayton and had a friendly smile that masked a tenacious competitiveness. Clayton had no doubt Castellano would someday be chief of the state police.

"Why the special handling for the ambassador?" he asked, wondering if there was anything else to the story Luis Mondragon had told him.

Castellano shrugged. "The governor wants to be a senator, but figures he's six years out. Next stop, if he plays his cards right, may be ambassador to the United Nations, then the Senate. Didn't Mondragon fill you in?"

"Not the specifics," Clayton replied.

"Now you know," Joe said as he scanned the crowd around the governor.

Meeting and greeting was what Governor Javier Alejandro Vigil did best. He had a knack for making folks feel he was truly listening to them. He introduced Francisco de Cardenas to the ranking university officials and local business leaders, and glad-handed everybody who sought him out. When the time came for his remarks, he ignored the podium, unveiled the plaque honoring Erma Fergurson, said a few words about her vision and generosity, and thanked all those assembled who'd helped to make the expansion of the center possible.

It took Davenport a few minutes to corral all the VIPs for the groundbreaking ceremony but soon she had them trooping outside with the governor. The guests followed, spilling off the portal onto the grounds.

Clayton checked the time and smiled. He'd get home early enough to shower and change before taking Grace out to dinner.

On the other side of the temporary orange construction fence, the backhoe rumbled into position behind the governor and the assembled VIPs, all with shovels in hand. In unison, they dug into the earth and discharged their ceremonial duty to much applause.

On cue, as the governor and VIPs turned to watch, the backhoe operator swung the bucket, lowered it, and dug into the ground, quickly depositing the dirt in a pile behind the fencing. He swung the bucket back, dug deeper, and repeated the operation. As the bucket swung into everyone's view with a third scoop of rocks and earth, the backhoe exposed part of a human skull wrapped in a fragment of cloth.

Shield in hand, Clayton ran forward yelling at the operator to stop, but it was too late. The skull, cloth, and what looked like a lower arm attached to a hand spilled onto the pile, completely covered over by the dirt.

Behind him, Clayton heard the crowd gasp as the backhoe operator shut down the machine. Clayton gazed unhappily at the mound of dirt, hoping the bones might be from some ancient burial. But until he knew differently, he had a homicide on his hands and hours of hard work ahead. He called Grace and apologetically told her to cancel their dinner reservation.

CHAPTER 2

It took two days of careful excavation to uncover all the residue of the skeletal remains from the burial site. Nobody, other than the news media, was happy about it, and Clayton caught the brunt of crabbiness coming from Santa Fe.

During the little time he spent at home to sleep and change his clothes, Grace had fallen silent. Her disappointment about their ruined anniversary trip cut deep. At the center, Cynthia Davenport constantly hovered outside the crime scene barrier, repeatedly asking members of the forensic team when they would be finished. Finally fed up, Clayton escorted her away and banned her from further loitering.

The general contractor, David Michael Jones, owner of DMJ Construction, nervously came and went, mumbling about lost job time. And by way of Luis Mondragon, Clayton learned the governor wasn't pleased that his opportunity to look like potential ambassadorial timber had gotten so screwed up.

All of it got synthesized into one very unambiguous message from state police headquarters in Santa Fe: clear the case ASAP.

The fact that the body had been in the ground for decades, that an old, rusted nineteenth century pistol had been found with the skeleton, and that there were entry and exit wounds from a bullet to the head, made that scenario unlikely. Additionally, the backhoe had severed the skeleton in half and shattered bones into shards, making evidence-gathering more time-consuming. Technicians were painstakingly reconstructing the skull, which was seriously damaged when the contents of the bucket had been dumped.

Nevertheless, the evidence gathered so far raised Clayton's hopes slightly. Analysis showed that the victim was a young Caucasian female, probably in her twenties. She had been wrapped in a blanket before being buried in a shallow grave less than twenty-five yards from the house, which meant the body had been moved from the original crime scene.

The cloth fragments found at the site were a combination of natural and synthetic fibers, which suggested, regardless of the presence of the old pistol, that the murder had been relatively recent, perhaps no more than fifty or sixty years ago. But that didn't rule out the possibility that the skeleton was very old, and along with the antique handgun had been wrapped in the more recent blanket and reburied. Fortunately, the need to bring in a forensic anthropologist proved unnecessary when the skull revealed dental work that conclusively put the victim in the modern era.

All that didn't ease Clayton's mind. In many homicides, especially cold cases, the crimes remained unsolved. Notwithstanding advances in technology and science, little had happened to change that unpleasant fact. Despite daunting odds against a successful arrest and prosecution, Clayton wasn't about to give up.

As he gazed at the tract of land that had been cleared and graded by the contractor prior to the groundbreaking ceremony, he wondered what it looked like before being scrubbed down to bare ground. He

glanced at the house. Why would a killer bury a victim close to a residence, heightening the risk of discovery? Or at the time of the murder
had the house even existed?

Clayton went looking for Davenport, found her in her office, and
learned that Erma Fergurson had built and moved into the house
in 1966.

"What did the land look like before the contractor cleared it for
the groundbreaking ceremony?" he asked.

"It was very rocky, with several sotol plants here and there," she
said. "Also, there were some boulder-size rocks, lots of mesquite, and
some old dead juniper trees, one of them huge."

"That's all? No structures or stand of trees?"

"No."

"Was the area used for anything?"

Davenport shook her head. "Not that I know of. None of the walking trails on the property go in that direction."

Clayton asked her to make a sketch of it.

"I doubt it would be very accurate," Davenport replied.

"Whatever you can remember will be very helpful."

Davenport quickly drew a rough map and handed it to Clayton.
In addition to the placement of several large boulders at the far corner
of the site, it showed a large dead juniper tree close to the spot where
the backhoe had revealed the human skull.

Clayton pointed to the juniper. "Are you sure before the site was
cleared the juniper tree was here?"

"Yes, I am. I remember it clearly because it died three or four years
ago and lost all its needles. I'd look out from the portal and think it
needed to be cut down. I just never got around to having it done."

"Thank you." Clayton folded the sketch and put it in his shirt pocket.

"When can we start construction?" Davenport asked.

"I'm going to talk to the contractor now," Clayton said, sidestepping the question. Outside, he told Garcia and Avery to have the crime scene techs go over every inch of the cleared ground once more, looking for anything that caught their eye, and drove to the office of DMJ Construction.

The construction yard sat south of town on a state road that featured feedlots, clusters of run-down houses, and the shuttered remains of failed roadside businesses, closed years ago because of the completion of the nearby interstate highway. Enclosed by a chain-link fence, the two-acre yard contained a modular office on concrete supports, several large toolsheds, and an old semi truck-trailer presumably used for storage.

Heavy equipment, dump trucks, and pickups littered the lot, haphazardly parked among the piles of rock and gravel, stacks of rebar and lumber, and an old conveyor that fed raw material to a separator. A junk pile of old tires, discarded wire spools, miscellaneous broken engine parts, and empty oil drums sat in the far corner of the lot in sharp contrast to the stark uplift of the distant Organ Mountains.

Clayton found Jones in a small office of the modular building. Five-eight, he had big round eyes and upwardly slanted eyebrows that made him look always surprised at something. He immediately wanted to know if he could put his people to work.

"Not quite yet," Clayton replied. Sitting across from Jones at a tiny, very dusty desk, he showed him Davenport's sketch and asked if she'd gotten the tree location correct.

"I'd say so."

"Did you walk the land before you cleared it?"

"Yeah, the whole site, twice."

"Did you see anything out of the ordinary? Trash? Old tires? Beer cans? Anything a person might have left behind?"

Jones scratched his chin. "Nothing like that, but there was an old rock campfire pit. It hadn't been used in years, but I knew what it was right away."

"How did you know?"

"I do a lot of deer hunting in season. It was man-made, for sure."

"Where was it?"

"Near the dead juniper."

"What did you do with the material you removed from the site?" Clayton asked.

"Hauled it here and separated what I could."

"And the trees?"

Jones nodded in the direction of the window behind Clayton. "In the yard, behind the gravel. I've got a guy coming to grind the smaller branches into mulch and cut up the rest for firewood I'll sell in the fall."

Clayton got to his feet. "Let's go look."

Jones led the way past the mounds of gravel, rock, and dirt, each at least twenty feet tall. Unless Clayton used an earthmover and had a squad of techs sifting through all of it by hand for weeks, whatever might be hiding there of value to the investigation was simply beyond his reach.

The dead junipers had been knocked down, loaded in pieces on a truck, and dumped along the fence. With Jones's help, Clayton pushed aside the branches partially covering the largest of the dead junipers to get a better look at it. Where it had snapped off at the stump, he did a rough tree ring count, and gauged it to be at least a hundred and fifty years old.

Under the bark of a four-inch-thick branch, a neatly coiled pattern protruded, as though something had been deliberately wrapped around it and become encased under the bark. Perhaps it was nothing more than a piece of baling wire twisted around the limb for some reason. Years ago on the rez, Clayton had come upon a tree that had virtually engulfed a small No Trespassing sign, so he knew such oddities were possible. He ran his hand over the pattern, backed off, and took a closer look. It looked and felt less substantial than baling wire.

"What is it?" Jones asked.

"I don't know," Clayton replied. "But I'd like to take this branch with me."

Jones sawed the branch off at the trunk, trimmed it into a four-foot length, and handed it to Clayton. "When can I get my people started on the job?"

He tucked the branch under his arm and started for his unit. "Tomorrow morning."

Jones smiled. "Great. Think you'll actually solve the case?"

"Officially, I can't comment, but I'm damn sure gonna try."

"Good luck with it."

"Yeah, thanks. Call me if you dig up any more bodies."

"I've got your number on speed dial," Jones replied.

———

In Clayton's absence from the center, a dust devil had swept through the job site, coating the crime scene vehicles and unmarked units with a sheen of dirt. He found Avery and Garcia, both sporting crusty faces, on the rear portal of the center with a rusted motor oil can peppered with bullet holes and a crumpled, empty cigarette package—the total haul from the latest sweep. He handed Avery the branch from the juniper tree and asked Garcia to tell the crime scene team to wrap it up and head out.

"Now the hard work starts," he added.

"What's the stick for?" Avery asked as Garcia hurried off to release the CSI personnel.

"It came from a dead juniper near where the victim was unearthed." Clayton pointed out the coiled pattern. "I want it X-rayed pronto." He handed it to Avery. "If it shows a foreign object embedded in the wood, find somebody, maybe an arborist or a botanist at the university, who can very carefully expose it without causing any damage, if that's possible."

"You got it." Avery swung the branch like a baseball bat.

"Enter it into evidence. I'll do the paperwork later to start the chain of custody."

Avery slapped the limb against his open palm. "This is a first, a dead juniper branch as evidence."

"Any progress with the pistol?" Clayton asked.

"It's a Colt Single Action Army .45, probably very early production model from the 1870s," Avery answered. "The cylinder and ejector housing are rusted to the frame, and we don't have serial numbers yet due to its poor condition. Pristine, it would be worth some big bucks. There's nothing like it in the National Crime Information Center database."

"The murder might predate the NCIC system," Clayton mused.

Avery nodded. "A depressing but likely thought. And because the body was moved, we may never know where the actual killing took place."

Clayton grimaced. There was another obstacle. With an approximate date of death somewhere between the 1960s and the 1970s, they faced a mountain of cold cases to sort through. "Tomorrow, we start with old New Mexico missing persons reports, and then go national if we have to."

Avery waved the juniper branch in the air. "Maybe this is the magic wand that will answer all our prayers."

Clayton grunted noncommittally.

"I'll call if I learn anything," Avery said.

"I'll be waiting." He walked with Avery through the house and veered outside to talk to Davenport, who wasn't in her office. Back at the center, he spotted her in Erma Fergurson's studio, which was now empty of the stage dressing, putting the unfinished watercolor that had been on the easel into the unlocked closet.

"You need a security alarm system," he advised. "And it wouldn't hurt to install closed-circuit TV monitors for the public spaces and the immediate grounds around the house."

"That's coming as part of the construction contract."

"Good. I thought you'd like to know the contractor can start tomorrow."

Davenport smiled happily. "Wonderful."

"Did you personally know Professor Fergurson?" Clayton asked.

Davenport smiled at the memory. "Oh, yes. Years ago, when she fell ill and couldn't work, she hired me as her assistant. Just prior to her death, she recommended to the university that I should be retained as the center's administrator. She was the most intelligent, talented, kind woman I've ever met."

"An impressive woman," Clayton said.

"I greatly admired her."

"I can see that. In all the time you've been here, has anyone come around who seemed odd or caused worry or trouble?"

"You mean like a trespasser or homeless person?"

"Yes, anyone like that," Clayton replied.

"Most people who show up uninvited are simply intrigued by the center and want to know more about it. But there have been a few who tried to camp on the property, which isn't allowed."

Clayton asked her to describe the events and made note of them. She'd called the campus police on one occasion about ten years ago to chase a vagrant away. She couldn't remember the exact year of a similar incident, but it had happened when Erma Fergurson was still alive, and had been handled by a deputy sheriff.

Clayton questioned Davenport more closely about the intruders, but she recalled nothing of value.

He handed Davenport his business card. "If you think of anything at all you haven't told me about those two events, please call."

"I will, Lieutenant."

He thanked Davenport for her time and headed for the office. Now came the fun part of the day, paperwork.

———

Clayton was about halfway through his reports when Avery came into his office and dropped an X-ray envelope on the desk. On his heels, Garcia arrived with the forensic firearm report in hand.

"You go first," Clayton said to Avery as he pulled the film out of the sleeve.

"As I should, being senior in service to Agent Garcia," Avery replied, grinning at Garcia.

Garcia shot him the finger as he sat down.

"Boys, boys," Clayton rebuked, feigning disapproval, as he studied the film.

Avery pointed at the X-ray. "Just as you thought, there's a foreign object embedded beneath the bark. It's definitely metal, type yet unknown, and approximately the thickness of common household string."

He held up his forefingers to show length. "The graduate research assistant at the university who examined the X-ray estimated that uncoiled the object would be about twenty inches long."

"Can he extract it from the wood?" Clayton asked.

"It's beneath what's called the cambia, which are cells between the wood and the bark. Cambia form into something called callus tissue that grows over an injured surface to help it heal." Avery frowned and consulted his notes. "I think I've got that right. Close enough."

"Can he get to it?" Clayton asked.

Avery settled into a chair across from Clayton. "Wood can't be melted, and it's tricky to try to dissolve it, so he's going to whittle out the object."

Garcia raised an eyebrow. "Intact?"

"He made no promises, but he's positive he can recover enough to do a metallurgical analysis."

"Did he have any idea how long ago it was left on the tree?"

"Not yet."

"Okay." Clayton swung his attention to Garcia and held out his hand. "What about the *pistola*?"

Garcia passed the report to Clayton. Forensics had managed to open the cylinder on the Colt .45 single action, find the serial number, and run it through NCIC. There was no record on file that the gun had been stolen, and no fingerprints had been lifted from the weapon. However, the one spent cartridge in the rusted cylinder had yet to be dislodged.

Clayton passed the report to Avery, who quickly scanned it.

"Once they get the cartridge out, they'll dust it for prints," Garcia added.

"Here's hoping," Avery said as he closed the folder and passed it back to Clayton.

Clayton slid the folder in a desk drawer along with the X-ray and turned to Garcia. "Is there any chance Forensics can determine if the entry wound to the head came from a .45-caliber bullet?"

"The techs are still piecing it together. They say we shouldn't count on a definite match and the best we can hope for is a strong possibility. They're working on it."

"That would be better than nothing," Clayton said. "It could be our perp has visited the burial site in the past, perhaps on the anniversary of the crime."

Avery's eyes widened in fake wonder. "A guilt-tripping perp? Wouldn't that be unusual?"

"Which might mean a boyfriend, husband, or lover," Garcia mused hopefully.

"That's possible," Clayton replied. He recounted what Davenport and the contractor had told him, and added that he'd asked the campus police and sheriff's office to conduct record searches for any reports about trespassing at the center. "The dates Davenport gave me are iffy at best, but maybe we'll get lucky," he added.

"If no damage was done, the responding officers could have simply escorted the subjects off the grounds and never filed a report," Avery ventured. "Who wants to bother with a court date for a petty misdemeanor?"

"Some skate who wanted the overtime would," Garcia commented. "But regardless of any circumstantial evidence we get from the records search, a murder victim without an identity means an unsolved case."

"Try to stay optimistic," Clayton counseled dryly. "We know a few things already and we're making progress. Tomorrow we dig in and start the search for our victim's identity. Once we know that, we'll look close to home for our killer."

"Let's hope we get a hit," Avery said.

"That would be nice, but if we strike out we'll expand our parameters," Clayton replied as he swiveled his chair to face the desktop computer and started back in on his paperwork.

With a clear message that it was time for them to do the same, Avery and Garcia retreated from Clayton's office. An hour later, he finished and called home to say he was on his way, only to get voice mail. He left a short message, trying to sound upbeat, hoping Grace would at least talk to him when he got there.

From long experience, he'd learned few things were more unbearable than being on the receiving end of the silent treatment from an Apache woman.

———

That evening, the children kept the family dinner congenial. Hannah's eyes flashed with pride as she shared the exciting news that on a lark she'd made the NMSU women's cross-country track team as a walk-on. She'd been an outstanding track-and-field athlete in high school, so the news came as no surprise. With the slightest hint of pleasure in her voice, she announced that her time in the 5K trial run had bested several other freshman girls who were on athletic scholarships. From across the dining table, Wendell gave his sister a big smile and a high-five.

Clayton followed suit, happy to have Grace distracted enough to stop radiating coolness in his direction.

"I'm very proud of you," Grace said with an approving smile, avoiding Clayton's eyes. "But will you have time to participate and keep your grades up?"

Hannah, who had her mother's slender figure and delicate frame, nodded as she pushed her food around her plate with a fork and selected a green bean. "I'm sure to make the dean's list again."

"My egghead jock kid sister," Wendell joked. At six feet, he had two inches on Clayton, and his pale complexion confused people into thinking he was of Anglo extraction. A starting running back in high school, he'd forgone college athletics to concentrate on his academic studies.

Hannah grinned devilishly at her brother and stuck out her tongue. "Have you gotten accepted into medical school yet?" she needled.

Wendell wrinkled his nose. "You know I can't apply until late next year."

"You'll get in," Hannah predicted as she rose to help clear the table. "After all, you're almost as smart as me."

"Smarter and wiser," Wendell challenged, as he pushed away from the table.

"No quibbling, you two," Clayton cautioned lightheartedly, glancing to see if Grace had warmed toward him at all. Maybe, but he wasn't sure.

He got a kiss on the cheek from Hannah and a fist bump from Wendell before they departed. Grace got kisses, but no fist bump.

Like most young people, Hannah and Wendell were not given to frequent displays of affection, but they knew their mother's occasional chilling silences well. Clayton figured they'd guessed the canceled twentieth wedding anniversary trip had put him in serious disfavor.

Grace didn't say a word as he finished clearing the table, silently watching as he filled the dishwasher. When he turned to apologize once again for ruining their anniversary plans, she waved her hand to stop him.

"When the case is over, let's plan to celebrate someplace where we can't possibly be bothered by work."

"Are you sure you can get time off?" Clayton teased, relieved to have her talking to him once again. As the program director of a bilingual preschool, she could set her own vacation schedule without difficulty.

"I'm serious, Clayton."

He studied her face. It was oval, with tawny, flawless skin, a thin nose, and thick eyebrows above dark eyes. She never failed to stun him with her beauty. "Where would you like to go?"

"Spain."

"I can see you've given this some thought."

Grace nodded. "Just the two of us. Wendell and Hannah can cope on their own for a week or two. In fact, they'll enjoy being rid of us for a while."

"Two weeks in Spain?" Clayton hadn't considered foreign travel. But Spain would be a good choice, as they both spoke the language.

"Why not?" Grace countered. "I don't want to wait until I'm your mother's age to see something of the world outside of New Mexico."

"Will this get me out of the doghouse?"

"You were never in it. My disappointment turned to anger, which you did not deserve. I fell silent because I wasn't able to talk to you about it in a good way."

"I was disappointed too," Clayton said, gathering Grace in his arms. "Let's go to Spain next April."

"Promise?"

"With all my heart."

"We could still celebrate a little in our bedroom, if you like," Grace whispered in his ear.

Clayton heard the front door slam as Wendell and Hannah left for the weekly evening meeting at the American Indian Student Center.

"I like," Clayton said, pulling her along by the hand.

CHAPTER 3

Clayton arrived at work early and found a message from Dav-enport asking him to call. She told him Erma Fergurson had periodically kept a journal, which, along with other documents, letters, and ephemera, she'd donated during her lifetime to the university library. Davenport didn't know what the old journals contained, but thought they might be helpful to his investigation.

"Why didn't you tell me about the journals when we talked after the remains were uncovered?" he asked.

"With the distraction of getting construction under way, I simply didn't think about it," she replied.

He thanked her for the information and called the library. Although it opened early during the academic year to accommodate students, the archives department supervisor, Eleanor Robbins, didn't start work until nine. He left a short message on her voice mail, identifying himself and saying he needed her assistance regarding urgent police business.

An hour later, Avery and Garcia rolled in just as he was about to leave to find Ms. Robbins. He directed Avery to goose the sheriff's department and the campus PD about the records check, and asked Garcia to get him an update from the lab on the cartridge lodged in the *pistola*.

"Where are you off to, *jefe*?" Garcia asked.

"The university library," Clayton replied. He told them why, added it might take a while, and instructed them to start pulling missing persons reports on subjects who matched the victim's age and physical characteristics.

"For now, stay within the time frame we discussed," he reminded them on his way out the door. "Work New Mexico cases first."

On the short drive to campus, Clayton contemplated what the journals might contain, his mind wandering to thoughts of his father. Quite possibly he'd find nothing of value to the investigation, but discover things about Kerney he'd never known. The idea of learning more about his history intrigued him.

At the library, he found Eleanor Robbins in her office. A tall, dignified woman in her late sixties with dark hair and clear light green eyes, she listened to Clayton's reason for his request, accessed her computer files, and regretfully told him the journals couldn't leave the library.

Clayton asked if the journals had been photocopied or digitized.

Robbins smiled apologetically. "Yes, but unfortunately we had a computer malfunction recently and lost some files, including the Fergurson papers. All we have are the original documents."

"Are they extensive?" Clayton asked, quietly miffed that nothing about the frigging case seemed to come easy. He wanted the journals *now*.

Robbins nodded as she pulled up the archive index file and did a fast scan. "Thirty volumes dating back to the late 1940s. There are thousands of pages that include handwritten entries, rough pencil sketches, quotations from other sources, ideas for student class projects, lists of daily things to do, notations on gallery representation and various museum acquisitions, thoughts on departmental faculty meetings, some notes on students, and comments about many of the important people and events in her life. It's quite a treasure trove of information."

"We're conducting a murder investigation and need to look at those journals as soon as possible," Clayton reminded her.

"I understand. As I said, the documents cannot leave the premises, but I can make them available to you here. I'll arrange a private room for you to use."

"That won't do," Clayton replied. "The journals may contain information pertinent to a murder and as such may become evidence. If you won't release them willingly, I'll have to serve you with a court order and seize them."

Ms. Robbins squared her shoulders in defiance. "I should speak to Dr. Janice Manchester, the library director, about this."

Clayton nodded at the telephone on the desk. "Please do it now, I'm in a bit of a hurry."

It took Robbins several attempts to reach Dr. Manchester. She explained the situation and within a few minutes Manchester, round and significantly shorter than Robbins, hurried in, a concerned look on her face, demanding a further explanation.

Patiently, Clayton explained how evidence-gathering was different than academic research, and how a chain of custody had to be established and preserved to have facts pertinent to a case admitted in court. To do that, he needed to take physical possession of the documents.

"How long would that be?" Manchester asked.

"I honestly won't know until we do an inspection. But I'll return them to you as soon as possible, especially those documents we find immaterial to our investigation."

"I see," Manchester said, turning to Robbins with a meaningful look. "I think we need to consult with the Office of General Counsel about this."

"Of course," Robbins replied, returning the look.

Clayton stood. "Tell your general counsel that I'll have a court order served on both of you before the end of the day. Please have the documents ready for me at that time."

He handed Manchester his business card. "Have your lawyers call if they have any questions."

Outside the library, students filled the walkways, some hurrying along to class, others sauntering, chatting in small groups. Clayton threaded his way to his unit through hundreds of young people, feeling decidedly middle-aged.

It was a quick drive from the university to U.S. 70, a highway that cut across the Tularosa Basin and through White Sands Missile Range. The recently built District 4 state police headquarters sat on a paved road off the highway, surrounded by raw land recently annexed by the city because of the area's continuing growth. Several big box warehouse stores next to a string of as yet untouched lots on a frontage road foretold more impending development.

Back in his office, Clayton prepared the search-and-seizure affidavit, called ahead to the local district attorney's office to say he was on his way, and arrived to find Henry Larkin, chief deputy DA, waiting for him.

"This better be good," Larkin said as he read the affidavit on his way to his office.

"You've heard from the Office of General Counsel?" Clayton asked.

"You betcha," Larkin replied as he settled into his desk chair. In his forties with a full head of curly gray hair and a John Kennedy smile, he was a shoe-in for district attorney once his boss decided to retire. Behind him, a picture window gave a great view of the city and the Organ Mountains beyond.

"What's the problem?"

"Seems an assistant art history prof at the university is researching a biography on Erma Fergurson, and is putting up a stink about releasing all the material to your custody. Their general counsel, Larry Babcock, who regularly loses to me on the golf course, wants our office to vouch that you need everything."

Clayton smiled. Robbins and Manchester had made their play. "I can't answer that until we see it."

"Granted. How long will you need the documents?"

Clayton shrugged. "I'll put people on it right away. Give me a week."

Larkin nodded and signed off. "That will placate Larry. I'll call when the warrant has been approved."

"Good deal," Clayton said.

"You should come out and play golf with me sometime," Larkin said as he walked Clayton down the corridor.

Clayton laughed. He hated golf and wouldn't watch or play it. "Find another pigeon to fleece, Henry. This town is teeming with ambitious young lawyers looking to get ahead politically."

"Yeah, but you'd be more fun to watch."

———

At the district office parking lot, Paul Avery pulled in right behind Clayton. As he exited his unit, Avery approached.

"We got zilch from the sheriff's office and campus police records search," he announced. "However, they did pass along lists of drunks, vagrants, psychos, panhandlers, trespassers, and homeless subjects who were either arrested or given a summons between ten and twenty years ago."

"How thoughtfully useless."

Avery waved a sheaf of papers at Clayton. "Three hundred and six individuals, several of whom I personally know to be dead and buried."

"Put it in the master case file."

"I predict the rest of the day will be just as fruitless."

"There's always tomorrow."

"You sure know how to bolster my spirits."

Clayton told him about the Fergurson journals and search warrant, and jokingly ordered him back to work with a growl.

At the end of the day, the victim remained unidentified, the partial thumbprint lifted from the cartridge was so degraded no definitive match could be made, and the piece of the metal whittled from the juniper branch proved to be a sterling silver chain of unknown origin. When the search warrant for Fergurson's journals came through, it contained a note from Larkin saying the NMSU library had until morning to assemble all the documents.

With Garcia and Avery sitting in his office, Clayton restrained his impatience, and reminded them that whatever they learned tomorrow would move the case along one way or another.

"When we find the perp, that partial print could help seal the case. We also need to think about why someone would wrap a sterling silver chain around the branch of a tree above a burial site."

"I got my wife a sterling silver necklace for Christmas last year, and it had to be exactly twenty inches long, to go with a pendant she had," Garcia offered. "When I went shopping, I found out real quick that's a standard size for a necklace."

"Twenty inches? That's the same length the grad student estimated the chain would have been," Avery said.

"So maybe it held a piece of jewelry that had a special meaning to the victim," Garcia speculated.

"Or the perp," Avery suggested.

"Left there and meant to be found," Clayton added. "But why?"

"To make sure the body would be discovered," Avery ventured. "The killer wanted to get caught. When the cops screwed it up, he just walked away."

"That's not unheard-of," Clayton said, staring at the thick piles of computer printouts on his desk, listing missing persons cases of young Anglo females from the 1960s and '70s. "I'm bringing in help," he announced. "Epperson and Olivas will join us tomorrow from the Alamogordo office."

"Good deal," Avery said. "Maybe everything we need will be in Fergurson's journals."

"Wouldn't that be lovely?" Garcia replied.

Clayton sent them home, checked his email for the last time, and thought about the Fergurson journals. He'd promised Larkin to release any unneeded documents back to the library as quickly as possible. But maybe not. As important as researching a biography about Fergurson might be to an assistant art history professor, it didn't trump murder.

He rose to leave, but another glance at the computer printouts gave him pause. Why simply scour old files when there was another possible way to ID the victim? He settled back in his chair and typed a draft public announcement asking any New Mexico citizen with knowledge about a young adult woman who'd gone missing in the 1960s or 1970s to contact the state police immediately. He sent it to Deputy Chief Robert Serrano, who oversaw the department's Investigation Division, as an attachment to an email, with a copy to Luis Mondragon, asking for approval to release it in the morning.

He powered off the computer and left the building, wondering how much time he had before a boot landed on his backside. If progress continued to inch along with no apparent breakthroughs, it wouldn't be good for his chance at a promotion.

His tenth year with the department loomed on the horizon, and he had another ten to go for a full pension. He was on the list to make captain, and the commander of District 8, headquartered an hour's drive away on the east side of the Tularosa Basin in Alamogordo, had announced his pending retirement at the end of the year.

If Clayton got the job, it meant leaving the Investigation Division, returning to uniform, and taking on greater responsibilities. It would be a perfect fit for the family, allowing them to stay in Las Cruces. Grace could continue her career in a job she thrived at, while Wendell and Hannah finished college without any disruption. It was only a possibility, but it would sure be nice if it all worked out.

He tossed wishful thinking aside, locked his unit in the driveway, and walked inside the house. Tomorrow he'd have Fergurson's journals in hand. He was eager to see where they might lead him.

CHAPTER 4

The Fergurson journals weren't ready to be picked up until late morning. While they waited, Clayton had his team—including the two additional agents—conduct a series of narrow, ten-year searches of missing persons cases. It yielded no results. The goal to identify a murdered twenty-something Caucasian female, approximately five-foot-five, killed forty, fifty, maybe sixty years ago, seemed insurmountable. Women and girls went missing far more often than any other demographic group, and with the sketchy victim profile Clayton had, record-searching was tedious and seemed almost futile.

Experience had taught him that a significant number of lost, vanished, or missing persons were previously unknown to law enforcement. Or, like this case, they were a murdered Jane or John Doe waiting to be discovered, often by accident.

Robert Serrano, the deputy chief in charge of the Investigation Division, had vetoed Clayton's request to issue a public service announcement asking for citizen help in identifying the victim, saying it was premature and failed to show progress, making the department look bad. Before hanging up, he noted Clayton could easily be replaced, which would kill any chance for promotion. He shrugged it off. Serrano liked to use threats in the mistaken belief it motivated people.

The library called to say the journals were ready. Robbins and Manchester were waiting for him in a staff conference room with the documents carefully packed in sturdy cardboard file boxes, each with cataloged contents. Liz Waterman, the campus police chief, and a lawyer from the general counsel's office were also present.

Clayton served the papers, did a quick inspection to make sure he had the real deal, and thanked Robbins and Manchester for their cooperation. It yielded tight-lipped smiles. He wondered why they seemed so put-upon. After all, he wasn't seizing the Book of Kells or the Gutenberg Bible.

Under the watchful eyes of Waterman and the lawyer, Clayton carried the boxes out to his unit, signed a receipt, and drove off, the backseat piled high.

Back at the district office, Avery and Garcia helped him unload. At the conference table they unpacked the carefully wrapped journals while Charlie Epperson and Carla Olivas hovered nearby.

Clayton surveyed the documents with a glimmer of hope. There were thirty volumes of personal history recorded in a hodgepodge of loose-leaf binders, pages from old writing tablets stapled together, cheap plastic spiral notebooks, sketchbooks that were a combination of drawings and writings, and expensive leather-bound journals filled with dated entries from end to end.

On the surface it seemed a jumbled, disorganized mess. But a quick look revealed Fergurson had chronicled events in her life stretching from her time as a young WAVE serving in the navy during World War II, to the year before her death. Many of the years overlapped in the individual volumes.

Fergurson's clarity of vision and attention to detail in her artwork carried over in her journals. She seemed to concentrate on important and memorable events, as opposed to idle musings. There were snippets of thoughts and observations, succinct yet detailed, that sparked Clayton's growing optimism there was something of value to be uncovered.

Until now he'd said nothing about his family connection to Fergurson. Although it was no secret that the legendary New Mexico cop Kevin Kerney was his father, he'd seen no need to mention Kerney's connection to Fergurson. But now the journals had surfaced, and it was likely they contained comments about Kerney and his parents. It was time for full disclosure.

"Professor Erma Fergurson was my paternal grandmother's lifelong friend," Clayton said. "During his college years in the sixties, my father, Kevin Kerney, rented an apartment from her. There may be entries about him, as well as my mother."

Clayton's revelation raised eyebrows.

"This investigation has suddenly become a lot more interesting," Avery said. "It's right during our time frame for the murder. Maybe we should haul Kerney in and give him the third degree."

He got a pinched look from Clayton and groans from the rest of the team. "Just joking," Avery said, backpedaling.

"Let's get to work," Clayton snapped.

After logging the journals into evidence, Clayton divvied them up, making sure everyone had sequential documents, including at least one that fell within their working time frame of the murder. He added the oldest two volumes to his stack as well, admonished everyone to bring him something they could use in the morning, and sent them off to do their homework.

When the office cleared, he returned to his desk and glanced at his watch. Grace was at the community college teaching an evening pre-school teacher-aide certification class, and the kids were on their own for dinner. There was no reason to hurry home. He had the rest of the afternoon and well into the night to dig into the material.

One by one, he examined the journals. The tantalizing impulse to start at the very beginning pestered him, but the years long before the murder were likely irrelevant to the investigation, and not what he needed to focus on. Instead, he opened the 1955 diary and began reading.

————

Suddenly awake, Grace reached across the bed for Clayton, who wasn't there. The blue light of the LED clock read two in the morning. Not surprised to find him missing, she puffed up her pillow, shifted on to her side, and tried unsuccessfully to go back to sleep, her thoughts dancing with speculations about the contents of the Erma Fergurson journals.

Curious when she found Clayton with binders and notebooks strewn across the kitchen table upon her return home hours ago, she'd asked what he was doing. He'd told her about the papers and why they could be important to the case. Usually, when he spoke about work, his comments were brief and matter-of-fact. But this time there was a touch of eagerness and apprehension in his voice. Grace worried that delving into Erma Fergurson's personal memoirs might rekindle Clayton's bitter emotions about his father.

She hoped not. Over the years, since Kerney and Clayton had met, their relationship had improved from chilly to civil. In Grace's mind, if it went no further that would be okay. Sometimes just getting along was good enough, especially if it was much more than one might expect.

She suspected Clayton had never fully let go of the idea that Kerney had abandoned his mother because she was pregnant, despite being told differently by both parents. If he found an inkling of support for that in the journals, it could easily result in a complete estrangement between the two men.

She slipped out of bed and went downstairs. He was still reading at the kitchen table, red-eyed, chin propped up by a hand.

"Aren't you ever coming to bed?" she asked warily.

He sighed, closed the spiral binder, and stood. "Might as well. There's no murder victim or suspect to be found in these pages so far."

"May I read them?" Grace asked, relieved not to find him fuming.

"Sometime, maybe," he replied, taking her by the hand to lead her upstairs.

"But not now?"

"Not now," he confirmed.

"Have you learned anything?"

Clayton stopped at the head of the stairs. "Yeah. In completely different ways, Erma Fergurson and Mary Kerney were two extraordinary women."

Grace continued to their bedroom. "Now you really have my interest up. What about your father?" she asked as casually as possible.

Clayton turned on the bedroom light. "Kerney's barely a teenager in the material I've read. Fergurson was like an aunt to him, and from her point of view he was one great kid."

"Does that surprise you?"

Clayton shook his head. "No, I've got two great kids of my own."

"It's all about the genetics," Grace proposed, hoping her fears would remain groundless. "On both sides. Come to bed."

"I'll be there in a minute."

———

Grace always marveled at Clayton's unique ability to mentally detach from events of the day, no matter how frustrating, trying, or gruesome they were. As usual, once in bed he fell asleep within minutes.

Although she worried about him every day he went to work, she never said a word or showed outward concern. Not once had she probed about the major felony cases he'd investigated, leaving it up to him to talk about them if he chose to do so. She was very good at being a homicide cop's wife, and he in turn spared her all the gory details of his job, for which she was grateful.

Until this moment in their marriage, it had never occurred to her to look through any of the work he brought home. But the Ferguson journals were different. They contained information about Clayton's ancestral family—people she knew little about, people her children were entitled to have knowledge of. What made Clayton think Mary Kerney was extraordinary? What made Kevin such a great kid?

Sleep wouldn't come. Quietly, she went downstairs, and found the journals tucked away in Clayton's attaché case on the shelf in the hall closet. She sat down at the kitchen table and started reading. She began with the first volume and quickly learned that Erma's friendship with Mary Ralston had blossomed during their service together in World War II. And how, after the war, Mary helped Erma escape from a disastrous marriage and convinced her to move with her to Las Cruces, where they rented an apartment and enrolled in college under the GI Bill.

She read how Matthew Kerney, a decorated veteran, blinded in one eye in Sicily, met Mary, courted her, took her to see the family ranch on the Tularosa, and married her in a whirlwind ceremony at a charming old hacienda in nearby Mesilla.

She was particularly fascinated by a small pencil sketch on the margin of a lined page with a notation identifying the subject as Clayton's great-grandfather, Patrick Kerney, a crusty-looking old frontiersman. His resemblance to Clayton and Kevin was remarkable, the same deep-set eyes, square shoulders, and lean frame.

She read Erma's detailed, loving description of the Kerney ranch on the edge of the San Andres Mountains, and its vast views of Sierra Blanca, ancestral home of the Apache people.

It made Grace recall the story she'd heard as a child of Crooked Running Woman, a famous Apache warrior who during the pony soldier wars had been saved by two White Eyes on a Tularosa ranch and returned safely home. Did Kerney's grandfather help save her? She would ask to hear the tale again from the old ones the next time she went home to Mescalero.

There were long segments in Erma's journals with no mention of the Kerney family, and while interesting, Grace skimmed them, her focus solely on learning more about Clayton's ancestors. She found rich material in several letters from Mary to Erma that had been folded in among the pages.

She was deeply engaged in one of Mary's letters when Clayton appeared in the kitchen. The stovetop clock read five a.m. He arched an eyebrow, but didn't say a word as he set up the coffee maker. As it gurgled and began to brew, he teasingly asked if she'd identified the victim and found the murderer.

"You're not upset at me for looking?" Grace replied.

Clayton shook his head. "It's too early in the morning to be upset about anything. It would only sour the day. Well, did you?"

Grace laughed. "Find the killer? No, but I did learn that Kevin's high school girlfriend was arrested and thrown into jail along with Erma Fergurson and some others at an anti-war protest in Las Cruces in the sixties."

"Jeannie Hollister," Clayton noted. "I read that. She was quite the budding young peacenik."

"You don't think she's the victim, do you?"

Clayton's expression turned thoughtful. "I don't know."

"Will you read all of Erma's journals?"

"Eventually."

"I worry that it will raise old issues for you."

The coffee maker beeped. Clayton poured two cups. "About all my past grievances with Kerney? I doubt it."

Encouraged by his tone, Grace joined him at the kitchen counter and looked him in the eyes. "Why is that?"

Clayton laughed. "Because it came to me recently that my mother and Kerney simply baffled each other and could never work it out. I can't get bent out of shape about that."

"What an interesting notion." She smiled and sipped her coffee. "I think you're right."

"Me, too." He put down his cup and kissed her. "I've got to get dressed and go."

Feeling reassured, Grace finished her coffee to the sound of the shower before returning Erma's journals to Clayton's attaché case and placing it on the table near the front door. Through Erma's entries of her visits to Mary, she'd learned a bit about Kerney's early boyhood days on the ranch, the family's relocation to Truth or Consequences during years of punishing drought, and Patrick Kerney's tragic descent into dementia. She decided to write down all she'd read so as not to forget it, and ask Clayton to let her read more.

———

While plowing through the papers, Clayton discovered that part of the problem identifying people Erma wrote about was her frequent use of only initials. At the office, he learned his bleary-eyed team had encountered the same difficulty. None of them had yet found anything that appeared relevant to the homicide.

A quick tally from the team revealed there were still thousands of pages yet unread. Faced with the possibility of many more people to identify, Clayton started a list of initials he'd run across on the whiteboard in the conference room. He told the team to add to it and nail down as many names, ages, and genders as they could.

"Cross off those that don't fit our victim's profile," he instructed.

Clayton returned to his office and settled at his desk with the door closed. He looked over the journals he'd yet to read after last night's marathon and opened to where he'd left off, silently hoping that somewhere inside the pages Erma had provided a clue to the victim's identity. If his team all stuck out, he'd be shit out of luck and starting from scratch.

———

Sometimes Paul Avery could be very funny, and sometimes, as he well knew, his attempts at humor were huge blunders that made him feel stupid for opening his big yap. Yesterday's joke about hauling Clayton's father in for questioning wasn't his worst faux pas in recent memory, but it sure had been a doozy.

The lieutenant was the best boss he'd ever had, and Avery felt he owed him an apology. But when Clayton's office door was closed it meant no interruptions unless it was something that couldn't wait.

The section of a journal Avery was reading contained Fergurson's notes on a summer she'd spent at her vacation cabin outside Ojitos Frios, a tiny Hispanic community in northern New Mexico. She'd done a lot of painting there, along with some entertaining, including a person identified only by initials who showed up rather frequently late in the evenings, and not to talk about art.

Fergurson's entries about her late-night visitor were lusty and erotic, causing Avery to question his decision to major in criminal justice in college. Perhaps he would have gotten a lot more action with the coeds if he'd been an art major. Except he stank at drawing even stick figures.

Fergurson's account of the bedroom antics clearly indicated her visitor was a male, so Avery added the initials to the whiteboard and promptly crossed them out to show they could not belong to the victim. Back at his desk, he glanced at the remaining journals awaiting his attention and hesitated. He had half a headache from all the reading and needed to stretch his legs and get some air.

He thought about his visit to Billy Boylan, the sergeant at the sheriff's office in charge of evidence and records, who'd told him no reports of any trespassing at the Fergurson Center had been located. Paul wasn't sure Boylan could be trusted to do a good job. Back in the day when they'd been rookies together at the SO, Billy had been a skate, always willing to avoid anything that required real effort or hard work. His father was the then-incumbent sheriff's first cousin. Thus, an accommodation had been made resulting in Billy becoming a fixture as supervisor of the evidence and records office.

He signed out for the sheriff's office, hoping Billy's boss would let him take a look for himself.

———

Billy Boylan's supervisor, Major Frank Casados, had been with the sheriff's office for thirty years and had no intention of retiring. He'd also been Avery's field training officer during his rookie year, and subsequently his patrol commander until Paul left the SO for the state police.

Now in charge of administrative services, a position created especially for him, Frank Casados had a spacious office with a trophy wall bookcase that held his various awards, plaques, and framed commendations. Casados smiled and clasped his hands around his substantial girth when Avery stuck his head in his open door.

"What are you doing here?" he asked genially, as Paul slid into a chair in front of his desk.

"It's that unidentified murder victim that got unearthed at the Fergurson Center," Paul explained.

Casados guffawed. "Oh, yeah, that one. Good luck with it. Must have seen the video clip a dozen times on the TV news. Boylan said he made a records check for you that came up empty."

"So he says," Avery replied pointedly.

Casados rolled his eyes. "Nice of you to be so polite about it. I bet you want to take a look-see yourself."

"Only without stepping on Boylan's toes. Can I look?"

Casados nodded. "You can, but I don't think Billy shortchanged you. I stayed on him to do a thorough job. If he missed something, it's in the basement storage room that's filled with records that were brought over from the old courthouse. Supposedly it's ancient stuff from before 1950, but you never know."

"Thanks."

Casados rose. "I'll take you down there. But you'd better be prepared to spend the rest of the day."

"That's okay," Avery replied. As they walked down the corridor to the elevator, he called and left a message for Clayton, reporting where he was and what he was about to do. To make sure he didn't immediately get yanked back to the journals waiting on his desk, he turned his phone off, which was sure to piss Clayton off if he called.

———

During a quick coffee break, Clayton listened to his messages. All but one of them were from Santa Fe, requesting updates on the investigation. He ignored them. The message from Paul Avery made him reach for the phone to order him back to the office pronto. He paused. Avery had good cop instincts. As an ex-deputy sheriff for Doña Ana County, he knew their internal operating procedures better than anyone else on the team, including Clayton. If he had reason to want to double-check the SO records, it wouldn't hurt to let him do it.

The conference room whiteboard was filling up with initials, most yet to be matched with names. The names that were listed had been crossed out with notations why, such as "deceased," "wrong sex," "too old," etc. Avery had entered and crossed out the initials NB but written no reason. Clayton skimmed the journal Avery had been reading and came across racy entries by Fergurson about her lovemaking with NB. He wrote "male" on the whiteboard next to NB's initials, thinking Erma Fergurson had been one helluva woman on many levels.

Hoping for some good news, he made the rounds of his team, only to be greeted with a shake of a head, a shrug of the shoulders, or a terse, negative reply. Back at his desk, he started in on a new journal that covered a sabbatical year in France and Italy, flipping through Erma's entries about painting trips in the countryside, visits to museums, meetings with galley directors, and social events with collectors and European artists. Several hours later, he'd moved on to another journal that dealt mostly with matters pertaining to her position at the university, with comments and observations, many less than flattering, about fellow faculty members and various high-ranking administrators. The words were starting to run together when Clayton looked up and saw Avery standing in the open doorway with a piece of paper in his hand, not looking at all happy.

"What have you got?" Clayton asked.

"During the move from the old courthouse, someone had mislabeled a box of 1973 field deputy reports by transposing the seven and the three, and it had been shelved with the 1930s records." What he held in his hand the lieutenant wasn't going to like.

"And?" Clayton prodded.

"First, I want to apologize about the stupid joke I made yesterday about Chief Kerney."

Clayton waved it off. "I already forgot about that. What's that in your hand?"

Avery stepped to Clayton's desk and handed him a copy of a field report dated Friday, April 27, 1973. "I was looking for missing persons reports and found this instead."

Written on a standard SO form used back in the day, it was a report made by Kevin Kerney, a guest at the Fergurson residence, of a stolen 1875 Colt Single Action Army model revolver. The responding deputy recorded that Mr. Kerney had found the handgun missing from a nightstand drawer in the guest bedroom upon his return to the residence with Professor Fergurson after they'd dined out, and that he'd last seen the pistol prior to going to bed the previous night.

Contacted by the deputy, Fergurson's renter, Maxwell Colley, a graduate student who lived in an apartment above the garage, noted he'd been home while Kerney and Fergurson were gone and neither saw nor heard any strangers arriving on the property. The only visitors to Mr. Kerney's room since his arrival two weeks ago had been his hostess, Professor Fergurson, and an old college friend, Kim Ward, a female who'd shown up unexpectedly and spent Wednesday night, 4/25/73, with him in the room. He had no reason to believe Ward would have returned and taken the pistol.

"It's an identical match to the Colt found with the skeletal remains," Avery added. "Minus the serial number, which the deputy noted as unknown."

"Holy shit," Clayton muttered, without looking up.

"Sorry," Avery said.

"Don't be," Clayton replied, his bile rising, eyes fixed on the report. "I want Kerney's fingerprint records sent to the lab pronto for a comparison with the partial from the cartridge recovered from the Colt. Handle it yourself and tell them it has the highest priority. I want an answer now, not next week."

"You've got it," Avery replied.

Clayton raised his head, his hand covering the field report as though to conceal the stark implications. "Ask the team to immediately focus on this Kim Ward. I want to know everything about her. Everything. Start running her down at the university. Concentrate on Fergurson's journal entries during Kerney's college years and after his return from Vietnam."

"I'll tell them to get on it."

"Tell them to keep a lid on everything," Clayton added. "No back-channel talk, no gossip, no pillow talk. Got it?"

Avery nodded. "Are you all right?"

"Yeah, fine. Close the door on the way out. I've got some calls to make."

When the door closed, Clayton's hand hovered over the desk telephone. Who in the hell was he going to call? Grace, to tell her Kerney had just become a possible murder suspect? The deputy chief in charge of investigations, who'd be on the phone to Clayton's immediate supervisor with orders to yank him from the case?

He pulled his hand away and took a deep breath. He wasn't about to step aside. Not yet. Not until he had more than some very shaky reasonable suspicion of Kerney's possible guilt.

The forgive-and-forget attitude about Kerney he'd expressed to Grace was fast evaporating. A lot of 'Nam vets had come home, lost it, and spent years paying for their crimes in the slammer. Did Kerney snap for some reason, kill the woman, and bury her on the Fergurson grounds? If so, why report the murder weapon stolen? Why bury it with the victim? Why kill her in the first place? The mere thought that Kerney might be a killer stunned him, angered him.

Clayton glanced at his wristwatch, and gave himself eighteen hours—the start of the day shift in the morning—to get some answers. Between now and then, there'd be no time for sleep.

CHAPTER 5

As the hours rolled on, Clayton and the team kept digging into Fergurson's papers, accumulating information that made Kerney at the very least a person of interest in the case. According to Fergurson, Kerney had, early in his first semester at college, introduced her to Kim Ward, and she'd entertained the couple at dinner several times. One entry noted:

> Kevin and Kim at dinner tonight. They could hardly keep their hands off each other. Resisted the impulse to tease them about their obvious mutual lust. They're so terribly sweet and young. Won't say a word to K's mother.

At the beginning of the second semester, after Kim joined the college rodeo team, Fergurson wondered if the romance had cooled. A month later, she wrote:

K and K no longer inseparable. Kevin unhappy but putting on a brave face. When he does see her, he lights up. I worry he'll get hurt. He's so completely loyal to those he loves.

Fergurson's next entry about Kim Ward came at the end of Kerney's freshman year:

Before K went home for summer break, I asked how he was handling the breakup with Kim. Very defensive, as expected. I told him not to be angry or to think badly of her. His good heart will overcome his bitterness, but it may take time. Still haven't said a word to Mary.

The final mention of Kim Ward came years later, while Kerney was staying with Fergurson after his separation from active duty:

Kim W., one of K's old college sweethearts, unexpectedly showed up asking his whereabouts. Had heard he was in town. Very disheveled, anxious, looking far too old for her age. Only wanted to talk to K, who took her to his room. I could hear their voices long into the wee hours. She was gone in the morning. Didn't pry, but K said she'd had a bad fight with her husband and left him to get away.

Clayton told Agent Carla Olivas to track down the husband, and asked Charlie Epperson to begin immediately concentrating on Kim Ward, or anybody with that given name or nickname, in all missing persons data banks. He reread the entries, wondering why Fergurson hadn't mentioned Kerney's stolen pistol, or the deputy sheriff's interview. Since the revolver was supposedly taken from a room in her home, wouldn't she have been worried other items might have been stolen? Perhaps a blanket from the guest bedroom? Did she know something bad had happened to Kim Ward, but was unwilling to record it? Did she help cover up a crime?

It was too much speculating. Clayton shook it off. Tucked in the journal was a letter from Kerney in its original envelope, mailed to Fergurson from Albuquerque months later. It read:

Dear Aunt Erma,

I've enrolled in graduate school at UNM under the GI Bill trying to figure out what I'm going to do when I grow up. I've met a girl who seems to like me. We'll see how that goes. You know I'm a sucker for the feisty ones. I've been thinking about Kim and wonder if you've heard from her. She was supposed to get in touch after the dust settled with Todd, but I haven't heard a word from her.

I'm living in a dumpy two-bedroom rental house on Cornell Street five blocks from campus with a guy who thinks he's the playboy of the western world. He's also hilarious. I'm taking pointers.

I'll come visit over Christmas break, if you'll have me.

Love,

Kevin

Clayton tapped the letter with a finger. Todd had to be the woman's husband. He stuck his head out the office door and gave Carla Olivas the news. "I bet that Kerney knew him," he added. "Otherwise, I doubt he would have referred to him by name in his letter."

Olivas took the letter from Clayton's hand and read it quickly. "Okay."

"Find the connection between the three of them."

Over her shoulder, he saw James Garcia pushing through the front door, carrying a load of books under one arm and not looking very happy. He dumped the books on his desk and approached.

"The college registrar won't cooperate," he said. "We'll need a court order to get Kim Ward's records."

Clayton held up his hand to keep Olivas from leaving. "Then do it. Work up a search-and-seizure affidavit with Carla pronto, and make it for three individuals, Kim Ward, Kevin Kerney, and Todd Somebody—last name unknown."

"Last name unknown isn't going to fly," Carla cautioned.

"Leave it blank for now," Clayton replied.

Garcia nodded at the books on his desk. "I borrowed some yearbooks from the college library that may give us Todd's last name. Kim Ward only shows up in her freshman and sophomore years, as a member of the rodeo team. Got a couple of good photos of her. Nice-looking girl."

Finally, there's movement, Clayton thought as he checked the time. "Get me a last name. Tell the registrar we'll be serving a warrant after their normal business hours, and to have someone standing by."

He turned to Carla Olivas. "Alert the campus police and ask for assistance in case we need to access other areas for the search. I'll call the DA."

"Ten-four," Olivas replied as Clayton returned to his desk and speed-dialed the DA. He finished the call just as Paul Avery plopped down in a chair with papers in his hand and sighed.

"Forensics says there's a seventy percent probability the victim was shot in the head with a bullet the same caliber as the Colt," he reported. "That's the best they can do. The partial fingerprint on the cartridge *could* be Kerney's, but it can't be absolutely confirmed. The lab gives it a sixty percent likelihood. Helpful for making a case for probable cause, but probably worthless in court. Any good attorney would be all over these little morsels at trial."

"Every little bit helps, and that's all I care about right now."

Avery stared disbelievingly at Clayton as he pushed the papers across the desk. "Jesus, do you *want* Kerney to be the killer?"

"I want to know the truth, one way or the other," Clayton responded evenly.

"Fair enough."

Carla Olivas stepped through the open door. "We've got a last name," she announced with a smile and a hint of excitement in her voice. "Todd Marks. He was on the rodeo team with Kim Ward. We faxed the search-and-seizure affidavit to the DA."

"How long?" Clayton asked.

"The DA has a judge standing by. Thirty minutes, tops." Olivas handed him a copy.

Clayton gave the form a thorough read. "Good job," he said, looking up to find the entire team clustered at the front of his desk. He pushed back his chair and stood. "I want everyone on the campus and ready to move as soon as the warrant is delivered. An ADA will hand-carry it to us."

The prospect of getting out and doing some fieldwork made everyone smile.

"Get ready for a long night," Clayton added.

———

The university administrators who'd been forced to stay late at work, or were called back to the office from their after-dinner evening in front of the television, barely maintained their civility as Clayton and his agents entered buildings, searched computers and storage areas, and printed or gathered up documents, records, and files. Two assistant district attorneys watched to ensure the search stayed within the legal limits of the warrant.

At Clayton's request, Liz Waterman, chief of the campus police department, had shown up with three of her officers.

They went from office to office, building to building, filling the trunks of several units with seized documents and computers. At their last search site, the university health center, a crowd of fifty activist students had gathered to protest state police being on campus. They shouted insults and recorded smartphone video.

Liz and her officers spread out to keep them at bay as the clinic administrator, a middle-aged woman, unlocked the front door and ushered the team inside. The woman read the warrant and shook her head in dismay.

"Is there a problem?" Clayton asked.

"For you, not for me," the woman replied. "Health records this old were put on microfilm years ago, and have never been converted digitally. We don't have the staff or funding to even organize it properly. I can't remember the last time anyone needed to access them."

"Well, we do, and right now, if you don't mind," Clayton said politely.

She turned on her heel, key ring in hand. "Follow me."

At the back of the first floor, she unlocked the door to a storage area and turned on the overhead fluorescent lights. Inside were dozens of tall, dust-covered microfilm storage cabinets, one long table with a microfilm reader on top, and an old wooden desk chair.

"How long do you think this will take?" she asked.

"A while," Clayton answered as the team fanned out across the room.

———

At four in the morning, with everything logged in, Clayton sent the team home with instructions to be back at noon. As he stood in the doorway of the Criminal Investigation Unit offices surveying the two folding tables filled with seized records and computers, he considered, out of spite, calling Deputy Chief Robert Serrano at home to report he had almost irrefutable evidence that Kimberly Ann Ward, age twenty-three, graduate of Deming High School and varsity member of the NMSU rodeo team, was their murder victim.

Forensics still had to make the final call, but Ward had broken her right arm at a rodeo meet during her sophomore year, and the microfilm X-ray in her university health records showed an exact match with the break in the recovered skeletal remains.

Deciding not to get ahead of himself and wait until Ward's dental records could be located to confirm her identity, he turned out the lights and locked the door.

In his unit, dispatch advised him that Captain Luis Mondragon was on a back channel waiting to speak to him.

Clayton switched frequencies. "What's up, Cap?"

"Heading home?" Mondragon asked.

"I'll be back at ten hundred hours. Did you call to say good night?"

Mondragon chuckled. "Not likely. Bobby Serrano, my friend and your headquarters boss, wants to know why you caused a riot on the NMSU campus."

"You're kidding, right?"

"Negative. Seems a complaint has been lodged about the disruption and inconvenience you and your agents caused during the search. There was mention of hundreds of students protesting your Gestapo-like tactics."

"It was no more than fifty," Clayton said.

"No matter. My take is that the whole thing was nothing more than a show put on by a fringe group of students who wanted to protest against the police and get some attention. Word has it through my brother-in-law the sorry spectacle will be on the early morning TV news with video showing you and your team supposedly storming the campus health center. Get the picture?"

"BS," Clayton grunted, too tired to give a hoot.

"The deputy chief would like you to call him."

"Tell him I will do so when I'm back in the office at ten hundred hours."

Clayton counted to ten before Mondragon broke the silence with a chuckle.

"You've got some *huevos*, amigo. I'll ask Bobby to chill. He owes me a few favors. I'll also find out what our Intelligence Unit knows about any radical student agendas on the NMSU campus. Catch some sleep."

"Roger that, and thanks," Clayton said as he wheeled onto the frontage road and headed home.

———

Clayton got up at nine to find Grace had delayed going to work to fix him breakfast. Over a cup of fresh coffee and the smell of scrambled eggs and bacon, he listened to Luis Mondragon on a local radio station dismiss the campus disturbance as nothing more than a small gathering of rowdy students bent on causing trouble. He went on to say that the ADA who accompanied the agents had issued a statement that all law enforcement officers had conducted themselves professionally. For having his back, Clayton figured he owed Mondragon a bottle of his favorite scotch.

As Grace served his breakfast, she smiled and said, "Did you crack the case?"

"Did I what?" Clayton asked, surprised by a question he'd never heard her ask before. Not asking *anything* about his cases was her norm.

"Isn't that what cops in murder mysteries do?" she replied teasingly. "Crack the case?"

Clayton laughed and reached for his fork. "No, but I'm ninety-nine percent sure of who the victim is."

"So, progress is being made?"

"Yes, but not quickly enough," Clayton replied.

"You're a patient man," Grace counseled. "You'll get there. By the way, your mother wants us to come this Saturday for dinner. The kids say they can make it."

Saturday was in two days. "Okay, sure."

"That will make her happy." She grabbed her purse from the kitchen counter and gave him a kiss on the cheek. "I'm off to work. Scrape and stack when you've finished."

"Yes, ma'am," Clayton said between mouthfuls.

———

Clayton telephoned Deputy Chief Serrano as soon as he arrived at work. Serrano's tone of voice indicated he was pissed that Clayton hadn't called back at four in the morning. At least the man held his temper. But he pushed hard, telling Clayton to positively ID Kim Ward as the victim and find the perp. He finished his badgering by implying there was the likelihood of a forced transfer out of investigations if Clayton didn't produce something substantial soon.

On the heel of Serrano's call came some good news. Fortunately, Kim Ward's dental records had been retained by the dentist who'd bought the practice. By the end of the day, Forensics confirmed Kimberly Ann Ward was the murder victim.

Clayton's second conversation of the day with Deputy Chief Serrano went a lot more smoothly. Serrano granted him permission to release a public service announcement asking for help locating Kim's mother, Lucille Ward, any of Kim's known relatives and friends, and her husband at the time of her death, Todd Marks.

Some years after Kim's disappearance, Lucille Ward had sold her house and moved away. Her current whereabouts were unknown, but there were local reports that she'd been seen in Lordsburg near the Arizona border, and in the village of Rodeo situated in the Bootheel, a sparsely populated part of the state that juts into Mexico, in a shape reminiscent of the heel of a cowboy boot. There were also several statements by those who'd known her that she'd remarried. One old-timer thought she was dead. Another said she'd become a heavy drinker.

Two of Kim's old high school friends still living in Deming also gave statements. One woman recalled Kim was into the drug scene. The other woman remembered hearing stories that Todd Marks had been two-timing Kim with a buckle bunny who couldn't keep her blue jeans on around rodeo cowboys. Both had lost touch with her.

Stories abounded, but none with reliable leads.

The PSA went out the next morning. Clayton, with every agent he could muster, fanned out across the southwestern quadrant of the state, from the Bootheel north to Catron County and the village of Reserve, where Todd Marks had been born and attended school before his family relocated to a small ranch in the tiny settlement of Glenwood.

Marks's parents, Ty and Heidi, were both deceased and the current ranch owner had no relationship to the family. Todd's brother and only sibling, Travis, lived in Reserve, directing an agricultural outreach program serving rural farmers and ranchers. Married, with three grown children, Travis told the agent who took his statement that he'd last seen his brother over twenty years ago, when Todd had shown up broke, drunk, and asking for money. Travis had put him up overnight, given him fifty bucks, and not heard from him since. The agent did verify that Todd had married Kim in Las Cruces, just before the couple dropped out of college and joined a pro rodeo circuit.

In his narrative report, the agent noted Travis Ward's description of his brother as an alcoholic deadbeat loser who drove their parents to an early grave.

The rodeo connection sent Clayton back to the NMSU campus to talk to the team coach, Lane Simpson, a young man in his mid-twenties with a band of freckles across his nose. He was at the ag barn checking animals and equipment for an upcoming event.

A New Mexican ranch-raised cowboy, Simpson was congenial, easygoing, and accommodating. Clayton explained what he was looking for. Simpson escorted him to his office, where it didn't take him long to find the documents Clayton had asked about.

"That team went to nationals both years," Simpson said proudly, handing Clayton several photographs, rosters, and statistical sheets. "We almost always do."

"That's something to be proud of," Clayton said, studying the photographs. Kim Ward and Todd Marks were easy to spot. He showed it to Simpson. "Do you personally know any of these team members?"

"I sure do," Simpson replied. "Rodeoing isn't something you give up easily. For most, it's in the blood. Even when they can't compete anymore, a lot of former team members stay involved either as boosters, sponsors, high school coaches, or judges."

"Do you know Todd Marks?"

Simpson shook his head. "I sure don't."

Clayton asked for the names and contact information of the team members who'd rodeoed with Todd Marks and Kim Ward.

"This is about that murdered girl from a long time ago up at the Fergurson Center, isn't it?"

Clayton nodded. "Kim Ward."

"I thought so." Simpson printed out a list from his computer, checked off a half dozen names of Kim's old teammates he personally knew, circled the rest, and gave it to Clayton.

"Do you have addresses for the ones you know?" Clayton asked.

Simpson nodded and scrolled through a computer file. "Most of them I checked off on that list still live in these parts." He studied the screen, jotted down some addresses and phone numbers, and gave the information to Clayton.

"You've been very helpful." Clayton handed him a business card and asked him to call if he remembered anyone else who might have known Todd and Kim back in the day.

On his way back to the office, Clayton heard from Carla Olivas that Lucille Ward supposedly had a relative, possibly a brother named Thomas, who once lived in Anthony, New Mexico, a small working-class community on the Texas state line.

"Nothing came back on a records check under the surname Ward," Carla said. "He'd be in his late eighties, if he's still alive."

A tough town, Anthony attracted the wounded of society, including the mentally ill, the marginally competent, and the indigent old, who signed over their disability or Social Security checks to unscrupulous landlords and lived in uninsulated garages, sheds, and condemned shacks, often with no running water or toilets. There was no law against it.

"I'm on my way there now," Carla added.

"Do you need assistance?" Clayton asked.

"Negative."

At five-foot-five and one hundred and twenty pounds, Olivas held black belts in tae kwon do and karate. She had an oval face and soft brown eyes that belied her toughness. To learn she was gay had disheartened many of the straight male officers in the department.

"Hang on a minute." Clayton pulled to the curb and consulted the list Simpson had given him. "Since you'll be in the vicinity, try to make contact in El Paso with Abby Hardin, maiden name Anderson." He read off the address and phone number. "She was Kim Ward's teammate."

"Ten-four, LT."

"Be careful," Clayton replied.

"Always," Carla said.

Clayton pulled back into traffic, hoping Olivas would come away with at least a single tangible lead from either Lucille Ward's brother or Kim Ward's rodeo teammate. Surely there was someone alive out there who could help turn things around.

He thought about Grace's "crack the case" joke at breakfast yesterday and smiled. Was she trying to cure him from spending too much time thinking like a White Eyes?

He decided to read Fergurson's entries about his father one more time.

———

For decades, much like its namesake across the Texas state line, Anthony, New Mexico, had been an unincorporated village. In a special 2010 election, voters decided to transform it into a city. Less than thirty miles from Las Cruces and halfway to El Paso, the town straddled a state highway that paralleled Interstate 10, the southernmost cross-continental highway in the nation. Originally an agricultural settlement, it was predominately Hispanic and poor. A good number of farms, dairies, and pecan groves still existed along the west side of town, extending into the rich Rio Grande bottomlands. To the east, neighborhoods of modest homes, many sorely in need of repair, were sandwiched between the interstate and the main highway through town.

Agent Olivas knew her way around because of a recent undercover assignment on a joint task force investigating illegal cockfighting in the area. Although outlawed, cockfighting with its attendant gambling still flourished in out-of-the-way rural areas of the state.

When the bust was made, over two hundred gamecocks were impounded, a hundred adults were cited for illegal gambling, and the owners of the birds arrested, along with the two families running the operation. Successful as it was, the officer in charge of the task force figured once all the parties made bail, they'd be up and running within weeks with new birds at a different location.

The fights were cruel and sickening. Before the bust, Carla had grown angry watching parents with their young children in tow, cheering on the bloody, gravely wounded birds, shouting with glee as the animals destroyed each other in the ring.

At a stoplight on the main drag, she put in a call to the Doña Ana SO asking for the whereabouts of Deputy Sheriff Orlando Guerrero, who'd worked with her on the task force and lived in the city. Told he was at home, she called his cell and asked if he had time for a cup of coffee. He agreed to meet her in ten minutes at a Mexican diner. He showed in less than eight, parked his patrol car outside the diner's picture window, and came in wearing sweats, running shoes, a faded Marine Corps sweatshirt, and a smile on his sweaty face.

Without asking, the waitress brought Orlando a diet soft drink along with Carla's coffee.

"That stuff's bad for you," she said.

Orlando took a swallow. "Tell me about it. What's up? You didn't drive down here to help me live a healthy life."

Carla laughed. "I'm looking for an elderly man named Thomas. His last name may be Ward. It's about the Kim Ward cold-case murder investigation."

"I figured, given the surname." Orlando shook his head. "I don't know a Thomas Ward."

"He'd be in his eighties. Maybe he goes by Tom or Tommy. Does that ring a bell?"

"There used to be a guy everyone called Old Tommy. I never knew his last name. He's dead."

"When?"

"Three months ago, in a hit-and-run on the interstate. The perp fled the scene. It was bound to happen to him. He constantly walked up and down I-10. Been doing it for years. Never crossed the state line into Texas. Said he didn't like the cops over there. He'd hike along the shoulder day and night. Sometimes he'd hitch a ride, most times not. He always looked skanky and smelled worse."

"Was he homeless?" Carla asked.

"I used to think so until a couple of years ago, when I saw him entering an old chicken coop at the rear of a run-down house that backs up to the interstate. I stopped by to check him out and found he'd been living there a long time, paying the landlord fifty bucks a month. No running water, a chamber pot for a toilet, an old surplus military bed, one ceiling light bulb fixture, and an outlet for a hot plate. When he wanted a shower, he walked to the big truck stop off the interstate to clean up. He'd wash his clothes at the Laundromat there."

"Did he have mental problems?"

"Yes. And he was basically harmless."

"Where was he living?"

"Better yet, follow me over and I'll introduce you to Nestor Vasquez, the guy who owns the place. Nestor isn't the brightest fellow and tends to get easily agitated with strangers."

"Let's go," Carla said, laying some dollar bills on the table.

———

Nestor Vasquez's house, a small mid-century ranch with a slumping front porch and peeling stucco, sat behind a waist-high, sagging, chain link fence. Behind it, five junky vehicles were parked helter-skelter in front of a shed and a chicken coop. The nearby roar of interstate traffic within yards of the property was loud and constant. The starkly beautiful Franklin Mountains rose in the distance to the east.

A frail-looking man in his late seventies, Nestor met Carla and Orlando on his front porch.

"Nestor, this is Carla Olivas. She's trying to find out if Old Tommy was a relative of a woman she's looking for. Have you rented out the chicken coop to somebody else since he died?"

Nestor eyed Carla suspiciously and shook his head. "No, it's too falling-down now. Tommy was my friend. Terrible somebody run him down."

"I'm sorry you lost your friend," Carla replied, almost certain she'd seen Nestor at the cock fights. "Do you know what his last name was?"

"He told me once, but I forgot," Nestor replied.

"Is there anything in the chicken coop that belonged to Tommy?"

"There's nothing there."

"Did you get rid of his stuff?" Orlando asked.

Nestor snorted at the question. "No, Tommy never kept nothing there."

"Nothing?" Carla probed.

"Not in the coop, but in the coupe," Nestor replied.

"Excuse me?" Carla said.

Nestor pointed a shaky finger at a rusty, 1960 two-door Ford Falcon sitting in front of the chicken coop. "In the car. He called it his closet."

"Can we look?"

Nestor shrugged. "It was his car."

On unsteady legs, Nestor followed Carla and Orlando Guerrero to the Ford, and explained that Tommy had bought the car for forty bucks from a junkyard and had it towed to the chicken coop soon after moving in.

Carla opened the driver's door and a family of mice scampered out from under the chewed-up bench seat and fled through the rusted-out floorboard. The interior was empty, but the glove box yielded a faded bill of sale from the junkyard and a key that opened the locked trunk. Inside the trunk were several plastic garbage bags filled with smelly clothes, a dopp kit containing a dozen pill bottles filled with expired psychotropic drugs, and a small suitcase. The suitcase contained old snapshots of young men in army fatigues, several military medals, a certificate of disability from the Veterans Administration, and an honorable discharge certificate made out to Thomas J. Trimble.

Held together with a rubber band was a packet of letters, all postmarked over twenty years ago, sent by Lucille Trimble. The return address was a Belen, New Mexico, post office box.

A fast scan of a letter brought a smile to Carla's face. Thomas and Lucille Trimble had been cousins, not brother and sister. In one passage, Lucille wrote of her continued, unsuccessful efforts to find her missing daughter, mentioning Kim by name. Carla now had a tangible lead—albeit an old one—on Kim's mother. Carla waved the letter at Orlando. "Kim Ward's mother. Maybe we've found her." She put the letters back in the suitcase, snapped it shut, hoisted it out of the trunk, and smiled at Nestor. "Thanks for your help, Mr. Vasquez."

Nestor scowled. "No more police come here anymore?"

"I can't promise you that," Carla said.

"That's okay," Nestor said, hobbling back toward his house.

Carla did a plain-view search of the empty chicken coop, thanked Orlando for his assistance, and headed for El Paso. A short drive down I-10 brought her to the home of Abby Hardin, who lived in a neighborhood near the El Paso Country Club. The housekeeper who answered the doorbell, an older, heavyset Mexican woman, told Carla that Mrs. Hardin and her husband were on an extended Mexico RV caravan tour of Yucatán and not due home for two more months. She added that they checked in by cell phone at least once a week.

Carla handed the woman a business card, asked to have Mrs. Hardin call her as soon as possible, and drove back to district headquarters eager to read Lucille's letters to Tommy.

———

Looking at the stack of documents on his desk made the notion of a streamlined, paperless workplace very appealing to Clayton. But such a fantasy would never fly in a cop shop. Nobody made a good arrest, served a legal warrant, testified correctly in court, or made an airtight case without paperwork, and lots of it.

He was too distracted to even think about wading through the field notes, investigative narratives, staff memos, and various other documents he was required to review. Instead, he looked expectantly at his desk telephone.

Carla Olivas had called in her discovery of Lucille Ward's old letters. Belen was a small city about forty miles south of Albuquerque along the I-25 corridor. A check with the post office revealed that a new patron had recently rented the postal box number once used by Lucille Trimble. Two agents from the north zone investigations unit were on their way for a meeting with a postal inspector to try and track her down. Clayton badly wanted them to succeed, and quickly.

He pushed aside the reports and reached for the leather-bound Fergurson journal that contained her entry on Kim Ward's stay in Kerney's bedroom before she vanished. Something about it didn't sit right.

Clayton read it again and realized it wasn't the content that bothered him, but the handwriting. It was choppy and untidy, and not at all like Fergurson's usual neat, flowing script. He scanned earlier and later entries, and it was the only one clearly out of sync. Perhaps what happened that night had really rattled her.

He closely examined the interior binding of the journal, where the pages had been glued and stitched together, and noticed that the page just before the Kerney entry had been carefully cut out. A thorough look confirmed no other pages had been removed. But what about the other journals?

With James Garcia's help, Clayton checked the remaining journals for missing pages. All told, at least thirty-six pages had been cut out from various journals.

"I guess there were some things Fergurson wanted kept private," Garcia said, closing the last journal.

"Or the pages were cut out by another person," Clayton replied as he headed for the door. "If Fergurson did it, chances are she destroyed them. But if it was somebody else, we need to find them. Call Eleanor Robbins at the campus library and radio me the office location for the art history professor who's researching Fergurson."

"You want company?" Garcia called out.

"Negative. I want some frigging answers."

CHAPTER 6

As a graduate of Western New Mexico University, a small col-lege in Silver City, for Clayton the size of the NMSU campus had always been a source of amazement. Today foot traffic seemed unusually heavy. After cruising past the university's stadium, he found his way to the building that housed the art history program and Dr. Nadira Shaheen's small office. She was a rather serious-looking woman of no more than thirty-five, with beautiful dark eyes. She wore a hijab that exposed her face but covered her hair and neck. Sitting at her desk, she smiled pleasantly at Clayton when he knocked at the open doorway.

"You're Lieutenant Istee, I believe. One of your colleagues called to say you were on your way."

"Yes, I am." Clayton showed his badge. "I need a moment of your time, Professor Shaheen, if you please."

"I am hoping you've come to say you are returning the Fergurson Papers to the library," she replied, her voice soft with a hint of a British accent.

"Not exactly." Clayton gauged her for any sign of anxiety, but saw none.

Shaheen's smile faded slightly as she gestured at an armless desk chair. "I'm disappointed. Please, sit and tell me what brings you here."

On the wall behind her desk were framed diplomas from the University of the Punjab, Cambridge University, and Harvard University, where she'd received her doctorate.

Clayton eased onto the chair. "There are thirty-six missing pages from the journals, and I need to recover them immediately."

Shaheen folded her hands and didn't blink at his insinuation. "Actually, the total number of missing pages is eighty-nine. If you have knowledge of where they are, I'd be most grateful if you told me."

"Perhaps you held them back for research purposes," Clayton pushed, hoping a frontal attack would rattle her composure.

"My goodness, why would I purloin documents I can easily make copies of?" Shaheen answered.

"Because of their inherent value or historical importance," Clayton countered. "Other academics have been known to do so."

"In this instance, your allegation is incorrect."

Clayton shrugged nonchalantly. "How do you know eighty-six pages are missing?"

"Eighty-nine," Shaheen corrected. "Because I am very thorough in my research, Lieutenant, and I examined every journal meticulously. But to answer your question more broadly, before he died last year, I recorded several interviews with one of Fergurson's closest colleagues in the art department, William Spenser Hurley. It was Hurley who told me Fergurson had removed some entries before bequeathing her journals to the university. She told him there were things from the past better left unrecorded."

"Did Fergurson share this information with anyone besides Hurley?"

"Not to my knowledge."

"Why did she tell Hurley?"

"To reassure him. They'd been lovers for a time during his marriage. When the affair was over, Hurley's wife, Barbara, subsequently became Fergurson's close friend. Erma saw no need to cause unnecessary strife with her. Thus, she removed the entries."

"Can I hear that part of the interviews?" Clayton asked.

"Yes, of course." Shaheen entered some keystrokes on her computer and sat back in her chair.

The raspy voice of an old man confirmed what the professor had said. It left Clayton with no doubt of Shaheen's truthfulness. "Eighty-nine pages?" he reflected.

Shaheen nodded. "Destroyed, I would imagine. I'd love to know what else Fergurson believed needed to be kept secret. So often, when recording in her journal, she was unconstrained, and personally revealing. What more had to be hidden from public view? It's quite an enticing mystery."

"Have you searched for the documents?"

"Everywhere. With Cynthia Davenport's assistance, I even went through the Fergurson Center files and looked at every folder and piece of paper. I've gone over all relevant Art Department archives, as well as associated library holdings. There is no place else to look."

Clayton stood. "Will it keep you from writing a good biography?"

"No, but I'll always wonder about the missing pieces."

Clayton flashed a sympathetic smile. "I can understand that."

He thanked the professor for her time, promised to get the journals back to the library as quickly as possible, and left wondering if her search had truly been exhaustive. Combing through papers was one thing. Academics were good at that. Probably better than cops in some ways. But what about searching places? Cops were much better at that specialty than art history professors.

It was time to go back to the Fergurson Center.

On his way to his unit, he got a call on his cell phone from Avery, who'd done a quick background check on Shaheen. Pakistani by birth, she had permanent resident status, and was married to a research scientist employed by NASA at the White Sands Missile Range Test Facility.

"Sorry, LT, she's legal. We can't deport her," Avery said flippantly.

"Did you know my ancestors were deported by the government?" Clayton replied. "Sent, shackled together in freight trains, from New Mexico to Florida."

"Yeah, I heard about that. They called it the Trail of Tears, right?"

"Wrong. That was an entirely different atrocity, and the victims were Cherokees, not Apaches."

"I guess not much has changed over the centuries," Avery said somberly.

"Try not to forget that," Clayton counseled.

———

A report by radio during Clayton's drive to the Fergurson Center brought frustrating news. The post office records search for Kim Ward's mother in Belen had stalled. The agents were back out in the field visiting residents and neighbors at the physical addresses where Lucille Trimble was known to have lived, hoping for a lead.

Clayton snorted in annoyance. He needed more than a lead, he needed a break in the case. He was way overdue for one. He slowed to a stop in front of the Fergurson Center and stared in astonishment at the mountain of dirt at the side of the house. A front-end loader was busily filling the bed of a dump truck, while two other trucks idled nearby, awaiting their turn. The excavation for the sunken amphitheater was huge and deep, almost swallowing up an earthmover blading dirt at the bottom of the hole. A cloud of dust and fine sand cloaked everything, thickening the air and reducing daylight by a third.

He parked behind a line of construction workers' vehicles and went looking for Cynthia Davenport. She was in the kitchen with the general contractor, David Jones, studying a set of drawings spread out on a counter. Clayton's sudden appearance triggered a passing look of irritation on Davenport's face. Jones, on the other hand, smiled affably.

"We're very busy, Lieutenant Istee," Davenport said. "Is it important?"

"I'm afraid so. I need to speak with you in private."

"Is that necessary?"

"Would you be more comfortable talking to me at district headquarters?"

With a dark look, Davenport grudgingly broke away and followed Clayton into the living room.

He continued toward the front door. "Your office, please."

Davenport sighed and followed him outside.

"What is it?" she demanded over the roar of heavy machinery.

Clayton didn't reply until they were seated in Davenport's office looking at each other across her desk, the construction noise reduced to a guttural rumble through the closed windows.

He had trained himself to read documents upside down, a skill helpful in his work. On top of the overflowing papers on Davenport's desk was a completed application to attend a memoir-writing workshop in Taos.

"I appreciate you telling me about Fergurson's journals," he began diplomatically. "I'd like to know more about your involvement with them."

Davenport blinked. "What do you mean?"

"As her last assistant, I assume you helped Fergurson put them in order before the papers went to the university library archives."

The lines around the corners of Davenport's eyes tightened, and she said slowly, "I assisted only in a small way. After all, they were Erma's personal writings. I only helped with the accompanying index. The catalog, so to speak."

Clayton showed no reaction, but it was hardly believable that Fergurson had donated her journals, minus eighty-nine pages, for all the world to see, without her trusted assistant ever getting a peek before they went into the archives.

"That makes perfect sense." Clayton smiled. "Did you know there are pages missing from the journals?"

Davenport cleared her throat. "I had no idea, until Professor Shaheen approached me about it."

"Of course, how could you know?" Clayton replied soothingly. "Do you recall any conversations with Erma about removing some of the entries?"

Davenport shook her head. "No. I discussed this with Professor Shaheen in detail. I even helped her search through all the center's files. Must I go through this again?"

"When you called to tell me about the journals, you didn't mention the missing pages," Clayton said.

Davenport looked at her wristwatch and stood. "I forgot about them, that's all. I was just trying to be helpful to you, Lieutenant. Now you've made me feel as if I've done something wrong. I really need to get back to my meeting with the contractor."

Clayton stayed seated. "I'd like to look at the files, Ms. Davenport. Maybe I'd have better luck."

Davenport shook her head. "Because Professor Shaheen is a university employee, it was permissible. But in this instance—a police matter—I'll need clearance from the administration."

"I'll arrange it." Clayton rose to his feet. "While I'm here, I'd like to take another look around the main premises."

"Whatever for?"

"I have a homicide to solve, and I want to make sure we haven't missed anything."

"From nearly a half a century ago? I doubt there's anything here for you to find."

"Humor me."

Davenport stepped around the desk to the door and opened it. "Be my guest."

Clayton followed her out, debating if she'd played straight with him or not. When it came to people doing wrong, he'd learned that acting like an injured party often signaled deceitfulness.

Davenport scooted away and Clayton wandered into the expansive, still-empty living room, thinking about Fergurson's "unconstrained" writing, as Professor Shaheen had put it.

Why were the missing pages from so many different years? From what he'd read at the office, some were gaps in sections of biting criticism about other artists and their work, several had been removed from Fergurson's running commentary about high-ranking university administrators, and there were two pages missing from a lengthy entry about a highly regarded, long-deceased former governor she'd actively supported with fund-raising dinner parties. Another intriguing break in a narrative involved a well-known feminist writer who'd been the editor-in-chief of a national magazine.

He studied the smooth plaster walls, the shiny tile floors, the long rectangular fireplace, looking carefully for any evidence of a hiding place. Nothing jumped out at him.

Fergurson had been a woman of means living alone in a some-what secluded setting. It wasn't unreasonable to assume she had a secure, secret place for valuables and important papers. Finding it was the problem.

He could hear Jones and Davenport talking as he walked down the hallway to inspect the bedrooms. The larger one was Erma's mas-ter suite, complete with a walk-in closet and adjacent bath. Two doors down, on the other side of a large linen closet, was the guest bedroom. It was opposite a full bathroom.

Clayton took his time with the closets and bathrooms, prime locations for wall or floor safes. He ran his hands over the smooth walls and tiles, hoping to feel a telltale irregularity in the surface. Using his pocketknife screwdriver, he removed the recessed medicine chest behind the sink mirror in the master bath, only to find a run of lath and plaster. He put it back and repeated the exercise in the guest bath, with the same disappointing results.

The kitchen and studio remained to be inspected. He bypassed the kitchen, where Jones and Davenport were still busy talking, and headed for the studio. It had been emptied after the staging for the groundbreaking ceremony. The view of the Organ Mountains out the two large picture windows continued to be spectacular. The room echoed the minimalist architectural theme of the living quarters, and, as before, Clayton saw nothing on the floor or walls that might signal a hiding place.

He glanced at the door to the large walk-in closet containing Fergurson's artwork. Davenport had not yet upgraded the lock or added surveillance cameras. Probably original to the house, the doorknob was of the keyed entry variety, likely with a turn button on the inside. Such locks had only a single cylinder, and were easily picked.

The door unlocked quickly on Clayton's first try. The racks, attached to the sidewalls and suspended a foot above the floor, held at least three dozen paintings stored on their edges, with thick pieces of cardboard separating each to prevent damage. He carefully tilted the paintings forward on the racks to look at the walls, and there on the back wall was a built-in safe with a standard tumbler combination lock.

He stepped out of the closet, locked the door, and went looking for Davenport. She was seeing Jones out the front door.

"Are you all done?" she asked, standing aside to let him pass.

"Not quite. I'd like you to open the closet in the studio."

She flinched slightly. "Only Professor Fergurson's paintings owned by the center are stored there."

"I'd like to look anyway," Clayton replied, noting her physical reaction. "Either right now, or within the hour with a court order."

"Very well," Davenport sighed.

She retrieved a key ring from a hook in a kitchen cabinet and opened the studio closet. Her shoulders sagged when Clayton removed the last painting that concealed the wall safe.

"Open it," he ordered.

"I don't know the combination," she blustered, stepping back.

Clayton closed the distance. "I think you do. If I have to call a specialist to open the safe, I will arrest you."

Davenport's trembling fingers jingled the key ring. "What for?"

"Concealing evidence, obstructing a criminal investigation, giving false information to a law enforcement officer, and probably a few more charges I'll think of before I'm done."

"You can't prove I've done anything wrong."

"I'm betting there are eighty-nine pages from Fergurson's journals in that safe with your fingerprints all over them. Pages you claim you never looked at. I'm guessing you took them, thinking they wouldn't be missed, because you planned to write a book about your years with Fergurson as her trusted assistant. A memoir, perhaps, containing some juicy exposés about prominent people she knew and startling new facts about mysterious events, such as the disappearance of Kim Ward."

Davenport covered her open mouth with her hand.

"I believe you didn't mean to interfere in a homicide investigation," Clayton added, seemingly sympathetic. "It just happened that way."

"Are you going to arrest me?"

"If you open the safe, I'd be inclined not to."

"Okay."

Under Clayton's watchful eyes, Davenport turned the tumbler, opened the safe, and took out a manila envelope. In it were the missing eighty-nine journal pages.

To protect the integrity of his investigation, he arrested her anyway.

CHAPTER 7

From Erma Fergurson's journal, Sunday, April 29, 1973:

I'm drained of emotion, wondering how to make sense of Kevin's behavior. It's been four days since Kim arrived unannounced and then vanished that very night, running away in the dark of night, K chasing after, trying to call her back. Her frightened screams, hurried footsteps on the floor, the slamming open of the front door, woke me from a troubled sleep. I heard her shout, "Leave me alone, get away, get away!"

From the open door, I watched them, Kim flying down the driveway as fast as humanly possible, clutching what appeared to be a shawl around her shoulders, K in pursuit, both disappearing into the darkness, voices fading, then silence.

An anxious sentinel, I waited in the living room until dawn for their return, the front door still flung wide open, the only sound a harsh wind whistling up from Mexico. In the kitchen,

my silver chain necklace I'd left on the counter the night before
was gone, and all the money in my purse was missing, the contents scattered about.

K's bedroom in chaos. Blood on a pillow case, damp bed
sheets kicked aside, a table lamp overturned, my small landscape
of Hermit's Peak askew on the wall, a tiny gash in the canvas,
pistol cartridges strewn on the floor—from whose gun? The
hunter-green wool bedspread missing. (The shawl Kim clutched
as she fled? Why did she run?)

My thoughts so jumbled. K so changed since Vietnam. That
warm, open young man now quiet, closed, wary. Tight smiles,
stingy conversation, long silences, easily distracted. The week
before Kim's arrival was tense. Not once did he speak of the war
or the tragic, heartbreaking death of his parents. Me, quiet, on
tiptoes, trying not to console or intrude.

Hours passed before his return. When he came back, shoes
caked with mud, clothes dirty, cactus needles clinging to his
pants cuffs, scratches on his arms, his face was flushed and etched
with anger. She'd taken some drugs—uppers—and gone crazy,
he said. She was an addict, had stolen his grandfather's ancient
pistol to kill her husband, he said. Why, he didn't know or
wouldn't say. He'd looked everywhere through the surrounding
hills to find her, but she'd vanished.

I said to call the police. He argued against it and wouldn't
relent, until I promised to say nothing other than his pistol had
been taken and Kim had spent the night. What was he hiding?
Why did he need me to lie? Why, after hours searching for Kim,
did he show no more concern for her safety?

I don't know if he did violence to Kim that night, but when
he returned his fury was palpable. I'd never seen him that way
before. I trembled when I asked why Kim had run away from

him. His answer, a tortured silence and dark look, left me shaken, fearing the worst.

Over these last few days, the silence has continued. He's leaving in the morning. I hope to God I've done nothing wrong.

———

With a low western sun painting the spires of the Organ Mountains shimmering gold through his window, Chief Deputy District Attorney Henry Larkin read Erma Fergurson's journal entries for a third time while Clayton waited patiently, seated at the other side of Larkin's desk.

In the foothills, he could see flashes of reflected light bouncing off the jib of a construction crane at the Fergurson Center, used to place massive boulders around the edges of the concrete pad at the bottom of the sunken amphitheater. As he waited, Clayton wondered how Davenport was feeling after her brief stint in the county jail. Although he'd made a call on her behalf to the best bail bondsman in town, which got her back on the street in a matter of hours, he doubted she held him in high regard. So be it. Lawbreaking had a price.

Larkin finally looked up. "This last entry by Fergurson, plus all the rest of the evidence you've gathered, doesn't get us to proof beyond a reasonable doubt of Kerney's guilt, which makes going to trial a real crapshoot. As it stands right now, even probable cause would be a stretch."

Clayton shook his head in protest. "We've got Kerney's revolver as the probable murder weapon, a partial of his fingerprint on the cartridge in the cylinder, a possible match of the fabric fragments found with the body and the type of bedspread Fergurson mentions in her journal, a falsified police report made about the revolver, and a handwritten account by Erma Fergurson of what was apparently a struggle or fight between Kerney and Ward."

Larkin clasped his hands behind his neck and leaned back in his chair. "But not an eyewitness account of the events in the bedroom, or what happened after Kerney and Ward went running off into the night."

Clayton sighed in agreement. "Okay, what Fergurson saw that night could be strongly questioned. There was a waning crescent moon on the night of April twenty-ninth, 1973, that set at five fifty-nine p.m. It was pitch-dark when Ward ran away."

Larkin sat up straight. "So Fergurson probably couldn't tell who was running down the driveway."

"She loved Kerney like a son," Clayton added.

Larkin chortled. "You're not helping your own case."

Clayton grimaced. "Kerney's comment that Ward was an addict was probably correct. Agent Olivas spoke by phone to an old rodeo teammate who reported that Todd Marks was dealing uppers and downers to contestants on the pro rodeo circuit and both Marks and Ward were using."

"Meaning?"

"Ward could have freaked out in the bedroom coming down off drugs, just as Kerney described it to Fergurson."

"I've never seen you so ambivalent." Larkin observed.

"It's worse than that. This is my father we're talking about. I don't know if I want Kerney cleared so I can get on with the investigation, or charged so I can step aside and wash my hands of the whole damn mess."

Larkin paused. "It might be wise to recuse yourself now."

Clayton shook his head. "Not until that question is answered."

"Kerney didn't raise you, did he?"

"Through no fault of his own. It's a long, sad story."

"And only yours to tell, if you want to."

Clayton smiled. "Don't go getting touchy-feely on me, Henry."

"Why, I'd never," Larkin replied, acting misunderstood. "Keep Kerney as your primary person of interest and continue digging. If you can't establish probable cause, maybe we can bring him in as a material witness. But I'd want to take that request to the grand jury, not a judge."

"Because?"

"For the simple reason that I'm not going to put my job on the line because you're conflicted."

"Fair enough."

"Has contact been made with Kerney to take a statement?" Larkin asked.

"Not yet. Voice messages have been left. He's out of the state in Missouri, attending his wife's retirement ceremony as the commandant of the army's military police school."

"You haven't been foot-dragging, have you?"

Clayton shrugged.

Larkin let Clayton's admission slide with a slight disapproving headshake. "His wife's an army commandant, is she? That must be a pretty high rank."

"She's a brigadier general."

Larkin whistled. "Gotta have some *huevos* to be married to a woman warrior."

"Tell me about it," Clayton replied.

"What do you want me to do with the Davenport charges?" Larkin asked as he rose from his chair. "Her lawyer's arguing that she had no knowledge of the contents of the safe."

"That's a lie, but she's no hardened criminal."

Larkin nodded. "I'll give it a week to let her sweat it out and then decline to prosecute. That should serve as punishment enough."

"Agreed." Dusk had shrouded the Organ Mountains, and the lights of Las Cruces stretched like long ribbons into the foothills.

Larkin walked Clayton to the door. "Enjoy the weekend."

"You, too," Clayton answered, suddenly remembering he'd prom-

ised to take Grace and the kids to Mescalero tomorrow for dinner with
his mother.

———

In tears, Cynthia Davenport left Hadley Hall, the university's administration building, and drove away fuming at Clayton Istee. Because of
her arrest, she'd been questioned, placed on administrative leave, and
ordered to stay away from the Fergurson Center until the Office of General Counsel concluded an investigation into the charges against her.

Nothing like this had ever happened to her before. In her entire
life, she'd gotten one traffic ticket for speeding and maybe three parking tickets, which she'd promptly paid. Now, facing the possibility of
losing her job, right when everything seemed to be going so well, she
was both frightened and angry. She was terrified of being a single,
middle-aged woman out of work, with a big black mark on her résumé,
and was furious at Lieutenant Istee for heartlessly deceiving her into
believing he wouldn't arrest her.

In hindsight, it had been a mistake to tell the lieutenant about
Fergurson's journals, and equally stupid to tell him she had no real
knowledge of the contents. But who knew a cold-case investigation
would become so all-encompassing, and drag her into it? All she'd been
thinking was how great it would be to have a sensational, decades-old
murder mystery solved to include in her book. In writers' workshops
she'd learned that true-to-life, sensational events made books more
marketable, turned them into bestsellers.

But her memoir hinged on a bigger lie, that of being Erma's closest
confidant for almost twenty years, privy to the most intimate details
about the important people in her life. She'd planned to dish all the
scandalous stuff Erma had removed from her journals with no single
main course, in which her surrogate nephew, Kevin Kerney, was by
no means front and center.

All the important particulars that were missing from the journals would be included in her book. The outline and proposal she'd submitted to a small university press had attracted the interest of an editor, and she'd hoped to have the book published to coincide with the grand reopening of the Fergurson Center.

But when Kim Ward's remains were found, her focus had shifted. Now she had a homicide that would be the centerpiece of her book. She'd tantalize readers with her uncanny ability to put together all the pieces of a missing-person cold case that had stymied the police for decades. And when the missing journal pages were discovered, although she'd yet to work out how exactly that would happen, it would confirm her role as Erma's most trusted confidant.

She'd told her lawyer that she had no knowledge of the contents of the safe, a story she stuck to at her meeting with her supervisor. Would it stand up under scrutiny? Lieutenant Istee had watched her open the safe's tumbler combination from memory. But she could argue that someone else with the combination could have placed the pages inside without her knowledge. She shook her head. It was a lame excuse. Her fingerprints were on every one of those papers she'd deliberately left in the safe to be "discovered" later and used to substantiate the damaging revelations in her memoir.

Her hands froze on the steering wheel. She was screwed. Lieutenant Istee had screwed her, ruined her life.

Home at the dining room table, a glass of Merlot in her shaky hand, she powered up her laptop and started an Internet search for Clayton Istee. He'd forced her to open the safe. Bullied and arrested her. What could she find to use against him? He deserved to be punished. There had to be something.

As expected, recent news stories about him leading the investigation into the cold-case murder popped up first, followed by older cases he'd successfully closed in the recent past. On the state police website only his name, rank, and position were listed, without an accompanying photograph or bio.

His two college-age children were on the usual social media sites, and his wife's work experience as a professional preschool educator and college instructor was also easy to access. Although there was little about the lieutenant, there was something familiar about his name. She recalled coming across it somewhere, long before he arrived at the center with his officers to provide additional security for the Spanish ambassador.

On a hunch, she retrieved a USB flash drive from the living room bookcase that contained the detailed outline of her memoir and all the names and dates she'd compiled from Erma's journals before delivering them to Eleanor Robbins at the university. A word search of the unusual surname Istee took her to Isabel Istee, mentioned in the 1969 and 1970 journals. The Internet yielded a news story of a ceremony honoring her for her service as a Mescalero tribal council member. It noted that her son, Clayton Istee, a tribal police officer at the time, and his wife and young children had been in attendance. Years later, there was another brief mention in the Ruidoso newspaper, reporting her retirement as head nurse from the Mescalero Public Health Service Hospital.

Okay, now she had something. Erma had known Lieutenant Istee's mother. What else did they have in common? Davenport sipped a second glass of Merlot, her spirits lifting, and went back to the flash drive. Kim Ward, the girl the police had identified as the murder victim, popped up. Now she remembered: Isabel Istee and Kim Ward had both been college girlfriends of the boy Erma suspected might have had something to do with Ward's disappearance. And his name, according to her outline, was Kevin Kerney, the son of Erma's oldest, dearest friend.

Davenport surfed dozens of archived Internet news items that chronicled his storied law enforcement career. So, he'd been a cop like Istee. Was that just a coincidence?

Nothing surfaced until she came upon an old news report about a manhunt and the killing of a wanted criminal in the rugged mountains of northern New Mexico. The headline stopped her cold.

FATHER AND SON COP DUO IN SHOOT-OUT
WITH WANTED KILLER

The story recounted how Kevin Kerney and Clayton Istee had tracked and shot to death an escaped convict who'd been on a murderous spree across the state.

Davenport was elated. Now it all made sense. Lieutenant Clayton Istee was protecting his father, Kim Ward's suspected killer. She smirked at the duplicity involved. If anyone else had been the suspect, an arrest would have certainly been made. Cops get away with murder. It happens all the time, shown almost nightly on the evening news.

She drained her glass, and poured another. God, if only she'd known. Her heart pounded in her chest at the thought of her life ruined by those two men. They'd stripped her of her job, destroyed her reputation, killed her dream of becoming a writer, and left her with nothing except an empty future. She had no family to fall back on, no children or husband, no close friends, no savings, a modest pension plan that, when cashed in, would run dry in a few years. The prospect of going to prison terrified her beyond belief. That, she couldn't face. She shuddered at the idea of being locked up surrounded by lesbians and brutal guards.

More than tipsy, she went to the kitchen, returned with another bottle of Merlot, and filled the glass. She hadn't eaten since breakfast but wasn't a bit hungry. At the laptop, with her fingers poised above the keys, she considered what to do. Over the years, she'd publicized numerous events at the center and had a sizable number of broadcast and print media contacts in her email address book, including reporters at the major television stations in Albuquerque and El Paso, and investigative journalists at the big newspapers in both cities, as well as an editor up in Santa Fe. Why not tell them what had happened? Ask them to find out why she was arrested after evidence found at the Fergurson Center implicated a former, highly respected police chief in a cold-case murder investigation that was being conducted by his son?

She'd propose that the police were trying to keep her silent. That Lieutenant Istee was engaged in a cover-up to protect his father. At the very least, why hadn't Kerney been questioned? And if he had, why hadn't the public been told?

She'd speculate that the conspiracy went to the top of the state police chain of command. And finally, she'd demand an apology from the police for being branded a lawbreaker for trying to do the right thing. She'd put everything she sent out on her Facebook page as well.

It could go viral. All it would take was just one reporter to show some interest. Davenport bared her teeth in a smile and began typing.

———

By lunchtime Saturday Clayton had almost forgotten about Kerney and the investigation. The drive home to Mescalero with the family in the morning to visit his mother had turned into a spur-of-the-moment gathering of uncles, aunts, and cousins he hadn't seen for some time. In the tall pines of the high mountains with the sacred Sierra Blanca in view, Clayton sat on Isabel's front porch watching Hannah and Wendell with his uncle James at the corral saddling up three ponies in anticipation of a short trail ride they'd take after everyone finished eating. Perched on the porch railing, his cousin Selena, who helped run the resort and casino for the tribe, was telling him about a Texas oilman who'd lost six hundred thousand at craps just before he had a fatal heart attack in the bar while his wife was busy playing the slots. Nobody, including the wife, shed a tear. Security moved the body out as quickly as possible to keep any lurking ghost at bay.

In the kitchen, Grace, Isabel, and the aunties had three different kinds of stews going, a meat and piñon nut that was Clayton's favorite, a vegetable with red chili, and a green chili with chunks of potato. There were two huge bowls of salad in the making: macaroni and a mustard-potato concoction—Grace's specialty. The delicious smell of fry bread filled the air, mixed with the spicy aroma of simmering chili sauce.

The staggering amount of food being prepared suggested more friends and relatives would be arriving throughout the day, although Isabel hadn't told him as much. It would be a feast, and Clayton looked forward to it. A day away from work, back in his ancestral homeland, surrounded by his people, felt cleansing, a release from all his doubts about Kerney. Starting out from Las Cruces, he'd gone so far as to turn off his cell phone to leave the case behind. But, if needed, Luis Mondragon knew where he was and how to reach him. He hoped that wouldn't be necessary.

In the front room, two more cousins and his uncle Bernard were gathered at Mom's new flat-screen television watching a satellite broadcast of a Chicago Cubs baseball game. Out back, several youngsters had a game of horseshoes going, and Clayton could hear the clink of metal against the stakes. In the driveway, Fred Peso, about the oldest Apache alive, leaned against the fender of his pickup truck talking politics with two retired tribal administrators.

It was about as perfect a day as it could get, and Clayton pondered coming home for good, not just occasionally on a stolen Saturday. The idea appealed, but any continuing thoughts about the future were waylaid by more arriving guests. It wasn't until later in the afternoon, after all had eaten their fill and Wendell and Hannah were back from their trail ride, that his mother had a moment to spare with him.

She joined him on the porch, where he occupied the same chair he'd claimed since morning, and kissed him on the cheek, announcing Grace was in the kitchen catching up with her mom and that Wendell and Hannah had taken off with some friends for a short drive to nearby Ruidoso.

The crow's-feet at the corners of her eyes and the wrinkles on her cheeks showed her age, but her eyes remained as shiny and clear as a young girl's.

"This was some great fiesta you threw," Clayton said. "Care to tell me what the occasion is?"

"Just a reminder," Isabel answered with a sly smile.

"Of?" Clayton waved her off before she spoke. "Wait, let me guess, where I'm from, who I am, where I belong."

Isabel nodded. "You know me well. It was also to celebrate the joy and pride I have for you and your family."

Kerney popped into Clayton's head. Right now he didn't have much pride and joy about him. Would it totally evaporate? He hoped not.

Isabel leaned close to him, searching his face. "What's the matter?"

"I hope I'm wrong, but my part of the family may not bring much happiness. Kerney is the prime suspect in the cold case I'm working on."

"The Kim Ward murder?"

Clayton nodded.

"Impossible," Isabel snapped. "Never in a million years. Have you talked to him?"

Clayton shook his head. "Not yet. For now, he's just a person of interest. There's not enough evidence to charge him with the crime."

Isabel's expression turned stormy. "He knows nothing about this? What are you doing even investigating him anyway? Why isn't another officer handling this?"

"It's my job, and I want to know if he did it, dammit."

"Call him in Santa Fe and ask him," Isabel ordered. "Tell him what you're doing. Let him defend himself, and then step aside. I am astonished that you would even consider him capable of such a thing."

Clayton thought back to a day years ago, when he'd broken his leg in a fall. It had happened when he was working alongside Kerney as they closed in on Craig Larson, a spree killer, in the rugged northern New Mexico mountains. Kerney had called for medical assistance and left him behind. When he returned, the target was dead.

Clayton had always wondered if Kerney had executed Larson. Among Larson's many victims was a young man who'd been Kerney's neighbor and friend. Larson had shot him down in cold blood at Kerney's front door.

He knew Kerney *was* capable. Under the right circumstances, he would be, too.

"I didn't think you gave a hoot about him," he finally said. "Besides, he's not home."

Isabel stood. "When I was young, unsure, and half afraid of the White Eyes' world, that man—your father—gave me much more than just you. Call him right now, wherever he is."

A black-and-white state police cruiser turned onto the long driveway to the house, emergency lights flashing.

Clayton pushed himself upright and started toward the oncoming unit. "This may not be the best time for that."

———

With a grim look on his face, Luis Mondragon opened the passenger door window and said, "Get in."

Clayton opened the door as he waved his mother away. "What's up?"

"It's all over social media that you've been shielding your father from murder charges. That Davenport woman went on Facebook about it, and she's got several TV reporters interested enough to ask for interviews about the allegation. Santa Fe is screaming for your head, and the DA told Henry Larkin to get a warrant for Kerney's arrest signed pronto."

"Shit."

"Larkin wants an exact location of Kerney's whereabouts, so he can have local authorities arrest and hold him for extradition."

"I don't have an exact location. I've already told Larkin he's in Missouri with his wife and son. Tell Larkin to call the army."

Mondragon nodded. "Okay, but you're coming with me. I bought you some time, and told Deputy Chief Serrano you were participating in an Apache religious ceremony at some secluded place on the rez but I'd try to track you down. Otherwise, a chopper would be here right now taking you to Santa Fe, so you could fall on your sword."

"Is it that bad?"

"Have you called or talked to Kerney?"

"Not once."

"If you can prove that to Internal Affairs, you might survive. But even with proof you didn't contact Kerney, they'll argue that you crossed the line."

"I should have punted this case to someone else as soon as I knew Kerney was involved."

"Ain't hindsight wonderful?"

Through the windshield, Clayton could see Grace hurrying toward the unit, with Isabel close behind. All the aunties had gathered on the porch, arms crossed, looking ready to go to war.

He took a deep breath and opened the car door. "Give me a minute."

"Make it quick," Mondragon advised.

He didn't like what he had to say to Grace and his mother. Didn't like it at all.

CHAPTER 8

Because he was an ex-cop, Kerney spent three days locked in a segregation cell for his own protection. Except for a phone call with Sara to figure out a strategy, a closed-circuit TV extradition hearing before a judge, and a meeting with the local lawyer Sara had retained, he was completely isolated. He hated every minute of it.

The lawyer, Roy Mossy, had given him a copy of the criminal complaint that had been prepared and signed by Clayton Istee. What had he done to that man, to be treated so outrageously? What in the hell was Clayton doing investigating him anyway? Clayton should have recused himself from the case the minute Kerney had become a person of interest.

There would be no answers until he got out of jail and could start his own investigation. It would be up to him to prove his innocence. But first he'd get Clayton kicked off the case. If it ruined his career, so be it. He wasn't feeling fatherly about him at all.

Clayton knew what kind of man he was. They had worked side by side as cops, gotten to know each other's families, built a cordial, if somewhat distant, relationship. If Clayton had asked Kerney about Kim Ward, he would have learned that she had been the first true love of his life, and that her disappearance had haunted him for years. It was Kim's disappearance that played a big part in his decision to become a cop.

An hour before Kerney was to fly home in the custody of officers from the New Mexico State Police, Roy Mossy told him his arrest for murder had gone viral on social media and been picked up by national print and television news outlets as a headline story. Pundits were calling him a fake hero, a rogue cop, a killer with a badge. Realizing he'd already been convicted in the court of public opinion, Kerney's spirits sank.

"You're national news," Mossy said. "They're going to perp-walk you out of here in front of a mob of reporters and cameras."

Kerney knew what to do: keep his head up, look straight ahead, stay composed, answer no questions. No smiling, frowning, or reactions that could be interpreted as anger or defiance.

He was glad Sara wouldn't be there to see it. She was in New Mexico retaining the services of Gary Dalquist, a top-flight criminal defense attorney with an outstanding record of winning acquittals in capital murder cases. She'd meet him at the Las Cruces airport when the plane arrived.

He wondered how Patrick was doing. It had to be tough on a kid of fourteen to have his father accused of murder.

Dressed in his wrinkled suit, Kerney processed out of jail, accompanied by two NMSP plainclothes officers, who cuffed his hands behind his back and guided him through a throng of converging reporters and cameramen, shouting questions and jabbing microphones in his direction. The scene played out again at the regional airport, where a chartered turboprop waited to fly him to Las Cruces.

During the flight, the officers kept Kerney cuffed to the back, which became increasingly painful. He kept his mouth shut and didn't complain.

On their approach to the little-used Las Cruces airport, it was clear Kerney was in for a repeat performance. State police officers had used their units to form a barricade to hold back a crowd gathered in front of the small terminal building. Vehicles filled the parking lot and lined the shoulders of the access road.

He deplaned accompanied by the two cops. His shoulders ached, his hands were numb, and his head throbbed with pain, but he kept his self-control and didn't wince.

He almost smiled when he spotted Sara in the crowd standing next to Gary Dalquist. Prosecutors hated to go up against Dalquist. With his deep, rumbling voice, cherubic face, and flamboyant personality, he could turn criminal proceedings into theater.

Kerney had known him for years. Now in his late seventies and semi-retired, Dalquist only took cases that appealed to him.

Kerney's escorts bundled him into the backseat of a waiting police unit while cameramen jockeyed for the best shots and reporters shouted questions.

As the young patrol officer wheeled his unit down the access road, followed by a small convoy of police vehicles, the glorious Organ Mountains came into view. Just the sight of them made Kerney feel better. He shook off the pain. He needed to be clear-headed in front of a judge, and by God he would be. Dalquist would have him out of jail in no time. Then the hard work of proving his innocence would begin.

The urge to call Clayton and tell him what a disappointing asshole of a son he was crossed his mind. That would have to wait until later.

———

On the short drive to the jail, Gary Dalquist suggested to Sara she should quickly get him home to the familiarity and comfort of their ranch, and, if possible, avoid talking about the case.

"No matter how prepared he thought he was to handle jail, trust me, it's a big shock to anyone's system," Dalquist commented. "He'll need to decompress."

"I'm sure you're right," Sara replied, as she slowed her car behind a pickup truck that turned in front of her.

Kerney's appearance as he deplaned at the airport worried her deeply. Although the police had hustled him to the waiting marked unit, a quick glance convinced her he'd been under considerable stress.

As she drove past the turnaround in front of the jail to the visitors parking lot, Dalquist proposed that they all meet three days hence in his Santa Fe office to discuss strategy. That would give him sufficient time to look over the discovery documents provided by the prosecution. In the interim, if the prosecution made demands to interrogate Kerney, he'd block it with a doctor's order certifying he was recovering from police mistreatment on the flight home, and unable to comply. Also, to ensure their privacy at home, he'd arranged for twenty-four/seven security at the ranch road entrance.

"That should stymie surveillance and keep any reporters at bay," he added.

"They'll use drones," Sara predicted as they walked toward the jail, a large modern facility close to the county administration building. "But every little bit of time we have out of sight will certainly help get us settled down and thinking straight."

Inside, the court hearing to secure Kerney's release would be conducted by closed-circuit TV. Sara had a bail bond agent standing by.

"Just make sure he stays put until our meeting," Dalquist cautioned.

"That may be hard to do. He doesn't like loose ends, and being arrested for murder is a pretty big rope left hanging."

"The case against him will never go to trial," Dalquist predicted with a smile. "It's about as bollixed as it can be."

"He's going to want more than that," Sara said.

"Of course," Dalquist replied. "Complete exoneration is our goal." He searched Sara's face. "Are you certain of his innocence?"

"Completely." Sara stopped at the front door and gave Dalquist a hard look. "Are you?"

Dalquist nodded as he stood aside to let Sara proceed through the front door. "I've known your husband for many years, and I know his character. He once helped a confessed murderer he arrested receive a greatly reduced prison sentence because he believed, as did I, that her action was justified."

"I didn't know that."

"Ask him about Nita Lassiter," Dalquist said. "However, our task is far more difficult, I'm afraid. To clear Kerney's name, we're going to have to find Kim Ward's killer, if that person is even still alive. Or produce irrefutable evidence that proves Kerney is innocent. And the police won't help us."

"I'm prepared to do whatever it takes," Sara said firmly.

"Well, then, let's get started," Dalquist replied, smiling to himself as Sara stepped inside. He couldn't have had a smarter, more competent investigator to work on Kerney's behalf. After but a few hours in her company, he'd concluded with certainty that Sara Brannon was an extraordinary woman.

———

Out on bail with court orders to surrender his passport and remain in New Mexico, Kerney slept most of the way on the long drive home from Las Cruces. He stirred awake as they crested La Bajada Hill, with Santa Fe, nestled in its shallow basin, stretched out before them, the still-snowcapped Sangre De Cristo Mountains spilling down to the foothills of the city.

"Welcome back," Sara said.

He stifled a yawn. "Jesus, I'm wrecked."

"We're almost there."

Kerney shook his head sadly. "Sorry I spoiled your retirement party."

Sara flashed him a smile and laughed. "You didn't mess up anything. Nice as they are, Tom and Margaret Benson would have bored you to tears, and the rest of the guests would've been gossiping about people you don't know, or debating Pentagon politics. Besides, what happened has made my retirement party legendary, something to be talked about for years to come at officers' clubs around the globe."

He half smiled. "Hopefully I've ruined any chance you ever had to be recalled to active duty."

Sara reached over and squeezed his hand. He no longer looked ghostly pale. "Well, we've found one good thing out of this mess we can agree on. I've no desire to be anything but a full-time civilian."

"Amen to that," Kerney replied.

He dozed again until they left the highway southeast of Santa Fe and turned onto the cutoff that led to the ranch road. At the gate, a polite, armed security guard checked their IDs, welcomed them home, and waved them through. They drove across the lower pasture and up the canyon to the ranch house, sheltered by a low ridgeline with views of the Galisteo Basin and Ortiz and Sandia Mountains coursing across the horizon. To the north, behind the low-slung, adobe house, the land rose gradually, hiding all but the night lights of Santa Fe from view, with only rolling pastures, lightly sprinkled with piñon and junipers, and the Jemez and Sangre De Cristo Mountains in sight.

Kerney sighed in relief. He was home.

Sara parked next to Kerney's truck. "I'm going to ask my parents to keep Patrick in Tucson for a few more days."

"Good idea." Kerney opened the passenger door. "I'll call him in the morning."

"He believes in you with all his heart, Kerney."

"I know that, but he deserves to hear me tell him that I didn't kill Kim Ward." His jaw tightened.

"What is it?"

"I just didn't keep her from getting killed."

"You don't know that."

He pulled himself out of the vehicle, his wrists still sore, his back still a tight knot. "Yes, I do."

"You need a drink, a soak in the tub, a good meal, and more sleep. Those are orders, not suggestions."

"Yes, ma'am," Kerney replied, as they walked together to the front door, accompanied by the sound of an approaching drone.

———

Sara woke to find Kerney gone from bed. In the kitchen, a carafe of fresh coffee and a rinsed-out mug signaled he was probably at the horse barn doing morning chores. Across the meadow, the sight of the old ranch pickup parked at the corral confirmed it. She decided to forgo coffee, hurried to dress, and drove to the barn under low clouds of a fast-moving April snowstorm, half rain, half snow, that promised to linger for a short while.

Kerney's dream to raise and train cutting ponies had ended when Riley, Jack Burke's son, was murdered while Sara, Kerney, and Patrick were living in London. They dissolved the partnership and sold the stud stallion, leaving only Kerney's horse, Patrick's pony, and Sara's mare stabled at the ranch, along with a small herd of cattle on the large pasture leased to a local producer. Kerney had talked about ending the lease and putting a few cows of their own on the land, but had yet to do it.

In the barn, she found him currying Pablito, Patrick's pony. Hondo and Ginger patiently waited their turn. The stalls had been mucked out, fresh straw laid down, water troughs filled, and feed put out. Some of the tension that had etched Kerney's face the day before had dissipated. She was happy to see it, and glad to find him with the horses—a sure sign he was bouncing back from the ordeal of the last few days.

"You're up early," Sara observed cheerily, as she stepped into Ginger's stall, patted the mare's muzzle, and started grooming her.

"I overdosed on sleep," Kerney replied, inspecting a small cut on Pablito's flank. "Besides, I need something to do other than brood."

"We should go riding when the storm breaks," Sara suggested.

"I'd like that."

The familiar sound of a truck diesel engine outside announced the arrival of Juan Ramirez, the producer's hired hand who drove down several times a week from Pecos to check on the cattle. As a side job, he also looked after the ponies and the ranch when the family was away.

He slid open the double doors and stepped inside, bundled in a heavy winter coat with his cowboy hat pulled down to the top of his ears. The storm had turned to heavy snow, and the cab of Juan's truck was covered in a good six inches of the wet stuff.

"We got three inches on the ground so far in Pecos," he declared, as he closed the doors, stomped his feet, nodded a greeting at Sara, and grinned at Kerney. "Hey, you're out of jail, man. That's good, real good. You ain't no killer, no matter what they say. I know that."

Kerney smiled. "Thanks for the vote of confidence, amigo." Many years ago, he'd busted a very young Juan Ramirez on a drug charge. After serving a year and a day in the county lockup, Juan had turned his life around. Now middle-aged, he had a weathered face from laboring at just about any kind of outdoor work he could find.

"Jail's no fun, *jefe*," Juan added knowingly. "It still gives me shivers to think about doing time."

"I didn't like it much, either," Kerney replied agreeably. "Come by for coffee when you're done with the cattle."

Juan grinned. *"Bueno, gracias."*

Sara smiled appreciatively at Juan. His straightforward, genuine belief in Kerney's innocence made a good start to the day even better.

———

After breakfast and a chatty coffee break with Juan, Kerney went into the library and called Patrick in Tucson. When he finished the call, he came into the kitchen smiling. Through the patio doors, the storm was clearing, leaving behind a lovely light blanket of sparkling snow on the grassy meadow.

"It went okay?" Sara asked.

"He was hesitant to talk about it at first, but he got over that in a hurry. He asked all the right questions. That boy would make a great cop."

"I'd much prefer he takes up ranching, and keep the family tradition alive for a few more generations."

Kerney nodded in agreement. "That would be fantastic. When are you going to quiz me about Kim Ward?"

"Do I have to?"

Sara's response caught Kerney by surprise. "I guess not."

"Then I won't. We're seeing Dalquist in two days to plan our counterattack."

Kerney shook his head. "That's too long to wait."

"No, it's not."

"Are you being firm with me?"

"You bet. Didn't we say something earlier about taking the ponies out for some exercise after the storm passed?"

"We did."

"Are you still up for it?"

"A short ride would suit me."

"Promise not to fall out of the saddle."

"I'm not that beat-up. But if I do wreck, just have Hondo drag me back to the barn."

"It's a deal. While we're saddling up, you can tell me about Nita Lassiter."

Kerney's eyes widened. "Dalquist told you?"

Sara nodded. "Well?"

"She killed a cop."

His answer stunned her. "There has to be more to the story than that."

Kerney reached for his coat on the wall rack near the patio doors. "There is."

"I'm listening," Sara replied as she tugged on her coat.

————

With Clayton pulled from the case and temporarily reassigned to Santa Fe, where he was inventorying seized vehicles for the next public auction, Paul Avery got tapped as acting supervisor. The brass didn't want to do it, as there were more experienced, higher-ranking agents within the division. But the department's ever-cautious chief legal counsel respected Gary Dalquist's ability to exploit any potential prosecution weakness, and felt disrupting the continuity of the case by bringing in someone new could be risky.

Not the least bit intimidated by a less-than-enthusiastic Deputy Chief Serrano, who'd assumed full administrative oversight of the investigation, Avery dug in. He had a saturation team headed by Carla Olivas looking for Kim Ward's mother in Belen and the surrounding communities. He had an agent down in Anthony doing an additional search of the chicken coop and junk car where Tom Trimble had lived, and interviewing everyone who knew him. Additionally, James Garcia was leading a team of three agents backtracking on everyone who'd already been interviewed in the hopes of shaking loose fresh information, while Charlie Epperson worked the list of Kim Ward's former college rodeo teammates.

Called up to Santa Fe to brief Chief Serrano, as well as a senior advisor to the governor, Avery drove into town early enough to stop at a roadside café on the south side of town and meet Sergeant Gabriel Medina, a supervisor in the Santa Fe County Sheriff's Office Investigations Unit. Gabe had been his best friend since elementary school in Albuquerque.

The café was a dive that smelled of greasy fried food and looked in need of major renovation, starting with demolition. Through the thin walls, the sound of power ratchets from the tire store next door reverberated.

"Have you found someone for me?" Avery asked as he joined Gabe at a back booth. His boyhood friend still wore the exact style of black-frame eyeglass that he'd had since kindergarten. He looked more like a high school science teacher than a cop.

Gabe nodded and glanced at his watch. "You owe me big-time. We're meeting him in an hour."

"Great."

"I'm hiking into the Gila Wilderness for some fly fishing this weekend," Gabe said with a wicked grin. "Want to come?"

Avery groaned. He'd accompanied Gabe on one such expedition and had returned from the mountains bored, leg-weary, and sick of eating fish. "Aren't you ever gonna stop ribbing me about that?"

Gabe grinned. "Never. Don't worry, though, I won't make the mistake of taking you with me again."

"Thank God." Avery paused as the waitress poured coffee and sauntered away. "So, tell me."

"Your CI is Juan Ramirez. He did a year in county a long time ago on a drug bust, otherwise his record is clean. Works for a small rancher in Pecos who leases pastureland from Kerney. He also looks after Kerney's horses and ranch when the family's gone."

"How did you manage to recruit him?"

"His sixteen-year-old nephew is a bit of a fuckup. I've got him in juvie on multiple charges stemming from an auto burglary and subsequent high-speed chase. Ramirez's sister doesn't want her boy to spend his next couple of birthdays locked up. I promised Juan I'd talk to the judge."

"Of course."

Gabe wagged a cautionary finger at Avery. "Ramirez is not a happy camper about this arrangement. He likes Kerney and his family. He could easily get agitated and want to bail on you."

"Will you babysit him for me? I can't do a lot of hand-holding from Las Cruces."

Gabe sighed. "You do know there isn't a serving or retired cop in Santa Fe who thinks Kerney killed that woman, and that includes a lot of your own people."

"Does that make what I'm asking you to do wrong?"

Gabe shook his head.

"I'm sure Kerney is going to work his own investigation, and I need eyes on him as much as possible. Overhead drones and surveillance tails aren't enough. I want to know what he's thinking, what his plans are."

"I'm not sure Ramirez can give you that, but I'll handle him for you. However, you have to meet with him first."

"To cover your butt?"

"Damn right."

Avery laid money on the table and stood. "Let's go."

"You haven't touched your coffee."

Avery stared at the oily, murky brew. "I'm a cautious man when it comes to food and beverage."

———

Assigned to deskwork in the vehicle maintenance building behind the Department of Public Safety headquarters in Santa Fe, Clayton had little to do except wait for the next round of interrogation, conducted by Captain Wayne Upham, head of Internal Affairs. He was a sour-looking hulk of a man nearing retirement, with no sense of humor, who seemed determined to find Clayton guilty of wrongdoing far beyond not recusing himself from the Kim Ward murder case.

Except for the windowless corner office Clayton sat in, the long, narrow building consisted mainly of large bay doors, hydraulic lifts, pits, diagnostic equipment, tool chests on rollers, and wheel-alignment and tire-mounting machines. The place reeked of motor oil and exhaust fumes, and the service and repair work constantly going on made for a noisy racket even with the office door closed.

There was no office phone, and the department had confiscated Clayton's personal cell phone for analysis. He was effectively cut off from everybody.

When he wasn't being grilled by Upham or one of his underlings, Clayton roamed the seized-vehicle impound lot, filling out the various forms and legal papers necessary for the upcoming public auction. Off duty, he drove an old, crappy unmarked unit to his room at a nearby Cerrillos Road motel, or one of the family-style restaurants that flanked a large southside shopping mall, whose mostly empty parking lot testified to the popularity of online shopping.

He wasn't physically locked up, but he could only use the vehicle for official business, personal errands, and meals. In the evenings, after a workout in the motel gym and dinner, he stayed in his room watching TV or reading a book, waiting for Grace to call. When they talked, he stayed cheerful and played down his misery, reassuring her all was okay and he'd be home soon. He wasn't fooling her, but thankfully she didn't challenge him about it.

Clayton knew Upham's attempts to demoralize and isolate him were part of a strategy to force him to a breaking point, a critical mile-stone in any interrogation. He'd already copped to poor judgment. But he wasn't about to crack under Upham's relentless pressure to confess that he'd deliberately contrived to conceal Kerney's guilt, and withhold evidence pertinent to the investigation.

At six the next morning, Upham's secretary called with orders for Clayton to present himself at headquarters in thirty minutes. Upham waited for him in a harshly lit interrogation room, sprawled back in a metal armless chair, legs crossed, reading a file, a cup of coffee on the tabletop close at hand.

Clayton sat across from him, facing the mirror that hid the video recording equipment and any interested observers. After a long silence, Upham looked at him and said, "I still don't understand something."

Hands folded on the table, Clayton silently looked at Upham.

"According to a statement made by Chief ADA Larkin, you took Erma Fergurson's incriminating journal entries about Kevin Kerney along with all the additional evidence against him for Larkin to review," Upham said. "Correct?"

"Yes."

"And argued in favor of an arrest warrant, citing Kerney's falsified police report about the allegedly stolen murder weapon, a partial of his fingerprint on the remaining cartridge in the cylinder, and a possible match with a bedspread from the house to a fabric fragment found with the remains. Is that correct?"

"Yes."

Upham leaned forward, took a sip of coffee, and studied a typewritten sheet of paper. "After all the conversation, the back-and-forth, didn't Larkin say to you, and I quote, 'It might be wise to recuse yourself now'?"

"He did."

Upham placed the sheet of paper facedown on the table. "Which you declined to do because you first wanted clarity as to Kerney's guilt or innocence."

"That's correct."

Upham smirked. "You needed clarity even though you were meeting with Larkin at the time, asking him to approve an arrest warrant for your father."

"Larkin didn't think we had enough probable cause."

"But you did. Otherwise why ask for a warrant at all?"

Clayton shrugged and stared at Upham's bushy eyebrows.

"Nothing to say?"

"I wanted a second opinion."

Upham smirked again. "With an affidavit for an arrest warrant in hand, you wanted a second opinion. Seems you wanted more than that." He paused for another sip of coffee. "You think your father is a killer, right?"

"I don't know," Clayton replied.

"When Captain Mondragon arrived to pick you up at your mother's house in Mescalero, you asked him to wait a minute while you spoke to her. What did you say to her?"

"I asked her not to contact Kerney."

"Why? Because she knew about the social media storm that Davenport caused by her Facebook posting?"

Upham dangled the proposed lie for Clayton to grab on to like fish bait. But Clayton, like most Apaches, didn't eat fish. "We hadn't heard about it. Captain Mondragon was the first to tell me."

"And then you told your mother."

"No, I'd already discussed with her that I was investigating Kerney as a possible suspect."

Upham shook his head sadly. "In clear violation of departmental policy. Tell me again, you're sure you asked your mother *not* to call your father."

"That's what I said."

"And you sent a text message to Kerney telling him *not* to answer if your mother called his cell phone number."

"Yes."

Upham leaned back, coffee cup in hand. "Hoping that your mother would call, and that your text message would ensure that he'd answer."

"That's not true."

"I think it is," Upham said. "I wish I could get you on an aiding-and-abetting charge, but it doesn't fit the statute. However, accessory after the fact does fit. Combine that with the multiple department policy violations you engaged in during your investigation, and I believe I have proof of your guilt beyond a reasonable doubt."

Clayton took a deep breath. He was hooked after all. "Make your pitch, Captain."

"Resign with an official admonishment in your file, which will allow you to keep your police officer certification, or be terminated with cause and face criminal charges."

Clayton nodded. "How do you want me to do it?"

With a friendly smile, Upham laid out the plan. Clayton would resign on the spot, and be immediately flown to Las Cruces, where he'd turn in all departmental equipment and clear out all personal items from his office. Additionally, for the remainder of the investigation and any court action subsequent to it, he would agree not to give interviews or make statements about the case or his resignation to the media.

"You simply say you resigned for personal reasons," Upham concluded, as he passed a prepared document across the table for Clayton to sign. "Our public information officer will say it was in the best interests of the department, and let it go at that."

Clayton's pen hovered over the signature block. Ten years on the job down the stinking drain. "You really get off on this, don't you, Upham?"

"In this case, no," Upham replied sincerely. "You had a tough call to make, and it went against you when you wouldn't back down and let go."

"That's comforting," Clayton said sarcastically.

"I know your father. He's a good man, and he was a damn fine officer. I doubt he's a killer, but if he is, I'd sure like to know the reason."

Holding still, Clayton wanted to scream, *What in the hell do you think I was doing?*

Upham gestured at Clayton to sign the resignation and agreement form. "I've known an officer or two who's been welcomed back into the department after a misstep. It's not unheard-of."

Clayton signed, stood, and tossed the pen on the table along with his shield, ID, and sidearm. "Are we done here? I'd like to go home now."

He didn't mean Las Cruces.

CHAPTER 9

Gary Dalquist's law offices were in an old red-brick cottage with a picket fence across from the recently abandoned, soon-to-be demolished county judicial building. Dalquist owned the cottage and wasn't about to move closer to the new courthouse in the revitalized railyard district that bordered downtown Santa Fe. From the shingles on neighboring buildings, several other lawyers apparently shared his sentiment.

The front room served as a reception and waiting area. It had a tongue-and-groove oak floor, and a hand-stenciled fruit-and-floral motif that ran along the top of the walls under the high plastered ceiling. There was nobody to greet visitors, but the door to Dalquist's back office was open, revealing him behind an antique oak standing desk with fancy turned legs. He looked up and waved Kerney and Sara in.

"On time, excellent," he said, as he sat with them in a comfortable area with a couch and two matching easy chairs. The brief snowstorm at the ranch had completely bypassed Santa Fe, and the long window at the back of the room provided a view of an old apricot tree covered in a riot of pink and white blossoms that draped almost down to the ground.

"Our enemies have not been forthcoming," he announced. In Dalquist's work, prosecutors and the police were adversaries. "Except for a list of all the people who've been interviewed, and the affidavit against you, I've yet to receive the rest of the discovery I requested. Nevertheless, we can proceed with what we know from the criminal complaint."

"Let's get started," Kerney said.

"A great deal hinges on what transpired between you and Kim Ward on the night of her disappearance."

"I understand," Kerney replied. "I'm assuming you want to know exactly what I'll say during any police interrogations."

"Indeed, *everything* you will say to the police, once we've all agreed upon it, word for word if necessary." Dalquist smiled at Sara, reached for the small digital voice recorder on the coffee table, and turned it on. "But let's first back up and talk about how you met Kim Ward and the prior relationship you had with her."

"We met during my senior year at the annual all-state high school rodeo competition held that year in her hometown of Deming," Kerney began. "I'd come down from T or C with my friend Dale, accompanied by our parents."

With a touch of shyness, he described the dance that was held for all the entrants and their families at the American Legion post the night before the rodeo, and how Kim had spirited him away to her house while her mother was at work. His description of that night in Kim's arms brought a mischievous little smile to Sara's face that almost made him stop. But he hurried on with the story, recounting how afterward they corresponded throughout the summer, and rekindled their romance at New Mexico State when they both started college in the fall.

He explained the affair ended during the second semester when Kim joined the rodeo team and took up with Todd Marks. He admitted she'd broken his heart.

"She was your first true love," Sara commented tenderly.

"She was," he acknowledged.

"What was your relationship with Todd Marks?" Dalquist inquired.

"In high school, at the rodeos, we were friendly but fierce competitors. He was by far the better cowboy. I wasn't angry at him for stealing my girl away, more hurt by Kim being so . . ." He struggled for the right word.

"Promiscuous," Dalquist suggested.

"Capricious," Kerney answered.

"That's an interesting distinction to make," Dalquist commented.

Before Kerney could respond, Sara shook her head in disagreement and said, "No, it's not."

"A much more forgiving attitude about lost love than one might ordinarily expect," Dalquist mused, with thoughtful glances at Sara and Kerney.

"Seasoned by becoming older and wiser," Kerney explained with a smile.

"Ah," Dalquist said, realizing Kerney's trust in the girl had been misplaced. A hard lesson to learn as a young man, no matter how mature he might have been. "Of course."

He probed Kerney about Todd Marks until he was satisfied there had been no animosity between the two prior to Kim Ward's switching partners. "What about afterwards?" he asked.

"I guess I brooded for a while, but there was no confrontation, if that's what you're getting at. I saw them on campus together occasionally until they dropped out to join the pro rodeo circuit. We may have given a nod or hello as we passed each other. I can't remember exactly. I never saw Kim again until the evening she showed up at Erma's."

"What about Marks?" Dalquist queried. "When did you see him last?"

"If you're asking if I saw him during or after the time Kim spent the night with me at Erma's, the answer is no. Last time I saw him was while I was a college freshman."

"Did you have sex with Kim that night at Erma's?"

Kerney glanced at Sara. "Yes." There was no reaction.

"Was it consensual?"

"I thought so."

Dalquist pursed his lips. "Thought so?"

Kerney shifted position. "Let me back up. Kim arrived in a panic after walking out on Todd during an argument. I was only recently out of the army and staying at Erma's. She'd heard where I was through a mutual friend I'd run into downtown, and wanted to be someplace where Todd wouldn't find her."

"Being in a panic doesn't tell me much," Dalquist interjected. "Can you describe her state of mind?"

"Frantic, frightened, emotionally fragile. I didn't realize it right away, but she was shooting up on speed—amphetamines—and was just coming down from a huge dose. Todd had gotten her started on drugs while they were working the circuit, driving from town to town for sixteen hours straight, doing rodeo after rodeo. She said she wanted to get away from Todd, rodeoing, and drugs."

"She told you this when?" Dalquist asked.

"Soon after she calmed down."

"Before or after you had sex?"

The question hung over Kerney's head like an ax. He'd gone to Erma's to recover from 'Nam, the death of his parents, jungle nightmares, and terrible feelings of loneliness that haunted him. The touch of a woman had been irresistible, the sensation of skin against skin overpowering. It had weakened his resistance despite knowing it was a bad idea.

"After."

"Then what happened?"

"I fell asleep. I thought she had, too, but when I awoke, I found her dressed and shooting up. When the speed kicked in, she went haywire, talking crazy stuff about killing herself, killing Todd, begging me to take her to Mexico—anywhere. Then, out of nowhere, she slapped me, called me a fucker, said all I wanted was sex, and started scratching at imaginary bugs crawling on her skin. She was screaming, 'Get them off, get them off.' "

"How was she able to get away?" Dalquist asked.

"She was completely uncontrollable, thrashing around. Because she was sweating heavily, I went to the bathroom to get a wet washcloth to cool her down. When I returned, she was gone, along with my grandfather's pistol from the nightstand drawer, and the blanket from the foot of the bed."

He went on to describe chasing her down the driveway to the county road and losing her in the dark, hearing a distant motor, and seeing tail lights dim in the distance, fading away.

"I don't know if she'd parked a car along the road and walked to Erma's, or if Todd found her. I kept looking until I finally gave up and walked back to the house, where Erma was waiting."

Dalquist turned off the recorder and stood. "Okay, I could use a cup of coffee. We'll stop here and take a break." He smiled at Kerney. "All of this so far is very good."

With a sad smile, Sara reached for his hand. "How awful."

"For her, not for me," Kerney rebuffed. "I was a complete jerk."

She shook her head in disagreement. "Not true."

———

Before they gathered at the kitchen table, Kerney took a quick look out the front-room window. A surveillance vehicle was still parked down the street. The kitchen, adjacent to Dalquist's office, was straight out of the 1950s, with black-and-white floor linoleum, matching countertop tile, and mid-century cabinets and appliances, including the sink, all in pristine condition. Through the backdoor window, the apricot tree danced in a slight breeze, hundreds of white petals slowly drifting to the ground. Sara thought it charming. For Dalquist, it was a convenient and refreshing refuge from the burden of office work.

"We can continue here, if you like," he said, refilling the coffee cups after some small talk. "There's not much more to cover." He went to his office, returned with the recorder, and placed it on the kitchen table.

"You want to ask about the lie I told that my pistol had been stolen by someone unknown," Kerney said.

"Precisely, and why you asked Erma Fergurson to do the same."

Kerney shrugged. "I was half convinced Kim would shoot Todd, or that something bad would happen, but I didn't want any of it to come back on me. I wanted nothing more to do with either of them. Reporting the pistol stolen by an unknown intruder seemed the best thing to do. Besides, I didn't want it to become a scandal for Erma."

"You were embarrassed," Dalquist suggested.

"What?"

"Ashamed of having taken advantage of a vulnerable young woman in crisis who came to you asking for help."

Kerney lowered his head and intently studied the yellow Formica tabletop.

"Perfectly understandable." Dalquist turned off the recorder. "The pistol story is the weakest part of our defense."

Kerney glanced at Sara. Was she okay with a bad mistake in judgment made decades ago, or just holding herself in check? "I know."

"We'll move on for now." Dalquist pushed a file folder across the table and turned on the recorder. "Inside is the current list of people the police have interviewed. Look at it carefully, and tell me who might be helpful to our side and who is missing that we need to find."

Thirty minutes later, they were done, with not a new name added and only a few people checked off as potentially helpful to their case.

After agreeing to meet again when Dalquist received the rest of the discovery, Kerney and Sara left. In the truck, he put a copy of the list of names Dalquist wanted him to study more closely in the glove box and waited a few seconds before cranking the engine.

"Are you okay?" he asked.

Sara nodded. "None of us is perfect, Kerney. I've a few indiscretions in my closet you don't know about. Maybe you never will."

He pulled away from the curb and watched in the rearview mirror as the unmarked unit did the same. "God, do I love you."

She leaned across the center console and gave him a smooch on the cheek. "Ditto. We will get through this."

——

Juan Ramirez was waiting in his truck when Kerney and Sara got home. Sara gave him a big wave as she scooted inside.

"*Bueno dias,*" Kerney said as Juan approached. "What's up?"

"*Bueno dias,*" Juan replied. "Maybe you could tell the security guards at the gate that I'm okay. They keep holding me up and poking around the bed of my truck when I try to get to the cattle."

"Sorry about that, amigo. I'll call down there and let them know you're family."

Juan grinned. "Thanks. Also, when you need me to look after the horses and the ranch, just let me know."

"The horses for sure, and pretty soon, I think. But Patrick's grandparents will be bringing him home this evening and staying over to look after him while Sara and I are gone, so you won't have to bother with the house."

"Where are you going?"

"We don't exactly know yet. But I'll give you a heads-up before we leave."

"Okay." Juan looked out over the meadow. "It's greening up fast. Spring came back in a hurry."

"It sure did," Kerney replied, wondering why Juan was hesitating and making small talk about nothing much, which wasn't his nature. "I'll call security for you."

Juan tipped his hat in thanks. "*Bueno.*" He looked skyward as a drone climbed into sight from the canyon below. "What's that for?"

"Surveillance."

"For you?"

"Of me."

"By the cops?"

"The enemy," Kerney corrected, borrowing Dalquist's character-ization. He never thought he'd think of cops that way.

Inside at the library desk, Kerney called the security guard at the gate and told him to give Juan free and unrestrictive access to the ranch.

"Pass it on to everyone," he added.

"Ten-four. Want me to shoot down the drones?"

Kerney hesitated. He'd forgotten to ask Dalquist if it would be legally kosher. "No, that won't be necessary."

On the desk in front of him was the list of names he needed to go over. He went through it several times, placing checkmarks by names he recognized and people he knew. Some, like Todd Marks's brother, he'd heard about but never met. Others were complete strangers to him.

He sat back in the chair and tried to focus on who the investigators were looking for. It had to be those people closest to the victim. Todd and Kim's mother, most certainly, if they were still alive. Thomas Ward, whoever he was, childhood friend, college friend, rodeo teammate, competitor on the pro circuit.

According to Kim on that night at Erma's, Todd had turned to drug dealing after a bad wreck in a rodeo event broke his leg in four places and ended his career. Kerney turned on the desktop computer to start a search for Todd. He knew a lot less than he needed to and it was time to start filling in the blanks.

As he waited for the machine to power up, he couldn't shake the feeling that there was somebody not on the list he was forgetting. When he finished searching for information about Todd, he'd look for more on Kim. As far as he knew, she'd been raised only by her mother, who'd given birth to her at sixteen or seventeen and never married. He remembered Kim mentioning one or two of her mother's boyfriends to him, but by first name only. Were those the names he was forgetting? He didn't think so, but there was somebody.

The search engine filled the screen and he started typing.

———

Sara's parents, Dean and Barbara Brannon, arrived at the ranch with Patrick several hours early. When everyone was settled in, Kerney turned to Patrick and invited him on a ride.

"We've been neglecting the ponies," he said. "They need some exercise, and so do we."

Patrick replied with an eager grin. "Let's go out to the old hacienda ruins."

"That's exactly what I had in mind."

Long and tall for his age, with his father's square shoulders and his mother's green eyes, Patrick had entered adolescence with an amazing growth burst that apparently had no end. His voice had deepened, and his body seemed to be gaining heft by magic.

In the barn, Patrick scratched Pablito's forehead, gave him half an apple, and looked him over thoroughly before saddling up. It pleased Kerney to see the care his son took with his pony, a sure sign of a good horseman.

With the sun hidden behind a single billowing cloud in an otherwise clear blue sky, they rode in silence up the hill behind the ranch headquarters, through rolling grassland. They stopped to open a ranch gate, continued along a trace into a draw bracketed by a low, rocky ridgeline, and drew rein at a pond encircled by marsh grass and cattails. An ancient willow sheltered some scattered foundation rubble, the only visible remains of a two-hundred-year-old hacienda that had once served as an overnight stop on the cartage road from the village of Galisteo to Santa Fe. A barbed-wire fence enclosed the site to keep the cattle away from the live water, but it didn't keep wild critters from getting to the pond. Fresh bobcat scat and puffs of rabbit fur signaled a recent kill.

"What was it like to be a policeman?" Patrick asked. "You never talked to me about it."

"You never really saw that part of my life, did you? You were just a little guy when I retired." Hondo pawed the ground, ready to keep moving. "I took pride in my work and enjoyed many things about it, especially helping people and keeping them safe when I could. But that's not your question, is it?"

"You've killed people," Patrick noted, eyes downcast.

"Yes."

"What's that like?"

Kerney sighed. "I hope you never find out. There's no simple way to describe it. You tell yourself it was necessary, that you had no choice. But each time it happens, a little bit of you withers away."

Patrick frowned. "That doesn't make any sense." Restless, Pablito raised his head. Patrick nudged him toward the pasture. "What withers away?"

Kerney turned Hondo to follow. "Your innocence, the good inside of you—call it what you will. You carry what you did like an invisible yoke."

"Is it like feeling guilty?" Patrick asked, as he dismounted to close the gate.

"Are you asking me about the murder of Kim Ward?"

"It's all over the Internet that you killed her, but I don't believe it."

"And you shouldn't."

Patrick remounted. "I'll get asked about it when I go back to school."

"What are you going to say?"

Patrick flung a leg over Pablito and loped the pony ahead. "That my father's not a murderer, and he'll prove it."

"Think I can?"

"I know you will," Patrick yelled over his shoulder as he urged Pablito forward.

Kerney held Hondo back slightly to watch his son—still so innocent, so caring, so effortlessly light in the saddle—joyfully gallop across the pasture through the fading light of early dusk. And for just a moment, the weight of the invisible yoke lightened.

———

An unsettling call from Dalquist that the district attorney was considering a high-powered special prosecutor to try the case ended Kerney's enthusiasm to continue his Internet search. Weary of sitting, he stepped outside on the portal. At the far end, lights were on in the guest wing, a two-bedroom suite with a full bath and combined kitchen, dining, and living area. It was comfortable and private, with great views of the Galisteo Basin.

Sara's family used it often on brief and extended visits. However, only twice over the years had Clayton and his family stayed there, and for a single night each time.

For a minute, Kerney took in the fresh evening air and deepening shadows before wandering to the guest wing, where Sara and Patrick were keeping Dean and Barbara company. They all sat together on the couch watching the local television news.

Kerney stepped inside, and Dean, his father-in-law, greeted him with a smile on his deeply tanned face. He had a mild manner, seasoned by decades of caring for big and small critters, working in bad weather, and dealing with the everyday disasters of ranch life.

His wife Barbara, her eyes glued to the screen, watched a report, broadcast live outside the Department of Public Safety headquarters, that Lieutenant Clayton Istee had resigned his position from the state police. The department's public relations officer refused to comment when asked if the resignation had anything to do with the ongoing Kim Ward murder investigation.

"Good," Kerney growled, his expression darkening.

"How can you say that, Kevin?" Barbara snapped. "He's your son. From what I've read, it was some woman he arrested who accused him on social media of covering up for you."

Kerney shrugged. Barbara was the ramrod of the Brannon outfit, running herd on her clan with the skills of a career diplomat and an army top sergeant. He loved her, but knew better than to quarrel with her.

"Give Clayton a chance to explain himself," Sara added.

"He knows how to reach me," Kerney replied. He retreated to the portal while the reporter droned on about the unusual circumstance of a police officer investigating his own father for murder.

He closed the door, took a deep breath, and let it out slowly. Even during the stormiest days of their truncated relationship, he'd respected Clayton, felt proud of him. It would take a hell of a lot of explaining on Clayton's part to restore any of those good feelings. Kerney wasn't sure it was possible.

CHAPTER 10

Paul Avery drove south out of Santa Fe feeling frustrated and angry. He'd met with Deputy Chief Serrano to request more agents to work the case. Instead of an expanded team or even a remotely sympathetic ear, Serrano had given him a lecture about the one hundred vacancies within the department's sworn personnel ranks, which might soon necessitate putting non-uniform officers temporarily back on patrol.

Even worse, Serrano had ordered him to reduce his team by the end of the week to James Garcia, Carla Olivas, and Charlie Epperson. Captain Wayne Upham, the IA commander who'd interviewed Clayton, would interrogate Kerney at Santa Fe headquarters. With a barely discernible smile, Serrano urged Avery to continue evidence collection, full speed ahead. Closure on the case was the department's top priority.

Avery couldn't tell if Serrano actually expected him to solve the case with inadequate resources, or if he was deliberately setting him up to fail. Regardless, it left him muttering curses under his breath on the long drive to Las Cruces.

It was late when he arrived at district headquarters. The building was quiet except for the occasional sound of radio traffic issuing from a monitor in an empty office. At his desk, he ran through all the daily field reports and logs, hoping somebody had finally tracked down credible information about the whereabouts of Kim Ward's mother or Todd Marks. He finished reading only to be disappointed once again. In a world filled with billions of people, vanishing wasn't all that hard to do. At times, reality sucked.

The door to Clayton's office was open. He'd moved out in the wee morning hours when no one was around to make things awkward. Given his forced resignation, it had been the smart thing to do.

Avery picked up the phone and dialed his buddy Sergeant Gabriel Medina at home. "Give me something substantial from Juan Ramirez," he begged when Gabe answered. "I'm drowning in a swamp of worthless leads and useless information with little ammunition and a big, hungry alligator circling."

Gabe laughed. "Don't sound so pathetic, amigo. Zero out the day, and be done with it. I've got nothing for you, other than Ramirez doesn't have to stop at security anymore to get onto Kerney's ranch. I'll see him tomorrow and give him a little goose."

"Well, at least Kerney still trusts him."

"There you go, then, progress."

"The high point of my day." Avery disconnected, wandered into Clayton's office, and turned on the lights. With everything personal cleared out, the room had been returned to institutional dullness, except for some scribblings in Clayton's hand on a calendar desk pad. On it, he'd written "Fergurson Photographs?" and circled it.

The question intrigued Avery and he thought for a long minute about what to say before dialing Clayton's home telephone. He decided to say nothing schmaltzy. When Clayton answered, he kept it light.

"Got a quick question. What were you thinking when you wrote a note to yourself about Fergurson's photographs?"

Clayton paused before replying. "Fergurson made numerous journal entries about photos she took of people she knew and places she visited. I was going to ask at the university library if they had any archives of her photography. If they did, I figured it would be worth a look."

"I bet they do," Avery predicted happily, smiling for the first time in hours. Any fresh bit of information that would strengthen the circumstantial evidence against Kerney would be invaluable. "We'll get on it in the morning. Thanks."

Without comment, Clayton disconnected, and Avery went from not being schmaltzy to feeling like a full-blown schmuck.

———

Clayton sat at the kitchen table, head bent over a pocket calculator, punching in numbers, the tabletop overflowing in bills, receipts, and sheets of paper from a yellow tablet filled with budgetary computations.

Grace took the accordion file organizer that held the family's financial records off a chair seat, put it on the floor, and joined him. "What are you doing?" she asked, knowing full well the answer.

Clayton looked up, his eyes narrowed with worry, his lips tight. "With my accrued leave time that's coming, my final paycheck, some—but not all—of our savings, and cutting back a bit here and there, I've got three to four months to find a new job."

"I don't think we have anything to worry about," Grace replied. "Who called earlier?"

"Paul Avery, he had a question about the investigation."

"Did you help him?"

"I answered his question."

Grace shook her head in dismay. "You're unbelievable."

"What?"

"Help your father, not Paul Avery."

Clayton leaned back and grimaced. "He'd probably shoot me on sight."

"No, but he might give you a good talking-to." Grace caressed Clayton's arm. "You're one of the most fair-minded people I know, but this time your judgment is clouded."

Clayton pulled his arm away. "Whose side are you on? I just wanted to find the truth."

"You've never once asked Kerney for the truth, have you?"

"Eventually that would have happened."

Grace sighed. "Why can't you get over your resentment of a man who has never done you harm—only good—and help him, now that you no longer have the power to hurt him?"

The sting of Grace's words was like a slap in the face. "I thought I was being impartial."

"No, you weren't. Will you help your family, or not?"

Her question struck Clayton's core. He'd never thought of Kerney as kinfolk, never included him as part of his Apache family. In his heart, he'd treated him with disrespect. And yet he *was* family, had been generous and honest in all his dealings with the family.

Clayton carefully cleared the table of all the papers and put them away in the file organizer. "I will help him," he finally said.

"Call him, tell him," Grace suggested, smiling approval.

"No, I will speak to him in person. I'll leave for Santa Fe in the morning."

"He will appreciate the gesture," Grace predicted.

"Or send me packing," Clayton replied ruefully.

Grace smiled and reached across the table to hold his hand. "I don't think so."

———

Dalquist called Kerney in the morning, just before he left with Patrick
to feed and water the ponies.

"You're to be at state police headquarters at nine a.m. I'll meet you
in the parking lot."

"Who am I up against?"

"Wayne Upham, Internal Affairs commander. Know him?"

"Slightly," Kerney answered, thinking back to his days as deputy
chief of the department, and remembering Upham as a spit-and-polish,
up-and-coming officer who liked things neat and tidy.

"My source tells me Upham conducted Clayton's interrogation."

"Interesting," Kerney replied. "See you there."

After cleaning the horses' stalls, feeding them, and shoveling horse
apples out of the corral with Patrick, Kerney fixed the clogged water
line to the outside trough and had just enough time for another cup of
coffee before leaving to meet Dalquist.

Sara looked him up and down as he reached for his truck keys. He
was unshaved, his hair limp around his ears, and wearing dirty jeans, a
sweat-stained plaid shirt, and horse-dung-encrusted boots. He didn't
smell pretty, either.

"My, my, aren't the state police in for a bit of a surprise," she commented with a look of approval.

"That's the whole point," Kerney replied, jamming his rattiest
cowboy hat on his head. He threw her a kiss on his way out the door.

———

The exterior of the New Mexico Department of Public Safety building on Cerrillos Road, which housed the state police headquarters,
showed no love to the thousands of motorists who passed by daily.

Plopped on a small hillock, buffered by a parking lot, and surrounded by a security fence, it reminded Kerney of a fortified blockhouse rather than a government office building. So much for the notion of community policing.

He arrived ten minutes early and parked his truck next to Dalquist's BMW. On the short walk to the visitors entrance, Dalquist gave him a once-over, a sniff, and raised a questioning eyebrow.

"It always helps to know your opponent," Kerney answered cryptically.

"I guess I should have worn a stronger aftershave," Dalquist mused.

At the reception window, they showed their IDs, signed the visitors log, and were buzzed through the electronic door to the main lobby. A young, uniformed female officer escorted them down a hallway to a bank of chairs along a wall opposite a row of interview rooms. As she hovered near where they sat, Kerney glanced at his wristwatch. They were right on time.

"Upham will make us wait," he commented softly to Dalquist.

"It's all strategy, isn't it?" Dalquist ruminated. "I've sometimes wondered how many of my clients survived the psychological onslaught by police interrogators."

"Sometimes being innocent helps," Kerney suggested.

Dalquist suppressed a smile.

Twenty minutes later, Upham appeared, wearing a crisp uniform and highly polished shoes, but was otherwise not the man Kerney remembered. A potbelly spilled over his waistband, and his face was puffy and sour-looking, with an unhealthy gray tinge. He clutched a thick file folder in his beefy hand.

He stepped close, wrinkled his nose, and looked at Kerney, who immediately got to his feet to keep Upham from establishing a dominant position.

He examined Kerney with a look of pure distaste. "You know the drill. Once inside, I'll Mirandize you again, and everything will be video- and voice-recorded."

"With my lawyer present," Kerney added.

Upham shot Dalquist an unhappy glance, wrinkled his nose again, and opened an interrogation room door. "Yeah. Let's go."

In the bleak, harshly lit room, after all were seated, Upham went through the legal formalities before he slowly opened the file, patting it affectionately as though it contained all he needed to send Kerney away for murder.

"If you don't mind, let's start with Clayton. What I don't understand is why he went after you so hard only to flip-flop and warn you."

"Is there a question?" Dalquist asked.

Ignoring Dalquist, Upham stared at Kerney.

"He didn't warn me," Kerney said.

"Well, if true, that's got to stick in your craw big-time. What kind of son would want to see his father go to prison for murder? I can't even imagine how steamed you must be at him. He thinks you're a killer, and worked hard to prove it. What does he know about you that we don't?"

Upham paused, looking perplexed. "Whether Clayton warned you or not—and I think he did—he must have some real, big emotional issues with you to be willing to throw his career away."

Kerney shrugged. "Can't say. I don't know him that well."

Upham leaned toward Kerney, nose wrinkling at the barnyard smell. "Maybe there was a time when you shared something with Clayton that gave him reason to believe you killed Kim Ward. Something said privately between a father and a son."

Dalquist raised a hand to stop the exchange. "Unless you stick to germane questions, Captain Upham, I see no reason for this interview to continue."

Upham leaned back and ran a forefinger over his nose. "What's not germane, counselor? All I'm asking Kerney is, did he ever confess to Clayton Istee that he murdered Kim Ward?"

"We'll not go down that slippery slope," Dalquist snapped, cutting Kerney off. The picture Upham wanted to paint of a son's knowledge of his father's crime could become an important weapon in the prosecution's arsenal, no matter what Kerney said to deny it.

Dalquist continued, "My client didn't kill Kim Ward, and therefore had no reason to engage in such an exchange with Mr. Istee, as you suggest. Now, can we get on with it?"

Upham nodded and patted the open file. He smiled agreeably at Kerney, but his nose kept wrinkling at the palpable stink of horse shit. "Walk me through how you first came to know Kim Ward."

Comfortable and relaxed, Kerney returned Upham's smile and told him about a pretty girl, a dance, and a high school rodeo in Deming, New Mexico.

CHAPTER II

Kerney's ploy to throw Upham off with his barnyard attire and the smell of horse apples wasn't a complete success, although the interrogation did end sooner than he expected. Upham called a halt after Kerney's disclosure of his early relationship with Kim and her flight from Erma's the night she disappeared. He showed Kerney and Dalquist the door, promising many more questions to come.

Standing between his BMW and Kerney's truck in the parking lot, Dalquist said, "Upham would have kept going, if he'd liked what he was hearing from you. He stopped so he could regroup and restrategize."

"That's what I thought," Kerney said, smiling broadly.

"You seem smug," Dalquist commented. "Is this a facet of your personality I've somehow missed?"

Kerney leaned against the door of his truck and laughed. "Upham did me a big favor, and I don't know whether to send him a dozen donuts or a bottle of whiskey. He jogged my memory about someone I've been trying to remember, a girl who was one of Kim's best friends in high school."

"Who might she be?" Dalquist inquired.

"I don't recall her name, but I know somebody who probably does. If it pans out and we can find her, we just might get some information the police don't have about Kim, her mother, and Todd Marks."

"That could be very beneficial." Dalquist stepped around to the driver's door of his BMW. "I retract my earlier remark."

"Retraction accepted," Kerney replied.

With a wave, Dalquist drove off. Kerney sat in his truck and called his oldest friend, Dale Jennings. Widowed, Dale still lived on the Rocking J Ranch in the San Andres Mountains, hard up against the White Sands Missile Range boundary, only now the outfit was run by his oldest daughter and her husband.

"I wondered if you were ever gonna call," Dale said when he picked up.

"I saw no reason to trouble you with my problems," Kerney replied.

"I figure if they do send you to prison, I'll have to come and break you out."

"I'd be counting on it."

"But you didn't call to chitchat."

"I did not, and I apologize for it."

"No need. What's on your mind?"

"That cute little gal you danced with at the American Legion Hall in Deming the year we took first in the team roping event."

"And you won the all-around championship," Dale added. "That was some great rodeo."

"The girl," Kerney prodded. "She was with Kim Ward when we met them at the arena, remember?

"I do," Dale recollected. "She was a cutie. Loretta Page was her name. We stayed in touch after I went into the air force. Wrote back and forth for a time while I was in 'Nam."

"I didn't know that."

"Not much to know. She lost interest in me, and that was that. Haven't seen or heard from her since."

"I need to find her, if possible. If there's anything about her you can recall in that ancient brain of yours, I'd be grateful."

Dale chuckled. "Insulting me ain't gonna make my noggin work any better. I remember she wrote me about some trouble she was having at home, and that she was going to stay with Kim's mother for a spell."

"You're sure about that?" Kerney asked. "Kim never mentioned it to me."

"I am."

"When was that?"

"Now you're really making me think. It was in her last letter to me, when she cut it off. I remember, because I was hoping to see her when I came home on leave. Instead, you got me drunk in a T or C dive."

Kerney thought back. Their excursion into drunkenness had occurred long after Kim had dumped him. "Anything else?"

"Nothing right now. I'll cogitate about it and let you know if something seeps through my muddled brain. Come see me before I drop over dead."

"Is that gonna happen anytime soon?"

"Not if I can help it," Dale said. "Oh, yeah, she was a year behind Kim in school."

"That's good to know. Did you keep Loretta's letters?"

"You're kidding, right?"

"Cops never assume and always ask. I take back my earlier insult. You're an exceptionally intelligent person with a razor-sharp memory."

"Damn straight I am," Dale said with a laugh.

———

Home and in an upbeat mood, Kerney found Sara in the kitchen and filled her in on his session with Upham, his phone conversation with Dale, and a possible lead to one of Kim Ward's high school friends.

"Let's hope it gets us somewhere," she said, as he retreated to the library to start an Internet search for Loretta. When security phoned twenty minutes later to say that Clayton Istee was at the gate, she decided to let Kerney make the call on what to do.

She opened the library door and said, "Your son wants to talk to you."

Kerney raised his gaze from the computer screen. "Is Patrick already back from town with Dean and Barbara?"

"Your *older* son," Sara said pointedly. "Security is holding him at the gate."

Kerney looked at the ceiling and sighed. "Jesus."

"Well?"

He half smiled and shrugged. "Why not get it over with?"

She came to his side and put a hand on his shoulder. "Do you want company when you see him?"

He shook his head. "I'll be fine."

"No fisticuffs, promise?" Sara demanded, half serious.

"It won't come to that. I'm over being angry."

"But not over feeling hurt."

"There is that," Kerney admitted.

"Good luck."

"Is that the sum total of your advice?"

"Just remember he's a lot like you in many ways."

"The poor man."

Sara smooched his cheek. "He's a good man, one of the best, like you."

Sara left, and his smile disappeared. He stared at the open doorway, wondering what in hell Clayton wanted with him. He couldn't think of anything pleasant. A sudden urge came over him to give the man a royal ass-chewing. He shut down the computer, pressed a fist to his lips, and bit back the impulse.

———

Clayton pulled to a stop next to Kerney's truck, killed the engine, and took a deep breath. It had been some years since his last visit, under different and more pleasant circumstances. The low adobe ranch house with faraway views of the Galisteo Basin and the great swath of rolling grassland that climbed the hill behind the horse barn looked much the same, except the windbreak trees were bigger and the landscaping more mature.

Sara met him at the patio door to the kitchen, and slid it open with a smile. "He's in the library."

"Thank you." His throat was so dry, it was all he could manage. He felt like a schoolboy about to be disciplined. He forced down his apprehension as he strode through the living room. He was middle-aged, no kid, and would make his apologies to Kerney man-to-man.

Through the open library door, he saw Kerney sitting behind his desk looking out the window. He knocked on the door. Kerney turned.

"Come in," he said tonelessly, his expression stern. Older now, with a little less hair, and wearing reading glasses, Kerney still looked fit and healthy.

Clayton stepped into the room. One side held a wall of floor-to-ceiling bookcases, with a shelf reserved for some of Kerney's police mementos. On another wall hung a rather large, nicely framed pencil sketch of Hermit's Peak, clearly the work of Erma Fergurson. Underneath it, two easy chairs were angled for conversation, separated by a table that held a mid-century pottery lamp.

Having memorized his short speech on the drive from Las Cruces, Clayton launched into it without preamble. "Over the years, I have not treated you kindly, and for that I apologize. You have been generous to me and my family, and I've been stingy, refusing to accept you as my father. For that, I am also sorry. You are part of my family and I should have been loyal to who you are. Instead, I was suspicious."

Taken aback, Kerney moved to one of the matching easy chairs and sat. "I wasn't expecting this." He waved at the empty chair. "Stop standing in the doorway and take a seat. Why were you suspicious?"

"For one, Erma was suspicious," Clayton replied as he joined Kerney. "You read her journal entry. She practically accused you."

"I've never told anybody this, but Erma was very stoned that night," Kerney replied. "She'd smoked a lot of grass before Kim showed up."

"Stoned?"

"Very. It was the seventies, and Erma liked to get high. She was always experimenting with art, with men, with life. There was no one like her."

"Were you high?"

Kerney's expression darkened. "Now you're sounding like a cop."

Clayton shrugged.

"I'd smoked a little with Erma that evening, but I was nowhere close to being stoned. When Kim showed up, I wasn't even buzzed." Kerney shifted in his chair to face Clayton head-on. "Was that your basis for coming after me?"

"Not completely. You've read the criminal complaint."

"You didn't have a thumbnail's worth of hard evidence. Why did you go for the arrest warrant?"

"It gets down to that, doesn't it?"

Kerney nodded. "You sure put yourself in a pickle."

"I kept thinking about the Craig Larson case we worked together."

Kerney sat bolt upright, his eyes cold. "That sonofabitch broke into

my home and killed a young man on my doorstep who I truly liked and admired."

"Although I didn't see you do it, I think you shot Larson down in cold blood."

"Why?"

"Because of what you just said." Clayton paused. "But before that, because of what you radioed back to me that day in the forest. Something like, 'He's almost dead.' You were watching him die, instead of calling for help."

"You didn't seem upset by the news at the time."

"Did you shoot him and let him die?"

"And that would make me what, a vigilante with a badge?"

"Did you kill an unarmed man who'd surrendered to you?"

"And that, in your eyes, would make me capable of murdering Kim Ward."

"Yes."

"What the hell did I do to make you distrust me so much?"

"I was asking questions, doing what any good cop does, looking to build a profile. Erma's journals made me think that maybe after killing Kim Ward, guilt made you want you to become a cop. To atone for your sin. It's not unheard-of. Or that you enjoyed killing so much, as a sworn officer, you'd be free to kill again without suspicion or punishment. These were theories I had to follow."

"You were profiling me on your own, solely based on some psychological mumbo-jumbo?" Kerney said disbelievingly. "No matter how conflicted you might have been about my guilt or innocence, you should have stepped aside. Instead, you went way over the line."

"I know that," Clayton snapped. "And I paid for it with my job."

Kerney snorted. "You get no sympathy from me on that account."

"You still haven't answered my question. Did you willfully murder Craig Larson, or at the very least let him die?"

Kerney got up and slammed the door shut. "Is this some sort of setup? Are you wearing a wire, trying to get a confession out of me?"

"Now who's distrustful?"

"Who's not answering questions now?" Kerney thundered.

"I'm not wearing a wire." Clayton stood and spread his arms out. "Pat me down."

Kerney stared hard at him. "I'll answer your question. I shot Craig Larson in self-defense," he lied. "That's what happened, and that's what the shooting review board confirmed."

"Whether that's true or not, he deserved to die."

Surprised by the comment, Kerney sat back down. "Sometimes I don't understand you at all."

His tension ebbing, Clayton sat. His thoughts turned to another killer, Samuel Green, who had blown up Clayton's home on the reservation to wipe him and his family out, all because he was Kerney's son. He'd later learned from the Lincoln County sheriff that Kerney had anonymously contributed a large sum of money to help him rebuild.

It had never been mentioned, and for a time afterward they'd gotten along fine, with a few family visits back and forth. But they'd stopped staying in touch. Maybe it was his fault; maybe nobody's.

"Nothing more to say?" Kerney asked.

"You once told Paul Hewitt that I was a good man, a good cop, and you were proud to be my father."

"I did say that."

"Not to me, you didn't."

Kerney sighed. "Well, I'm backing off on the good cop part for the time being. But you are a good man and I'm still proud of you, despite being pissed off at what you've done."

"I truly don't know if you are innocent, but you're my father and part of my family, so I must help you, with or without your consent."

"You're serious?"

"Yes."

Kerney put his elbows on the chair arms and leaned forward. "I've always felt that you're more Apache than gringo like me, so tell me what this is really all about."

Clayton met his gaze directly. "I am your son. I've apologized and want to help. Isn't that enough?"

Kerney exhaled. "For chrissake, you're impossible. I was not trying to pry."

"I know that," Clayton answered.

"It will look like collusion to your old bosses if you help me. You'll probably never get your job back."

"That doesn't matter. I want to make it right between us."

"Seriously?"

Clayton nodded.

Kerney studied Clayton. He'd been willing to risk his career to find out if his father was guilty of murder, and was now prepared to torpedo his future in law enforcement to help Kerney prove his innocence. "Go home to your family, Clayton. You've made your amends, and I thank you for it."

"I can't do that," Clayton replied stubbornly.

Kerney knew him to be a fine detective with great instincts. He certainly could use the help. "If we do this, I run the show."

Clayton nodded. "Understood."

"And you stay with it for the duration."

"Of course."

"Okay, we'll start with you telling me everything you know, with nothing held back."

Clayton held up a hand to call a stop, and turned to the Hermit's Peak pencil sketch on the wall. "First, tell me about the drawing."

"It's by Erma, of course. Sara found it in a Tucson art gallery and gave it to me as a present before we got married."

"An oil of Hermit's Peak was in Erma's guest bedroom the night Kim Ward came to see you."

Kerney nodded. "It's a study for that painting."

"I thought so."

The door opened, and Sara stepped inside. "It was quiet enough in here to suggest either coffee or something stronger, if you like."

"Coffee will do just fine," Kerney replied. "And join us. Clayton was just about to run down all he knows about the investigation. He's signed on with us for the duration."

Sara's smile lit up the room. "Brilliant, as my opposite number in the British army used to say."

———

By the time Patrick and his grandparents were due to return from town, Clayton had finished his briefing on the investigation up to the point of being pulled off the case. From there, they worked out an operational strategy and set priorities.

Kerney and Clayton would handle the fieldwork and Sara would run a one-woman command center at the ranch. She'd do phone research and Internet searches, coordinate with Dalquist, manage communications, and—if possible—keep the state police investigators in the dark or at bay.

In the morning, Kerney and Clayton would travel south to Deming in separate vehicles to begin the search for Loretta Page. Before Clayton's surprise arrival, Kerney had found three different area listings under the last name Page in online directories. If none of those sources panned out, they'd dig into city and county public records.

It was a long shot, at best, but it was also the only lead to the whereabouts of Todd Marks and Lucille Ward the police didn't have.

"We've got a plan," Kerney said, exchanging looks with Sara and Clayton. "Let's hope it takes us somewhere."

Clayton reached in a pocket and took out his smartphone. "Grace will want to know."

"Of course," Kerney said.

"Let me say hello when you finish," Sara said.

"I will," Clayton answered with a smile, feeling a whole lot better about himself than when he'd arrived.

CHAPTER 12

Early morning began with a heated discussion in the kitchen between Kerney and Patrick, who adamantly demanded the right to be included in finding Kim Ward's killer, despite being fourteen years old and required by law and his parents to go to school, which had resumed on Monday. They argued about it throughout their barn-cleaning chores, until Kerney finally decreed the matter closed to further discussion. But the decision unraveled upon their return to the house, where Sara announced she didn't think it necessary to remain behind while Kerney and Clayton did the fieldwork.

"There's no earthly reason why I can't manage all the phone research, do Internet searches, and stay in contact with everyone on the fly," she noted. "I'm coming with you."

"I can help too," Patrick pleaded defiantly, squaring his shoulders to resist the inevitable rejection of his offer, looking to Clayton for support, who was studiously stirring cream in his coffee to avoid getting pulled into the debate.

"You will help, by looking after the ranch in our absence," Sara told Patrick. "We need you here to stay on top of things and keep us informed."

"You'll be our eyes and ears, in case the police come calling or try to pull some funny stuff," Kerney added.

"Funny stuff?" Patrick queried, not fully satisfied with his sudden promotion to chief of home security.

"Tapping our phones, intercepting our mail, searching the house in our absence, planting listening devices, trespassing on our land," Kerney enumerated quickly.

Patrick's eyes widened. "I didn't think about that."

"That's why we need you here," Kerney added.

Outnumbered and outgunned, Patrick groaned in reluctant agreement. "Okay."

"That doesn't mean you can skip school," Kerney cautioned.

"I know that," Patrick huffed, offended by the remark.

"Then it's settled," Kerney said, extending his hand.

Still feeling left on the sidelines, Patrick grudgingly shook his father's hand. "How long will you be gone?" he asked.

"A few days at the most," Sara guessed.

"If it runs over that, you can all come down to Mescalero for the weekend," Clayton suggested.

Sara flashed him a big smile. "Oh, that would be wonderful. Get the whole clan together. I love it."

"Cool," Patrick said, excited by the prospect. "But who'll look after the ranch?"

"Juan Ramirez will," Kerney replied. "He's already offered."

Pleased with achieving a reasonable degree of family harmony, they rounded up Dean and Barbara from the guest quarters for a family confab, and laid out the plan over coffee at the kitchen table.

"We'll be fine here, with Patrick running the show," Dean said. "I'll give him a hand with the chores and whatever else he says needs doing."

Patrick grinned at his grandfather's compliment.

"It would be wonderful to see Mescalero and meet your family, if that works out," Barbara said to Clayton.

"Let's make it official," Clayton said impulsively, looking around the table. "Mescalero this weekend, agreed?"

"I'm all for it," Kerney said with gusto as he pushed his chair back from the table. "Why let a trumped-up first-degree murder indictment stand in the way of a long-overdue family gathering? Let's all plan to meet in Mescalero Friday evening, no matter what. And we'll convoy out of here this morning. If nothing else, that should throw the cops into a tizzy for a little while."

For a moment, Kerney's constant worry over an uncertain future lifted. His world had exploded at Fort Leonard Wood, but with the unwavering help of his incredible family, everything had to turn out right.

One by one, Kerney hugged them all.

———

Gabe Medina, supervising sergeant in the Santa Fe County Sheriff's Office Investigations Unit, sat in his unmarked unit outside a popular roadside diner on the Old Las Vegas Highway. Juan Ramirez was already fifteen minutes late. Punctual by nature, Gabe hated being kept waiting, and he was bored watching geriatric transplants to Santa Fe climb out of their shiny SUVs and hobble inside for breakfast. Ramirez arrived just in time to grab one of the last parking spaces.

"What took you so long?" Gabe grumbled as Juan got in his unit.

"I got a job, you know," Ramirez replied.

"What have you got for me?" Gabe countered.

"Everybody left the ranch this morning. Nobody's there."

Gabe gave Juan a disgusted look. Every state, county, and local cop knew about the convoy of four vehicles leaving the ranch through a neighbor's adjoining acreage. After a scramble by law enforcement agencies, all those vehicles and their occupants now had tails. Kerney's in-laws were browsing the aisles at a southside discount store after dropping the grandkid off at school. Kerney was driving south on I-25. Clayton Istee was also southbound on a secondary highway that would take him to Alamogordo, if he didn't veer off. Kerney's wife was taking the scenic route through the Jemez Mountains on her way to who knew where.

"That's it?" Gabe asked.

"No, Kerney called me to say I need to look after the place this coming weekend, starting Friday afternoon. Until then, Patrick and the boy's grandparents will be there."

Gabe's interest spiked. "Go on."

"They've got a weekend planned away, that's all I know."

"That's not enough."

Juan shrugged. "He didn't tell me nothing more."

"Does he usually let you know where they'll be?"

"Yeah, but not this time."

Gabe sighed. "What did you do to make him suspicious?"

"Nothing, I swear. It's just this murder thing has him not himself. All uptight and everything."

"You think he murdered that girl?" Gabe asked.

Juan licked his lips. "Man, I don't know. I didn't think so until I saw on some TV show he'd shot and killed six people while he was a cop. Killer with a badge is what some people are saying."

The breakfast crowd was emptying out. "I need to know where Kerney is going today, and I need to know as soon as possible. Also, find out where everybody is going for the weekend."

"I'll talk to Patrick after he gets home from school," Juan proposed.

"But be cool about it," Gabe cautioned.

Juan nodded. "What about my sister's kid?"

"I'm not ready to talk to the judge about him. You got a few more things to do for me."

"Like what?"

"I'll tell you when the time comes."

Juan shook his head. "I'm not happy about doing this."

"Yeah, well, you won't be very happy if you have to tell your sister you blew getting her son out of juvie."

Juan grunted and opened the passenger door.

"Call me as soon as you know anything," Gabe ordered.

"*Hijo de puta*," Juan muttered under his breath as he walked to his truck.

Gabe pulled out of the parking lot just as the geriatric early lunch crowd began arriving.

———

Halfway between Las Cruces and Lordsburg along the Interstate 10 corridor in the southwest quadrant of the state, the small city of Deming sits in the Chihuahuan Desert with the menacing skyline of the barren Florida Mountains as a backdrop. Only when Sara drew close did the mountains appear less formidable, but still no more inviting.

Last night she'd read in a guidebook that before the 1854 Gadsden Purchase of almost thirty thousand square miles of land from Mexico, there was nothing here other than an unmarked border crossing, which was now thirty-three miles south in the small village of Columbus, made famous by Pancho Villa's 1916 murderous attack against unwary American citizens.

Even in April, Deming was hot, dry, sun-blasted, and windy. Gusty winds peppered her Jeep with fine sand, and the air-conditioning kept her from sweltering. To get oriented, she made a tour of the town. It was tidy and unpretentious, with modest houses, an assortment of mobile home trailer parks, and some appealing older buildings in the downtown core. A four-lane street paralleled the interstate and ran through the heart of the business district past the usual assortment of gas stations, car dealerships, small businesses, fast-food franchises, and moderately priced family-style chain motels.

It was too early to meet up with Kerney, so she drove south of town, where farms and ranches predominated. There were irrigated fields of chili, cotton, and hay, and dryland ranches watered by windmills and stock tanks. But the desert still dominated, with vistas of far-off shimmering mountains and expanses of sand-encrusted scrublands.

Kerney called her with his ETA and she rendezvoused with him in the parking lot of a motel on the main strip. Clayton would arrive later. He'd stopped off in Las Cruces to see if he could tease out information from his former staff about the status of the investigation. They made a reservation for Clayton and checked into their room. Hungry, Sara called the front desk clerk and asked about a good place to eat. The clerk recommended a nearby diner famous for its green chili cheeseburgers and home fries.

With state police in an unmarked vehicle following in plain sight, they drove together in Sara's Jeep to the diner, a retro 1950s eatery off the main drag with chrome and red leatherette counter stools and booths. Over lunch, Sara asked Kerney if he'd been back to Deming since his high school rodeo days.

"Not really," he answered. "Occasionally I've driven through it on my way to someplace else."

"No nostalgia about the old days?"

Kerney smiled and shook his head. "Not since the cops barged into our hotel room at Fort Leonard Wood. Before that, I had pleasant recollections about my youthful indiscretions."

Sara grinned. "Is your sense of humor returning?"

Kerney squeezed her hand. "It's possible."

They munched on the remaining home fries, and discussed how to use the remainder of the day. Kerney would track down the three area telephone listings for Page, and Sara would try the county courthouse and school administration to find any historical and current information about Loretta Page.

Sara crossed her fingers. "Let's hope we get lucky."

Outside the booth window, an RV with British Columbia plates eased to a stop, engulfing three parking spaces. "I'd settle for the truth," Kerney replied. "It's out there somewhere."

———

Growing up on the Mescalero Reservation, Clayton knew Alamogordo well. It was a raw, unpolished city, dependent on the huge federal payroll from nearby Holloman Air Force Base and adjacent White Sands Missile Range. A growing community of thirty thousand due to an influx of military retirees, it continued to expand along a raggedy commercial corridor that stretched for miles. Only the rugged escarpment of the Sacramento Mountains towering to the east above the city, and the Tularosa Basin with its billowing sand dunes and distant mountains to the west, saved it from drabness.

In the early evening, on a middle-class residential street in the foothills, Clayton parked inconspicuously behind a pickup truck and waited for Agent Carla Olivas to arrive home. He'd ditched his tail in Las Cruces by borrowing Wendell's twelve-year-old Jeep Wrangler and using unpaved, rough back roads to leave the city.

Carla's spouse, Monica Shaw, had just pulled into the driveway, returning from her job as a civilian systems analyst at Holloman. Clayton hoped Carla wouldn't be far behind. As a sergeant in the state police uniform division, he'd been her field-training officer during her probationary year with the department. He'd guided her through a couple of personal rough patches, including a temporary breakup with Monica, then only her girlfriend, before his promotion to lieutenant and transfer to criminal investigations. After Carla had served two years on patrol, Clayton had recommended her for transfer to investigations, where she'd quickly blossomed into a fine agent. She was his best chance to learn any fresh information in the Kim Ward murder investigation.

When the familiar silhouette of her unmarked unit turned onto the street, he left his truck and hurried to meet her.

"Got a minute?" he asked, as she opened the car door.

"Lieutenant," Carla said, stifling her surprise. "I can't be talking to you."

"Then don't talk, just listen," Clayton replied. "If I say something that's true, nod. Did Avery look at the Fergurson photography archives at the university?"

With an angry stare, Carla nodded.

"Did it yield anything new?"

Carla remained motionless.

"Has anything developed with the search for Lucille Ward?"

Carla nodded, her expression darkening.

"Have you found her?"

Carla didn't react. "Stop this," she said sharply. "I can't help you. You know that."

"One more question," Clayton pleaded. "Have you located Todd Marks or any trace of him?"

"I'm going inside my house and calling in your location," Carla replied with a slight, negative headshake, looking around for Clayton's pickup truck. "I brushed you off and we didn't speak to each other. Do you understand?"

Clayton nodded. She was giving him a short head start before a new surveillance tail could pick him up. "Thanks."

As he hurried away, he heard her whisper, "Good luck."

————

After Clayton checked into the Deming motel, he met Kerney and Sara at a nearby Mexican restaurant to compare notes. The constant sound of tire rubber on the pavement from I-10 drifted through the thin walls of the diner, adding a whiny background hum to the surrounding patrons' chatter.

"Apparently they've made progress on finding Lucille Ward," Clayton reported after the waitress passed around menus and left to get them water. "But that could mean anything from a good lead to her confirmed death. Todd Marks is still MIA, and Fergurson's photo archives at the university proved unhelpful. That's all I got."

"They're stalled," Kerney declared. "Which is good."

Sara leaned across the table toward Clayton. "What were your reasons for chasing down Lucille Ward and Todd Marks?"

"I was looking for anything that would punch holes in Kerney's defense," Clayton replied. "If Marks is found and swears he hadn't seen Kim either before or after she was with Kerney at Erma's, and we could prove it, that would weaken his case. Also, if the mother knows of any contact between Kerney and Kim after his arrival at Erma's but before Kim's sudden disappearance, that would further damage the defense."

"Good points, but still not conclusive proof of guilt," Sara observed.

"No, but every little bit helps," Clayton countered. "What have you got?"

The waitress returned with water and took their orders. On her way to the kitchen, she skipped around a four-year-old boy who was loitering on the floor behind his mother's chair.

"At the high school, I posed as a distant relative looking for Loretta Page," Sara said as she slid a copy of a page from a high school yearbook to Clayton. "That's her photograph. All I learned is that she dropped out and failed to graduate for reasons unknown."

"Pregnant?" Clayton suggested.

"Likely," Sara replied. "For many small-town girls, the sixties free-love hippie movement didn't eliminate the shame of being pregnant and unmarried."

"I wonder if she had an abortion, which is why she went to live with Kim Ward's mother for a time," Kerney speculated.

"That makes sense," Sara said. "If she chose to have an abortion, it was still illegal in most states."

"But not in nearby Mexico," Clayton noted.

"Exactly," Sara replied, consulting her notes. "Loretta had an older brother who school officials told me died while serving in Vietnam. Through the Armed Forces Records Center, I confirmed that army Private First Class Louis Page of Deming died from wounds he received in combat at Long Binh during the 1968 Tet Offensive. His parents—Loretta's as well—Jack and Jann Page, also of Deming, were beneficiaries of his life insurance policy. The proceeds were mailed to them at a residential address here in town. It's a small house now owned by a retired railroad engineer and his wife. They'd never heard of the Page family."

Clayton studied Loretta Page's photo. With her curly hair and upturned nose, perky-looking was the best way to describe her. "I wonder if there may have been another reason she wound up leaving her parents' home and staying with Kim Ward's mother."

Kerney shrugged. "Unknown. But I can tell you the people named Page listed in the phone book have no family connection to Loretta. One is a retired, widowed nurse from Cedar Rapids, Iowa, another is an African-American man who works at the local green chili pepper processing plant. He lives with his Mexican-born wife and her two children in a trailer park. The last listing was for Kenneth Page. Originally from California, he's a vintner who owns a small winery on some acreage outside of town. Runs it with his second wife. His only child, a son, is grown, married, and living in North Carolina."

Kerney paused for a sip of water. "He said when he first moved here some twenty years ago, the old-timers asked if he was any relation to Jack and Jann Page."

"So, we've got that tidbit to follow up on," Clayton concluded. "At least it's something."

"Everything we know, the police will also know by tomorrow," Sara added. "They'll be out looking for who and what we're searching for."

The waitress, tray in hand, delivered plates of enchiladas smothered in green and red chili, smiled, and left, again sidestepping the ignored four-year-old boy on the floor behind his mother.

They ate in silence, their spirits slightly dampened, until Clayton smiled across the table at Kerney and Sara and said, "We're smarter than the cops."

Kerney nodded in agreement. "Plus, we have a head start."

Sara pushed aside her half-eaten meal. "Stop congratulating each other, gentlemen, and start thinking of what we're going to do next. I want this over with, so I can start enjoying my retirement."

"Yes, ma'am," Kerney and Clayton replied in unison.

CHAPTER 13

Early in the morning, still half asleep in his Pecos single-wide, Juan Ramirez got yelled at when Sergeant Medina called and discovered he still didn't know where Kerney and his family were going for the weekend. Ramirez wanted to tell Medina to stuff it, but didn't have the *bolas* to do it. Instead, he said he'd find out right away.

He was microwaving a cup of leftover coffee when his sister stopped by to bitch at him about not getting her boy out of juvie. Gritting his teeth while she dumped her frustrations on him, Juan didn't mention that the cops were threatening to keep her *hijo* locked up indefinitely. *Madre de dios*, he'd be in deep shit with the *familia*, especially his mother, if he let that happen.

To make the start of the day even worse, he was badly hungover from too much *cerveza*. He had to hurry, or he'd be too late to talk to Patrick before his grandparents drove him to school.

He splashed water on his face, yanked on his boots, found his truck keys, and barreled down Interstate 25 through Cañoncito at Apache Canyon. On U.S. 285, he crested the hill overlooking the Galisteo

Basin and turned off the pavement onto a gravel road that led to Kerney's ranch gate, where the security guard waved him through.

He came out of the canyon, saw Kerney's old truck parked in front of the horse barn with the doors wide open, and sighed in relief. He'd made it in time.

He ground to a stop in front of the open barn doors, saw Patrick and his *abuelo* inside, and called out a *buenos dias*.

"Juan," Patrick replied with a smile, replacing his pitchfork on the wall rack by the doors. "*Que pasa?*"

"I got salt for the cows, Patricio," Juan replied, getting out of his truck and nodding a wordless greeting to Patrick's grandfather. It was no lie. He had several fresh salt licks in the truck bed. "And I came to look after the ponies, *tambien*. I thought you were going away."

Patrick shook his head. "Not yet. I think my dad told you Friday."

Juan shrugged sheepishly, stuck his shaking hands into his pants pockets. He quickly looked away from Patrick's grandfather, who was standing inside one of the stalls staring at him. "I guess I forgot."

"We'll leave from town after school," Patrick replied.

"Okay, I'll be here after that."

"Thanks."

The headache in the back of Juan's skull made it impossible to be subtle. It wasn't his strong suit anyway. He forced a smile. "Where are you going again?" he asked bluntly, gritting his teeth at his stupidity. "I think I had too much *cerveza* last night."

"Mescalero," Patrick answered with a big grin. "The whole family is gathering."

Fuzzy-headed, Juan couldn't remember where that was, but decided not to ask. With a tense smile, he stepped back to his truck. "*Bueno*. Have fun. See you."

"*Adios*," Patrick replied. He turned to his grandfather and whispered, "I've never seen Juan hungover like that before."

"That *vaquero* seemed nervous as well as hungover," Dean commented as Juan drove away.

"About what?"

Dean shook his head. "I don't know, but it's not a good sign. Best we tell your father about it."

———

In Clayton Istee's former office, Paul Avery sat and listened with deep misgivings as Agent Carla Olivas described her encounter with Clayton the previous evening. Advised by dispatch as soon as Olivas called in Clayton's location, Avery didn't like the way she'd handled it.

When she finished, he shook his head and asked, "Why didn't you report this directly to me then?"

"I saw no need to bother you," Carla replied. "As I said, I refused to speak to him."

"Yes, as you said," Avery snapped.

Olivas stiffened. "I'll put it in writing."

"Did you help him, Carla?"

"Why would I have done that? Besides, except for learning that Lucille Ward supposedly moved away from Belen, whereabouts still unknown, we've gotten nowhere since Clayton resigned."

"Did you tell him that?"

"Stop being such a dickhead, Paul."

Avery sighed. "All right, let's drop it. We know Clayton is with Kerney and his wife in Deming. I want you there finding out what they're looking for. I'm uneasy that they know something we don't."

"Okay."

Olivas turned and left. For a moment Avery questioned his decision to take on the responsibilities of a supervisor. He could have said no. A call from Gabe Medina shook him out of his musing.

"*Compadre*," Medina said cheerfully. "My CI reports Kerney et al.

will gather at the Mescalero Reservation for the weekend, starting late Friday afternoon."

"Shit," Avery replied.

"I know, I know," Medina consoled. "It's a sovereign nation, and you have no jurisdiction."

"Worse than that," Avery muttered. "Apaches don't like meddlesome gringos or non-native cops hovering around."

"Better circle the wagons in case they go on the warpath."

"Very funny. Can Ramirez get into Kerney's house after everyone leaves on Friday?"

"He has a house key and the owner's permission," Gabe replied. "That makes his entry legal. What do you want him to do?"

"Just report back on what he sees in plain sight. Notes on a wall calendar or stuck on the fridge, maybe papers on top of a desk or a bedside table, phone numbers jotted on a desk pad—that sort of thing. Ask him to write down exactly what he sees but to leave everything as he found it."

"That stretches the boundaries," Gabe warned.

"No, it just makes him a nosy guy."

"You're joking, right?"

"No, I'm not."

"I won't do it."

"Come on," Avery pleaded.

"Come on, shit," Gabe replied. "Kerney isn't some lame civilian who thinks he knows everything about criminal law because he watches TV cop shows. If he gets one whiff of this, his lawyer will be all over your ass."

"You won't do it?"

"Hell, no. As your friend I won't do it, and to cover my own ass with my department I won't do it."

"Okay, I'll leave you out of it," Avery said. "Tell Ramirez to expect a call from me."

"Jesus, you're serious."

"I've got a stalled investigation and the brass on my tail. You bet I'm serious."

"Okay, I'll tell him. But I'm out of it from now on."

"Thanks."

"*Por nada*," Gabe Medina grunted as he disconnected.

Avery gazed out the window. Maybe Gabe was right, but he had to push the envelope. Asking Ramirez to look around Kerney's house wasn't that big a deal, and it was worth a shot.

———

Sara's after-dinner computer searches had yielded some interesting information. She'd found birth records for both Jack and Jann Page, as well as their children, Loretta and Louis, but only a death certificate for Jann, who'd died in Silver City several years before. Their son, Louis, killed in combat in Vietnam, was buried at the Fort Bayard National Cemetery outside Silver City. The whereabouts of Jack Page, if he was still alive, were unknown. Born in 1929 on a ranch outside the small settlement of Hachita southwest of Deming, Page had enlisted in the navy during the Korean War. He'd been medically retired with the rank of petty officer third class after suffering burns to his hands and arms during a boiler explosion on a heavy cruiser off the North Korean coast.

Page had received the Navy Commendation Medal for saving the life of a more seriously burned shipmate, and the Purple Heart for wounds suffered in a combat zone. Upon retirement he'd received a twenty percent permanent disability pension for his wounds. Electronically deposited monthly government checks had sat untouched in a dormant bank account for years, until the account was declared abandoned and the balance transferred to a state-administered unclaimed assets program. At that point, the federal government had stopped all payments.

There was no record that Jack Page had died. Likewise, there was no record he'd been buried at the Fort Bayard, Santa Fe, or El Paso National Cemeteries or the recently opened state veterans' cemetery north of Las Cruces.

Sara was waiting to hear from a contact in military intelligence about a deeper records check on Page at the Department of Veterans Affairs, the Social Security Administration, and the Department of Defense Finance and Accounting Service. That should tell her if Page was alive and, if so, where he could be found.

Over breakfast at a restaurant chain that specialized in platters of bland, overcooked eggs and undercooked bacon, Sara, Kerney, and Clayton decided to expand their search to additional southern New Mexico counties. Loretta and her father, Jack Page, might not have strayed too far over the years. The expanded search would focus on county courthouse records for marriage licenses, district courts for divorce decrees, and county public health and social services offices for any records of treatment or assistance.

Kerney and Sara would concentrate on the southwest corner of the state, and Clayton would cover Doña Ana and other several south-eastern counties. It meant splitting up and traveling long distances, but they'd keep in touch by cell phone. If it turned into a washout, they'd regroup in Deming and take another tack, yet to be determined.

Kerney's phone rang as they were about to leave. He smiled and answered. "Patrick."

"Gramps and I think Juan is acting weird."

Kerney's smile faded. "How so?"

"Like nervous and asking questions. He wanted to know where we'll be this weekend."

"And you told him?"

"Yeah. Was that wrong?"

"Not really, you'll be followed there by the police anyway. Besides seeming nervous, how else was he acting?"

"He was really hungover."

Kerney had never known Juan to show up at the ranch in such a condition. "You're sure?"

"Gramps says he knows a hungover cowboy when he sees one."

Kerney laughed. "I bet he does."

"Is there anything I should do?" Patrick asked.

"If Juan shows up again before Friday, just behave normally. If there is something going on with him, it's best he isn't tipped off that we're suspicious."

"You don't seem surprised about Juan," Patrick said.

"I'm not. You did good."

"Thanks," Patrick said with pleasure in his voice. "Got to go."

He disconnected before Kerney could turn his phone over to Sara for a quick hello.

"What is it?" she asked.

"Apparently Juan Ramirez has been recruited by the cops to spy on us," he answered.

"Seriously?" She laughed.

"Yes. What's so funny?"

"Juan Ramirez is the best they could do?"

"Apparently." Kerney grinned as he gave the waitress his credit card. "There is a certain humor to it. I wonder what carrot and stick the cops are holding over poor Juan's head."

"Will you fire him when you get back to the ranch?" Clayton asked.

"On principle, I might have to."

Kerney's phone rang before the waitress returned with his charge slip.

"Upham wants you at state police headquarters at eleven this morning for another round of questioning," Gary Dalquist announced.

"I'm in Deming," Kerney replied. "Tell him to reschedule."

"I know where you are, Kerney," Dalquist said testily. "And we're not rescheduling. Upham would love to tell the prosecutors and a jury you were uncooperative. They'd wrap that tidbit up as part of a telltale allusion to your guilt in their closing statement. I have a chartered plane en route to the Deming Municipal Airport. I'll meet you when you land in Santa Fe."

"Okay."

"Don't ask me what it will cost. You can afford it."

"I wasn't going to. What's Upham's agenda?"

"He wouldn't budge when I asked. Expect him to try to throw you off."

"That's what I'd do."

"Your plane will be on the ground in thirty minutes. The pilot told me he was an aviation officer for the state police when you were deputy chief. You two should have a lot of catching up to do."

"Only if he thinks I'm innocent."

"He does. Safe travels." Dalquist disconnected.

Kerney smiled at Sara. "You're on your own today. Upham wants me in his office at eleven. Gary's sending a plane. I should be back by late afternoon, if not sooner."

"I'll concentrate on Luna and Hidalgo Counties," Sara replied.

"I'm off to Las Cruces," Clayton noted. "That's home ground for me. Maybe I'll get lucky."

Kerney nodded. "I'll give you a heads-up once Upham kicks me loose." He stood and gave Sara a quick smooch. "Something's got to give," he added wistfully.

"It will," Clayton predicted, as he walked with Kerney and Sara to their parked cars, where three unmarked state police units waited, engines idling.

———

The short, uneventful flight to Santa Fe left Kerney with his ears ringing from the nonstop chatter of the pilot, Steve Sather, who spent the entire time recounting stories of rescue missions into the high country, drug interdiction operations along the Mexican border, air surveillance on human trafficking convoys traveling the interstate, and the VIPs he'd shuttled around the state in airplanes during his twenty-five years on the job.

It was better for Steve to talk than cry. In the past year, he'd lost his wife to cancer and his only child to a Taliban attack while serving in Afghanistan. Kerney deplaned thinking Steve's heartbreak made his own troubles seem minor.

Dalquist was waiting outside the small, Santa Fe–style terminal. On the curving exit road to the highway they passed the sprawling auto junkyard that gave arriving passengers a slightly different view of Santa Fe as a tourist mecca. In Kerney's mind, the rusted, broken, and wrecked vehicles were tangible proof that despite the historical neighborhoods, the downtown plaza, the cultural institutions, and the stunning backdrop of the beautiful Sangre de Cristo Mountains, much of Santa Fe was like any other southwestern city.

At the Department of Public Safety, Upham made them wait twenty minutes under the watchful eye of a uniformed officer. He appeared, lumbering down the hall wearing a wrinkled business suit that hung loosely on his heavy frame, a thin file folder clutched in his hand. He pointedly sniffed the air as he drew near. Kerney gave him a big smile.

Upham grunted. "Let's go."

In the same uninviting interrogation room, he recited all the necessary legal mumbo-jumbo, and stared in silence at Kerney from across the table for a good long minute.

Kerney waited him out.

"When you arrived at the Fergurson house to begin your stay as her guest, who was there to greet you?" Upham inquired.

"No one," Kerney replied. "Erma was on her property near Hermit's Peak, and didn't get back for another four days."

"Wasn't that the large ranch outside of Las Vegas Fergurson willed to you?"

"That question is irrelevant to this inquiry," Dalquist sharply noted.

Upham ignored him. "Did Fergurson give you permission to stay at her home in her absence until her return?"

"Of course."

"There's no mention of it in her journals," Upham noted.

"She didn't write in her journal every day," Dalquist countered.

"Erma was like family," Kerney said. "Do you have a point to make, Upham?"

Upham consulted his file. "What about Maxwell Colley, the graduate student who rented the apartment above the garage? Was he at home when you arrived?"

"No, I didn't meet him until several days later. He'd been out of town on a research trip."

So, for three or four days, you had the Fergurson residence all to yourself."

"That's right."

Upham thumbed through some papers. "During that time, did you invite any old friends to stop by?"

"No."

"Did anyone come by?"

"I wasn't there every minute, so I can't say. But while I was at

Erma's I was alone until Colley returned from his trip, although we saw very little of each other afterwards."

"You were alone at the house," Upham echoed.

"Do you have a point?" Dalquist asked.

Upham leaned forward toward Kerney. "Did Kim Ward visit you at the Fergurson residence prior to the night of April twenty-fifth, 1973?"

"No," Kerney answered flatly.

"Did *anyone* visit you prior to that date?"

"No."

Upham smirked. "Fergurson's renter, Maxwell Colley, says otherwise. He recalls a young woman coming to the residence looking for you prior to the night Kim Ward stayed with you. He is clear that it occurred before he was questioned by the police about your allegedly stolen pistol. Colley saw her enter the house and noticed your vehicle parked in the driveway. He remembers her staying for about an hour before driving away."

"Did he ID this woman?" Dalquist inquired.

"His description as to height and weight matches Kim Ward's."

"That's not an identification," Dalquist said. "Did Colley see this woman with my client?"

"No, but it's helpful information nonetheless, and your client has just lied to me."

Kerney shook his head. "I saw nobody."

Dalquist put his forefinger to his lips to silence Kerney. "I need access to Maxwell Colley."

Upham kept his gaze fixed on Kerney. "Dr. Colley is a professor emeritus of geology at Adams State University in Alamosa, Colorado." He handed Dalquist a business card. "Here's his contact information."

Dalquist glanced at the card and pocketed it without comment.

Upham leaned closer to Kerney. "If you weren't in the house, and your car was in the driveway, where were you when this young woman came to see you?"

"Don't answer," Dalquist said.

"I could have been hiking," Kerney replied. "I often took a trail from Erma's up to the Organ Mountains. It was a good way to clear my head."

Upham shifted back in his chair. "Why would she wait an hour to see you, if you were off hiking?"

Kerney shrugged and held Upham's gaze.

"Who do you think it could have been waiting to see you?"

Kerney shrugged again.

"On to other matters, then," Upham said, breaking eye contact and selecting another piece of paper from his file, this time an eight-by-ten photograph. "Were you at the Stallion Bar on Main Street in Las Cruces on the night of April twenty-third, 1973, when a fight broke out between soldiers from White Sands Missile Range and some local cowboys?"

"I don't recall that."

Upham handed Kerney the photograph. "This was taken by a staff photographer for the daily newspaper showing the arrest of some of the brawlers. We think one of the onlooking spectators in the photo is you."

Dalquist snapped the photograph from Kerney's hand. "Don't answer."

"One of the cowboys arrested that night was Todd Marks," Upham added with a wicked smile. "Didn't you tell me you never saw him after he and his future wife dropped out of school to join the rodeo circuit?"

"You have his prior statements," Dalquist interjected quickly, studying the photograph. "I see no one here with the slightest resemblance to my client."

"We believe with computer enhancement you will." Upham turned to Kerney. "Are you in the photograph, Mr. Kerney?"

Dalquist waved Kerney off from replying. "I'll require a copy of this photograph as part of discovery," he said, handing it to Upham.

"Of course." Upham put the photograph in his file, stood, and looked down at Kerney. "How's your private investigation going?"

Kerney rose. "I'm pleased with our progress." He stepped around Upham and walked out the door.

———

Dalquist held his questions until they reached the parking lot. With Cerrillos Road traffic resonating in the background, he asked Kerney if he'd witnessed the brawl at the Stallion Bar.

"I don't remember being there," Kerney replied.

"Do you remember a woman coming to see you at Erma's house, as Maxwell Colley has alleged to the police?"

Kerney shook his head.

"Was it Kim Ward?"

"As far as I can recall, I had no visitors, male or female, until Kim showed up the night she disappeared."

"Did you see Todd Marks or Kim at the bar?"

"I know I did some bar-hopping in town at night, but I can't recall seeing either of them."

"Why is that, Kevin?"

"Because for three days I was staggeringly drunk. I was angry, depressed, and lonely. Emotionally numb from 'Nam, the army, and the crash that killed my parents. I walked out of the army a civilian, with nobody waiting for me and no place to go, except Erma's. When I got there, I fell apart. She sobered me up and saved me."

Dalquist sighed. "Is there anything else you haven't told me?"

Kerney smiled and patted Dalquist on the shoulder. "Don't worry, that's the whole story."

He got in the passenger seat of Dalquist's BMW. On the drive to the airport he called Sara and Clayton and filled them in. They reported no progress locating Loretta.

CHAPTER 14

When Clayton learned Upham had a newspaper photograph that purportedly placed Kerney in Todd Marks's presence a night or two before Kim Ward's arrival at Erma's house, he went looking for Dewey Bullard.

At the time of his retirement a decade ago, Dewey had spent fifty years as the news photographer for the local paper. Now he concentrated on photographing historic churches and old ruins throughout the state. If he wasn't location-scouting on remote private ranches or two-hundred-year-old haciendas, he'd set up a table at the farmers' market on Main Street and sell his framed photographs cheap to art lovers who knew a bargain when they saw it.

One Saturday morning, Grace had tugged Clayton to Dewey's table, and they bought a large framed image of the Apache cathedral at Mescalero. It hung in the living room over the couch.

Bullard shared his photographic archive with local and state historical societies and preservationist groups. He prided himself on having kept the negatives of every picture he'd ever taken, including hundreds of images that showed the changing landscape of Las Cruces over six decades and counting.

He wasn't listed in the phone book, but he had a website where interested customers could browse through selected images. Clayton tried the phone number on the website, and got a voice message saying Dewey was either out taking pictures or in his darkroom. He left a message and sent an email through Bullard's website with little hope of a quick response.

On a hunch, he checked the back of the photograph and found Bullard's business card taped to it, with a cell phone number. Dewey answered on the first ring, and said he'd be more than willing to help solve a cold-case crime.

Clayton wrote down his address and hurried over. It was a small cottage near the university in a neighborhood that sprang up after World War II and had been popular with young families. Over time it had been transformed into rentals, duplexes, and some blocky apartment complexes that catered to college students.

Clayton found Bullard waiting for him on his front porch, a look of pleased anticipation on his face.

"Now, what's this cold case all about?" he asked eagerly as Clayton approached. Once tall and in vigorous good shape from frequent hikes with his equipment to remote sites, Dewey was now stooped over and used a cane.

"There was a brawl at the Stallion Bar on Main Street on April twenty-third, 1973, and you took the photo of an arrest that was published in the paper the following morning."

Dewey laughed. "I got dozens of great late-night shots of brawls at that dive before it closed down. This isn't about a bar fight, is it?"

"No, it's about a girl who went missing around the same time and whose remains were recently uncovered."

Dewey nodded. "Kim Ward. I read about it. And about you having to quit the state police because of it."

"I'm here as a civilian," Clayton confirmed. "Would you happen to have the roll of film from that night?"

"It's ninety-nine percent certain that I do." Dewey opened the screen door. "When I bought this place, it had a crawl space under the floor, and tiny as it is, I couldn't squeeze a darkroom in anywhere. So I dug out a basement, and that's where I store all my old negatives and develop my prints. Still shoot thirty-five millimeter at times, but now I'm doing mostly digital work."

He led Clayton to a rear kitchen and down a corner circular staircase to a large basement room containing enough cameras and equipment to fill a store. Dozens of film storage cabinets lined the walls.

At a vertical film cabinet, he read the labels on the drawers, found what he was looking for, and did a quick search. "This is it," he said, plucking out a proof sheet. "Took some good crowd scenes outside the bar that night."

He handed it to Clayton, along with a magnifying glass. "The first twelve images are of an amateur golf tournament at the old country club earlier in the day. You can skip those."

Clayton studied the shots taken at the bar. Two showed Todd Marks in handcuffs being led away, full face and from the back. In another, Kerney clearly stood out as one of the onlookers outside the open front door of the bar. Although he couldn't be positive, because her face was partially in shadows, at the edge of the last photograph it looked like Kim Ward had also been there.

"Can you make me a copy of this sheet?" he asked.

"Can do," Dewey replied.

"Thank you. When I leave, the police officer who followed me will question you. Tell him exactly what you did, and give him what you gave to me."

"You don't want me to lie for you?"

"No, sir, I don't."

Dewey smiled. "Fair enough."

A short time later, Clayton left Bullard's house, with evidence in hand and his stomach in knots. Had he been wrong to believe in Kerney's innocence?

———

Born and raised in northern New Mexico in a small village outside of Taos, with towering mountains and the stunning chasm of the Rio Grande Gorge nearby, Agent Carla Olivas was no fan of the stark desert that overwhelmed Deming and all that surrounded it. Particularly on this day, she was no admirer of the almost constant dry, dust-laden wind that sapped moisture from everything, including her small frame. Despite starting on her second six-pack of bottled water, she felt totally dehydrated. Her eyes were red and irritated. She was ready for a long dip in the motel pool, a siesta, and a drink.

She'd been trailing Sara Brannon over a two-county area, documenting every courthouse, government building, schoolhouse, social service agency, and public health office she visited, passing the information on to other agents tasked with finding out who she was talking to and what she was looking for at those places. All they had so far were two names: Jack Page and Loretta Page. Queries of state and federal databases were under way.

Eager for something interesting to happen, Carla sat in her unit with the AC running at the Deming Municipal Airport on the outskirts of town, in plain view of Sara Brannon, who was parked fifty feet away in her SUV waiting for Kerney's return from Santa Fe.

The seldom-used airport had few facilities and served only small general aviation planes. There was no good place to hide. Bored, Carla kept gazing at the Florida Mountains in the distance, glancing back at

Brannon's vehicle, squinting at the ribbon of traffic on Interstate 10, or scanning the delivery trucks leaving the sprawling chili processing plant nearby. When she looked back at her target, Brannon was out of her SUV, thirty feet away and closing fast.

With a sigh, Carla rolled down her window. "Can I help you?" she asked when Brannon arrived.

"Indeed, you can," Sara replied with a smile. "Stop this constant harassment. It's tiresome, unnecessary, and possibly illegal. You have no cause to follow me."

"Is that what you really wanted to say to me?" Carla retorted.

"Fair warning. I've been video-recording you all day," Sara answered. "If you continue this surveillance, I will file a civil rights complaint against you personally."

"Go right ahead, ma'am," Carla said, as she tapped the automatic window button to block her out. She watched the retired army general walk away. She didn't know if Brannon's civil rights were being violated, but the threat of legal action was worth reporting.

By radio, Carla repeated Brannon's threat to Paul Avery, who ordered her to continue her assignment. He'd let the lawyers at headquarters know about it, and unless he got a legal opinion to cease operations, surveillance would continue.

Over the sound of the AC, Carla heard the distinctive roar of a twin-engine aircraft. Through the windshield she saw a plane bank and turn on final approach. Kerney was arriving.

———

The sound of the propellers as the plane taxied for takeoff masked Kerney's question as he climbed into Sara's SUV. He closed the passenger door and asked again, "Who's shadowing you today?"

"A young, attractive female agent," Sara answered. "I've just threatened to slap her with a civil rights violation suit."

"On what grounds?"

Sara smiled and shrugged. "I thought I'd leave that part up to Dalquist."

Kerney laughed. "Smart."

"I thought so. Is it you in the newspaper photograph Upham sprang on you?"

"Possibly. That was a very drunk time in my young life."

Sara's expression clouded. "Not good."

"No."

She checked the rearview mirror as they left the airport. The unmarked unit stayed back a polite distance. "Jack Page used to have his government benefit checks electronically deposited to an account at an Arizona bank. Years ago, the bank declared the account dormant, and sent the proceeds to a state agency that manages unclaimed assets. As a result, all federal payments into the account were discontinued."

"How much was in the account?" Kerney asked.

"Over twenty thousand dollars."

"That's a lot for anyone to voluntarily give up. Is he dead?"

"Unknown. He last surfaced at the Fort Bayard Veterans Center, where he'd been admitted for medical treatment. According to a records clerk, Page voluntarily left the center six months ago, supposedly to receive home care by a family member. Because of confidentiality rules, I know nothing more than that."

The time display on the dashboard information system showed four-thirty. "Let's go to Fort Bayard," Kerney said.

"We won't get there until after normal business hours."

"Exactly," Kerney said. "There will be fewer bureaucrats there to guard the gates."

"Smart," Sara said, flashing him a smile.

"I thought so. Any word from Clayton?"

She shook her head.

Kerney speed-dialed Clayton. "Where are you?" he asked when he answered.

"Just leaving Las Cruces coming in your direction."

"Can you lose your tail?"

"No problem."

"I'm with Sara. Meet us at City of Rocks."

"Okay."

"Have you got anything?" Kerney asked.

"Yeah," Clayton said tersely. "I'll go over it with you there."

"Roger." The reason for Clayton's brusque tone would have to wait. Kerney disconnected, turned to Sara, and said, "We need to lose our surveillance as well." He accessed the dashboard GPS system. "Take Highway 180 north towards Silver City and grab a right at a county road on the outskirts of town. It's unpaved and leads to a remote, low-lying mountain off Highway 61. She won't be able to keep up off the pavement and you can lose her there." He pointed at a cutoff that would take them to an abandoned settlement.

"Why City of Rocks?" Sara asked.

"It's an out-of-the-way state park and a perfect place to make a switch without drawing undue attention. We'll wait there until after sunset, and then I'll go on to Fort Bayard with Clayton, while you head back to the motel in Deming, hopefully picking up your tail along the way."

Sara swung onto Pine Street and headed for the 180 junction.

———

On the graveled county road with civilization fast disappearing in her rearview mirror, Sara's SUV threw up a dust cloud that completely obscured the unmarked unit. The road deteriorated into a washboard that had Sara and Kerney bobbing in their seats. Where an old arroyo had reclaimed the road after a cloudburst runoff, only the Jeep's four-wheel drive got them through the sandy bottom. There was no way the unmarked unit could follow.

Back on the highway, it was a short drive to City of Rocks State Park, a square mile of high desert volcanic rock columns, pinnacles, and uplifts separated by narrow pathways and road-like corridors. It resembled the stunning ruins of an ancient city or the sculpted remnants of an extinct, alien culture. A low, golden sun on the western horizon gave the park a mystical glow.

A few dimmed night lights showed through the windows of the closed visitor center. The only sign of activity came from an area reserved for recreational vehicles, where some elderly folks were sitting on lawn chairs admiring the sunset. Several unattended tents were scattered around the perimeter of the park.

Sara stopped at the trailhead to the botanical garden, and Kerney called Clayton to give him their location. He arrived within ten minutes, got into the back of the Jeep, and tossed a manila envelope into Kerney's lap.

"What's this?" he asked.

"You tell me," Clayton snapped.

Kerney turned on the interior lights, pulled out the proof sheets, and scanned the images.

"You were with Todd Marks and Kim Ward at the Stallion Bar hours before she showed up at Erma Fergurson's," Clayton announced. "Have you made a fool of me?"

"Not you." Kerney passed the proof sheet to Sara and turned to face Clayton. "Me. I was the drunk fool. I honestly didn't remember."

"You were that drunk?" Clayton challenged.

"Let me give you the short version of what happened to me after that wrong-way driver killed my parents, so that you'll understand. I was coming home from Vietnam and they were driving to meet me at the Albuquerque airport. They never showed up. I called home, got no answer, and waited for hours until a cop paged me. They'd found my flight information in the wreckage and located me through that. At the crash site, I identified their mangled bodies and arranged to get them transported to a funeral home. An officer drove me home. After I buried them, I cut short my leave and applied for compassionate separation from active duty."

He reached up, switched off the interior lights, and continued in the darkness. "The army took its time processing my request. The only way I could cope was by shutting down and doing everything by the numbers. All the time I waited, I was a spit-and-shine, by-the-book executive officer of a rifle company. There were no cracks in the armor, no falling apart, no drinking, no weed-smoking—nothing. I was a perfect soldier and a total zombie. When I got out, I did fine until I reached Erma's and could totally let go. I stayed in a drunken stupor for days. That's why I've never been completely sure of exactly what happened."

He turned to face Clayton. "But I know I didn't kill Kim Ward. I just didn't save her."

"The department has the proof sheet," Clayton said.

"But it doesn't prove I killed her. You can bail out on this, if you want to."

"I didn't say that. I'm in."

The last tip of the sun faded in a cloudless, orange-streaked sky and the City of Rocks turned foreboding in the gathering night. "Good. Let's go to Fort Bayard and pretend we're still cops."

CHAPTER 15

Clayton coasted to a stop in front of the Fort Bayard Medical Center, a state-run long-term care facility that included a designated veterans center. Kerney took a deep breath, stepped out of the vehicle, and looked around. The new facility had been built some distance away from the old historic fort with its row of stately two-story officers' quarters and the squat adobe headquarters building that faced the large grassy quadrangle.

Kerney wanted to see the quadrangle again before they left the campus. He clearly remembered the monthly trips he'd made with his parents to the now-demolished old hospital to visit Patrick Kerney, his sick and dying grandfather. He'd loved that old man with his rough-hewn ways, and had reveled in grandfather's stories about frontier years on the Tularosa, the outlaws he'd known, his service in Cuba with the Rough Riders, and the famous charge up San Juan Hill with Teddy Roosevelt. But most of all, Kerney had loved doing chores with Grandpa, working the ponies, learning the old-time cowboy ways, taking evening rides with him when the day had cooled and the breezes were pleasant, before he got too sick to sit a horse.

In the hospital at his bedside, Kerney had sat and stared at the fragile old man who no longer spoke, mentally willing him to open his eyes and talk to him one more time, just to say goodbye. It never happened. After a massive heart attack, his grandfather had been moved to the VA hospital in Albuquerque, where he died in his sleep, on the same day the U.S. Army took possession of the Kerney family 7-Bar-K Ranch, the last privately owned outfit on the Tularosa.

"Are you all right?" Clayton asked, pulling Kerney out of his memories.

He nodded wordlessly as he approached the pillared and roofed entrance. The automatic sliding glass doors to the medical center were locked, but there was a buzzer and intercom speaker for after-hours callers to use.

Kerney waved Clayton off as he reached for the buzzer. "Let's not announce ourselves just yet. Maybe we can find a back way in."

They wandered through a large, well-lit, landscaped courtyard to a loading dock at the rear, where a middle-aged man in blue scrubs sat on a folding chair under a shielded exterior light, smoking a cigarette.

The unexpected sight of two strangers surprised him. He stood and quickly ground out his smoke. "Hey, you can't be back here."

Kerney stepped close, flashed his retired police chief badge, and introduced himself as Agent Blackburn with the New Mexico State Police. "My partner is Agent Clauson," he added.

"Is something wrong, Officer?" the man asked in a worried voice. He had a narrow forehead and a wide nose accentuated by a bushy mustache that covered his upper lip.

Kerney flipped the badge case closed. "Not at all. We're just in need of some information."

"I can get the charge nurse for you," the man said. His staff ID badge identified him as Robert Ripple, nursing assistant.

"That might not be necessary," Clayton replied. "We're trying to get in touch with Jack Page, who was in the veterans unit."

Ripple laughed. "Old Jack. He left here some time ago. Got taken home by his son after complaining for months that he didn't like living with old people." He snorted humorously. "Getting on to ninety and didn't like old people."

"His son came for him?" Clayton asked, exchanging looks with Kerney. Supposedly, Jack's son, Louis, had died in Vietnam.

"That's right."

"Remember his name?" Kerney queried.

"Not right off. I think he lives somewhere in this neck of the woods, because I've seen him in Silver City every now and then."

"When did Jack leave the center?" Kerney inquired.

Ripple thoughtfully tapped a finger to his lips. "Six, seven months ago, I'd say."

"We need to see Jack's file," Clayton said.

Ripple shook his head. "No can do. Except for routine medical charts, patient records are kept locked up because of confidentiality and all that. You'll have to come back when the records administrator is here."

Kerney smiled. "Of course. Did Jack make any close buddies while he was staying here?"

Ripple nodded. "Despite being grumpy and pretty much a loner, he was good friends with another Korean War navy vet, Bud Elkins."

"Is Bud still here?"

"Oh, yeah," Ripple answered. "He's probably playing pinochle in the dayroom right now. It's really a living room, but the vets have their own words for things."

"Can we talk to him?" Clayton asked.

Ripple hesitated. "Well, you're supposed to get admitted through the front entrance and sign in, but seeing that you're the police and all, I'll take you to him."

"That would be great," Clayton said.

Ripple led them through a large storage room and down a corridor to the veterans wing. In the living room, about two dozen patients, some in wheelchairs, some with walkers close at hand, and some there under their own steam, were busy with after-dinner socializing, reading, playing cards, and watching TV. Bud Elkins, an overweight, rosy-faced fellow in a T-shirt with U.S. NAVY printed across the front, shorts, and white knee-high diabetic compression socks, looked irritated when Ripple interrupted the card game and said the police wanted to speak with him.

"What the hell for?" Elkins grumbled.

"We've recovered a stolen vehicle belonging to Jack Page's son," Clayton said. "We'd like to locate him so he can get his property back."

"Apparently the vehicle registration information is out-of-date," Kerney added, picking up on Clayton's improvisation. "Do you know his whereabouts?"

Elkins put his cards down and gave Kerney the once-over. "Aren't you a little long in the tooth to be a cop?"

"I'm a reserve officer," Kerney replied with a smile that took in Elkin's cardplaying buddies. "It's something I enjoy doing for the community. Do you know his whereabouts?"

"Louis? What Jack told me was he had a little place up some remote canyon. An inholding in the national forest. Ran some cows on a grazing allotment."

"Can you be more specific about where Louis lives?" Clayton asked.

"It started with an *M*, I think," Elkins said. "Or maybe it was the name of the ranch. I don't remember."

"That's it?" Clayton nudged.

Elkins snorted. "All Jack told me was his boy liked to live where nobody could find him, and that was okay by him."

"Can you describe Louis?" Kerney asked.

"Only saw him that once, when he came to pick Jack up," Elkins replied. "Maybe your age, but with his gray hair pulled back in a pony-tail, and a scraggly gray beard. Looked sort of like a guy who didn't bother much with people."

"Yet he took his father under his wing," Clayton commented.

"Jack said he wanted to be with family and his son was willing. Can't fault either man for that."

"No, you can't," Kerney agreed, turning to Ripple, who hovered nearby. "How was Jack's health when he left?"

"Good," Ripple answered, eager to help. "Sharp as a tack men-tally, but needing a walker because of two bad hips and a busted leg. The docs thought he was too old for replacements. Jack didn't want them anyway."

"Well, that's it, then," Clayton said. "Thanks for your time."

Elkins scooped up his cards. "When you see Jack, give him a howdy and tell him that I miss the old curmudgeon."

"I'll do that," Clayton replied.

Ripple escorted Kerney and Clayton to the front entrance and had them sign the visitors log. Under the watchful eye of a CCTV camera, they averted their faces and signed using their fictitious names.

When the automatic doors closed behind them, Kerney squeezed Clayton's shoulder. "Good work."

Clayton laughed. "You, too. Think we got away clean with this one?"

Kerney shrugged. "I wouldn't count on it. When cops show up anywhere it's usually an event, and all eyes were on us in the dayroom."

"We could get busted for impersonating police officers," Clayton reflected.

"Yeah, but it's a lesser change than murder," Kerney noted.

"For you," Clayton said. "So far, I've never been busted."

"Let's hope it stays that way."

"Do you think Louis Page is alive?"

"Likely not," Kerney conjectured. "But we've got a lot of ground to cover to find out."

"Find out what?"

Kerney shook his head. "I don't know. We'll start with asking the Forest Service who has grazing allotments in the Gila National Forest."

"There are probably dozens," Clayton predicted.

"If we strike out, we'll move on to the Bureau of Land Management."

Clayton groaned. "How in the hell do we pull that off without police powers?"

"It's all computerized public information," Kerney said. "If the Forest Service won't cooperate, I bet the Sierra Club will have what we need. Tomorrow's Friday. We'll work a short day accessing the data banks and head off to Mescalero early. It's not like we've got fresh tracks to follow."

"Amen to that," Clayton said.

Before heading back to Deming, Kerney asked Clayton to drive him around the old Fort Bayard grounds. As they slowly passed by the remaining old buildings bordering the quadrangle, Kerney told him the story of his grandfather and his visits to see him during the last year of his life.

"So that's who Patrick got his name from," Clayton said. "I never knew that."

"Now you do," Kerney said, glad the dark vehicle hid his sudden feelings of sadness.

———

On Highway 180 five miles north of Deming, an unmarked unit picked up Sara's Jeep and followed her into town. She didn't know if the cop behind her was the young agent she'd provoked earlier in the day, and didn't care. Coming back from the City of Rocks, away from Kerney and Clayton, she'd deliberately let down a little bit to shake off the intense worry that had obsessed her since that bizarre, awful night at Fort Leonard Wood.

Impulsively, she pulled off on the shoulder of the road and called Patrick at home. He told her all was well, the cops were still watching them, and Juan Ramirez would take over the barn chores tomorrow afternoon.

"Granddad and Grandmom will pick me up after school and we'll drive straight to Mescalero," he said excitedly. "I'm all packed."

"It will be a wonderful weekend," Sara predicted.

"I know," Patrick said. "Tell dad I figured something out."

"What have you figured out?"

"Just some tech stuff I think he'll like," he answered, sounding pleased with himself.

"But you won't tell me?" Sara teased.

"I didn't mean it that way. I'll show it to both of you tomorrow, okay?"

"Okay, I won't be pushy," Sara said. "'Bye, kiddo."

"'Bye, Mom."

She disconnected, feeling calmer than she had in days, and decided she would not sit in the motel room waiting for Kerney and Clayton. The Deming morning newspaper had featured a story about a special evening fund-raising event open to the public at the local museum, which was housed in a historic National Guard armory. She'd driven past it several times and was curious to find out what treasures it housed.

Back at the motel, she did a quick fix of her face and hair, changed into a clean blouse, wrote a note for Kerney and Clayton, and made the short drive to the museum. The three-story brick building was lit up, the parking lot full of cars, and people were climbing the wide concrete stairs to the arched entrance.

She found a spot, and hurried up the stairs, eager to have an hour of normalcy surrounded by people unconcerned with murder.

———

Agent Carla Olivas waited several minutes before following Sara Brannon into the museum. At the lobby desk near the front entrance she stood in line behind folks registering for the event. When her turn came, she filled out a membership application form and paid the five-dollar annual fee rather than identify herself as a police officer. She took a contribution brochure and promised to seriously consider making an annual donation to support the museum's operating costs.

In the main hall, people were wandering past cabinets filled with crystal, china, teapots, and glassware, displays of veterans memorabilia from the infamous Bataan Death March in World War II, and Native American collectibles. Sara Brannon was nowhere in sight.

Carla passed through various rooms where couples and families were studying shelves of antique dolls, inspecting an authentic old jail cell, examining a genuine ranch chuck wagon, and scrutinizing a glistening gem and mineral collection. She passed through an early 1900s furniture display and spotted Brannon approaching a docent in the lobby. Carla caught Brannon's eye just as her phone rang. It was Paul Avery.

"What's up?" Carla asked.

"Deputy Chief Serrano has called off all surveillance," Avery said grumpily. "Says it's too expensive and we've enough evidence to go to trial. Chief legal counsel and the district attorney agree. Pack it in and go home."

"Are you okay with that?" Carla asked.

"Orders are orders."

"Did you find Kim Ward's mother?"

"Negative. If she's still alive, she's not in Socorro, Belen, Los Lunas, or anyplace in between."

"Ten-four." Carla pocketed her phone and headed for the lobby, sidestepping clusters of happily chatting people. She slowed as she reached Sara Brannon, who smiled charmingly and nodded politely. With an equally well-mannered nod and smile, Carla walked by.

Two thoughts occurred to her as she wheeled out of the parking lot. There was no doubt that Brannon was a classy lady, not to be underestimated. And, while she was happy to be going home, the case against Kevin Kerney was far from being a slam dunk.

———

After the agent left the museum, Sara returned her attention to the docent she'd been questioning about a photograph in the Old Timers Room. It showed a man standing next to a fence with two young boys, and it was labeled underneath in capital letters: "JACK PAGE WITH HIS SONS LOUIS AND EARL AT THE FAMILY RANCH."

"As I said, I didn't know Jack Page had two sons," Sara repeated. "I'm a very distant cousin, and family genealogy is very important to me."

The docent, Edith Grunwald, an older woman with a chubby face and pleasant disposition, shook her head. "Oh, my, I'm not the one to ask. Wait here, and I'll go find Mr. O'Dowd. He's who would know."

Grunwald disappeared into the throng of people in the main room. A few minutes later she returned with a very old, slow-moving man in tow.

"This is Alan O'Dowd," Grunwald said. "He's sort of the unofficial historian of the old timers' photo collection."

"Thank you for speaking to me," Sara said sweetly.

O'Dowd looked up at Sara. "I understand you may have stumbled upon a previously unknown relative."

"Yes, I think so."

"Show me the photograph," O'Dowd said as he shuffled toward the Old Timers Room.

Inside the room, they had to wait a minute until a line of people viewing the photographs moved past the picture of Jack Page and his boys. O'Dowd got up close for a good look.

"Yep, that's Jack with his boys, Louis and Earl. Earl's the older one. Jann's by her first marriage to Sam Matson. I don't recall if Jack ever adopted Earl or not, but he treated both boys as his own. If you're related to Jann, Earl's kin."

"I am," Sara lied delightedly. "This is such interesting news. Do you have any idea how to contact Earl?"

O'Dowd shook his head. "Earl was a bit wild, as I recall, and left Deming to avoid the Vietnam draft, or something like that. The family never talked about it. Don't know what happened to him."

"Would anybody know?"

"Can't say that I do."

"What about his natural father, Sam?"

"Passed years ago," O'Dowd replied.

"And Jack's daughter, Loretta? What happened to her?"

O'Dowd shook his head. "She got in some trouble and left town also. That's all I know."

Pleased with what she'd learned, Sara thanked O'Dowd and left the museum. The young woman agent following her was nowhere to be seen. Had the state police called the surveillance off? And was that good news or bad news?

———

On the way to the motel, Kerney had Clayton stop at a gun shop that stayed open late for customers who used the indoor shooting range. He turned down the owner's offer to test-fire a new Beretta semiautomatic, and bought a Bureau of Land Management map of New Mexico that showed all federal, military, tribal, state, and private lands, including inholdings in the national forests.

He walked outside to find Clayton and his vehicle gone. He was reaching for his cell phone when Clayton pulled up. Kerney opened the passenger door and the smell of take-out pizza filled the air.

"Dinner," Clayton announced. "My treat."

At the motel room, they unloaded the extra-large pizzas, drinks, and dinner salads, found Sara's note explaining her whereabouts, and decided not to wait for her return.

Kerney spread the map out on the bed and, with a slice of pepperoni and green chili in hand, began studying the private inholdings around the Silver City area. At the desk, Clayton was doing a one-finger laptop computer search for federal grazing permits, his free hand otherwise occupied with a slice of cheese and veggies. They were finishing their second slices when Sara arrived.

"Dinner in," she said. "How charming."

"Clayton's treat," Kerney explained. "There's also salad and iced tea."

"Wonderful." She slipped out of her shoes, claimed a slice of cheese and veggie, and sank into the bedside easy chair. "So, who wants to go first?"

Quickly, they exchanged facts. Louis Page had allegedly returned from the dead to rescue his father, Jack, from the veterans center, and taken him to live on some remote ranch outside Silver City. The discovery of a new family member in the person of one Earl Matson, Louis, and Loretta's half-brother. Once considered a little wild, his current whereabouts unknown. His natural father Sam Matson reportedly deceased. And finally, Loretta, who had gotten into unknown trouble and left town years ago.

"One more thing," Sara added. "I'm fairly sure surveillance has been pulled."

"Great," Clayton said. "Now we can keep spinning our wheels unobserved."

"The fact that none of this seems to make any sense means we're missing something," Kerney proposed.

"What if we find out that it has nothing to do with proving your innocence?" Clayton asked.

"We tell Dalquist to delay going to trial as long as he can, and we keep digging," Sara answered emphatically.

"But not this weekend," Clayton cautioned. "My mother and the aunties are preparing a feast, and Grace, Wendell, and Hannah will be joining us."

"How wonderful." Sara sighed. "Two days with family. I'm ready."

"Me, too," Kerney said, wondering how many more days he'd get to spend with his family.

CHAPTER 16

Clayton finished his pizza and left for Las Cruces to continue his computer search at home. He and his family would see them in Mescalero tomorrow afternoon.

Alone with Kerney, Sara watched as he sat at the desk studying the map and making notes. His determined expression couldn't hide his fatigue. Standing behind him, she could see the futility of the task. Large areas of the land within a hundred-mile radius of Silver City were controlled and managed by the BLM, the state of New Mexico, and the federal Department of Agriculture. An enormous chunk of it was designated wilderness, and there were hundreds of square miles of land in private ownership that abutted remote areas with limited access.

"Stop it," she ordered.

Startled, Kerney looked up. "What?"

"You heard me. You're exhausted and what you're trying to do right now is impossible. What Jack Page's pal at the veterans center told you about a remote ranch may or may not be true. But this is no way to find it."

Kerney tossed his ballpoint pen on the desk, took off his reading glasses, and rubbed his eyes. "What do you suggest?"

"Let's assume that Louis Page died in Vietnam and verifying it as fact would waste our time. If someone is using his identity, there must be a good reason for him to do so, and we need to find out what it is and who he is. What if it was Earl Matson who took Jack out of the veterans center? The docent I talked to at the museum told me Jack treated Matson as his own flesh and blood. Wouldn't it be natural for Page to refer to him as his son?"

Kerney pushed back from the desk and stood. "Sure, but why tell Bud Elkins his son's name was Louis?"

"Unless Jack is demented, why indeed?" Sara replied. "If he knows the difference, that makes him complicit."

"Which may or may not be a big deal. According to the nursing assistant, he's got all his marbles."

"Let's say Jack lied for an important reason. My command sergeant major at Fort Leonard Wood retired about a year ago and went to work for Homeland Security. He's now a senior special agent in the Office of the Inspector General. In the morning, I'll call and ask him to research Earl Matson through the National Security Agency database."

"Without a DOB, a Social Security number, a reliable physical description, or other identifiers, that could generate hundreds of names."

"You don't know NSA," Sara responded. "We can assume he was born or lived much of his life in New Mexico. Bud Elkins told you he had a gray beard and long hair pulled back in a ponytail. That's a start. I'll give my guy some additional parameters as to approximate age and location, which should help narrow the field."

"And if it's a dead end, as Clayton intimated it might be?"

Sara reached up a hand and smoothed down Kerney's hair. "We move on."

"What would I do without you?"

"You'd be in big trouble."

The wastebasket next to the desk was stuffed with leftover trash from dinner, exuding a strong smell of pizza. Their room, in probably what amounted to the best motel in Deming, approached depressing. Bland prints on the walls, mass-produced furniture, and the awful floral curtains covering the one big window above a noisy combination air conditioner/heater, almost made Sara shudder. The previous night, they'd been kept awake by an hour-long argument between a couple next door.

She reached down and picked up the wastebasket. "Mind making a trip to the nearest trash bin? Eau de Pepperoni is not my favorite fragrance. While you're gone, I'll put on some fresh lipstick, and then we'll go out for a drink. We both could use one."

Kerney smiled. "Good idea." Wastebasket in hand, he gave her a quick kiss and went out.

There were two kinds of customers in Trino's Lounge, a bar that catered to real and faux-cowboys, serious drunks and casual drinkers. But the place was clean and quiet, and there seemed to be no brewing disagreements between the pool players at the back of the room.

In a booth away from the dozen customers gathered at the bar, they sipped shots of tequila and didn't speak until the final chords of Marty Robbins's classic "El Paso" faded away on the jukebox.

"We promised Patrick he could spend the summer with my brother and his family at the Montana ranch," Sara said.

Kerney put down his shot glass. "We can't go back on that."

"Even if—"

He raised his hand to stop her. "Yes, *even if*. It would be too much of a letdown to take that away from him. He's been looking forward to it all year. Besides, with what I'm putting him through, he'll need a big dose of family sanity. I'll talk to Dalquist when we get home and find out when he thinks the prosecution plans to go to trial. Which we won't let happen, because we're going to blow their case apart."

Sara lifted her shot glass. "Here's to you."

"For what?"

"For reminding me that you're a man who never gives up."

Kerney winced. "I have been less than optimistic lately, haven't I?"

"You've hidden it well."

They clinked glasses, finished their shots, and left Trino's as Johnny Cash's "Don't Take Your Guns to Town" started playing.

———

There were no sounds of domestic squabbles or raucous partying from the adjoining rooms, and soon Kerney was asleep. Sara curled up next to him, listening to his steady breathing. Fortunately, the firestorm of publicity about him had died down, but to have his whole career called into question by one false accusation had hurt him deeply. She drifted off wondering what else she could do to ease his anxiety.

In the morning, she woke to an empty bed, the sound of the shower in the bathroom, and the smell of coffee. She poured a cup from the in-room carafe and called retired Command Sergeant Major Otis Roderick at his new job with the Department of Homeland Security, counting on his thirty-five-year-old habit of always being first to report for duty. He answered on the first ring.

"Command Sergeant Major Roderick, this is Sara Brannon," she said. "Hello, how are you, how's the family, and I need a favor."

Roderick laughed. "Good morning, ma'am, I'm fine, the family is fine, and what can I do for you?"

She asked for a full background check on Earl Matson, gave him what little information she had, including some history about Louis and Jack Page, and told him the reason why.

"I've heard about your husband's difficulties," Roderick said diplomatically. "I'll get on it ASAP, General."

"Thank you, Otis."

"You were the best boss I ever had. Would it be inopportune of
me to congratulate you on your recent retirement? It's been the talk of
the town, so to speak."

"Not at all," Sara answered lightheartedly. "Thank you. We'll
come out on the right side of this shitstorm."

"I wouldn't bet against you, ma'am," Roderick said.

Sara disconnected just as Kerney emerged from the bathroom in a
T-shirt and skivvies, rubbing a towel through his hair.

"We've been going about this all wrong," he said.

"How so?"

He sat on the corner of the bed. "By treating everything as if it
were an isolated thread. What if it's all connected? Kim's murder, her
friend Loretta going missing, the disappearance of Kim's mother and
Todd Marks."

"Tied in with Jack Page and Earl Matson?"

"Why not? With the epicenter for all of it right here in Deming."

"How do we connect the dots?" Sara asked, delighted to hear reignited enthusiasm in his voice.

"We start with Flavio Sapian. This is his hometown. After he
retired from the state police, he joined the Deming PD and worked
his way up to chief before retiring a second time. If anyone can tell us
where to look for buried secrets, it's Flavio."

"How do we find him?"

"If I recall, everyone knows Flavio. All we have to do is ask."

———

Years ago, while pursuing a smuggler and murderer, Kerney had met
with Flavio at his home on some acreage outside of the Deming city

limits with a fine view of the Florida Mountains. Like so many New Mexicans rooted to the land by ancestry and choice, Sapian still lived there, expanding what had once been a small, mid-century ranch-style house into a two-story home and an attached two-car garage. A late-model motor home was parked nearby on a concrete pad. At the rear of the house, a covered deck shaded a hot tub, an expensive barbecue grill, and a wrought-iron dining table with enough chairs to accommodate a dozen people. It was a fine example of the New Mexico tradition of moving up the socioeconomic ladder without moving out of the family home.

Except for a few more pounds and a slightly sagging jawline, Flavio hadn't changed much. Burly and thick through the chest, with stout legs and strong arms, he could be an intimidating presence, which had given him a great advantage during his law enforcement career. But just as readily, his calm nature and friendly smile could quickly put people at ease.

Under the welcoming shade of the rear deck with a cool breeze moderating the growing heat of the morning, Flavio served iced tea and explained that his wife, Rosemary, was in Albuquerque visiting one of their children, a daughter attending UNM.

"As soon as she gets back on Monday, we're heading out in the RV to Yellowstone," he added. "We want to see it before it gets over-crowded with summer tourists."

"That sounds wonderful," Sara said.

Flavio nodded in agreement. "It will be great." He swung his attention to Kerney. "Knowing the trouble you're in, I bet this isn't a social call."

"It's not." Kerney laid out his theory of connecting all the dots to the people they were searching for in Deming and asked Flavio for his help.

Flavio rubbed a hand across his chin and gave it some thought. "It might be a stretch that Kim Ward's murder was connected to something in her past, and not because of a drug-fueled marriage gone bad. Granted, all those people except Todd Marks are from Deming, but Kim Ward and Louis Page died in totally unrelated circumstances, and Jack Page, Earl Matson, Loretta Page, and Kim's mother haven't lived here for years. Plus, if Jack is alive and living off the grid somewhere with Earl, what's the glue that holds everything together?"

"I don't know," Kerney answered. "But it seems odd that an entire family has either gone missing or deliberately into hiding."

Flavio sipped his iced tea. "That's true."

Kerney waited a beat for more, but Flavio remained silent. "You've put a pretty big dent in my theory, and I'll understand if you don't want to get involved."

Sara reached for her sunglasses on the table. "Thank you for your time."

"No, it's not that," Flavio said with a wave of his hand. "I was just wondering what I could do to be helpful. I've got the weekend here by myself before Rosemary gets back and nothing but small chores to do. Let me turn over some rocks with a few of the old-timers I know."

"That would be great."

Flavio stood up. "No promises. Will you still be staying in town?"

"No, we're heading out to Mescalero for a family weekend," Sara replied.

"Good. If there are any secrets to be found, it's best that I work this on my own. Deming may call itself a city, but it's really still a small town."

"And strangers are strangers," Kerney said.

"Exactly."

Flavio walked them to the front of the house. "I'll call after I've turned over those rocks."

Kerney extended his hand and Flavio shook it. "Thanks."

"You didn't kill that girl," Flavio said in parting. "I know it."

—

Following behind Kerney's truck on the way to Mescalero, Sara received a text message from Otis Roderick that read: "No joy in Mudville unless Earl Matson Page from Deming, New Mexico, is your boy."

Jack Page *had* adopted Earl after all. Sara pulled over to the shoulder of the highway, called Kerney, gave him the news, and said she'd be along after talking to Roderick. Up ahead, Kerney coasted to the shoulder and waited for her.

"That's our boy," Sara said when Otis picked up.

"Can you positively ID him?"

"Why?" Sara asked.

"Because this Earl Matson Page was an undercover DEA Special Agent in Colombia who disappeared in the jungle over twenty-five years ago with five million dollars in confiscated drug money to be used to recruit a confidential informant close to one of the major drug kingpins. He's been legally declared dead. Can you positively ID him?"

"No, but there may be someone who can."

"I can only hold on to this information so long."

"Understood," Sara said. "How long?"

"Monday. I'll send you his photograph as soon as we disconnect. I've got a sketch artist working on an updated rendering, complete with ponytail and beard. You'll get it in about an hour."

"Can you push your deadline past Monday?"

"If you can confirm his identity, I'll hold off until Tuesday morning. But once I report to the inspector general, he'll want to move quickly on this."

"Thank you. Did NSA have any tracking information on him?"

"Negative. Not under Matson or Page. He's completely off the radar, and that's almost unheard-of these days."

"We may have a general location."

"Try to nail it down. If it is Earl Matson Page, he's a dangerous, crooked cop and the DEA wants him. It's against the rules, but I'll send you his personnel jacket. Give me your most secure email address."

Sara rattled off the information.

"Be careful, General," Roderick warned.

"Affirmative, and thanks again." She disconnected, flashed her headlights at Kerney, rolled to a stop behind him, and got in his truck.

She held up her cell phone with Earl Matson Page's official DEA photograph on the screen. "He's a former DEA agent who went missing twenty-five years ago in the Colombian jungle with five million dollars. Supposedly dead."

Kerney whistled. "If he isn't dead, that might explain using his brother's name. What now?"

"We've got until Tuesday morning to wrap him up. I should have an artist's sketch of how he might look today in about an hour, plus a copy of his personnel jacket."

"Forward it to my laptop," Kerney said. "You go on to Mescalero. I'm going to the Fort Bayard Veterans Center to have another talk with Bud Elkins."

Sara shook her head in dismay.

"I know, this could ruin the family weekend. But only for me, not for you, Patrick, or your parents. Tell Clayton that I may need him for backup, but please stay put for Patrick's sake."

"This man is dangerous," Sara said.

"I'll be careful. If I get nowhere with Bud Elkins or the staff at the veterans center, I'll be in Mescalero in time for dinner."

"Promise?"

Kerney nodded and kissed her. "Promise. I'll give Flavio a heads-up."

She followed him until he got off the interstate at the next exit and turned back toward Deming, the silhouette of his pickup disappearing in the steady stream of westbound traffic.

———

Flavio Sapian kept two old horses and some weed-eating goats on his acreage, not just to reduce his state property tax assessment, but also for the pleasure of seeing critters on the land other than rabbits, road-runners, and rattlesnakes. After Kerney and his wife left, he fed and watered the horses, let the goats out of the pen to roam in one of the small pastures infested with ragweed, and went to talk to Elias Lopez, his wife's ninety-six-year-old great-uncle and the former sheriff of Luna County.

On the road, Kerney called with information about Matson that made Flavio's willingness to help more interesting. He felt his old cop instincts begin to kick in.

Elias lived with his eighty-six-year-old sister, Carmella, in a neighborhood of small homes not far from downtown. In the tiny front room filled with Carmella's prized Victorian furniture, sipping a cup of her terrible coffee, Flavio waited patiently for Elias's favorite television game show to finish. When the last winner went running and screaming off the stage, Elias muted the TV.

"So, why do you come to see this old man?" Elias asked. With his full head of hair slicked down, his new dentures in place, and dressed in pressed, faded blue jeans, he looked ready to go to the grocery store, one of his favorite outings. Still able to get around without a cane or walker, and sound in mind, Elias was proof old age didn't have to be all that bad, even though the thought of it made Flavio wince.

"I need your help, *Tio*. When you were sheriff, did you have any dealings with a couple named Jack and Jann Page and their children?"

"Is this about the cop they say killed Kim Ward?"

"Yes, Kevin Kerney," Flavio acknowledged.

Elias studied Flavio with his cloudy eyes. "Are you helping him?"

"I am."

Elias smiled. "Good."

"Jack and Jann Page, *Tio*," Flavio gently nudged. "Did you know them?"

Elias nodded. "Besides his ranch down here, Jack had a small place he'd inherited outside Mimbres where they used to run a few cows in the summer. I was with the Grant County Sheriff's Office back then when a call came in about somebody killing his cattle. There were five dead cows and two dead calves, all shot in the head. We never did find out who did it. Jack used his tractor to bury them."

"Can you remember where Jack's property was?" Flavio asked.

"That was a long time ago, but it was up a canyon away from the village. There wasn't much to the place except an old trailer, a couple of sheds, and a pasture. Ask in Mimbres how to get there. Somebody will know."

"*Gracias, Tio.*"

"*Por nada.*" Elias's second favorite game show was starting. He turned on the sound.

———

At the veterans center, Bud Elkins hobbled out of the physical therapy suite, his face flushed from exertion, breathing heavily. Kerney held up his cell phone with the forensic artist's drawing of Earl Matson Page as he might look now.

"Is this the man who took Jack Page home?"

Elkins scowled and refused to look. "I know who you really are. Why should I tell you anything? Coming in here and lying to everybody like you did."

"I apologize for misleading you, but I have a lot at stake."

"Go to hell."

Elkins shuffled away. The sound of heavy footsteps and the clicking of heels caught Kerney's attention. He turned to face an older, uniformed security guard and a stern-looking, middle-aged woman dressed in a conservative gray pantsuit.

"You are to leave the premises immediately," she snapped.

Kerney stepped back from the guard's attempt to guide him by the arm. He had the bearing of a man who knew his job, probably a retired cop.

"This is a public building," he replied genially.

"And you're causing a disturbance," the woman countered. "Leave now before I call the police."

There was no sense in arguing. She led the way to the main entrance and remained in the lobby watching as the guard accompanied Kerney to his truck.

Kerney opened the driver-side door and paused. "Is Robert Ripple on duty?"

"Bobby? He works swing shift only."

"Know how I can find him?"

The guard smiled. "Now, why would I tell you that?"

Kerney shrugged and got behind the wheel. "I can tell you're retired law enforcement. Give me a hand here."

The guard nodded. "Thirty-two years with the San Diego PD, Traffic Division. I don't know if you're guilty or not, but Bobby's not hard to find. He works part-time in the lumberyard at Big Jim's Home Improvement Store on Highway 180. Usually puts in his hours there before he starts his shift here."

"Did you ever see or meet Jack Page's son?"

"Can't help you with that one, pal, but good luck." He closed the truck door and retreated to the entrance, where he waited until Kerney drove away.

———

According to the lumberyard supervisor, Bobby Ripple wasn't due to clock in for an hour. At a truck-stop diner, Kerney killed time over a cup of coffee and a stale cheese Danish. After the first bite, he realized the Danish had been a big mistake and pushed it aside. He was on a coffee refill when Patrick called.

"Where are you?" Kerney asked.

"On the road to Mescalero with Gramps and Grandma," he answered. "Where are you?"

"Silver City," Kerney said. "I'll be along shortly, I hope. What's up?"

"Before we left, I put the home security video app on my phone. You've got to see this."

When they were traveling a lot to visit Sara at her duty stations, Kerney had installed an expensive video security system at the ranch, but rarely checked it. "See what?" he asked.

"Juan snooping around inside our house."

"Okay, hang on." Kerney touched the app icon and watched a replay of Juan going from room to room, looking at the family calendar on the fridge, poking through the papers on Kerney's desk in the library, even wandering through the guest quarters. If Juan was acting under police orders, the video would cause serious damage to the prosecution's case against him.

"That was a smart thing to do, son," he said. "This is going to be a big help."

"Thanks." Pride filled Patrick's voice.

"Do one more thing. Show it to your mother, so she can call our lawyer. He'll know what to do with it."

"Okay."

"And thanks again. You're one sharp hombre."

He disconnected, dropped some bills on the counter, and got back to the Big Jim's ten minutes before Bobby Ripple clocked in. His eyes widened in surprise when Kerney closed in on him at the doorway to the staff lounge.

"Jesus, I never expected to see you again."

"Did I get you in trouble?"

"Just a slap on the wrist, but I got a great story to tell. Guys will be buying me beers at the VFW for months."

Kerney held out his phone with the age-enhanced forensic drawing of Earl Matson Page on the screen. "Is this Louis Page?"

Bobby Ripple nodded. "That looks like him."

"You're sure?"

"Yeah, he even introduced himself to me when he came for Jack. I remember it clear as a bell, because most folks don't wait until after the evening meal to take a family member home. It isn't usual."

"Will you write out a statement to that effect?"

"Right now?"

Kerney handed him a pencil and a tablet. "Right now."

With Bobby's written statement in his pocket, Kerney called Sara from the truck and gave her the news. "Now all I have to do is find him," he added.

"I'm leaving for Silver City right away."

Kerney cranked the engine and turned on the AC. "Don't do that. If I need help, I'll ask Clayton to jump in. For now, it's just legwork."

"Where will you start?"

"At the Grant County Assessor's Office."

———

Many times, Flavio had passed through Mimbres on his way to his favorite mountain fishing holes. More a settlement than a village, it was named for the river that trickled through the lovely valley, the foothills of the Black Range of the Gila National Forest pressing against it. A two-lane blacktop rose into the high forest and dead-ended at a popular lake and tourist vacation spot.

Flavio stopped at three houses in the village without any luck. His next stop, a house on lush river bottomland, was protected by several towering cottonwoods. On a driveway fencepost a sign read FRESH EGGS FOR SALE. The name on the mailbox was B. Velarde.

He heard chickens cackling from behind the house. He knocked on the front door and a woman stepped onto the porch. In her early seventies at most, she stood no more than five-foot-one and weighed at best a hundred pounds. Browned by the sun, wearing a weathered sun bonnet, she greeted him with a smile and a shake of her head.

"No more eggs until tomorrow. I always forget to take the sign down."

"My bad luck," Flavio said, as he flashed his retired police chief badge. "I'm Flavio Sapian. Actually, I'm looking for somebody who knows Jack Page and his son."

"Bianca Velarde," the woman replied. "They haven't been here for years. He only used it to keep a few cows." She sat on the porch step and patted it with a hand.

Flavio accepted the invitation and joined her. "Any ideas on where they went?"

Bianca shook her head. "No one in the valley ever heard from them again."

"Where is Jack's old place?"

Bianca pointed her chin in a northeasterly direction. "One canyon up, all the way to the end of the road, if you can call it that. It gets really rocky and rutted about a mile in."

"Does anyone live there?"

"Oh, yes, TM and Lucille Trimble. She's old now, in her late eighties and feeble. I don't see her much."

"And the man?" Flavio nudged. "What about him?"

"Younger than Lucille and not real friendly. He's disabled, and walks with a bad limp."

"Not friendly?"

Bianca shrugged an apologetic shoulder. "They both keep to themselves, but that's not unusual for older people nowadays. I'm getting to be the same way."

"Does TM have a name?"

"I don't know him by anything other than TM. Maybe Deanna Madrid, our postmistress, does."

Flavio asked for a description. She described TM as five-ten, clean-shaven, and mostly bald.

"He walks with a limp in his right leg," she added.

"Have you visited with TM and Lucille at their home?" he asked.

Bianca shook her head. "Oh, no. I've only been there once, years ago when I was still active in our volunteer fire department. We had to use their road to reach a brush fire started by a dry lightning strike. It's posted. No one goes up there."

Flavio got to his feet. "Thanks."

With a concerned look, Bianca rose. "Have they done something wrong?"

Flavio shook his head. "Not as far as I know. Next time I'm in the neighborhood, I'll stop by early enough for a dozen eggs."

"You won't regret it. My chickens produce the best eggs in the county."

"I bet they do."

At the post office, Deanna Madrid, the postmistress, refused to give Flavio any identifying information about TM and Lucille Trimble. It made him miss the authority cops had getting around roadblocks to learn information quickly. He suspected it was even more frustrating for Kerney. Back in his truck, he tried calling Kerney but couldn't get a signal.

A few miles back, a road sign advertised a coffee shop off the highway. He decided to get something to eat and try Kerney from there.

———

In one way, Silver City reminded Kerney of Santa Fe with a historic, interesting core and a lot of nondescript strip malls, franchise retail stores, and fast-food chains. Located along a main highway through town, the building housing the county assessor's office was no better. A faux-Southwest façade hid a single-story rectangular box, and the small scrubby hill behind it offered no reprieve to the dullness.

Inside, the assessor's online property search program had Kerney hoping the visit might be worthwhile after all, until he turned up goose eggs. No property in the country was owned by Jack Page, Louis Page, Earl Matson Page, or Loretta Page. He tried Jann Page, and got nothing back.

With sinking expectations, Kerney called the four property owners listed with the same surname, only to have his suspicions confirmed. None claimed any knowledge of or kinship to Jack and his children. Just in case someone was lying, he wrote down their names, addresses, and phone numbers.

On his way to his truck, traffic noise on the highway and a hot sun that promised a spring afternoon scorcher in the high, thin air damped his spirits. His phone rang, and he answered Flavio's call.

"Do the names TM and Lucille Trimble mean anything to you?" he asked. "The TM guy walks with a limp in his right leg."

Kerney stopped in his tracks. "That's who I'm looking for. Are you packing?"

"Affirmative. Concealed-carry permit. You?"

"Same," Kerney replied. "Do you have a location?"

"Roger that. Meet me in Mimbres by the post office."

"I'm bringing some sheriff deputies with me, if they'll come. ETA within the hour."

"Ten-four."

Kerney disconnected and walked to the sheriff's office, where a secretary informed him both the sheriff and the undersheriff were at a conference on terrorism in Honolulu. However, Lieutenant Steven Campos, commander of the Patrol and Traffic Division, was available.

She called Campos, and within a minute he appeared from a back office.

Tall and solidly built, Campos sized Kerney up. "What can I do for you?"

"You know who I am?" Kerney asked.

"Of course."

"And what I'm charged with?"

Campos nodded.

"I've got a solid lead on Todd Marks, the man I believe killed Kim Ward, the woman I'm accused of murdering. I'd like you to come with me and take him into custody."

The lieutenant's expression changed from doubtful to interested. "You're serious?"

"I'm very serious. Flavio Sapian is waiting for us in Mimbres."

"I know Chief Sapian. I served under him at the Deming PD."

"Then you know this is no joke." Kerney speed-dialed Flavio and held out his phone to Campos. "Here, talk to him."

Campos took the phone, identified himself, and asked Flavio for an explanation. He listened, disconnected, and asked Kerney if there were outstanding warrants for Marks or the woman he lived with.

"I don't know. But Marks is a person of interest in a murder investigation. The state police have been looking for him. You have the right to identify, question, and take him into custody as a material witness."

Campos pursed his lips and thought it over. "And you won't interfere?"

"I will not."

After writing down Kerney's number, Campos handed him the

phone and turned to the secretary. "Have dispatch contact Corporal Little and tell him to meet me at the Mimbres post office. No lights or siren."

He returned his attention to Kerney. "You'll ride with me, but first I'm going to check for wants and warrants on the subjects."

"I'll be waiting right here," Kerney replied as Campos stepped away.

Within a few minutes, Campos returned and reported no outstanding wants or warrants. As they left the building, Campos said, "You'd better tell me all you know."

"Absolutely," Kerney said.

———

After meeting up at the post office, Corporal Jim Little parked his street cruiser at the turnoff to the canyon, and joined Lieutenant Campos in his four-wheel drive unit. Kerney rode with Flavio in his truck, with instructions to stay back and away from any action. GPS put the Trimble property five-plus miles in at the head of a canyon on a mostly bad road.

"Do you have your *pistola*?" Flavio asked Kerney.

"It's back in my truck."

He popped the glove box to reveal a Smith & Wesson two-inch revolver. "Be my guest."

Kerney gladly grabbed the weapon. "Where's the rest of your arsenal?"

Flavio tapped his right cowboy boot. "My baby Beretta. Did you convince Steve Campos that you were innocent?"

The road turned crappy. Up ahead, the SO unit dipped and swayed over and around rocky obstacles. "I've got him questioning my guilt, *un poquito*."

Flavio laughed as he worked the steering wheel. "What are you going to do if TM turns out to be your man?"

"I suggested Campos ask him to confess."

Flavio laughed even harder. "You didn't call your wife, did you?"

"No need to worry her." Up ahead, Kerney could see they were losing ground on the SO unit. "Speed it up, will you? I don't want to miss out on all the fun."

The canyon widened, with mountains beyond and some overgrown fenced pastureland on either side of the bone-rattling road. Soon the outline of an older double-wide appeared in the distance, with a tall TV antenna tethered on the roof by three steel cables. A single electrical line on a series of poles crossed a side canyon and connected to both the double-wide and a small, windowless building that looked to be a pump house. Across from the double-wide, a large, tin-roofed, open-air shed held enough firewood for at least two winters. An ATV and a battered Ford four-wheel drive truck were parked a few yards beyond where the ranch road ended.

"Looks peaceful enough so far," Kerney said as he checked the cylinder of the revolver. It was fully loaded.

CHAPTER 17

Todd Marks put the phone down and went into Lucille's bed-
room. As usual, she was asleep in her reclining easy chair, snoring with
her mouth open. He liked her that way. Awake, she'd be wandering
through the double-wide, talking trash, bumping into things, turning
on the stove burners for no reason, or straying into the fields outside.
Decades of boozing had pickled her brain.

When he had to leave her to tend his marijuana crop up in the
high country, he'd lock her in her bedroom. She remembered to use
the bathroom some of the time, but he was always cleaning her up.

Marks paid the bills by supplying high-quality marijuana to an
Albuquerque dealer. He kept production small to avoid drawing
unwanted attention.

He pulled a chair next to Lucille and sat. He'd watched the television reports about the Kevin Kerney murder investigation. Although
it had taken forty-five years to pin the crime on Kerney, Todd had
started to think he'd finally pulled it off. He couldn't believe the dumb
cops had never found the silver chain he'd wrapped around the juniper

branch where he'd buried Kim. But now that a cop was asking questions about him at the post office, he was starting to worry that somebody had wised up.

He bent close to Lucille. "You still sleeping?"

She snorted and turned away.

"That's good. Remember all those letters I sent you long ago saying I was looking for Kim and wouldn't stop until I found her? It was pure bullshit. I knew where she was, but I wanted you to believe I'd done nothing wrong."

Marks leaned back. "I always thought you suspected I'd killed her, and I didn't want you saying that to the police. I truly didn't mean to do it. She just got me so pissed off."

He shook his head. "I never expected you'd write back to me. If you hadn't, I would probably be still locked up for knifing that old man in Canada. I had no one to run to except you. You saved my ass."

He paused to listen for any sound outside. All was quiet. "I guess I needed your forgiveness, and you needed to believe Kim was alive. I know you miss her. Sometimes I do, too."

Marks chuckled, reached for weed he kept in a pouch in his shirt pocket, rolled a joint, and lit up. "The cops are coming for me, and this time I've got nowhere to go. Do I put a bullet in your head and kill myself, or take on the cops?"

Lucille didn't move. He flicked an ash off the joint, took a long drag, and smiled. It was a no-brainer. He'd take on the cops. Maybe Kerney would be with them. He'd heard on the news that he was trying to solve the case with the help of a hotshot lawyer.

He thought about waking Lucille up and giving her a sleeping pill, and decided against it. Instead, he covered her with a blanket, went to his bedroom, took his Barrett fifty-caliber sniper rifle from the gun cabinet, and set it up on a table under an open window in the spare bedroom that had a clear view of the road.

He sat on a straight-backed chair, rolled three more joints, placed them next to a jar lid he used as an ashtray, and waited. Minutes passed before he heard engines on the road. He got to his feet, stubbed out his joint, lit another one, and settled on his knees behind the fifty-caliber. Soon two vehicles came into view, a sheriff's SUV followed by an unmarked four-by-four pickup. Through the scope he could see two occupants in each vehicle.

He put his smoke on the jar lid, sighted on the SO unit, and fired two rounds, one into the engine block, the other through the windshield. The SUV careened into a fence post and ground to a stop, its hood dug into the bottom of the post, rear tires in the air. Marks switched to the truck and pumped two rounds into the passenger door as the driver pulled a quick one-eighty. It retreated under a cloud of road dust.

He relaxed, took another hit off the joint, and waited for movement inside the sheriff's unit.

———

Crouched below the dashboard, Steve Campos watched blood pour from Jim Little's head wound and puddle on the seat. He keyed his radio, told dispatch he had an officer down, and called for backup.

"We're taking fire from an active shooter," he added. "Roll SWAT, send every deputy to my location, and put a medevac in the air right now."

He dropped the microphone and called Kerney's cell phone. Flavio Sapian answered.

"You okay?"

"Yeah, but Kerney's not. He's hit in the shoulder and the chest. I've got pressure on the chest wound but it looks nasty."

"Can the shooter see you?"

"Negative."

"Stay put," Campos ordered. "My corporal has a bad head wound and I'm pinned down."

His first-aid kit was tucked away in the back of the unit, out of reach. Campos struggled out of his shirt, ripped it up the middle, and tied it around Jim Little's head. It turned red in seconds.

He needed that first-aid kit. Slowly, he opened the driver's-side door. Two fifty-caliber slugs almost tore it off the hinges.

Dispatch radioed a fifteen-minute ETA.

Campos doubted help could get there fast enough to save Jim, but *Jesus*, he hoped so.

He huddled below the dashboard, listening to radio traffic, and watched Jim Little die, wondering what he'd say to his wife and four-year-old daughter. Occasionally the shooter fired another round at the unit. The explosion of lead on steel as the bullets tore into the SUV jangled his already frayed nerves.

Volunteer firefighters were the first on scene, and Campos listened as an EMT radioed his assessment of Kerney's wound to a surgeon at the Silver City hospital. The prognosis was guarded. Chopper ten minutes out.

Flavio was unharmed. At least there was *that* good news. Campos broadcast a description of the crime scene, and the shooter's location inside the double-wide. On a back channel, he requested State Police Sergeant Scott Thorndike's assistance. Thorndike had two Afghanistan tours and over a dozen Al-Qaeda kills under his belt as a Marine sniper. He was one of an elite few. Within minutes, Thorndike radioed he was in the air. He wanted information about surrounding terrain he could use as cover.

Not able to see a damn thing with his head tucked below the dashboard, Steve lateraled the request over to Flavio, who suggested two promising locations, both about three-quarters of a mile out with good cover and direct line of sight to the shooter's location.

"That's what I need," Thorndike replied coolly.

The welcoming wail of sirens echoed up from the valley, signaling arriving backup units led by Sergeant Jessie Gomez, the on-duty shift supervisor.

Campos keyed his microphone. "When you get here, set up out of sight from the double-wide."

"Roger," Gomez replied. "You okay?"

"So far, so good."

"And SO Seven?"

That was the call sign for Little's unit. Campos paused. He hadn't reported Jim's death, half hoping it might go away like a bad dream. But the puddle of blood on the seat dripping from his wound was now splashing onto the floorboard. It was too much blood for make-believe.

"SO Seven?" Gomez repeated.

Campos answered in a whisper. "Negative."

Gomez's radio went silent.

The thudding sound of a chopper's rotor began to fill the air, and the pilot called for an LZ location.

"You're good on either side of the road," Flavio said. "But come in fast and low, the shooter's using a fifty-caliber."

"Hot LZ," the pilot replied calmly. "Ten-four."

Sporadic fire from the double-wide continued, but it was no longer coming at Campos. After the next round he snuck a look. The shooter was framed in the open window lighting what looked like a hand-rolled joint. He watched as the man took a long drag before settling back behind the scope. After the next shot, he repeated the same behavior. He radioed his observation to Thorndike.

"That's what I like to hear," Thorndike replied. "A sniper with bad habits."

"He's either already stoned or getting there," Campos said.

"It doesn't matter," Thorndike said.

The second chopper came in fast and low, creating a brief dust storm that swirled dried weeds, grass, and dirt into the air. Small pebbles pelted the roof of Campos's battered unit like hail, punctuated by the booming sound of the fifty-caliber. He unracked his pump shotgun, loaded it with slugs, and radioed Thorndike he'd distract the shooter with cover fire.

"Affirmative," Thorndike replied. "Are there any other shooters?"

"None visible."

"Any other perps?"

"Unknown."

"I'm on the ground, moving into position now," Thorndike said.

The shooter was firing erratically at the choppers and several firefighters who'd broken cover to load Kerney. Campos couldn't wait.

"Get there soon," he snapped, dropping the microphone. Gripping the shotgun, he rolled out, rose to his knees behind the partially demolished driver's door, and pumped three slugs into the open double-wide window. Before he could duck, the fifty roared twice and something that felt like a rocket slammed into his chest.

I'm dead, he thought, eyes closed, as the sound of the choppers began to recede. Still breathing, he opened his eyes to the remains of the vehicle door resting on his chest. Dizzy from the impact, he pushed it off and crawled backward, eyes on the shooter, who took another hit before settling down behind the scope.

Okay, now I'm dead, he thought just as the man's head blew apart, spewing a geyser of blood and brains.

Thorndike's voice came over the car radio. "You okay?"

Campos crawled to the rear of his unit, felt his chest, and didn't find any holes. He keyed his handheld and replied, "I'm good, I think."

"I've got you covered. Medics are on the way."

"Okay," Campos replied, fighting back a wave of double vision that didn't want to let go.

"You're not going to believe this," Thorndike said.

"What?"

"There's an old woman—I mean a really old woman—teetering on the top step of the double-wide."

"Unarmed?" Campos felt woozy, about to faint.

"Seems to be," Thorndike noted.

"Don't shoot her."

"She just collapsed on the step."

"Rescue her," Campos said before he lost consciousness.

———

From the sidelines, Flavio watched technicians, uniformed personnel, and investigators work the crime scene. It would be hours before they finished, likely lasting long into the night. Although his truck was drivable, it wouldn't be released to him until all the forensics were wrapped up. That could take days. Until then it would be impounded.

He didn't give a hot damn. After what had happened to Kerney, he'd never step inside that vehicle again, no matter how perfectly restored it might be. The minute it was fixed, he'd tow it to the dealer and get a new set of wheels. He was overdue for a new ride anyway.

If it meant delaying the Yellowstone trip, so be it. That was a minor inconvenience. Rosemary would understand, without explanation. Thirty-plus years a cop's wife, she knew all his coping mechanisms.

He'd resisted the impulse to call her in Albuquerque. He'd do that after he got home, had a shot of tequila, and could calm down and tell her the whole story.

A reserve deputy was coming to drive him to Deming. Flavio didn't mind the wait. But it was hard not having anything to do except give a statement. For the first time in years, he didn't enjoy being retired. This was no time to be a civilian.

As EMTs painstakingly removed Corporal Little's body from the bullet-ridden unit, all activity ceased. Standing stone-silent, everyone watched as he was carried to a fire rescue vehicle and driven away, the flashing emergency lights washed out by a fierce sun that somehow felt angry.

Flavio's spirits lifted when word came from the hospital Kerney had survived the first round of surgery. If he remained stabilized in post-op, he'd be medevaced to the university hospital in Albuquerque. His prognosis remained guarded, and his identity had not yet been released. According to Campos, state police were in the process of contacting Kerney's family. Corporal Little's wife would learn of his death within the hour when a knock came at her door. Flavio didn't envy the bearers of such horrible news.

Badly bruised but intact, Campos refused medical treatment and remained on-scene and in charge. Flavio watched him work with a certain amount of pride. He'd recruited him as a rookie with the Deming PD, and now he was a seasoned commander, doing the job and doing it damn well.

Evidence collected from inside the double-wide identified Todd Marks as the shooter and Lucille Trimble, Kim Ward's mother, as the old woman. In transit by ambulance to the hospital, Trimble had been unable to confirm her identity and broke down in hysterics.

Flavio wanted to be there when Kerney learned that Todd Marks had been living with the mother of the woman he'd allegedly murdered. Whatever the reasons, it was more than a little bit weird.

He also wanted to be a fly on the wall when state police bigwigs learned their team of crack agents had been bested by two retired, over-the-hill cops. There'd be butt-chewing galore up and down the chain of command, of that Flavio was sure. The thought made him smile briefly.

Nasario Valdez, the deputy assigned to drive him home, was a sixty-year-old retired Spanish professor who'd joined the reserve deputy program to do something different. He wasn't chatty on the bone-jarring ride out of the canyon. Flavio appreciated the silence.

A roadblock at the mouth of the canyon kept a gathering crowd of newshounds and curious citizens at bay. Waved through by a member of the state police mounted patrol, and thankfully back on pavement, Flavio asked Valdez to make a quick stop at the Mimbres post office.

In the parking lot, Flavio borrowed Valdez's miniature digital recorder, switched it on, stuck it in his shirt pocket, and went inside. He waited patiently while Deanna Madrid, the postmistress, retrieved a package from the back room for a patron. She was a heavyset woman in her fifties, with a perpetual frown etched across her forehead.

The patron left, and Flavio stepped to the counter. "Remember me, Ms. Madrid?"

Madrid's face turned florid. "Why, yes. What's going with all the sirens and helicopters?"

Flavio ignored her question. "Earlier in the day, I showed you my badge, told you I was a retired police officer, and asked you about TM and Lucille Trimble. Do you remember that?"

Madrid's lower lip trembled slightly. She nodded her head. "Yes."

"You called him, didn't you?"

Madrid dropped her shaking hands below the counter, out of sight. "No."

"You called and told him a police officer was asking questions."

Madrid shook her head.

"Answer me," Flavio demanded.

"No."

"TM told us you did," Flavio lied.

Madrid's eyes teared. "He told you?"

Flavio stared at Madrid until she looked away.

"What are you going to do to me?" Madrid's voice cracked.

"Did you warn him?" Flavio snapped.

"Yes."

"That's better," he said consolingly.

"What happens now?" Madrid pleaded.

Flavio shrugged. "A police officer is dead. Get ready to have every cop in the state pissed off at you." He paused, hand on the exit door. "Did you know the typical driver violates the traffic code on average once every five minutes? Or is it five times, every five minutes? I forget."

"I didn't mean anybody any harm."

Flavio smiled with his teeth. "I'd watch my driving very, very carefully from now on, if I were you. And stay available. The police will want to talk with you."

In Nasario Valdez's unit, Flavio played back the conversation and asked him to make sure Lieutenant Campos got it.

Nasario groaned in dismay. "Good God, she caused Corporal Little's death."

"Or contributed to it," Flavio replied, thinking maybe he had, too, by asking Madrid about Trimble in the first place.

He sank back against the passenger seat and closed his eyes. He really needed to talk to Rosemary. "Take me home, please, Nasario."

CHAPTER 18

Kerney woke up slowly in an anesthetic daze. Sara was sitting at his bedside holding his left hand.

"Hey, you," she said gently, relief flooding her voice.

"Hey." Kerney squinted in the dim light of the room, trying to get his bearings. "I got shot, didn't I?"

"Yes."

"What hospital am I in?"

"University Hospital, Albuquerque."

"How long have I been out?"

"A day."

Gradually, his mind began to clear. "What did the doctors do to me?"

"They cut you open, fixed what was broken, and stitched you back up."

Sara's lighthearted answer made Kerney smile. "Can you be a little more specific?"

"Your smashed right shoulder has been repaired, but you'll need additional surgery later. A bullet fragment penetrated your chest and did some muscle damage. The surgeon successfully removed it. A tiny piece of shrapnel lodged in your skull has also been removed. The surgeon thinks it was a glass shard from Flavio's truck."

Kerney touched his forehead. It was covered with a bandage. "Was Flavio hurt?"

"Not a scratch. He may have saved your life."

Kerney looked at his right arm. It was in a cast and he couldn't feel any sensation. "Is the arm going to be any good?"

"Eventually, with more surgery and physical therapy."

Kerney groaned. "I'm a mess."

"Your words, not mine."

"But I'm gonna live, I take it."

Sara smiled. "Yes, and everyone wants to see you, starting with your son."

"What about the two sheriff's officers?"

"One deputy died, the lieutenant is okay."

"Damn." Kerney took a deep breath. "Is Todd Marks in custody?"

"He's dead, shot by a state police sniper. Lucille Trimble is alive and in the Silver City hospital under guard. According to the doctors, she has Alzheimer's or alcoholic dementia, and may not be much help to us."

Kerney swallowed his disappointment. A bouquet of fresh flowers rested on the dresser under the wall-mounted television. "Who sent the flowers?"

"Flavio. It came with a note." She flipped open the card and read it. "'Dear Kerney, Thanks for helping me decide it was time to buy a new truck. Get well soon.'"

Kerney laughed. "What a warmhearted guy. Who's here with you?"

"Patrick, my parents, Grace, and Gary Dalquist."

"Where's Clayton?"

"When we got word you'd been shot, we had a family powwow in Mescalero and decided Clayton will take over the investigation while I get you settled at home. Dalquist will pitch in to help Clayton as needed."

"What's left to investigate?"

Sara patted his hand. "Don't despair, Kerney. I lied to the feds about Earl Matson Page. I left them a voice message that our lead turned cold."

Kerney couldn't repress a laugh. It made his chest hurt. "You lied?"

"I did. Hopefully they'll lose interest. Clayton will follow that thread."

"You mean our last thread," Kerney replied grimly.

Sara smiled. "We'll see."

"I'm sorry I ruined the weekend."

"Don't be silly." Sara stood and kissed him on the lips. "That's from Isabel. She sends her love."

Kerney's eyes widened in amazement. "Really?"

Sara nodded. "Yes. I believe you've been the love of her life forever."

"I'm flabbergasted."

"You shouldn't be. I feel the same way about you. I'm very glad she gave you up." She kissed him again. "That one was from me. I'll get Patrick. The doctor says to keep the visits short."

"Yes, ma'am."

Sara opened the door and Patrick burst in, his face a mask of worry.

"Hey, sport," Kerney said.

Patrick slid to a sudden stop next to the bedside chair. "I've been waiting to see you for hours."

"I guess I needed my beauty sleep."

Sara stepped back inside and closed the door to the corridor.

Patrick's gaze jumped from the bandage that covered his dad's head to the cast on his right arm, the drip tube connected to his other arm, his drawn, ashen face, and the bank of instruments above the bed flashing vital signs. "I was worried you'd never wake up."

Kerney smiled. "I'm not going anywhere, sport. I've been think-ing, when I get back on my feet, we should get a dog or two and buy a couple more ponies to train as cutting horses, like my pa used to do. Would you be up for that?"

Patrick grinned with delight. "That would be okay by me."

"We'll cancel the grazing lease and run some of our own cows. But I'm gonna need a good hand to help me."

"I can do it."

"Good." Kerney stuck out his good hand. "Shake on it."

Smiling, Patrick grabbed it tightly. "I'm not going to the Montana ranch this summer," he announced.

"Oh, yes, you are," Sara corrected from the foot of the bed.

Patrick's smile faded as he searched Kerney's expression for sup-port. "I should stay here to help you and Mom. We're firing Juan, right? Somebody has got to do all the chores. And what if the trial starts while I'm away?"

"The trial won't start while I'm stove up like this," Kerney said. "And the chores will get done as soon as we hire Juan's replacement."

"Who's going to fire him?" Patrick asked.

"I'll have Mr. Dalquist do it."

"But I'm the one who caught him."

"Yes, you did, and you get a lot of credit from me for the smart way you pulled it off. But Mr. Dalquist can do it in a way that helps my case and makes the police look as dumb as they are."

Patrick nodded. "Got it."

Sara opened the door. "Out, mister," she ordered. "There are oth-ers waiting their turn."

Patrick leaned over and kissed Kerney on the cheek. "I'm glad you're gonna get better."

"Me, too," Kerney said, trying to recall the last time his fourteen-year-old son had kissed him. Quite some time ago, he reckoned.

Kerney spent a few minutes reassuring Dean and Barbara that he was going to be just fine, and then chatted with Grace about rescheduling the aborted family gathering in Mescalero. When Grace left, Sara ushered in Gary Dalquist. She remained in the room, as she had during all the visits.

"The media is calling what happened the 'Shoot-out at Barranco Canyon,'" Dalquist said. "The coverage has been relentless."

"Is that the name of the place?"

Dalquist shrugged. "I guess so. They're reporting that you impersonated a police officer. Several staff members at the Fort Bayard Veterans Center came forward and gave TV interviews to that effect. True?"

"True."

Dalquist groaned. "Did you impersonate a police officer at Barranco Canyon?"

"Absolutely not. The police were there at my request. Tell me about the deputy who was killed."

"Corporal Jim Little," Dalquist answered. "Married, father of a four-year-old girl. Six-year veteran of the department."

Kerney remembered Campos and the corporal jawing at the mouth of the canyon with the easy camaraderie common between good friends. "Find out what we can do for his family," he said.

"Of course," Dalquist said solemnly. "On a different matter, I'll arrange a meeting with Juan Ramirez posthaste. I'll record it and get a transcript to you. It should be informative and entertaining, at the very least."

"I need some light reading," Kerney joked.

Dalquist stood, and peered down at Kerney. "You look in need of a nap." He turned to Sara. "When will he be discharged?"

"The day after tomorrow, if all goes well."

He patted Kerney's good shoulder. "Excellent. Rest now and recuperate."

Dozing off, Kerney yawned his reply.

———

Clayton's attempt to interview Lucille Trimble in her hospital room had been rebuffed by both the Grant County Sheriff's Office and the district attorney. Trimble would remain in police custody until released to a long-term care facility. An Adult Protective Services caseworker had been assigned to manage the necessary paperwork needed for the transfer. First, the issue of Trimble's placement eligibility had to be addressed.

Clayton's calls to the caseworker went unreturned, but a supervisor in the office told him the process could take weeks. In the meantime, a temporary emergency transfer to a nursing home was in the works. Since Trimble had no known family, only authorized government representatives would be allowed to visit her at the facility.

Clayton called Dalquist and explained his dilemma.

"She may be demented like they say, but I still need to talk to her," Clayton added.

"Let me see what I can do," Dalquist replied. "I'll get back to you as soon as I can."

He reached out by telephone to Louise Fowler, a Silver City lawyer specializing in services to senior citizens.

"This involves the Kevin Kerney case and the killing of Deputy Little, correct?" Fowler probed.

"Correct. The woman in question, Lucille Trimble, suffers from Alzheimer's or dementia, so an interview may not yield much, but we'd be wrong not to try. She has no known relatives. Can you help?"

"Perhaps. I do a fair amount of pro bono family guardianship cases for elderly clients. The judge might be willing to grant me temporary guardianship until all the placement issues can get sorted out. She's not a big fan of Adult Protective Services."

"That would be of enormous help," Dalquist said. "I expect you to bill me for your services."

"Who's your investigator?" Fowler asked.

"Clayton Istee."

Fowler sighed. "Kerney's son? What are you dragging me into?"

"His services on behalf of his father are completely voluntary and under my direct supervision."

"Give me his contact information," Fowler said. "But be advised, I will be present when he interviews Trimble."

"Of course."

Dalquist gave Fowler what she needed, and asked when she might be able to approach the court.

"I'll have to check her docket, but later today isn't out of the realm of possibility."

"Thank you," Dalquist said. "Please stay in touch."

———

At six that evening, accompanied by Louise Fowler, Clayton entered Lucille Trimble's hospital room. She was sitting up in bed, watching cartoons on a muted, wall-mounted television. Clayton sat at her bedside and touched her hand. Only then did she turn away from the TV and look at him.

"Are you a fucking wetback?" she asked harshly, staring at his face.

"I'm Apache," Clayton answered. Trimble was ancient. Deep wrinkles cascaded down her cheeks. Her eyes were hollow and sunken. She looked as if she could die any minute.

"You're a damn wetback," she hissed.

Clayton smiled. "Whatever you say."

Trimble laughed bitterly. "Where's my Todd?" she asked in a sing-song baby voice.

"At home, waiting for you," Clayton lied. "Is he your son-in-law?"

Trimble held up her left hand and wiggled her ring finger, circled by a yellow gold band. "He gave me this."

"Can I see it?"

"Promise to give it back?"

"I promise."

She took off and handed him the ring. Engraved inside were the initials TM and KW, for Todd Marks and Kim Ward.

"Your daughter's wedding ring," Clayton commented, handing it back.

"Mine," Trimble snapped, as she replaced it on her finger. "It's all written down."

"What is?"

"Not my fault!" Trimble snarled. Suddenly she started to cry.

Clayton waited until Lucille's sobs ceased. "I'm sorry."

"My little pills," she said, baby-talking again. "I want them."

"Tell me what's written down," Clayton nudged.

"The letters. *A, B, C, D* . . . I forget."

Trimble turned away from Clayton and said no more.

Fifteen minutes of continued silence convinced Clayton there was little chance he'd learn anything else that night.

"We can try again in the morning," Fowler suggested as they left the hospital. "But I must say that was pretty weird."

Clayton nodded. He liked Fowler. Late middle-aged and motherly, she exuded an air of nonjudgmental compassion. "I wonder what's written down."

Fowler laughed. "Other than the alphabet?"

"Yeah."

Fowler hit the unlock button on her car's remote. "See you tomorrow."

———

With twilight fading and a full moon on the rise, Clayton drove to the Barranco Canyon cutoff, where a solitary volunteer firefighter had his truck blocking the road.

"No entry," the Hispanic man said.

"The cops aren't securing the area?" Clayton asked.

"Only during the day shift. The sheriff doesn't have enough deputies. We're covering at night in four-hour shifts."

"Any people trying to sneak in?"

"Like you?" the man asked suspiciously.

Clayton laughed. "I'm not that curious."

"That's smart, because it's a rough road or a long walk to the site."

"That's good to know." Clayton put his truck in gear. "Take care."

The firefighter waved as Clayton drove off. Out of sight a quarter mile up, he parked behind some trees lining the highway, got out a backpack containing emergency food and water, grabbed a flashlight from the glove box, and began hiking to the rise that defined the mouth of Barranco Canyon. If Lucille Trimble wasn't talking complete nonsense, there was something important written down at the double-wide, and he was determined to find it.

pickup parked outside might have belonged to Todd Marks. Clayton made no assumption. He slowed, veered off the road behind the
bullet-riddled sheriff's unit, and quietly circled the dwelling. Crime
scene tape secured the front door. A window facing the road was also
crisscrossed with tape.

With his semiautomatic in hand, he cautiously climbed the creaky
front steps, stood to one side, and slowly opened the unlocked front
door. He called out, got no response, and waited a beat or two before
entering low and fast. He cleared the residence room by room, turning
on all the lights as he went.

The place was a shambles, with kitchen cabinets torn from the
walls, furniture upended and smashed, broken glass littering the frayed
carpet, bedroom dresser drawers ripped apart, mattresses cut open.
Someone had ransacked the place, and Clayton was certain it wasn't the
police. No matter how angry officers might have been about Corporal
Little's death, tempers would have been checked and the proper search
protocol observed.

Was the culprit looking for something specific or merely on a ram-
page? Either way, something might have been missed. He also wondered what evidence the cops had gathered and removed.

He snapped on a pair of latex gloves and started a search in the
master bedroom. Even amid the disarray he could tell that Lucille
Trimble had occupied the room alone. There was no men's clothing
in the closet, empty boxes of women's diapers littered the floor, some
prescription bottles dumped in the adjoining bathroom sink were in her
name, and the medicine cabinet contained only female toiletry items.

The closet had the musty smell of limp, old clothes. He searched
every item, went through the jumble of women's shoes on the floor and
a messy pile of wadded-up sweaters on the single high shelf.

Back in the bathroom, he did a thorough search. A wastebasket

CHAPTER 19

Clayton dropped into Barranco Canyon far enough away from the roadblock to avoid being seen or heard. Under a moonlit sky, he set a steady pace up the rocky, rutted road. Here in the middle of the Mimbres Apaches homeland, he could feel the tug of ancestors whispering in his ear. He gained stamina and speed as he followed the twisting canyon into higher terrain, remembering the famous Apache warrior Victorio, who during the Indian Wars had found sanctuary with his people in the black mountains that loomed above.

His footsteps broke the silence of the night, and his thoughts strayed to his days as a young Mescalero police officer patrolling the remote reaches of the reservation high in the Sacramento Mountains. It had been among his happiest times. Maybe the ancestors were beckoning him to return. The idea made him smile.

Without realizing it, he'd started into a trot along a sandy stretch of roadbed that crossed an arroyo. Up ahead, tumbled rocks and half-buried boulders forced a slower pace, but he kept on without pause.

The double-wide came into view with a light on inside. The old filled with soiled adult diapers that smelled of old urine and dried feces made him want to retch.

He moved on to a smaller bedroom that had obviously served as Todd Marks's sleeping quarters. A twin-sized box springs and mattress sat on the floor under a pile of bed linens. A computer cable dangled to the floor from a combination printer-copier on a small bookcase, but the computer was missing. No doubt the police had taken it. A gun cabinet, empty of weapons, sat against a far wall.

He pawed through bills, receipts, and junk mail strewn around an upended side table. On the floor next to the bed, an ashtray filled with cigarette butts was amazingly undisturbed.

The hope that he might find something written down that would help exonerate Kerney suddenly seemed foolish.

He pushed aside his doubts and kept looking, going through all of Todd's clothing before moving into the living and dining area, where an overturned faux-leather couch and matching chair faced the smashed screen of a large analog television. A corner woodstove leaned precariously against the tiled wall, the unattached chimney flue hanging perilously from the ceiling. A dusting of black soot covered everything.

In the kitchen, he found the refrigerator unplugged and food rotting inside. He searched around the electric water heater in the small closet next to the half bath and finished up in the bedroom where Todd Marks had set up his fifty-caliber. The back wall was crusted brown with his blood.

He returned to the living area and took a second look, hoping to discover something of a personal nature, some evidence of a family history—a book of treasured snapshots, a framed rodeo poster from Todd's glory days on the pro circuit, perhaps a belt buckle Kim Ward had won for barrel racing. But the place seemed scrubbed clean of any past life or treasured memories. Surely the police wouldn't have taken every family memento.

Clayton sat on the front step, wondering if the vandalism was a cover-up of some sort. If so, who would have done it, and why? Drawing a blank, he walked to the truck. There was no key in the ignition, but he found a vehicle registration in Lucille Trimble's name tucked in the visor along with an out-of-date auto insurance certificate. He searched the glove box, looked under the seats, and examined the debris and bags of smelly household trash in the truck bed. He had a feeling Marks either dumped or burned his trash somewhere on the property. That search, if necessary, would have to wait for another day.

He leaned against a front fender and shook his head. It made no sense. People didn't live in the same place for years without accumulating and keeping some personal stuff.

He poked around the woodshed and inspected the well house that revealed the petrified remains of a dead bull snake curled up in a corner. He circled the double-wide, shining his flashlight on the aluminum skirting covering the concrete block pillars that elevated and held the dwelling in place. A portion of the skirting had been cut out and replaced with a rough-sawn wood cap. He pulled it loose and peered inside. His flashlight beam caught a scurrying rat headed for darker recesses, and six cardboard packing boxes resting on a warped piece of plywood just out of reach.

He made a full, careful sweep with his flashlight for any more disturbed or angry critters before crawling in. He pulled the boxes out one by one, and carried them inside.

At the dining table, he opened a box and found the personal mementos that had been missing from the house. There were rodeo trophies, belt buckles, ribbons, awards Kim had won in high school, and several high school yearbooks. There were programs of events she'd entered, a scrapbook of newspaper clippings, a diary with some sketches of horses, favorite quotes, and observations about boys she liked.

The second box contained some legal papers, including a divorce decree granted six months before Kim's birth to Lucille Ward from Joseph Ward, but no marriage certificate. There was also a copy of a thirty-year-old restraining order against Douglas Butler, ordering him to permanently stay away from Lucille. Attached to it, and dated a year later, was a copy of a district criminal court proceeding, sentencing Douglas Butler to a year and a day in jail for stalking. Included with it was the victim's statement Lucille Ward had given to the court. Another legal document, dated three months after Butler's conviction, changed Lucille's surname from Ward to Trimble.

The reasons for changing her name made sense, but why Trimble? Was it a family name?

In the third box was a packet of old handwritten letters from Todd to Kim. One accused her of infidelity. It was postmarked from Lubbock, Texas, and mailed to her at her mother's address in Deming. It read in part:

> *I know you've been sleeping around. Don't think you can sweet talk me with your bullshit, and don't try to run and hide like you did last time, because I'll find you.*

It had been sent a month before Kim went missing from Erma Fergurson's house.

In an earlier letter, Todd begged Kim to forgive him for hitting her, promising never to do it again. In yet another, he blamed his drinking for slapping her at an El Paso bar. It wasn't the jackpot that could completely clear Kerney's name, but it was solid evidence that bolstered his defense.

He went through the remaining boxes. In the bottom of the last one he discovered another packet of letters from Todd written to Lucille. Some were addressed to her in Belen, others had been sent to her post office box in Mimbres. They were short notes, spanning the years 1974 to 1990, and mailed from places throughout the West and Canada. In each, Todd wrote of his continuing search for Kim, telling Lucille where he'd been looking for her, and that he'd never give up. It was pure claptrap.

Clayton felt pumped about what he'd uncovered, but it had to be used properly. He'd broken the law by trespassing and tampering with evidence at a crime scene. If he gave the actual letters and documents to Dalquist, the court would rule they were illegally obtained by the defense and therefore inadmissible. Plus, he could be charged with larceny. If he was found guilty, three misdemeanor counts against him, that would be more than enough to revoke his police officer certification.

Clayton used his smartphone to make copies of everything of value he'd found, and put the boxes back under the double-wide. Early dawn had arrived, and chances were good the police would be returning. He splashed water on his face at a frost-free spigot and ate an energy bar before dialing Agent Carla Olivas's cell phone.

"I need your help," he said when she answered.

"Oh, for chrissake, just turn yourself in and make bail," Olivas replied.

"What?"

"You don't know? There's a warrant out on you for impersonating an officer. Kerney's already been placed under arrest and is under guard at the hospital. Where are you?"

"Where are you?" Clayton countered, masking his surprise. Not three, but four misdemeanors. Whoopie. It just kept getting better.

"Home in Alamogordo. I'm on my two days off."

"Good. I'll call you in three hours."

"About what?"

"Overlooked evidence."

"What overlooked evidence? Where?"

"Don't push me, Carla. I'm doing you a favor."

"I'll take your call, but I'm reporting this conversation."

"Of course." Clayton disconnected, filled his water jug at the spigot, and started down the ranch road.

He'd been up all night, but he didn't feel tired. It felt good to be moving, and he kept a steady pace. Near the mouth of the canyon, he heard the familiar squawk of a police radio. He scrambled up a low ridgeline and hurried to his truck.

The sight of it brought him to a full stop. It was half stripped. The tires and wheels were missing, along with the tailgate, the hood, the battery, the optional fog lights, and his tool bed box. The multimedia navigation system had been ripped out of the dashboard, and the front bucket seats were gone, along with the floor mats.

Muttering, he hot-wired the ignition to make it look as if the truck had been stolen, removed the license plate and vehicle documents, zipped them in his backpack, and started walking toward Mimbres. As soon as he got a signal, he called Wendell in Las Cruces. Fortunately, his first class hadn't started.

"Hey, Dad," Wendell answered.

"Come get me. My truck has been stripped and I need a ride."

"What? Where are you? Are you okay?"

"I'm fine. I'll be at the coffee shop in Mimbres. It's a village east of Silver City. You can't miss it."

"That's a couple of hours away."

"Yeah, I know," Clayton replied, as he walked past an older reserve deputy standing next to his unit at the Barranco Canyon roadblock. He waved cheerily and kept moving. "Don't get stopped for speeding. See you when you get there."

"I'm on the way."

At the coffee shop in a back booth, he ordered a big breakfast and considered calling his insurance company. He decided against it. The truck, or what remained of it, would be found sooner or later. He'd deal with it then.

For now, it was talk to Dalquist, get home, and find out from Sara what was happening with Kerney. A cup of hot coffee helped clear his head. Jeez, what a night.

Right at the tail end of his three-hour promise, he called Agent Olivas and said he'd changed his mind and had nothing more to tell her.

CHAPTER 20

Otis Roderick played back General Brannon's voice message for the umpteenth time. Although he wanted to believe her attempt to locate Earl Matson Page had suddenly turned cold, he didn't buy it. He'd served with the general and knew how she operated. One of her cardinal rules was to communicate important and sensitive information directly. That meant you didn't send an email or leave a voice message. You made personal contact. Second, although Brannon sounded matter-of-fact, he'd never known the general to give up so easily. It wasn't her style.

Granted, her husband had been shot and seriously wounded, an unnerving and terrifying event. But if finding Earl Matson Page meant clearing Kerney of murder charges, Sara Brannon would be nothing less than relentless.

Roderick sighed. The general was lying.

He opened the case file on Page. Of all the DEA agents he'd served with in Colombia over twenty-five years ago, only one, Oliver Muniz, remained with the agency, now the special agent in charge of the El Paso Division Field Office.

Roderick reached for the telephone and dialed Muniz's number.

———

Oliver Muniz hung up the phone, reached for the bottle of antacid tablets in his desk drawer, and quickly chewed a chalky handful. Earl Page, his old partner, his onetime best friend, and the man who had almost ended his career, was apparently alive and living off the grid somewhere in southern New Mexico.

Signing the department chit for the five million dollars that vanished along with Page had cost Muniz a scheduled promotion and three years of brain-numbing backwater assignments. It took that long to outlast lingering suspicions that he was in on the theft. Even so, Muniz knew he could have, should have, risen further through the ranks.

Roderick wasn't one hundred percent sure of his facts, but Muniz didn't give a tinker's damn. The evidence was strong enough to embark on a personal manhunt.

He washed the chalky antacid taste from his mouth with the last of his coffee. As special agent in charge of the El Paso Division Field Office, he supervised West Texas and all New Mexico DEA operations. Which meant Page was on his turf. What good luck was that?

Page was somewhere near Silver City, being looked for by that retired police chief accused of murder, who'd gotten himself badly shot up. Muniz snorted. Probably another ill-trained, cowboy-type lawman, all too common to these parts.

Although it was prime-time news, Muniz hadn't followed the case closely. He'd correct that. He buzzed his second-in-command, and asked her to prepare a briefing report on the Kevin Kerney murder investigation ASAP.

"I want an update on the current status of the case, with as much information you can get," Muniz added. "Go through the normal channels."

"Are we jumping in on this one?" Samantha Hodges asked.

"Not officially, Sam. If someone wants to know, just say we're gathering information on a person of interest."

"Anything else?"

"Get me two experienced field agents, and have them ready to mount a special operation within twenty-four hours. This is strictly a need-to-know assignment, so keep a tight lid on it. I'll be in command."

"Who are you going after?"

"An old friend of mine I can't wait to see again."

Ordering a clandestine, off-the-books field operation wasn't something division bosses normally did. Commanding one was even rarer. Sam had but one guess, and she voiced it. "The legendary Earl Matson Page is alive?"

"Apparently so." Oliver chuckled.

She'd never heard Muniz sound happier.

———

Clayton didn't pick up his phone again until Wendell arrived at the coffee shop. While his son dug into a green chili cheeseburger and a mound of fries, Clayton stepped outside, called Dalquist, and told him what he'd found. He read some of the pertinent sections of letters that substantiated a history of violence between Todd and Kim prior to her disappearance. Dalquist was clearly delighted. He wanted everything sent to him immediately.

"I'll alert Kerney and Sara," Dalquist said. "Well done."

"There's more to come, I hope," Clayton replied. "How's Kerney?"

"Recovering peacefully, now that the police officer outside his hospital door has been removed. Guarding a seriously wounded individual who wasn't going anywhere was simply ridiculous. I found a district judge who agreed."

"That's good," Clayton said.

"Call me after you've turned yourself in and made bail. Impersonating a police officer. How impertinent of you."

Clayton laughed, disconnected, and dialed Paul Avery. "Did Carla Olivas tell you I called?"

"She did," Avery replied. "What's this about overlooked evidence?"

"I've changed my mind," Clayton replied. "Why should I make your job easier?"

"Come on, Clayton, give. You wouldn't have even mentioned it unless it helped your case. Where are you? Let's get together and talk."

Clayton checked his watch. Avery needed about fifteen more seconds to pinpoint the nearest relay tower that was bouncing his cell phone signal. That should be clue enough as to where to look.

He decided to drop a bigger hint in case Avery had suddenly turned completely dim-witted. "Check the Barranco Canyon crime scene." He turned off the phone and put it in his shirt pocket.

Inside the café, Wendell was dipping the last of the fries in a puddle of ketchup on an otherwise empty plate.

Clayton paid the bill and put a tip on the table. "Let's go. When we get to Las Cruces, drop me off at the jail. Ask your mother to come and pick me up."

"Busted for impersonating a police officer, right?" Wendell asked.

"Right."

Wendell grinned at his father as he gunned the Jeep down the highway. "This is more fun than hitting the stacks at the library."

Clayton grinned back. "I'm always up for some quality father-son time with you."

———

Juan Ramirez waited in the reception room of Dalquist's law offices in downtown Santa Fe. The day before, he'd received a letter from the lawyer, asking him to keep a two o'clock appointment to discuss his continued employment at the Kerney ranch.

Juan wasn't sure what to think. But he figured maybe Kerney wanted him to stay on, with more hours and better pay. A contract or something like that.

Juan liked getting the cash Kerney paid him. But if he made more in a paycheck, he could quit the *pinche* rancher who worked him like a dog and never gave him any raises. That would be *que bueno*.

At two o'clock, the door to a rear office opened and a man Juan assumed was Dalquist stepped out. Short, old, with a round face, he smiled broadly and shook Juan's hand firmly. Up close, Juan recognized him as the gringo lawyer he'd see on television every now and then.

"Thanks for coming in, Mr. Ramirez. I'm Gary Dalquist."

Juan removed his hat. "I've seen you on TV."

"An unfortunate aspect of my profession, I'm afraid," Dalquist said. He gestured at a closed door adjacent to his office. "Please, come to the kitchen for a cup of coffee. I won't take much of your time."

"It's about work for Senor Kerney, right?" Juan asked as he followed.

"Exactly," Dalquist replied, stepping into a small kitchen that reminded Juan of his *tia* Sophia's, with the same old fashioned black-and-white linoleum floor and big cast-iron kitchen sink. On the table were two coffee cups, a sugar bowl, and an open laptop computer.

"I want to show you something," Dalquist said as he fetched a carafe from the stove and poured coffee.

"What is it?"

"You'll see," he said, sitting down. He turned the laptop screen toward Juan and played the surveillance video of Ramirez inside the Kerney residence.

Juan froze as he watched himself looking through papers on the desk in Kerney's office, searching a built-in desk in the kitchen, open-

ing bedroom dresser drawers, pawing through the contents, and snooping inside closets.

"I was just checking that everything was okay," he said lamely. "I've
got a key for when they're away."

Dalquist shook his head in dismay. "You broke the law, and with
a felony conviction on your record." He let the thought of jail time
hang in the air.

"I was just trying to help get my sister's son out of juvie," Juan
explained, his face flushed with anxiety. "I was doing it for a cop. He
said it would be okay."

Dalquist smiled sympathetically. "I knew there was a reasonable
explanation." He placed a digital recorder on the tabletop. "Is your
nephew still incarcerated?"

Juan nodded. "That *pendejo* cop has done nothing to help him."

"What are the charges against the boy?"

"He stole some things from a car and ran away from the police."

"Nothing more serious?"

Juan shook his head.

"Does he have legal representation?"

"The public defender."

"Good. If you agree to cooperate and tell me everything, I'm sure I
can convince Mr. Kerney not to press charges against you. Also, I might
be able to help get your nephew released from juvenile detention."

Juan searched Dalquist's face. "There is no more work for me at
the ranch, is there?"

"Sadly, that's correct. But your sister could well have her son home
soon, and you can continue to have your reputation intact with no one
the wiser to what you've done."

"I can't pay you."

"You don't have to. Do we have an agreement?"

Juan nodded. "I'm sorry for what I did."

Dalquist turned on the recorder. "Shall we begin?"

An hour later, Dalquist thanked Juan for his time, made an appointment for him to return in the morning to sign a transcribed copy of the recording, and told him his caretaker services at the Kerney ranch were no longer required.

Juan handed him the ranch keys. "You'll help my nephew?"

"As promised," Dalquist replied.

"And if that state cop calls me?"

Dalquist gave Juan his business card. "Say nothing about our meeting and have the officer contact me."

"Okay."

Standing in the open front doorway, Dalquist watched Ramirez trudge dejectedly to his pickup. Manipulated by the police, he was more victim than culprit, and Dalquist felt a twinge of regret for the price he was going to pay. He pushed down an impulse to speak to Kerney on the man's behalf, and returned to his office smiling. Picking up the phone, he left a message for Lynn Stavish, the chief district public defender, asking her to call him at her earliest possible convenience.

Stavish would jump at the opportunity to use his pro bono services on behalf of Ramirez's nephew.

He played back his Q&A with Ramirez. If Kerney's case went to trial, he'd smear egg all over Agent Avery's face, as well as the incompetent bureaucracy of the New Mexico State Police.

———

Juan sat in a Pecos bar brooding over his second shot of tequila. He'd lost a half day's pay meeting with that lawyer, thinking maybe a better job was waiting for him. Instead, now he'd have even less work and less money. He should have told that lawyer *nada*.

He took out Dalquist's card and studied it. Why should he follow the *abogado*'s advice and say nothing to the police? He was *loco* to think the man would help his nephew, just as he was *estupido* to believe the cops. He'd been royally screwed by all of them.

He deserved to get something out of it. The police paid informants, didn't they? That's what he'd been doing for Sergeant Medina and Agent Avery, wasn't it? Five hundred dollars, Juan decided. That's what he wanted, and he wouldn't take less. If they blew him off, he'd talk to Rudy Velasquez, an old high school classmate who worked for the Santa Fe daily newspaper. Tell him the whole story of what they made him do. With Kerney being accused of murder, it would be front-page news. Maybe Rudy would pay him for—what's the word?—an exclusive.

He downed the shot of tequila, paid his tab, and left the bar. From home, he called Sergeant Medina at the Santa Fe Sheriff's Office.

"Get my nephew out of juvie today," he demanded.

"Can't do it," Medina replied. "The chief juvenile probation officer refuses to cooperate. Says there are additional charges pending from another auto burglary the city police are investigating."

"Do it, and get me five hundred dollars, cash."

"I can't do that, either. You were assisting the state police, not me."

"Tell your state police *compadre*, no money, I go to the newspapers. I've already met with Kerney's lawyer. He's got a video of me in the house looking for stuff. Says he won't do nothing about it."

"Are you sure about the video?"

"I saw it. I want five hundred dollars. You tell Avery."

Juan hung up. For the first time today, he felt good. *Chinga* all of them.

———

Avery brought Carla Olivas and James Garcia with him to the crime scene at Barranco Canyon. They didn't find a thing of interest until

Garcia noticed dirt disturbed in front of a wooden lid covering a section of the skirting. They pulled it off and saw six boxes. Fresh scuff marks in the dirt showed that someone had recently removed and then replaced them.

"Clayton?" Garcia proposed.

"Possibly," Avery replied.

Carla laughed. "Of course it was Clayton. The sheriff's office would have hauled them away as evidence."

Carefully they went through the contents piece by piece, logging everything as evidence.

When they finished, they loaded the boxes in the SUV Avery had borrowed from the uniform division, and started for Las Cruces.

"I wonder what Clayton took," Avery said as they bumped down a stretch of washboard ranch road.

"Nothing," Carla said snappishly. "He wouldn't be so stupid as to steal evidence from a crime scene. That would be big trouble."

"Well, he was stupid enough to get shit-canned from his job, wasn't he?" Avery shot back.

"He's smart enough to have found those boxes the Grant County SO missed," Carla replied. "I bet he copied what he needed, and would love to have us withhold it from Dalquist."

"We don't know what he found," Avery retorted. "Maybe it was something else entirely and he took it."

"That's ridiculous."

"Give it a break, you two," Garcia groaned from the backseat. "Clayton was a damn good boss and our friend as well. Stop beating up on each other because the man disappointed us."

"I'm just trying to do my job," Avery muttered sourly.

At the roadblock to the canyon road, Avery asked the reserve deputy on duty if he knew that the crime scene had been disturbed.

The old deputy shook his head. "No, I didn't know that."

"Well, tell your supervisor it's been trashed big-time. He may want to investigate."

"I'll call it in," the deputy said as Avery drove away.

They were on the highway to Deming when Avery's phone rang with an incoming call from Gabe Medina at the Santa Fe SO. He pulled off the road and answered.

"Your CI got busted by Kerney's lawyer," Gabe reported. "And he copped to it."

"What?"

"The lawyer has video of Ramirez rifling through belongings in Kerney's ranch house. Juan wants five hundred dollars and his nephew out of juvie or he goes to the press."

"What?"

"Pay attention, Paul, you've got a problem."

"I'll take care of it." Avery disconnected, took a deep breath, and slowly eased back into traffic.

Garcia leaned forward from the backseat. "Is there a problem?"

"Nothing I can't handle," Avery replied, fervently hoping it was true.

CHAPTER 21

Before Kerney's discharge from the hospital, Gary Dalquist held a strategy meeting with the family in a small second-floor conference room. Kerney walked in with Sara and was greeted by Dalquist, Clayton, and Sara's parents.

"What's the agenda?" Kerney asked as he gingerly settled into a comfortable padded chair.

Dalquist smiled. "It's time to look at where things stand and go from there."

"Where do things stand?" Kerney asked. He took Sara's hand as she sat beside him.

Dalquist opened a folder. "On the positive side, we have some good news. The letters Clayton found at the crime scene show a history of violence between Todd and Kim that predates her disappearance." He passed copies he'd printed at his office to Kerney.

"If we must go to trial, that's very powerful ammunition." He paused to give more papers to Kerney. "Additionally, Juan Ramirez has made a sworn, notarized statement that he was coerced by New

Mexico State Police Agent Paul Avery to conduct an illegal search of your house. I'll use that to call into question all their evidence against you, and hammer away at police stupidity and ineptitude."

Dalquist thumbed through some papers. "Clayton also discovered legal documents detailing the reasons Lucille Ward changed her name, and a series of letters Marks wrote to her about his made-up attempts to find Kim. I've copied everything for you."

"Good," Kerney said.

Dalquist closed the folder and clasped his hands. "Lastly, while getting shot was gravely unfortunate, it eases our worry about going to trial too soon. I have doctors who will certify you need a lengthy convalescence. We'll have more time to prove your innocence, which we must use wisely."

"What are the negatives?" Kerney asked.

"Before we get to those, let's deal with the charges against you and Clayton for impersonating a police officer," Dalquist replied. "From what Clayton has told me, at the Fort Bayard Veterans Center, you introduced him as a cop, but he displayed no police credentials, and did not identify himself to anyone as an officer."

"That's correct," Kerney said.

Dalquist beamed. "You'll sign a statement to that effect, and we'll confirm it with the people you spoke with at the center. A first-rate Silver City attorney I know will act as Clayton's counsel and handle the details. I'm sure she'll be able to get the case dismissed, which removes any question of Clayton losing his police officer certification."

"That's a relief," Kerney said.

"You bet it is," Clayton added, cracking a smile.

Dalquist gave Kerney a pointed look. "As for you, we'll enter a not-guilty plea and delay a court appearance for as long as possible."

"When will that be?" Kerney inquired.

"After we've proved you innocent of murder," Dalquist answered.

"Now for the negatives we must deal with. You're still the prime suspect and the last person known to have seen Kim alive. The documented evidence the prosecution will use to prove your guilt includes Erma Fergurson's journal entries, residue evidence gathered at the burial site, the police report you filed about your stolen pistol, and the photograph of you and Kim Ward outside the Las Cruces bar the night Todd Marks was arrested."

"What does the photograph prove?"

"That you lied in your statements to the police."

"I didn't remember being there," Kerney rebutted.

"Do you hear how that sounds?" Dalquist gently challenged.

Kerney nodded grudgingly. "Yeah."

Dalquist took the papers back from Kerney and put them away. "Let's move on. With Marks dead, and Kim's mother too ill to be of any use to us, our best hope to clear your name before trial rests with Kim's girlhood friend, Loretta Page, assuming she knows anything at all of value."

Kerney's expression darkened. "A long shot at best."

Dalquist shrugged. "We don't know that yet, which is why finding her is important." He opened a second file. "We do know that she lived for a time with Kim's mother, after Kim had left home. And it's possible Loretta was pregnant, although we're not certain. Beyond that, we have nothing current about her or her family."

He ran his finger down the page. "Until six months ago, when her half-brother, Earl Matson Page, surfaced masquerading as Louis Page and removed his adoptive father, Jack Page, from the veterans center at Fort Bayard."

"We also know," Sara said, "that two years after Earl stole the five million in drug money, Jack Page and his daughter, Loretta, disappeared."

"Where did they disappear from?" Kerney asked.

"Duncan, Arizona," Dalquist replied, looking up from the file. "Although we can't pinpoint their current location, the anecdotal information we've gathered suggests they live somewhere outside Silver City, perhaps in or near the Gila National Forest."

"How was Jack Page's veterans center bill paid?" Kerney asked.

"Fort Bayard has refused to give us any payment for services information," Sara replied. "Since we could find no claims for federal or state insurance reimbursement, the best guess is cash or cashier's check."

"Do we even know if Loretta Page lives with her father and half-brother?" Kerney asked.

"We do not," Dalquist replied. "But on to a different matter. Tomorrow you'll be discharged and go home with Dean and Barbara, who've agreed to look after you, Patrick, and the ranch. With Ramirez gone, Dean and Patrick will handle the ranch chores."

Dean grinned and nodded at Kerney. "Looking forward to it."

"Also, a registered nurse will be on call, should her services be needed," Dalquist added.

"We'll take good care of you," Barbara said.

Kerney turned to Sara. "This was all figured out in advance, wasn't it?"

Sara nodded. "Clayton can't work this alone, and you're in no shape to help. Now that the feds know about Earl Page, we must move fast. I doubt my lie about losing Page's trail will keep them at bay for long. They're probably out looking for him right now."

Kerney clenched his teeth and shook his head. "Just let it go. I'll take my chances at trial. I don't want anybody taking any more risks. Don't do—"

"All three of us will be working on this from Silver City," Dalquist calmly interrupted. "I've hired a wilderness guide to help us narrow the scope of our search."

"We're giving it a week," Clayton said. "We'll regroup after that, if necessary."

Kerney sighed. "Is Grace in on this?"

Clayton smiled. "Everybody is. Grace, Wendell, Hannah, and my mother as well. You're outvoted."

Kerney shook his head. "I surrender."

Dalquist's cell phone rang. He glanced at the screen, answered, and listened for a minute before thanking the caller, disconnecting, and breaking into a big smile.

"What is it?" Kerney asked.

"Better that I show you." Dalquist pulled his tablet out, powered it up, found the Internet page he'd been directed to by the caller, and handed it to Kerney. A breaking news story from the *Santa Fe New Mexican* read:

MAN USED BY POLICE TO SEARCH
FORMER CHIEF'S HOUSE

New Mexico State Police declined to comment on an informant's allegation that an agent pressured him to search former Santa Fe Police Chief Kevin Kerney's house. Currently under indictment for the murder of Kim Ward, a college girlfriend, who disappeared in 1973, Kerney is hospitalized in Albuquerque recovering from gunshot wounds sustained in what is now being called the "Shoot-out at Barranco Canyon." The incident left two people dead; a Grant County deputy sheriff killed by Todd Marks, Kim Ward's husband, and Marks himself, who was shot by a state police sniper. The informant, Juan Ramirez, a part-time caretaker at the Kerney ranch, claims he was promised the release of his nephew from juvenile detention if he agreed to cooperate, but that he did so reluctantly. The boy is still in detention. More in tomorrow's edition.

"Don't you just love good news?" Dalquist asked with a chuckle as the tablet got passed around.

CHAPTER 22

On a bright, windy morning, Earl Matson Page, who made it a point to use only his last name, made his weekly trip to Silver City to pick up mail and run a few errands. In the post office box among the usual stuff was an envelope addressed to Jack from one of his pals at the Fort Bayard Veterans Center, postmarked five days before.

Page tore it open and read:

Jack,

Some cops came by looking for Louis about a stolen vehicle or some such thing. Wanted to know how to find him. I didn't tell them squat. Thought you'd like to know. Hope you're doing okay. Come see me.

Bud

There was no date on the letter, no telling if it had been written and sealed up for any length of time before the postmark.

Page forgot about the errands, threw the mail on the passenger seat of his truck, and tore out of town in a hurry. When he'd hatched a plan to steal five million dollars in DEA-confiscated drug money allocated to recruit an informant close to a major Colombian drug lord, he'd discussed his scheme with Loretta. To get away clean, he needed a new identity, an escape route from Medellín to the Panamanian border, and someone trustworthy waiting with transportation to get him home. It had to be her.

Loretta loved the idea of being part of a five-million-dollar caper. It would give them all the money they needed to be together forever. She suggested using Louis's identity. They traveled to Juárez, and with Louis's birth certificate had a forged passport and driver's license within a day. They celebrated in a luxury room at the best hotel in El Paso.

It was also her idea to charter a boat in Panama. They got quotes. Paying in advance for a bare-bones charter and Loretta's airfare would eat up most of Earl's savings. Nothing fancy would have to do. He cleaned out his account and gave her the cash.

They studied maps and decided to rendezvous just over the Colombian border at a small fishing village. Earl would call to wish her a happy birthday. That would be her cue to be offshore in two weeks.

It went off without a hitch, except for some bodies Earl left behind in the jungle to ensure no trace of his escape would be found. He figured Loretta didn't need to know about that.

When they arrived home, Earl immediately set about making the family as invisible as possible. He promised Jack a full partnership in the scheme if he let his bank account fall dormant so that he couldn't be traced. Page would cover all expenses with the stolen drug money, including Jack's lost income.

The chance to ranch again was a no-brainer for Jack. He'd lost his small ranch to drought and a rare parasite that killed most of his livestock, and he was tired of getting by on day wages from area ranchers and his puny benefit checks. Besides, he was getting too old to make a hand.

Safe and sound back in New Mexico, Page hid the money in water-proof containers under the foundation of a cabin he'd inherited from his biological father, Sam Matson.

Almost inaccessible, with no road and only a faint, unmarked trail for access, the cabin and one square mile of land abutted wilderness to the north and east, and a patchwork quilt of private and state-owned land to the west and south.

Starting out, he used some of the cash to buy a new truck, along with several handguns and rifles, and rent a grader to build an all-weather road to the cabin. When it was finished, he installed a locked gate and spent months fencing the section with NO TRESPASSING signs posted every hundred feet. Only then did he turn his attention to making the off-the-grid cabin livable.

He designed and built a water catchment system, installed solar panels with heavy-duty battery packs for electricity, and put in indoor plumbing using gray water for outside irrigation. His infrequent trips to town consisted of library visits to study how-to books, post office stops to pick up mail and technical manuals he'd ordered, and shopping for necessary equipment, food, and supplies. For nearly two years he lived in virtual isolation, venturing away from the homestead once a month to visit Jack and Loretta, across the state line in Duncan. Although he tried to argue Loretta out of visiting, she'd occasionally appear at the cabin unannounced and interrupt his day. He couldn't keep her away.

At the entrance to the ranch road, Page punched his access number into the keypad that opened the solar-powered gate, and then gunned his truck toward home. Over the years, his one section had grown to ten sections of combined private and leased state land totaling sixty-four hundred acres.

He'd been careful with the drug money, building it back up slowly

to four times the original five million through conservative investments, profits from the cow-calf operation, and income from a highly
regarded quarter horse breeding program, all operated as part of a
corporate entity.

The original cabin had blossomed into a family compound and
ranching operation, with Jack ensconced in his own comfortable quarters a mile away from the main house, where Page and Loretta lived as
man and wife. Additionally, there was permanent housing for a ranch
manager, a large horse barn, and a modular garage for repairing ranch
equipment. Nearby were several large corrals, loading pens, and a practice track for the ponies.

The entire perimeter of the headquarters' compound, including the
airstrip and metal hangar for Page's four-passenger turboprop aircraft,
was protected by a state-of-the-art electronic surveillance system.

As the land holdings and ranching operations had grown, he'd
been able to hide in plain sight by requiring all employees, contractors, and service providers to sign binding confidentiality agreements not to disclose anything about him, Loretta, Jack, or the ranch
with outsiders.

Furthermore, he insisted that his employees, who were hired
through an out-of-state recruitment firm, be single and undergo extensive background checks. Page didn't want anyone working for him
who had personal or family connections in New Mexico or Arizona.
Local contractors and service providers were heavily screened by private investigators to ensure they could be trusted to be discreet.

As business prospered, rumors grew about the eccentric millionaire
who lived on a remote showcase ranch. Gossip was Page owned a cos-
metic company, was heir to a fast-food chain, or had made his money
in a Silicon Valley tech company. Nobody had yet fingered him as a
rogue DEA agent who'd built his little empire with stolen narco money.

He paid very well, and most staff honored their employment contracts. Those who stuck with him for five years or more got a bonus. The money was so good, nobody quibbled about the company rules.

Over the years, only three employees broke trust, and Page killed them. Other than those anomalies, there were no other hiccups.

Jack's house was timber-frame, just like the main residence. Smaller in size, it had exposed beams and tresses, and a pitched roof that defined an open living space where Jack could stretch out in his adjustable easy chair in front of a mammoth TV and binge on his favorite movies, shows, and sporting events. There were satellite dishes on both houses for television and Internet access.

Page found Jack in the kitchen, standing behind his walker, heating canned soup on the stove. Behind him, the kitchen table was set for lunch along with a bottle of his favorite pilsner and a slice of buttered toast.

Although over ninety, Jack could still see to his own needs. He'd shrunk a bit, and his cowboy days were over, but he wasn't ready again to take up residency in a nursing home, and probably never would be.

"Want some?" Jack asked. He hated the ponytail and beard on the boy. Not fitting for a man his age, despite it being a disguise. His adoptive son even drove an old pickup and dressed like a hardscrabble farmer when he ran his errands, which was not an unusual sight in a town that had its fair share of eccentrics, vagrants, and old hippies. Jack understood the need for caution. Secrets and lies had a way of falling apart if you didn't tend to them.

"Not hungry," Page answered. "You got a letter from your buddy at Fort Bayard."

"What does it say?"

Page read Jack the note.

Jack stopped stirring the soup. "Cops looking for you? That's not good. What for?"

"You tell me."

"Tell you what?" Jack snapped as he turned the heat off under the pot. "All Bud knew was my son Louis was coming to fetch me home."

"You're sure of that?"

"Damn right I am." With a steady hand, he poured soup into a bowl. "What are you going to do about it?"

Page put the bowl of soup on the table for him. If Jack hadn't fallen off his horse, fractured his leg, and demanded to rehab at the Fort Bayard Veterans Center, this wouldn't be happening. He loved the old man, who'd been more than a father to him, and there was no cause to fault him. "It's worrisome, but not a problem. I'll look into it."

Jack snorted. "I told you the time would come when somebody started snooping around. Nothing stays hid forever."

Page helped Jack slide into his chair and moved the walker to one side, close at hand. "Rest easy. I'll handle it."

"I'll give old Bud a call after I finish my lunch."

"Wait until I bring you a new cell phone to use," Page replied.

"Nothing wrong with my old one."

"Where is it?"

Jack motioned at the kitchen cabinet drawer, where he also kept his wallet and keys.

Page retrieved the phone and stuck it in his jeans back pocket.

"Nothing wrong with it," Jack grumbled again.

"It's time to replace all the cell phones anyway," Page said. He kept a dozen prepaid throwaways in his office with brand-new numbers, and changed out the old ones monthly.

Jack slurped some soup. "Fine with me. I hardly ever use the damn thing."

"I'll be back in a little while."

Jack nodded as he bit into his toast.

———

Page drove to the horse barn, where he had his ranch office, too distracted by Bud Elkins's troublesome note to enjoy the ponies loitering
in the pasture or the sweep of high wilderness mountains that filled
the skyline.

His air-conditioned office couldn't completely eliminate the
unmistakable, pungent smell of horses, but he didn't mind. Through
the walls he could hear the occasional snorts and stomps of ponies still
in their stalls. It was one of his favorite indoor places on the ranch.

Because he used the office to conduct business with stock haulers,
beef buyers, repairmen, and others, he displayed nothing personal, just
some framed prints on the walls by well-known contemporary cowboy artists and a small bronze sculpture of a saddled pony on his desk.

He opened a wall safe, grabbed two fully charged cell phones,
and used one to call the Fort Bayard Veterans Center. He asked for
Bud Elkins, and was put through to his room, but the telephone went
unanswered.

He sat back in his desk chair, wondering what the fuck was going
on. Cops trying to find him for what? He'd always known that if
anyone seriously started looking for him, chances were good he'd be
found. To make the search more difficult, the ranch and all his assets and
investments were managed through an offshore trust, which reduced,
but didn't eliminate, the risk of discovery.

Page sighed in frustration. What were his crimes, for chrissake?
Walking out on a job he'd come to hate? Stealing millions from a
Colombian drug cartel? Killing some bad hombres in the jungle who
wanted to kill him during his trek to Panama to meet Loretta? Silenc-
ing some untrustworthy blabbermouths? Putting thousands of dollars
every year into the local economy?

He drummed his fingers on the desktop. First he needed to know if there was a palpable threat. He knew Kevin Kerney was looking for Loretta. She'd told him why when they saw the news that the retired police chief had been arrested for Kim Ward's murder. But the gunfight in Barranco Canyon where Kerney had been seriously wounded diminished the threat. Wouldn't the cops assume Marks was guilty of Kim's death?

Since the shoot-out, he hadn't been paying close attention to the news. He opened the laptop, went to the electronic edition of the Silver City newspaper, and scrolled through the articles. In the weekly police notes column, he found the risks had escalated. Arrest warrants for impersonating police officers at the Fort Bayard Veterans Center had been issued for Kevin Kerney and his son, Clayton Istee.

He headed out the door to talk to Loretta at the ranch house. In the distance, Jack's place sat nestled at the edge of a grove of piñon and juniper trees, like a modern version of a gatekeeper's cottage along the ranch road.

Near the main house, a large solar array occupied what had been a small pasture, sheltered from view by a thick stand of evergreens. At the edge of a landscaped lawn, a tall, hand-laid rock wall hid a propane-fired generator with a huge tank capable of powering the enclave for days.

The pitched front of the timber-frame house was elevated, with a deep covered porch perfect for sunset-viewing. Large picture windows climbed the two-story structure, and there were cozy balconies off the two upstairs master suites.

He parked at the head of the circular driveway and paused, remembering how Loretta would tease him about never wanting to leave the ranch. When would he take her to Berlin, or to see the Taj Mahal? Would he really force her to stay in a dismal three-star San Francisco hotel the next time they were shopping in the city?

Away from the ranch and Silver City, they enjoyed trips for a theater

night in New York, a museum opening in Los Angeles, or a weekend of jazz in New Orleans. Only rarely did they take longer excursions.

Loretta's teasing ended earlier in the year when she was diagnosed with fourth-stage colon cancer. With the aid of a full-time, live-in nurse, she was spending her remaining days in the second master bedroom, with her hospital bed positioned in the middle of the room to take in the view, a table nearby with issues of her favorite magazines and a pile of books she wanted to read, a television on a stand she almost never turned on, and several monitors the nurse used to check her vital signs. There was a beeper close at hand to call for assistance.

He hurried inside, climbed the staircase to her bedroom, and found her snoozing, an open book resting on her chest. Quietly, he positioned a chair close to her side and took her hand.

She was still beautiful. Her light brown hair was streaked with gray, and her brown eyes were no longer lively due to the pain medication. She'd kept her figure except for a few lost pounds, and despite some wrinkles her face looked the same as it did when they were kids, adolescent lovers living under the same roof as brother and sister.

It had been an inevitable outcome of their attraction to each other. From a very early age, they'd intuitively known it would happen. In the dark of night, away from Jack and Jann, where Louis could not hear, they had whispered about it, thrilled about it, looked forward to it.

Loretta's eyes fluttered open. "Hey, you," she said squeezing his hand.

"Sleepyhead," Page replied, giving her a kiss.

She saw the worry in his eyes. "What's wrong?"

"Jack got a note today from his buddy at the veterans center that the police had been around looking for me. They were imposters. Guess who?"

Loretta sighed. "Kevin Kerney and his son. Isn't Kerney seriously wounded and in the hospital?"

"That won't stop him or his family."

"How can he possibly know I can prove he didn't kill Kim?"

"He doesn't have to know, just believe that it's possible," Page said. "This is happening at a bad time."

"What are we going to do?"

"Shut everything down, just as we've always planned."

"But nobody's looking for you."

"We don't know that. You can bet the state police are on Kerney's tail. One way or another, this unravels for all of us."

Loretta smiled grimly. "We were supposed to fly away, if this happened. We can't do that now, can we?"

"I can charter a bigger plane to fly us out."

"So I can die someplace else? No, thank you. Besides, you'll never get Jack to leave here."

"Then we all stay, and I send everyone else packing."

"Do that," Loretta said. "We've never talked about what would happen to this place after we were gone or arrested. Why didn't we prepare a will?"

Page laughed. "Dead or in prison, a will wouldn't mean a thing. The government will seize everything based on the principle of ill-gotten gains. With no heirs to challenge the surrender of our assets, Uncle Sam gets it all. Think of the federal government as our one and only charitable cause."

Tired and sleepy once again, Loretta smiled. "I suppose it's only right."

"Poetic justice," Page said as he patted her hand. "I'll go tell Jack."

Loretta turned her cheek for a kiss. Page obliged, then hurried from the bedroom. She watched as he drove away in his truck, thinking back to the night long ago when they'd told their parents she was pregnant and they wanted to get married. Jack understood, but Jann freaked out,

demanding that Loretta get an abortion and Earl leave home immediately. Jack agreed to the abortion and that Earl and Loretta should
be separated for a long spell. But he wasn't prepared to say they never
should be together again.

It was Jack's idea for Earl to move to Houston, live with a second
cousin, and apply to the police department, a career he'd shown some
interest in. The Houston PD needed new recruits, and draft deferments
were granted to applicants who made it through recruit training and
agreed to serve with the department a minimum of two years.

If Earl and Loretta still felt the same way about each other after two
years, Jack said, they'd all talk about it more.

Jack's open-mindedness ruptured his marriage. Jann couldn't toler-
ate the notion of such an incestuous relationship. She left him, moved
to Silver City, went to work as a secretary at the university, and had
nothing more to do with him or her children until she died.

It was four, not two years, when Page returned with news he'd been
recruited out of the Houston PD Narcotics Division to join the DEA, a
job he dearly wanted. Until he finished training and had a permanent
assignment, they'd have to wait to live together. When it turned out
he'd be back in Houston as part of an undercover task force, the wait
got longer.

After Houston, each new posting took Page deeper into narco-
trafficking assignments, making it impossible for any normal home
life. They made do with his infrequent visits, short vacations together,
and some long holiday weekends when he could manage to get away.
Occasionally, when he wasn't undercover, she'd go to him, if he was
stateside.

Loretta continued to live with Jack on his ranch, and found a job as
a school secretary, which gave her summers free and long holiday and
spring breaks from work. It was the best she could arrange in order to

be easily available to Page. It dragged on that way for years until his Colombia assignment changed everything for the better.

That made Loretta smile. Drowsy from the opiates, soothed by old memories, she fell asleep with the premonition that none of them was going to leave the ranch alive. And that was okay.

CHAPTER 23

Sara, Clayton, and Dalquist left for Silver City by chartered plane. As they flew over the rugged Gila Wilderness, Sara pondered their chances of success. With no roads or settlements, few structures, and no motorized vehicles allowed on over a half million acres, was it possible that Jack, Loretta, and Earl were down there, tucked away where nobody could find them? In a wilderness used primarily by commercial outfitters, adventure backpackers, experienced campers, and Forest Service personnel, it seemed unlikely. But there were places less remote in the state where hermits, cult members, and wanted fugitives had lived undiscovered for years.

The landscape below changed with the appearance of dirt roads, buildings, and occasional water tanks reflecting flashes of morning sunlight. They were on the ground at the Grant County Airport within minutes. Located on a flat plateau south of Silver City, there wasn't much to the airport except one major runway, a few hangars for small aircraft, and the facilities for the Gila National Forest Aerial Fire Base, which provided air support to fight forest fires throughout the

Southwest. Three all-wheel drive, high-clearance vehicles were waiting, watched over by four employees from the local dealership that had rented them to Dalquist.

He tipped the employees and passed out ignition fobs to Sara and Clayton. "I doubt our new vehicles will deter the state police from discovering our presence in the area," he commented with a smile. "But in the backcountry, we may be able to lose them."

He shook his key fob at them. "I hate these things," he said, as he walked toward the red SUV. "This one is mine. I understand they're fun to drive. Follow me."

They convoyed into town through the historic district, past the city's renowned two-story Victorian hotel, to a side street where a small restored adobe cottage sat next to a church. A sign in front of the cottage announced the law offices of Sheila Russell.

Inside, they were greeted by Russell, a forty-something woman with a short haircut and the toned physique of a marathon runner. Several framed photographs on her office desk documented her participation in the sport.

After handshakes all around, they gathered at a circular conference table.

"I've booked you into a bed-and-breakfast that has a separate cottage with three bedrooms away from the main house," Russell said. "It comes with a fully stocked kitchen and it's within the city limits, a five-minute drive from downtown. You'll have privacy and convenience."

Dalquist beamed. "Excellent."

Russell smiled in return and passed out maps to the B&B. "Mr. Dalquist, I suggest you and Ms. Brannon check in right away, while I accompany Mr. Istee to see a magistrate judge."

"You have two in Grant County," Dalquist noted. "Which one?"

"Of course you'd ask," Russell replied amiably. She turned to Clayton to explain. "We have two magistrates, one with a law degree, the other without. We're going to visit Alejandro Armenta, who only has a two-year degree from a community college, but is fair-minded and knows the ropes."

She picked up a file from the table. "We're due there in twenty minutes. I'm asking for dismissal of the charge against you. I believe I have everything we need."

Grinning, Sara reached over and squeezed Clayton's hand. "Good luck."

"I'm ready," Clayton said, breaking into a smile.

Dalquist nodded his approval and stood. "As soon as that's cleared up, we'll meet at the cottage."

"As you wish," Russell said. "I'll call you when we're leaving court."

Outside, Clayton got into the passenger seat of Russell's compact Honda, still feeling a bit apprehensive. Judges were as quirky as any other professional group, maybe more so, and his anxiety wouldn't lift until the charge against him went away.

They drove out of Silver City to the small town of Bayard and parked beside a brown-stuccoed building at the intersection of two highways. A portion of the building housed the magistrate court, where Judge Armenta waited in his cluttered office.

Wiry and in his fifties, with a prominent chin, Armenta was casually dressed in blue jeans and a western shirt. He rose to greet Russell with a smile, motioned for Clayton and her to sit, and settled behind his desk.

"Thank you for seeing us, Judge," Russell said.

"Of course. I've read the statements from Chief Kerney and the witnesses at the veterans center, and it is clear your client did not openly identify himself as a police officer."

"That's correct," Russell said.

Armenta paused and looked sternly at Clayton. "However, it could be argued that you permitted the deception. By that, I mean you helped perpetrate the belief that you were indeed a serving police officer."

"If you're asking did I deny it, no, I did not," Clayton answered.

Armenta nodded. "I appreciate your honesty, which is exactly what I wanted to hear from you. I'm dismissing the charge."

Clayton held back a sigh of relief. "Thank you, Your Honor."

"You do know that under state law the arrest record cannot be expunged," Armenta continued. "Fortunately, the charge does not automatically result in revocation of your police officer certification. However, the Law Enforcement Board has latitude in deciding what constitutes misconduct sufficient for revocation or suspension."

"I understand that," Clayton replied.

"Good." Armenta smiled at Russell. "Anything else?"

"No, Judge. Thank you for your time."

As they drove away, Clayton looked back at the nondescript building with the big MAGISTRATE COURT sign planted by the front door.

"It's not the hallowed halls of justice by any means," Russell commented.

"Appearances can be deceiving," Clayton said.

Russell laughed as she reached for her phone to call Dalquist. "You've got that right."

———

Away from the main house, the two-story cottage at the bed-and-breakfast was surrounded by tall pine trees with private parking. The front living room had a deep fireplace, and comfortable chairs with side tables and reading lamps. A large country-style kitchen included a dining table capable of seating eight. The large stair landing held a writing desk connected to Wi-Fi, and the second floor had three large bedrooms with full baths. There wasn't a television anywhere to be found, but each bedroom had a small radio next to an old-fashioned dial telephone.

Clayton threw his luggage on his bed and went downstairs. Dalquist, Sara, and Russell were at the dining table chatting with Sid Bonnell, the wilderness guide Dalquist had hired. Covering the table-top were several large maps of Gila National Forest and its three designated wilderness areas, the Gila, the Aldo Leopold Wilderness, and the Blue Range Wilderness.

Somewhere in his forties, Bonnell didn't top out over five-five. He was muscular and deeply tanned.

"I was telling your partners I'd be glad to pack you into the high country," Bonnell said. "But it would take several weeks to cover the areas where folks might have set up permanent residence in the wilderness, and cost you a pretty penny, to boot. And I'm willing to bet you'd come up empty."

"Why is that?" Clayton asked.

"It's a dry, hard country," Bonnell explained. "On some of the south-facing slopes at nine thousand feet or more, desert plants thrive. If people were gonna live there, they'd need a reliable source of year-round water, and there just ain't a lot of it."

"No hidden springs or forgotten micro-wetlands?" Sara asked.

Bonnell snickered. "The Forest Service may have its failings, but one thing they've got a handle on is where the water is and where it ain't. I've been to all of them, and there aren't any people living there."

"Are you suggesting we don't bother looking?" Dalquist inquired.

"Didn't say that." Bonnell waved a hand over the maps. "Scout it by air."

"How long to cover that much territory?" Sara asked.

"A full day in a small plane, with a good spotter." Bonnell tapped his chest. "That would be me."

"I'll go along for the ride," Sara said.

Bonnell nodded. "A friend of mine is a contract pilot for the Gila Aerial Fire Base. He's got a sweet Cessna that's perfect for low-level reconnaissance. I can set it up for tomorrow, if you like."

"By all means, do so," Dalquist said.

Bonnell rolled up the maps and looked at Sara. "Sunrise tomorrow at the airport."

"I'll be there."

Bonnell excused himself and left. Clayton announced that in the morning he'd start working the businesses in town that catered to ranchers and farmers. Dalquist asked Russell to help him with a search of county property and tax documents. The meeting broke with no one feeling particularly optimistic. Sara went to her room to call home.

———

Bonnell's pilot friend, Danny Crowley, a burly, jovial retired battalion chief with the Boston Fire Department, owned a twenty-year-old Cessna 172 Skyhawk, a four passenger, fixed-wing, 180-horsepower single-engine aircraft. Sara was familiar with the plane, which for years had been used for initial military pilot training and was still widely in service with the Border Patrol.

They took off at dawn, provisioned with a cooler Sid had filled with a twelve-pack of bottled water, prepackaged sandwiches, and assorted snack food. A peek at the contents made Sara regret skipping breakfast to grab a little extra shut-eye.

With Sid spotting from the passenger seat next to Crowley and Sara in the backseat, they flew west to avoid the rising sun, gaining altitude quickly before dropping over a sweeping mountain range into the heart of the Gila Wilderness. Sara could see what Sid had meant by a parched, empty landscape. Forest roads were few, trails were faint, creek beds were dry, and in places large burn scars from forest fires arched up and down tiers of ridges.

She saw deer moving through the shadows of trees near a meadow, and an occasional tent campsite thrown up along a trail. Above, an eagle circled warily before veering away in the direction of a high pine forest.

At each location Sid pinpointed, Crowley did several slow flyovers, while Sara and Sid scanned with binoculars, looking for the slightest sign of human activity. At one location next to a live stream, two back-packers waved a friendly greeting. Crowley dipped a wing in response and flew on.

With a steady hand, Crowley kept the flight smooth and the turns gentle, except when an occasional wind burst buffeted the plane. As they skipped from place to place throughout the morning, the constant need to stay focused kept Sara's hunger at bay. But when Sid broke into the cooler and started handing out ham-and-cheese sandwiches on white bread, she couldn't resist. The sandwich was almost tasteless, except for the mustard and mayonnaise she slathered out of small pack-ets onto the bread. She ate quickly and washed it down with water, eyes glued to the landscape below.

Finished scouting west, Crowley flew into the Blue Range Wilder-ness. It was remote and dense with dark tree cover in areas spared from wildfires. Even along the foothills Sara saw no signs of settlement. For-est roads were virtually nonexistent, and the Continental Divide Trail section Crowley pointed out to her was almost indiscernible. He flew them over the thin ribbon of the Mimbres River, where the mountains rose precipitously and relentlessly, lurching into the distance. Scanning carefully through binoculars, Sara saw nothing worth a closer look.

Crowley circled to return to the airport. "Sorry this has been such a washout," he commented. "We've got fuel and time to spare, if you want to widen the search."

Sara nodded in approval, and consulted her map. "West of the wilderness is a checkerboard of federal, state, and private land spread out between small ranching communities along the highway to Reserve. Let's make a pass over the areas closest to the mountains."

"Ten-four," Crowley confirmed, turning the Cessna west, into the sun.

Sara picked up her binoculars.

Civilization dotted the landscape as they crossed out of the wilderness. The Gila River twisted through pastures and bosque. A stretch of a two-lane highway weaved through the valley, following the low-lying contours of the land. Sporadic clusters of roadside buildings gave way to ranches, some large, some small, with the pattern repeated farther down the highway. Near the river, dense tree stands cloaked houses and barns. On the ground there would be a helluva lot of places to cover in one of the least-populated areas of the state.

The enormity of the search made Sara's throat tighten. Would they ever catch a break?

On a series of sweeps, Crowley took them out of the valley, following ranch and forest roads deep into the foothills, climbing high to crest the mountains before descending to pursue another route.

In a sky suddenly filled with fast-moving thunderheads, a microburst hit the Cessna as they topped out over a high ridge. Lightning flashed around the aircraft, and Crowley struggled to keep control. A huge bolt hit them, followed by a deafening thunderclap, and the engine sputtered and died.

"We're going down," Crowley yelled above the roar of the storm.

Sara couldn't hear a word, but knew what he was saying. The steel-gray, rain-whipped storm enveloped the Cessna, and she had no idea what they'd hit, only that any chance of survival was slim.

Preparing for impact, she bent over, covered her head with her hands, and waited.

———

Jack Page stood outside watching the storm roll through, clouds racing by like sailing ships on a turbulent ocean of murky gray sky, the thunder and lightning now off in the distance near the Arizona state line.

He'd seen the small plane come and go a couple of times, once right over the ranch, before losing sight of it. Was somebody spying on them?

Up in the high country, the sky was clearing fast. He caught sight of a thin plume of smoke whipping above treetop silhouettes. Had a lightning strike started a fire, or had the plane crashed and ignited it?

The way the wind was blowing it could race down on them. Jack pulled the cell phone out of his pants pocket. He didn't mind staying here with family and shooting a few lawmen when they came to arrest Earl. Hell, he looked forward to it, wouldn't have it any other way. But damn if he'd see this place burn.

He dialed 911 and reported a possible airplane crash and a forest fire.

CHAPTER 24

Crowley kept the Cessna right-side up during its rapid descent until it hit belly-first, the fixed landing gear ripping away as the plane dug nose-first into the ground, the sound of the propeller a metallic scream as it shredded into fragments. The right wing buckled against a boulder, the strut twisted into splinters, and the fuselage came to rest at an angle.

The impact threw Sara into the back of Sid Bonnell's seat. It felt like a hammer blow to the head, but she didn't black out. She sat up to find Crowley unconscious and slumped over the flight yoke. Sid was awake and moaning, his head bleeding profusely.

She opened the door, dropped a few feet to the ground, and stood light-headed, swaying for a second, her eyes closed to regain her balance, then looked around to get oriented. With the towering mountain wilderness to her back, she could see the foothills and the narrow river valley below in a clearing sky. To the west, the thunderheads tumbled on.

The Cessna rested on a sharply angled ridgeline with scant tree cover. An overwhelming smell of aviation fuel filled the air. She unstrapped Crowley from his seat, removed his headset, and yanked him out of the plane by his upper arms. His body thudded into her and knocked her to the ground. She pushed him off, regained her footing, and pulled him away from the smoldering airplane.

Sid had managed to get out on his own and was stumbling around blindly, hands to his face, blood streaming down his cheeks.

She led him to Crowley, had him sit, and ran back to the Cessna. She grabbed the fire extinguisher and first-aid kit and sprinted back to the two men just as the fuel tank exploded, knocking her to her knees.

She checked Crowley's pulse. He was dead. From the unnatural angle of his head, probably from a broken neck. The gash in Sid's forehead was long but shallow. She worked quickly to close it using a large sterile bandage covered by absorbent fabric wrapped around his head.

"Is it bad?" Sid asked.

"No." She flushed the blood out of his eyes with an emergency bottle of water from the first-aid kit. "Can you see okay?"

"Jesus, I ain't blind," he said with great relief, his eyes blinking rapidly. He glanced at Crowley. "Is he dead?"

"Yes."

"Jesus."

Sara pointed at duff that smoldered under a nearby grove of small, scrawny junipers, caused by a slender lick of fuel that had spilled from the wreckage. "Can you stamp that out before it spreads?"

Sid nodded and stood unsteadily.

"Are you sure?" Sara asked, propping him up with a hand on his back.

"I can do it." He lumbered away, pulling off his shirt to use as a blanket to smother small flames lapping at the base of a juniper.

She grabbed the fire extinguisher and approached the burning plane. The smoke was thicker now, rising into the clear sky, pushed by gusty winds westward over the foothills into the valley.

It was lucky they'd crashed on the extreme edge of the wilderness within sight of civilization. The heat scalded her face as she emptied the fire extinguisher on the flames and retreated. Sparks flickered and reignited the blaze in the cabin. Surely someone by now had seen the smoke and called it in.

Were they close enough to civilization to get a signal? She pulled her phone from her pocket. The screen was shattered and there was no reception. She turned to find Sid facedown and unmoving in the smoldering duff. She yelled and ran to him, lugged him clear, and rolled him on his back. His face and chest were burned, and he wasn't breathing.

She started CPR, and kept it up until Sid coughed and started breathing.

"What happened?" he asked in a broken whisper.

"Hush. Just stay quiet." She propped up his head, and gave him ibuprofen from the first-aid kit.

She glanced at Danny Crowley's body. During her army career, she'd survived a stateside military helicopter crash that claimed six lives. She'd lost men and women under her command to combat in Iraq, consoled seriously wounded warfighters who'd sacrificed their arms and legs in service to their country, and grieved with families who'd lost loved ones.

Here she was, grieving again over the loss of another good man, with no help in sight. Which was worse, she wondered, dying or bearing witness to the death of others? At that moment, bearing witness seemed more harmful to her soul.

———

Ed Sandoval, manager of the Gila National Forest Aerial Fire Control Base and a decorated former army helicopter pilot, got the call of a small plane crash and fire. He thought about Danny Crowley, who'd left early in the morning for a wilderness flyover with Sid Bonnell and another passenger. He tried radioing Danny several times, only to be greeted by dead air.

As far as he knew, there were no other small planes in the air on a flight plan across the wilderness. But that didn't mean much, as general aviation pilots frequently didn't bother filing on short hops or when logging flight time.

It was too early to call out a fire suppression team, especially with strict guidance from on high to let wildfires burn in the forest if no lives or structures were in danger. Ed got the general coordinates of the sighting provided by 911 dispatch and took off in one of the rescue helicopters.

He gained altitude quickly, looking for smoke on the distant horizon north and west of Silver City as he overflew the town. Nothing. He topped Goose Lake Ridge on the Pinos Altos Range and caught sight of a faint smoke plume near the western escarpment of the Mogollon Mountains. Sandoval dipped the bird lower, pushed its speed to over a hundred miles per hour, and radioed Crowley, hoping for a response.

He dropped into the valley, the smoke plume almost invisible. He took the chopper over a saddleback break in the foothills and made a steep ascent to the crest, where sunlight glinted on a shattered cockpit. A hundred yards from a precipitous drop-off, the burned wreckage tilted at an angle, the fire almost out.

Below, a woman who was sitting on the ground with an arm wrapped around Sid Bonnell waved. Stretched out next to her was Danny Crowley, and he wasn't moving.

Sandoval veered to a clearing behind the downed aircraft. As he set the bird down, he called in two survivors, one possible fatality, and scrambled a crew to the crash site.

As the rotor blades slowly churned to a stop, he ran to the woman.

With her help, he wrapped Danny's body in a tarp and loaded it on the chopper. Once they had Sid strapped into a seat, Sandoval took off.

"Are you okay?" he asked the woman. Her face was smudged and there was a big welt on her forehead.

"I'll make it. It's Sid who needs the hospital."

"We're on the way."

CHAPTER 25

Forty-eight hours into his hunt for Earl Matson Page, Oliver Muniz remained optimistic. What he knew from Otis Roderick's phone call, the current status of the cold-case murder investigation, and his personal knowledge of Earl convinced Muniz that Earl was somewhere close at hand, just waiting to be found.

In Colombia, he'd spent endless hours with Earl on stakeouts and field intelligence operations, sidestepping embassy and headquarters bureaucrats, running confidential informants, dealing with corrupt Colombian officials, and drinking *cervezas* in some of the trendy Medellín bars and nightclubs frequented by narcos.

Both had been single at the time, and for two years they spent practically all their waking hours together. As a result, Muniz knew about Earl's dream to own a ranch that would be the most modern and successful operation in the Southwest, and how he planned to have his father help him run it.

The ranch had been Earl's obsession, to the point that whatever free time he had was devoted to learning about state-of-the-art range management and cattle breeding practices. He'd return from stateside with magazines and books about modern ranching methods. There were stacks of them in his small apartment.

Earl had been recruited by the DEA out of the Houston PD, but he was a New Mexico native, and that was where he wanted his ranch to be. Where, as he put it, you could actually see the horizon, the weather was warm and sunny, and monsoons didn't last forever.

A city boy from a low-income Chicago neighborhood, Muniz had his own dreams, which were to stay with the department and move up through the ranks to become a high-echelon boss.

But he'd signed for the five million dollars Earl disappeared with, screwing him. Because of Earl, he'd never rise higher than his present position.

Starting out in Deming, Earl's hometown, Muniz and his two agents had swept west and north, often in the wake of state police investigators and the accused ex-police chief and his family cohorts. They'd concentrated on the larger ranches, trying to pick up any information about Earl and his family that others might have missed. So far the only new tidbit Muniz had uncovered was that during Earl's time in Colombia, his father and sister were living in Duncan, Arizona. That intelligence came not from knocking on ranch house doors miles off the pavement, but from information on a survivor and beneficiary form Earl had submitted to Human Resources prior to his South American posting.

Tomorrow they'd go to Duncan, but tonight they were staying over near the hamlet of Glenwood, on the highway to Reserve, in some rustic tourist cabins.

Muniz's cell phone rang as he was toweling off after a shower. He sat on the squeaky double bed with the towel wrapped around his waist and listened as his boss, Warren Lee Kelso, DEA operations chief in Washington, read him out over the phone.

"Did you really think I wouldn't hear about this?" Kelso snapped. "I swear to God, Oliver, with anybody else I'd be telling them to put in their retirement papers. Send those two agents back to El Paso immediately."

Muniz said nothing. Kelso probably thought him nuts. The scope of his search for Earl was mind-boggling. Looking for someone in four New Mexico counties comprising over seventeen thousand square miles with a population approaching sixty-five thousand people was a preposterous undertaking.

"Are you listening to me?" Kelso demanded.

"I hear you," Muniz replied, wondering who had squealed on him. Was Samantha Hodges, his number two, really that eager for his job? It didn't matter. Cop shops of any shape or size were like sieves when it came to keeping secrets. "You know what this is about, right?"

Kelso snorted. Back in the day, he'd served briefly in Colombia with Page and Muniz, and knew in detail what had happened. "Of course I do. But you can't do this on the agency's time."

"I'll send them home, but I'm staying. Make it official, Warren, and reopen the case. Let me catch this bastard."

"Not a chance," Kelso replied. "The agency buried this embarrassment long ago and doesn't want it exhumed. Page died in the jungle, killed by drug lords while on an undercover mission, and his body was never recovered. He died a hero. End of story. Take annual leave, you've got over half a year accumulated, for chrissake."

"Okay."

"And if you find him, don't kill him. I'll make him disappear from my end."

"I can't promise you that, Warren," Muniz replied.

"Do as I say," Kelso replied heatedly. "And don't make me call you again. You've got a week, and either you're back at your desk or you're retired."

The phone went dead. Muniz got up and looked out the window. At the diner across the road, the two agents were waiting on him. Should he tell them before or after they ate? He decided to buy them dinner and then send them home.

His cabin had a small analog color television with a digital convertor and rabbit-ears antenna sitting on top of a 1950s dresser decorated with a row of carved cowboy lariats on each of the legs. The TV received only three over-the-air broadcast channels, two of them grainy and fuzzy. The local news was on, reporting the breaking story of a downed civilian airplane in the Gila National Forest. Muniz turned up the volume. The pilot, Danny Crowley, was dead. Two surviving passengers, Sara Brannon and Sid Bonnell, were being treated at the local hospital.

Wasn't it the ex–police chief's wife who'd contacted Roderick about the search for Earl Page? Apparently she was still looking, despite lying to Roderick about it.

Had she been looking for Earl when the crash occurred? Muniz consulted a map. According to the news report, the plane had gone down in nearby mountains, close to a large swath of privately owned land that stretched northward through the valley. Had she found Page? Before he got excited about the prospect, he needed to know exactly what ground she'd covered.

With the Mexican border so close, and the high-security White Sands Missile Range less than a hundred air miles to the east, it was possible some federal agency had tracked the flight. His best hopes were the Border Patrol, the U.S. Army at White Sands, and maybe even NSA.

He made some calls requesting information, got dressed, and, feeling slightly more chipper than before, crossed the empty highway to the diner. He decided he'd try the T-bone steak dinner.

———

As soon as the news broke about the state police using a civilian to search Kerney's residence, Deputy Chief Serrano quickly disbanded the Las Cruces–based murder investigation team, officially censured Agent Paul Avery, and assumed personal oversight of the case, using headquarters personnel to do the fieldwork. According to what Avery had heard, the new team had accomplished nothing more than a paper review of the investigation since day one.

Serrano also assigned a newly promoted lieutenant as acting deputy commander of the Southern Zone Investigation Unit with orders to clean up the "Las Cruces mess."

For Avery, tucked away in a cubicle with boxes of evidence from closed cases to sort through for possible destruction, it meant Siberian desk duty, and a very cold shoulder from most of the district civilian and sworn personnel, James Garcia excluded.

When Garcia told him about the airplane crash in the Gila, Avery nodded and sat silent, mesmerized by the news. Ever since the Barranco Canyon shoot-out and Clayton's search of the property, he'd been convinced that the locus for finding Loretta Page was somewhere around the Gila. If that's where Clayton and Brannon had zeroed in, that's where he wanted to be.

He spent a long several minutes working out a plan that would make that happen before appearing at Luis Mondragon's open office door.

"No, you don't," Mondragon cautioned, waving a finger at Avery as he stepped inside. "Talk to your lieutenant."

"Come on, Cap," Avery pleaded. "Hear me out."

Mondragon scratched his almost bald head and rubbed a sore shoulder from an overzealous morning workout. "Two minutes."

Avery stepped in front of Mondragon's desk. "I fucked up, and I

know it. Serrano was right to slap me down. Put that aside for a minute. Ever since Kerney appeared in our crosshairs as the prime suspect,
this case has been all balled up, and why?"

"You tell me," Mondragon said.

"Because part of the time we've wanted Kerney to be guilty, so we
could show the world that we'll clean our own house, no matter how
far the high and mighty fall. The rest of the time, we wanted Kerney
to be innocent, because he's one of our own."

"Go on," Mondragon said.

"I know I bungled it badly."

"You did get in a bit over your head," Mondragon commented
dryly. "What's your point?"

"I want to know the truth about this case, not what some judge or
jury may decide."

Mondragon hesitated. He liked to think Kerney was innocent, but
after years on the job, ugly realities still jumped up and surprised him.
"What do you want from me?"

"You're short five uniformed officers, correct?"

Mondragon raised an eyebrow. An officer retiring soon would
make it six, and the next academy recruit class didn't start until late in
the year. He was stretched thin, with no relief in sight. "That's right."

"I'll transfer to patrol duty effective immediately, if you'll agree to put
me on a three-day special assignment before I have to report in uniform."

"Three days doing what?"

"What I just said, find the truth," Avery replied. "Call it a special
assignment under your direct supervision."

Mondragon liked Avery's vagueness. "Your transfer means you'll
have no seniority for shift preferences," he noted.

Avery nodded. "Understood."

Mondragon leaned forward. "Do you think in three days you'll
know the truth?"

"I'll know that I tried."

Mondragon ran a finger over his lips. Serrano might huff and puff at him about it, but it was within his jurisdiction to do as Avery suggested. Also, he'd be delighted to get rid of Avery. As a bonus, Mondragon would gain a uniformed officer with experience, not a snot-nosed rookie requiring months of constant field supervision.

"Turn in your transfer request to me before you leave the building tonight, and report for duty in seventy-two hours. You'll start on the graveyard shift."

Avery smiled. "Thanks, Cap."

Mondragon waved him away. "Get out of here before I change my mind."

———

Clayton had spent his day talking to area merchants, heavy equipment and automobile dealers, feed and fuel suppliers, veterinarians, and anyone else who might have ongoing business dealings with ranchers in Grant County and beyond. He passed himself off as a process server looking to deliver court papers, and flashed the age-enhanced sketch of Earl Page to everyone. He didn't get one positive response. On his way to canvass the small surrounding villages, on impulse he stopped at a salvage yard on the outskirts of Silver City.

A jungle of wrecked vehicles and discarded farm machinery surrounded a tin shack that served as the sales office. A sign next to the door read PULL YOUR OWN PARTS. A decidedly different way to interpret the meaning made Clayton crack a smile.

The man behind the counter was late middle age, overweight, and smoking a hand-rolled cigarette. He introduced himself as Carl Yeager, and nodded when Clayton held up the sketch.

"Jack Page's son," Yeager said without hesitation.

"You're sure?"

"That's what my pa said."

"Can I speak to him?"

"Dead," Yeager replied. "Several years back."

"Sorry for your loss." Clayton waved the sketch in Yeager's face. "You're sure this is Jack Page's son?"

"Can't say I know it for a fact. He's been in here many times, brought the old man with him once or twice."

"Jack Page?"

Yeager looked at Clayton like he was an idiot. "That's who my pa says he was. We weren't formally introduced."

"How did your father know Jack and his son?"

"Before my pa bought this place, he ran an auto repair shop in Duncan. He knew Jack back then when he had a small ranch."

"Did you know the family?"

Yeager shook his head. "Nope. I came here from Barstow to help out after my wife left me."

"Do you know where Jack and his son live or work?"

Yeager paused. "Not for sure. There was a fella in here once the same time they were. After they left he told me they ran a big ranch. He used to be a regular customer, and I was gonna ask him more the next he was in, but he never came back."

"Do you remember the customer's name?"

"Called himself Vic."

"Did Vic have a last name?"

"Don't know it."

"How about the name of the ranch?"

Yeager shook his head.

"When was this?" Clayton inquired.

"Maybe three years ago. What's Jack's boy done?"

"Domestic matter," Clayton replied.

Yeager smirked. "Yeah, I know all about that shit."

Clayton asked Yeager to describe Jack's son, and he guessed six-foot, medium build, and in good physical shape. He couldn't remember any unusual scars, birthmarks, or tattoos.

On the highway heading to the state line and Duncan, hungry and thinking about dinner, Clayton wondered if he'd been lulled into thinking Jack and Earl had a small, remote ranch somewhere in the national forest because of what Bud Elkins at the veterans center had said. Was it just pure BS on Jack's part that Elkins had swallowed?

And why was Earl so hard to identify among the locals? Robert Ripple, the aide at the veterans center, had seen him around Silver City, and the salvage yard operator knew him by his father's surname. But nobody else?

An old hippie type with a scraggy beard and long, gray hair pulled back into a ponytail would have surely drawn his share of attention. While they weren't an endangered species by any means, they were decidedly noticeable. But not according to all the other folks Clayton had spoken to that day.

He was less than eight miles from Duncan entering the sleepy, picturesque farming village of Virden, New Mexico, along the Gila River, when his phone rang. It was Dalquist. Sara's plane had crashed in the mountains. She was alive and going to be okay.

Clayton made a quick U-turn and gunned the SUV back toward Silver City. His visit to Duncan would have to wait.

CHAPTER 26

Page always kept a lot of cash on hand for emergencies, and by the end of the day he'd laid off everyone except Alice Sherrell, the live-in nurse who cared for Loretta. He handed out pay packets that included regular wages, accrued vacation time, and four-figure bonuses to most staff. New employees got less, but everyone had to re-sign their confidentiality agreements before they got paid and could leave. He gave his ranch manager, Preston Higgins, who'd been with him over ten years, the ranch's newest, one-year-old king cab pickup truck for his services. Additionally, because of all the personal stuff he'd accumulated over the years, Preston had an extra twenty-four hours to clear out.

To show his appreciation to Alice, Loretta's nurse, he paid her in advance through the end of the year and deposited an additional fifty thousand dollars in her bank account.

Nobody complained, and nobody asked any questions. They all knew the drill. They were to leave the state, keep their mouths shut about their past employer, and never come back. The money and the threat of legal action were good enough to make the rules stick. Although in this case Page didn't think it mattered anymore.

He'd considered selling all the livestock on the ranch and decided against it. There was enough browse and sufficient water to carry the animals for several weeks without causing any hardships. Late in the afternoon, with Preston's help, Page moved all the ponies to fresh grass, and watched as they cantered friskily across the field. The cattle, spread out on different pastures, would do fine on their own.

To celebrate the end of a good long run, he had Preston and Jack up to the house, invited Alice to dinner, carried Loretta downstairs, and cracked open a three-hundred-dollar bottle of single-malt scotch. On the back deck of the house looking out on a spectacular expanse of the Mogollon Mountains, he grilled up thick rib-eye steaks, roasted ears of corn, and put the final touches on one of his special salads.

He'd told Loretta about the planned cookout, and she'd insisted on attending, getting herself gussied up with Alice's help in a fresh blouse, blue jeans, and a touch of lip gloss and eye shadow. Page told her she looked beautiful. She beamed with pleasure. Jack, Preston, and Alice chimed in to confirm it.

The conversation didn't turn to the ranch shutdown until dinner was over and the scotch was almost gone. Logs blazed in the outdoor fireplace, keeping the chill of the evening at bay.

"I can be gone by early morning, if that's what you want," Preston remarked. A slow-talking man with not much to say unless it had to do with business, he was by far Page's favorite employee.

"That might be wise," Page answered.

"Will there be trouble?" Alice asked. She'd be a pretty woman if it wasn't for her beak of a nose.

"Not for you," Loretta said with a reassuring smile, snuggled in a warm blanket Alice had fetched for her. "My husband will keep you safe."

Alice gave Page an anxious look.

"Don't you worry," Page said.

"If you want, I can stay on and help you keep the hostiles at bay," Preston offered.

Page gave him a questioning look. "Why do you think there will be trouble?"

"Well, for one, you're shutting down in a big hurry. That means trouble to me."

"True. What kind of hostiles do you think they'd be?"

"Bankers in suits, lawyers with briefcases," Preston replied. "Maybe the taxman or the police wanting to serve papers. Makes no never-mind to me. I'd hate to see this place get sold off piece by piece at auction. It's the best damn spread in the state and has been a good home to me for years."

Jack laughed. "I like your gumption."

Page nodded in agreement. "What if it's drug lords or federal agents with guns?"

Surprised, Preston sat up straight in his chair. "Why would drug lords or federal agents come here?"

Page laughed. "That's the five-million-dollar question, isn't it?" He leaned back and smiled devilishly at Loretta. He'd never even hinted about the stolen millions to any outsider before. It felt almost cleansing. He relished the feeling. Loretta looked totally astonished, and Jack completely dumbfounded. Page laughed in delight again.

"Are you serious?" Preston asked, still half believing it was a joke.

Page's smile vanished. "Dead serious, and it's not your fight."

Preston stared blank-eyed at Page as he got to his feet. "I think I'll make tracks now, rather than wait until morning."

"Good idea." Page rose, shook Preston's hand, thanked him, and watched as he walked way. "That went well," he announced sardonically.

Jack's expression had altered to disbelief. Loretta was smiling, eyes bright.

"I can't stay here," Alice said, clenching her shaking hands.

"You'll be fine, I promise," Page replied. "You'll have a safe place in the house, if need be."

"What safe place?" Alice demanded, her eyes fearful.

He walked over to Loretta and picked her up in his arms. She quickly kissed him and snuggled against his chest. "I'll show it to you in a little while."

He kissed Loretta on the cheek. "Are you doing all right?"

"I am. Do me a favor."

"Anything."

She leaned close to his cheek and whispered in his ear.

Page listened and laughed. "Of course I will. After you get settled for the night."

He carried her upstairs, helped her change into her nightie, and promised to return shortly. In the library, he showed Alice how to open the wall of books that hid the safe room. It contained all the necessities: a bed, toilet, hand sink, small refrigerator, cooktop, and a week's supply of food and water.

"Come here if you get scared."

"What about Loretta?"

"I'll take care of her. You won't get hurt, Alice. I promise."

"What's going to happen?"

Page shrugged. "Actually, I don't know. But you'll be just fine."

He left her at the foot of the stairs and joined Jack on the deck, the fire crackling, the smell of piñon wood wafting in the night air. "You reported the downed plane, didn't you?" he said.

"I did. Wasn't about to let this place burn down, unless we torched it ourselves."

Page nodded understandingly. "Why don't you spend the night here with us?"

"Nope, I sleep better in my own bed."

"Suit yourself."

"Do we have a plan?" Jack asked.

"When the shooting starts, protect yourself."

Jack nodded. "You can count on it." An anguished look welled up. "I know this is all because of me, making you put me up in the veterans center after I busted my leg, just because I got plain lonely for some new company."

Page squeezed Jack's shoulder. "You did nothing wrong. I let my guard down. I should have said no."

"I guess that's true." Jack pulled himself upright, reached for his walker, and started for the double patio doors at the back of the house. "I'll come up in the morning for breakfast."

"See you then."

Page waited until Jack beeped his horn to signal he'd made it safely to his truck. He doused the fire and went upstairs to his bedroom. It took him a while to do as Loretta had asked. When he finished cutting off his beard and ponytail, he hacked off more of his hair to shorten it, shaved, showered, dressed in fresh jeans and a T-shirt, and padded barefooted into Loretta's bedroom. She was in bed, half asleep with a book on her lap.

He stroked her face, her eyes fluttered open, and she stared at him in amazement, smiling delightedly. "How handsome you are. You look ten years younger."

He squeezed her hand and grinned. "Don't try to sweet-talk me unless you mean it. We can still fly out of here. Say the word."

"For another hospital bed and a view out a window?"

"It would be a breathtaking view. A change of scenery might do you good."

"What about Jack?"

"I could bind and gag him, and toss him in the plane."

Loretta shook her head. "He's right to stay put. We'll stay with him."

"Affirmative." Page kissed her. "Get some sleep."

"Send Alice in, please."

"Will do." He kissed her again and turned to find Alice entering the bedroom. He said good night and went downstairs for a nightcap.

He'd often speculated how they'd get caught, but he never thought an old murder he had nothing to do with, and Loretta's long-lost friend, would be their undoing.

———

"Close the door," Loretta said to Alice after Page left. Alice did as asked, and approached the bed with pills and a glass of water in her hand. Loretta waved them away. "Not yet. In the nightstand you'll find my phone. Do you know how to use it?"

"Of course."

"Please get it. I want you to video-record a statement I'm going to make." Using the remote, she adjusted the bed so she could sit upright. Alice stifled a quizzical look, got the phone, and checked to make sure it was charged. "What's this all about, Loretta?"

"You'll see." She'd left her makeup on to look better. "Do you know how to upload video from a phone to a computer and stream it on YouTube?"

"Yes."

"Promise me you'll do it?"

"I promise."

Loretta smiled her appreciation. "Good. Put a copy on my tablet and the library computer as soon as we're finished, and wait to stream it until you leave the ranch. If you can't do that, take a copy to the police."

"When will I be leaving?"

"I think very soon. Ready?"

Alice stood at the foot of the bed, pointed the camera phone at Loretta, and nodded.

Sara refused to leave the hospital until Sid was stabilized and moved to ICU. He was scheduled for surgery in the morning and his doctor predicted the chances of a full recovery were good. At his bedside, Sid squeezed her hand and thanked her for saving his life. Sara gave him a peck on the cheek and told him to get well fast.

Driven back to the cottage by Clayton and Dalquist, she arrived with a bruised forehead, a stiff back, and some painkillers she promptly threw away. After sending them out of her room and calling Kerney to reassure him, she collapsed into a dreamless sleep and woke twelve hours later, groggy and still a little sore. One look in the bathroom mirror at the lump on her head convinced her that near-death experiences did nothing for a woman's looks.

A hot shower, fresh clothes, and some makeup improved her disposition. She sat in a bedroom chair by an open window listening to the sweet sound of a songbird for a minute, before calling Kerney again as promised.

"I was starting to get worried," he said when he picked up.

"Sorry to be so late calling," Sara replied. "I'm just now fully awake."

"That's okay. How are you?"

"Except for an ugly lump on my head and a tiny headache, I'm fine."

"I never know what fine means when you say it."

"I'm okay, although I feel I could sleep another twelve hours. How are you?"

"Getting better every day. I'm on my feet and the physical therapy for my shoulder is helping. I've been thinking, maybe we should back off, give the ball to Dalquist, and take our chances at trial."

"What made you even think something so preposterous?"

"Two men are dead, including a young police officer. I've been shot, and you almost got killed in a plane crash. Then there's Clayton's ruined career and putting Flavio in harm's way. That's enough. I don't want anybody else getting hurt, physically or otherwise."

"We can't stop now," Sara said firmly.

"We're stalled and not making any progress."

"Listen to yourself. Let's declare defeat and slink home, tail between our legs."

Kerney groaned. "That's not what I'm saying. Come home for now."

"I'm not coming home yet. We'll see this through. I love you, Kerney, but I have to go. Give Patrick a kiss for me."

She disconnected and went looking for Dalquist and Clayton. They were downstairs in the guest cottage kitchen, sitting at the table. Both men looked at her with concerned expressions. The stove clock read ten-fifteen. She poured a cup of coffee and joined them.

"Sorry I slept so late," she said.

"Are you okay?" Clayton asked.

"I'm coming around." She took a sip. The coffee was perfect.

"Perhaps you should go home for a while," Dalquist advised.

Sara smiled. "Kerney said the same thing, and as much as I appreciate your advice, I'm staying."

"I didn't mean to sound paternalistic."

"You didn't." She took another sip. "Let's stay on mission. Apparently, Earl and Jack Page are not survivalists tucked away in a remote area of the national forest. So, where are they?"

"Clayton raised an interesting point last night," Dalquist replied. "Jack Page lied to his buddy at the veterans center about Earl's identity. He well could have lied about the ranch."

"Describing it as inaccessible could mean a lot of things," Clayton added.

"Such as?" Sara asked.

"I talked to a man yesterday whose father knew Jack Page when he ranched in Duncan, Arizona. The guy owns a salvage yard that Earl and

Jack occasionally patronized. He swore he knew nothing about them, other than who they were. He knew zero about the ranch, where it is, or who works there, except for a guy he hasn't seen in a couple of years who may have known the Pages."

Sara's expression brightened. "We've been thinking small, when we should have been thinking big, both in terms of who and what we're looking for."

Dalquist nodded. "Our best strategy might be concentrating on large properties on both sides of the New Mexico–Arizona line. Focusing on those property owners—individual, corporate, full-time, part-time, absentee, or otherwise—who value their privacy."

"Other than the salvage yard operator, nobody admits to knowing Jack or Earl," Clayton added. "I suspect some of those I talked to were lying. What if Page has confidentiality agreements with employees, suppliers, contractors, and anyone who visits the ranch?"

"A common thing among celebrities and the very rich," Dalquist noted.

"Maybe we've been thinking small in terms of Page's current net worth, as well," Sara replied. "What's next?"

Clayton consulted his notepad. "We've been doing Internet research. Duncan is a tiny village with not much to it. Seven, eight hundred citizens; rural folks who tend to stay put. We start there and if necessary move on to the closest town, Stafford, about forty miles west. Somebody has got to know something."

"I'll keep researching large private landholdings between here and Stafford," Dalquist proposed. "So far we've identified two across the state line we hadn't considered before."

"Let's do it. But first, I desperately need food."

Dalquist rose. "I'm considered a fair cook. Would soft-scrambled eggs, bacon, and toast do?"

"Perfect," Sara replied.

CHAPTER 27

After finding his truck burglarized and stripped near the mouth of Barranco Canyon, Clayton had canceled his appointment to interview Lucille Trimble a second time.

On their way out the door to Duncan, he told Sara that he'd arranged a late morning meeting with Trimble at an assisted living facility in Hurley, where she had been temporarily placed.

"Louise Fowler, her court-appointed guardian, will meet us there," he added.

"Is it worth the effort?" Sara asked.

"Trimble was basically incomprehensible when I spoke to her. But she was traumatized by the shoot-out and Marks's death, so we might have better luck this time. We can go together, if you like."

Sara climbed into the passenger seat of Clayton's SUV. "Did you learn anything of value from her the first time around?"

"Just what you already know. She has a nasty mouth, and seems to think she was married to Marks, which is delusional and more than a little weird. There was no marriage certificate among the legal docu-

ments I found at the double-wide, and according to Steve Campos, the
SO doesn't have it in evidence."

Clayton wheeled the SUV off the secluded grounds of the B&B
and onto the pavement. "Talking to a woman might be less stressful
for her," he said. "Want to take a crack at it?"

"Definitely." Sara had grown accustomed to the ugly strip of commercial and retail clutter along the highway leading out of town and
now barely noticed it. "She wasn't totally incoherent?"

"No, she knew her ABCs," Clayton replied with a grin. "At least
some of them."

"That's a start."

Clayton's phone buzzed. It was Dalquist. The Grant County Sheriff's Office had just booked two drug addicts into jail on vandalism and
burglary charges. They'd been caught with items from the Barranco
Canyon double-wide. That tidied up a loose end. Clayton gave Sara
the news.

———

Hurley, a working-class mining village, bleeding jobs and losing population, hugged the east side of the highway to Deming. The family-
owned assisted living facility sat on a side street across from a vacant
lot. Originally a sprawling ranch-style family dwelling, it had been
transformed by a second-story addition that loomed over a front yard
of freshly cut grass, an old, carefully pruned ash tree, and two flower
beds filled with yellow marigolds that bordered the walkway to the
front porch.

The proprietors, a middle-aged couple named Onita and Angus
McFarland, greeted them in a large, modern kitchen that had been
tacked onto the rear of the original house. Beyond, through a sliding
glass patio door, a tall concrete-block wall enclosed a rear yard with
benches, picnic tables, and several large shade trees.

Louise Fowler had yet to arrive.

With a rosy red nose and lopsided smile, Angus McFarland loomed over his petite, brown-skinned wife, who was busy wiping down the stainless-steel sink.

"Lucille has been no trouble at all," Angus said reassuringly, as he gestured for Clayton and Sara to sit at the long, rectangular dining table. On the wall next to the kitchen door, a state license to operate the facility was prominently displayed along with a health department food inspection certificate.

Sara eased into a chair. "That's good to know." Pots and pans hung on a rack above the sink. A nearby footstool allowed Onita to reach them.

Onita turned away from the sink, drying her hands on a dish towel. "Louise said to wait for her before you see Lucille."

"Of course," Clayton said. "Has Lucille been talking at all?"

"Oh, yes," Onita said. "But not to make any sense or have a real conversation. She refuses to leave her room. We sit with her regularly."

"She does keep asking for Todd," Angus added, as he served mugs of coffee to Clayton and Sara. "From what we know happened, it's very sad."

"Indeed, it is," Sara replied.

While they waited for Fowler, the McFarlands told them about their facility. They lived on the premises in a second-floor apartment, and served a maximum of ten residents, whom they referred to as "guests," each with their own private room.

Because Lucille would be with them for only a short time, she'd been given a furnished room specifically used for short-term placements. At Fowler's request, a deputy had fetched some of Lucille's clothing and a few personal items that had been taken into evidence from the double-wide.

"Most of our guests keep family mementos in their rooms," Onita explained. "In Lucille's case, there wasn't much to bring."

"Perfectly understandable," Clayton said. "What personal items did the deputy bring?"

"I have it right here." Angus said. He reached for a three-hole binder on a shelf behind the table. "We do an inventory for each guest."

He paged through the binder, found the inventory, and passed it to Clayton. Sara scooted closer to get a better look.

In addition to an accounting of all of Lucille's clothing, the list included toiletries, a purse containing a wallet, a framed photograph of a young sailor in uniform, and a black leather pocket prayer book.

"Where are these items now?" Sara asked.

"In her room," Angus answered.

Just as Sara was about to ask for permission to meet with Trimble, Fowler arrived.

"Sorry to be late," Fowler said, smiling apologetically, explaining she'd been delayed by a phone call from a judge.

Sara got to her feet and shook Fowler's hand. "No problem. I'm Sara Brannon."

Fowler smiled and put her purse on the table. "Nice to meet you."

"And you as well." Sara replied. "I'm sorry to be so abrupt, but can we proceed?"

Fowler glanced from Sara to Clayton. "Is there a rush?"

"Lucille has some items in her room we'd like to look at," Clayton answered. "It might be helpful."

"I see." Fowler glanced at Onita and Angus McFarland. "I'll escort them. We won't be long."

She ushered them through a communal living room where two old ladies at a card table were busy working on a large puzzle, and down a long hallway where open bedroom doors gave glimpses into the small rooms, some filled with treasured furniture and objects, others sparsely decorated. In one room, an old man sat in a rocking chair, eyes closed, snoring softly.

The door to Trimble's room at the end of the hall was open. She sat stiff and unmoving at the foot of her bed staring out a window that gave a view of the front yard and brought sunlight into an otherwise tidy but bleak room.

The photograph of a sailor sat on top of a chest of drawers next to a candlestick bedroom lamp. Her purse was on the bedside table, but the wallet and prayer book were nowhere in sight. A small padded armchair positioned in a corner near the closet was the only other furniture in the room.

Fowler's cheery greeting went unnoticed. To get Lucille's attention, she gently tapped her on the shoulder. Lucille remained unresponsive.

"Except for asking about Todd, she's only spoken gibberish and curse words since she left the hospital," Fowler explained.

Sara knelt in front of Trimble and said, "Lucille, we'd like to look around your room if that's all right with you."

Lucille's eyes fluttered open.

"Would it bother you if I took the photograph out of the frame?"

Her eyes fluttered shut.

"Would you like to talk to me about Todd?"

Lucille shook her head.

"Do we have your permission to search?" Clayton asked Fowler.

"Go ahead." She stepped into the open doorway to watch.

The sailor in the black-and-white photograph was very young, yet somehow familiar-looking to Sara. He wore a traditional navy jumper with two stripes on the left sleeve denoting a very junior rating as a seaman apprentice.

Sara carefully removed the photograph from the frame. Handwriting on the back read: "Jack home on leave, 1951."

She looked more closely at the young man's face. Was it Jack Page? Stamped on the back was the name of the photographer who'd taken the portrait: "Charles Stedman, Hotel Cochran, Main Street, Duncan, AZ."

It had to be Jack Page. She turned to tell Clayton, who held up the pocket prayer book he'd found tucked between the mattress and box spring of the bed.

"Listen to this entry from the back of the book," he said. " 'Maureen Trimble married Elliot Page in 1927. They had two children, Jack, born in 1929, and Lucille, born in 1932. Lucille had Kim born in 1949, father unlisted. Jack had two children with Jann, Louis born in 1948, and Loretta in '51. Trimble was her mother's maiden name.' "

Sara handed Clayton the photograph. "Here's Jack, before he shipped out during the Korean War. Jack Page was Kim's uncle."

"And Loretta her first cousin," Clayton added.

Sara shook her head. "One night in Deming, Kerney suggested everybody we were looking for was somehow connected. Kim's murder, her mother gone missing. Todd the same. All tied to Jack and Earl. Throw in Loretta, and the picture is complete. What was in her purse?"

"A wallet, some facial tissues, three pennies, and a lipstick. There are some old snapshots of a young boy and girl on horseback in front of a ranch house, inscribed 'Jack and Lucille' on the back."

Clayton handed Sara the faded, hand-trimmed prints. "That's it. I don't think Lucille and Todd were married. The first time I spoke to her, she showed me the wedding band she's wearing. It belonged to Kim."

"How did she get that?" Sara asked.

Clayton shrugged. "Maybe Todd took it off Kim's body." He turned to Fowler. "I saw a printer-copier in the kitchen. Do you think the McFarlands would mind if we use it?"

"I'm sure they won't."

Sara knelt in front of Lucille, who hadn't moved an inch since the single shake of her head. "You'll get everything right back, I promise."

Lucille's eyes fluttered open.

"Would you like to tell me about Todd?" Sara gently urged. "Is there something about him you'd like to say?"

"Go fuck yourself," Lucille replied.

CHAPTER 28

Oliver Muniz got nothing useful from White Sands Missile Range or the Border Patrol about Sara Brannon's reconnaissance flight over the Gila National Forest. He left Glenwood hoping for a solid lead in Duncan, Arizona.

Never a fan of small-town America, Muniz didn't find much to like in Duncan, although he had to give the town credit for trying to stay alive. It was situated along the Gila River with a highway and a railroad running through it. Many of the old buildings that fronted the road, occupied or vacant, had been given a fresh coat of paint. Recently installed replicas of old-fashioned lampposts lined the street, and an inviting town park sat near one of the village restaurants.

Duncan boasted two celebrities in its past, retired Supreme Court Justice Sandra Day O'Connor, whose family had ranched nearby, and Charles Stedman, a photographer who chronicled the community until his death in 1960. Justice O'Connor had a memorial walkway along the highway near the high school, and a dozen of Stedman's most iconic regional photographs commanded a wall in the town hall.

Three hotels, all early twentieth century brick buildings, served
tourists and travelers, including the Hotel Cochran on Main Street.
Muniz had booked himself into the spacious Charles Stedman Suite,
complete with a private bath. Owned by Stedman's grandson, the hotel
featured framed landscapes by the locally renowned photographer, copies of which could be purchased in the lobby.

The tourist season hadn't started, and Muniz was the only guest for
the night. He signed the hotel register as a civilian.

The Cochran sat directly across from a hotel that had been converted into a bed-and-breakfast catering to vegetarians. A meat-and-
potatoes man, Muniz had thankfully discovered a local steakhouse
within walking distance on the highway.

The address Earl had listed on his DEA beneficiaries form was on
High Street, a dirt road a few hundred yards away from the hotel at the
base of a small hill with a Veterans Park at the summit. A decommis-
sioned Air Force F-100 Super Sabre jet mounted on a pedestal, poised
as if on takeoff, crowned the top of the hill. On the road to the park,
the local American Legion post occupied a single-story former schoolhouse with peeling pale stucco.

The High Street address took Muniz to a weedy lot filled with
concrete rubble and badly charred roof timbers scattered around the
crumbling remains of a fireplace and chimney. Next door, a small travel
trailer, minus tires and wheels, sat on a concrete pad with a handicapped
ramp leading to the door. A boxy faded green Subaru station wagon
parked near the ramp sported an Arizona disability license plate.

The young, overweight woman who answered his knock eyed him
suspiciously, until he showed his DEA credentials.

"You're not from the welfare checking on my mom? She's asleep
right now."

"No, I'm interested in knowing what happened to the house
next door."

The woman shrugged, and her double chin jiggled. "It's been that way since we moved in."

"How long is that?" Muniz asked.

"Three years, but I heard the place burned down a long time ago."

"Do you have neighbors who might be able to tell me more?"

"We keep to ourselves. Did something bad happen there?"

Muniz shrugged. "I don't know. Thanks for your time."

At his vehicle, he debated if a door-to-door canvass during working hours would be worth the effort. Dilapidated cottages and neglected single-wide trailers on concrete blocks along the street were obviously lived in, but an absence of vehicles suggested few, if any, people were home.

Jack Page's dossier included a summary of his service during the Korean War. Perhaps Page had been a member of the American Legion. But as Muniz expected, there was no one to answer his knock at the door.

Surely, in a town of eight hundred, somebody knew something about Jack Page and the burned-down cottage. Muniz decided to start with his innkeeper. Charles Stedman lived in the building adjacent to the Hotel Cochran, which, according to the plaque outside, had once been Mendelsohn's Mercantile Store. Stedman was more than willing to answer Muniz's innocent questions about Duncan.

Settled into an easy chair in the front living room, the walls filled with gold-tone portraits of early Duncan pioneers taken by his host's grandfather, Muniz learned about the big flood in the seventies that had almost destroyed the town, the birders who came to wander the riverside walking trail with binoculars in hand, and, of course, the personal history of Grandfather Stedman, who'd set up his photography studio in the early twentieth century.

When Stedman paused for breath, Muniz asked about Jack Page. "I was friends with his son Earl a long time ago," he said. "I'm hoping to reconnect."

"Everyone knew Jack and his daughter, Loretta. They lived up on High Street."

"I stopped by there," Muniz said. "Nothing but rubble."

"Place burned down about a year after Jack and Loretta left town. Fortunately, nobody was staying there at the time. Fire chief said it was arson, probably kids."

Muniz wondered if Earl had burned the place down. He'd always been attentive to small details. "Do you know where Jack moved to?"

"I sure don't," Stedman replied. "Up until a year or so ago, he'd return occasionally to visit his buddies at the American Legion. I'd see him down at the steakhouse with some of the other old vets, sharing a meal and telling war stories."

"I tried the legion hall."

"With the old-timers dying off and the younger vets who've come home not interested in joining, membership has dropped. Your best bet would be talking to the post commander, Tim Lunt. He's a Vietnam vet who was a good friend of Jack's. He manages the county fairgrounds."

"Where are the fairgrounds?"

"Take Main Street across the river, turn left at the church, and you're there. What's your connection with Jack Page's son, if you don't mind my asking?"

"We worked together in law enforcement. Now that I'm about to retire, I decided to look him up." Muniz hoped retirement wasn't imminent. It would be nice to serve a few more years with the stain of Earl's betrayal scrubbed clean.

Stedman nodded. "That explains the car you're driving. I thought it looked very much like an unmarked police vehicle."

"It is," Muniz confirmed as he got to his feet. The black Explorer with the distinctive antennas and U.S. government license plates was hard to miss. "Tim Lunt is the fairground manager?"

"Yes. He shouldn't be hard to find."

———

Muniz took the first left over the river, drove past the Mormon church, and turned onto the fairgrounds parking lot entrance a few hundred feet down the road. The manager's office was in a white building next to a racetrack. According to a sign mounted on the wall, the office was open from nine to four, Monday through Friday, and Saturday by appointment. A scribbled note taped to the door read: "Back in Twenty Minutes." Muniz waited an hour for a white pickup truck to coast to a stop next to his SUV.

A lanky man in his late sixties got out and asked if he could help.

"Tim Lunt?" Muniz asked.

"That's me," Lunt said. "Hope I haven't made you wait too long."

"Not at all." Muniz displayed his credentials. "I'm trying to find Jack Page. I've been told you're a friend of his."

"What do you need to see Jack for?" Lunt asked warily.

Muniz smiled reassuringly. "Nothing bad, I assure you. In fact, it's good news. Mr. Page is entitled to a supplemental beneficiary payment recently approved by my agency. I just need to get his signature on a few forms so we can cut him a check."

Lunt's concerned look passed. "Jack would never turn down free money. He's been gone from here a good twenty-five years or more. He lives over in New Mexico, I don't know exactly where."

"Can you point me in a general direction?"

"It's a ranch, I know that. He used to come visit at the legion post and brag about it being a big, fancy spread. Never gave us an address, but one time I was driving up to Socorro to see my sister, and he was right in front of me on the highway. Recognized his truck. I was about to wave him over when he turned off onto a dirt road, so I just kept going."

"Where was that?"

"On 180 near Alma. I asked him about it the next time I saw him. Said he was just visiting a friend."

"That's north of Glenwood, right?"

"Yes, sir."

Muniz opened the driver's door to the Explorer. "I appreciate your time."

"Say howdy to Jack when you see him."

Muniz responded with a toothy grin. "I sure will."

———

Back at the Hotel Cochran, Oliver Muniz consulted his maps. There were a half dozen county dirt roads that branched off from U.S. Highway 180 near Alma. He'd drive every one of them and probably find a few more that weren't on any maps. He switched to his tablet, searched for information about Alma, and discovered that the famous outlaw Butch Cassidy had once cowboyed at a nearby ranch. Interesting stuff.

There wasn't much to the unincorporated settlement, and the only lodging he could find was a rental bunkhouse at a ranch a few miles away. It offered a stocked pantry and advertised a once-in-a-lifetime cowboy experience. He called, and fortunately it was available.

He opened the bottle of scotch he'd packed in El Paso and poured himself a generous shot. Not to celebrate, but as a reward for progress made.

Muniz raised his glass and said, "Here I come, Earl, ready or not."

CHAPTER 29

Paul Avery waited an hour to interview Bud Elkins at the Fort Bayard Veterans Center. When he finally showed up the meeting started out poorly.

"I've got nothing more to say to the police," Elkins sputtered.

Avery put his shield away. "Why is that, Mr. Elkins?"

"I read in the paper yesterday that a magistrate judge dismissed the charges against one of those jokers who came here impersonating cops."

"I can understand how that would upset you."

Elkins leaned forward in his wheelchair. "Cops, lawyers, judges. Phooey!"

"He's an ex-cop trying to solve a murder. That's not a bad thing, is it?"

Elkins raised an eyebrow. "You're on his side."

"No, I'm not," Avery replied emphatically. "He screwed up and lost his job. But I also want to solve the murder. I'll do it the right way, if you'll help me."

Elkins gripped the arms of his wheelchair. "Jack Page is no killer. He's a good man."

"I believe you." Avery shifted closer. "I'm not looking at Jack as a murderer. That hasn't entered my mind. But he—or someone in his family—might know who killed a pretty, young woman many years ago. I just need to find them and ask a few questions."

Elkins sneered. "You're trying to clear that ex-police chief's name."

Avery shook his head. "If he's guilty, I'll gladly do my best to make sure he goes to prison and stays locked up for a long time."

Elkins looked doubtful.

"I mean what I say." Avery paused to let his words sink in and then took a different tack. "Jack was a good friend, wasn't he?"

Elkins's expression softened. "Damn good friend, while he was here. Least he got to leave. I ain't going nowhere. Got Lou Gehrig's disease. Pretty soon I won't be able to get out of this damn wheelchair and walk around."

"I'm sorry to hear it. That's got to be hard on a man like you."

Elkins nodded appreciatively. "Jack knew how much I hated the idea of becoming completely housebound. We'd talked about me going to the ranch on a furlough before it got too bad. Man, I was really looking forward to it."

"Maybe you can still go," Avery suggested. "I'll remind him about the furlough idea when I see him. Did he ever talk about the ranch?"

"He was real proud of it. Said he had his own place, and his boy lived with his wife in a beautiful ranch house a mile away. They even have a ranch manager."

"Did he say where it was?"

"Not really, except one time he grinned and said it was near where the Wild Bunch once roamed."

"The Wild Bunch?"

Elkins nodded. "An old-time cowboy gang of thieves and robbers, is what he told me."

"Have you been in touch with Jack since he left?"

"I sent him a note and he called after he got it."

"Why did you write?"

"So that he'd know cops were looking for his boy. At the time, I didn't know they were imposters."

"What did you talk about?"

"Same thing, those two ex-cops who came here pretending to be the real McCoy."

"That's it?"

"More or less."

"Do you have his address?"

"In my room."

Avery followed Elkins, who refused to let him push the wheel-chair, into the patient living area, down a long hallway with private rooms on each side. Bud's room had a shelf of paperback novels and a large reproduction of an old navy recruiting poster featuring a pretty WAVE, framed and hung on the wall. A photograph of young Elkins in uniform standing on the foredeck of a destroyer sat on his bedside table. On the table was a cell phone.

Jack Page's address was a box number at the Silver City Post Office. Avery wrote it down, and asked Elkins if he'd received Jack's phone call through the center or on his personal cell phone.

"On my cell phone, why?"

"Did you save the number?"

Elkins grabbed his phone. "I never erase anything."

"I'd like to have that number."

"I don't have to give you that. You've already got his mailing address."

Avery shook his head in dismay. "This is not the time to become uncooperative, Bud."

"Why is that?" Elkins snapped.

"Because it's a crime not to assist an officer conducting a lawful investigation when you have the ability to do so. It's called obstructing justice."

Elkins snorted and handed Avery the phone. "There's a law against everything. Damn country is going to hell."

Avery scrolled through the incoming call log. There were dozens of entries. "When did Jack call?"

"I don't remember, but it was the last call I got."

"You're sure?"

Bud nodded.

Avery found it, wrote down the number, which had a 907 area code, and handed the phone back to Elkins. "Thanks."

"You gonna leave me alone now?" Bud grumbled.

"If that's what you want."

He shook Bud's hand and left. In the parking lot he looked up the 907 area code. It covered Alaska except for a tiny community in the southeastern part of the state near the border to British Columbia. He dialed the number and got a "no longer in service" message. Probably a burn phone, he figured. He headed for the post office.

————

North Hudson Street, a major thoroughfare, ran past the historical part of Silver City where the charm of the town was safely encapsulated and out of sight of the sprawl of relentless growth. The post office was a relatively new facility. Inside, Avery learned that Jack Page had been a box holder continuously for over twenty-five years. The street address on the original application was on High Street in Duncan, Arizona. The box had been renewed annually by credit card.

Without proper authorization from a postal inspector, no further information could be released.

He left a note asking the inspector to call, and drove to his no-frills budget motel on the U.S. 180 strip. Inside his room, he cranked up his laptop, searched for "wild bunch," and came up with two different gangs. The Doolin-Dalton Gang had operated out of Oklahoma. Butch Cassidy's Gang had worked on a ranch near Alma, New Mexico, for a time. Avery knew about Butch Cassidy and the Sundance Kid, had seen the movie years ago, but didn't recall anything about a New Mexico hideout.

Was it a true story, or just a folktale? He needed verification. He found an online magazine article that gave credence to the story, citing a British army captain who'd met Cassidy at a ranch near Alma, where he'd been employed as the assistant ranch manager under the alias Jim Lowe.

A website out of Wyoming had Cassidy owning a saloon in Alma, also under the name of Jim Lowe.

To be certain it wasn't all malarkey, Avery searched for one more citation, and found it in a South Dakota historical journal. The article said that William Ellsworth Lay, one of Cassidy's best friends and gang members, had signed on with him at the Alma ranch in 1898.

That sealed it for Avery. Alma was where he had to go. But first he wanted to pinpoint the location. Nearly all prepaid cell phone providers piggybacked on the major communication networks. He accessed a website that would identify the cell towers between Silver City and Reserve, the county seat of Catron County. Four major cellular phone companies used common towers in the area that extended to Glenwood, sixty miles north. But beyond Glenwood to Reserve it was almost a dead zone, with only two towers operating. Both were rated poorly, with spotty reception and weak signal strength.

About to give up, Avery scrolled through consumer reviews on the off chance Jack Page may have complained about his service, until an advertisement popped up about cell towers or cell sites private individuals could lease. It hadn't occurred to Avery that ordinary folks could do that.

Maybe Jack Page was forced to drive somewhere to get adequate reception to make a wireless call. Or maybe he had access to a privately leased cell tower.

A quick search told him there were over three hundred thousand cell towers in the country. Avery found a federal government website that showed the location of cell towers nationwide. He zeroed in on a map of the western half of New Mexico, and there it was, a cell tower leased and operated by SM Enterprises outside of Alma, New Mexico.

He switched to a search for accommodations in Alma, found only one, a ranch bunkhouse already booked, and settled on a cabin in Glenwood, a few miles south. In ten minutes he was packed, checked out, in his unmarked unit, and on his way.

———

The owner of the Glenwood cabins, Darryl Wheatley, took Avery's state–government–issued credit card, looked at the unmarked police unit parked in front of the office, and shook his head as he processed the charge.

"What?" Avery asked.

Wheatley scratched his mustache. "Must be something going on. I had DEA agents staying here. Last one left yesterday. Now you."

Avery's interest was piqued. "DEA? You're sure?"

"Yeah, looking for some fugitive hiding out in the woods, or something like that."

"That's what they said?"

Wheatley nodded in the direction of the diner across the road. "That's what they talked about over dinner."

"You know that for sure?"

"The wife runs the place. Ask her."

"I will. Know of anybody in the area around Alma with a cell tower on their property?"

Wheatley's congenial expression faded. "Can't say that I do." He handed Avery his credit card and a key. "Cabin three. Enjoy your stay."

At the diner, Avery ordered lunch and, while he waited, questioned Wheatley's wife, Karen, a woman with thick arms and a wide body.

"They were sure looking for someone," Karen said, "but I didn't catch a name. Two of them left that night while the other one stayed on. Are you looking for the same fella?"

"Right now I'm trying to find a cell tower. Know of any nearby?"

"Don't think there is one, or I'd have heard about it. Your meal will be up shortly." She stepped away to clear a recently vacated table.

Avery's cell phone had a signal strength of two, meaning there was wireless service, but not what he'd hoped for. As he waited for his meal he studied the landscape watercolors of local scenes hung on the walls, all painted by Eunice Sommerville, an eighty-nine-year-old resident. He wondered if Eunice would also lie to him if he asked her about a cell tower.

Who were the DEA agents looking for? Somebody growing pot in the national forest? A Mexican mule running drugs across the border? His meal came, and he dug in. No sense ruminating on an empty stomach. After dinner, he'd get the names of the cops who'd stayed at the cabins and run their license plate numbers from the guest log.

CHAPTER 30

Before breakfast, Clayton gave Dalquist his notes and asked him to find a way to run a quiet background check on Carl Yeager, the salvage yard owner. He reached out to a small-town New Mexico police chief who owed him a favor. When the report arrived, it showed Yeager had lied about never living in Duncan. Plus, he'd been busted twice for DWI and arrested once for failure to pay child support. He was currently thousands of dollars behind in payments for his three children to the California Department of Child Support Services.

Dalquist decided to pay Yeager a visit. He found him alone in his small office, eating a microwaved burrito.

"What can I do for you?" he asked between bites.

Dalquist smiled. "The more important question is, what can I do for you?"

Yeager looked at Dalquist in his expensive suit, white shirt, and tie, and scowled. "You a lawyer?"

Dalquist nodded.

"How did the bitch find me?"

"She hasn't yet. That's entirely up to you."

"How so?"

"Answer a few questions, and I won't tell her where you are."

"What questions?"

"You spoke to a colleague of mine recently about a man named Jack Page."

"Yeah, I remember."

"Do Jack and his son pay you for your silence?"

Yeager's eyes widened. "Not me, but I've heard about that from some folks up in Catron County."

"Did you hear it from a man named Vic, who might have worked for the Pages?"

Yeager nodded.

"Tell me about Vic," Dalquist said.

"Like I told the other guy, I just knew his name, that's all."

Dalquist shook his head. "I'm thinking either Vic was a good customer you got to know, or you knew him from before. Why didn't you admit you'd lived in Duncan?"

Yeager licked his lips. "Vic isn't from Duncan."

Dalquist smiled. "So you do know him. What's his full name?"

"Knew him," Yeager countered. "Victor Landis. I haven't seen him in several years."

Dalquist pushed. "Why lie about not knowing him?"

"He asked me to. Said he'd get fired if his bosses found out he had any family in Duncan."

"Why is that?"

Yeager shrugged. "He didn't say. He grew up on a ranch outside of Willcox and when his parents divorced, his mother remarried. Her and her new husband bought an old, rundown hotel in Duncan, fixed it up, and turned it into a bed-and-breakfast."

"How did you meet Vic?"

"He came into my pa's auto repair shop needing a new water pump for his truck. He was visiting his mom at the hotel. Wasn't like we were best friends."

"What's the name of the hotel?"

"The Gleason Hotel."

"What happened to Vic?"

Yeager shook his head. "Man, I don't know. He just stopped showing up. I figured he moved on to another job. Maybe his mom knows."

"You've been very helpful."

"You won't tell my ex-wife where I am?"

Dalquist smiled. "Of course not. I'm a man of my word."

In his car, Dalquist searched the National Missing Persons Database for Victor Landis. He'd been reported missing three and a half years ago by his mother, Renee Gleason, of Duncan. His last known address was a ranch at an undisclosed location in Catron County, New Mexico.

Dalquist called Sara, who was with Clayton. They were thirty minutes outside of Duncan. He updated her about Victor Landis, his mother Renee, the Gleason Hotel, and a mysterious ranch somewhere in Catron County.

"You and Clayton should return after you finish in Duncan," he suggested. "All roads seem to be leading to Catron County. It would be nice if you can get an actual location."

"I agree," Sara replied. "We'll let you know what we find out."

Dalquist disconnected, and dialed the California Department of Child Support Services. When he finished squealing on Carl Yeager while preserving his good word not to call his ex-wife, he called Merlin Root, the Catron County sheriff, and asked if he could meet with him at the diner in Glenwood the next morning at eight.

"What's it about?" Root asked.

"The Kerney investigation. I may need some law enforcement assistance."

"Should I bring a deputy?"

"No, I'm hoping to have a peaceful conversation with an Alma rancher, but I may need your help gaining entry to his property."

"Who's the rancher?"

"Louis Page and his father, Jack."

"I'll see you in the morning," Root replied.

———

Sara Brannon had come to appreciate the harsh beauty of the desert and the formidable barren mountain peaks that drew her attention no matter how close or far away. But she yearned for a greenery different from the high mountain pine forests of the Gila Wilderness and the vast lowlands mesquite and creosote. Entering the verdant farming settlement of Virden along the Gila River took her breath away.

Sheltered on both sides of a valley by the shoulders of soft hills, rich farmland stretched along the river, lush and green. So different from the stark dryness and the bleak scale of the desert, Virden gladdened Sara's eyes.

In Duncan, they parked in front of the Gleason Hotel on Main Street, which wasn't by any means the town's principal thoroughfare. That honor belonged to U.S. Highway 70, which cut through the village along the nearby Gila River.

The hotel, a two-story brick building with a bed-and-breakfast sign hung above the locked front door, faced another inn across the street. There was no response when Clayton rang the bell, but a garden gate at the side of the building was open. At the rear of the building they came upon a woman tending a large fenced garden. At the far end of the lot stood a sizable commercial-grade greenhouse. Several housecats lazed about on garden benches and under shade trees near the hotel's back door.

"Can I help you?" the woman asked, as she stepped out of the gar-

den and approached, trowel in hand. It was hard to see her face under
her cowboy hat, but she was trim-looking in a pair of blue jeans and a
long-sleeved pullover.

"Are you Renee Gleason?" Clayton asked.

"Yes."

"We'd like to talk to you about Victor," Sara said.

Renee Gleason's lips trembled. "Have you found him? Do you
know where he is?"

"We have an idea, and hope you can help," Clayton said.

"Yes, yes, of course." Gleason gestured at the back door. "Come
in, please. Let me get my husband."

She ushered them to a small sitting area adjacent to the front lobby
and hurried upstairs. Framed drawings and watercolors of botanical
plants were nicely arranged on the walls.

They sat on a small Victorian-style love seat with a large front
window behind them, facing two wooden armchairs across a coffee
table covered with magazines. Renee and her husband, Ed, soon joined
them, both looking anxious and unsettled.

Ed was about the same height as his wife and just as trim. "What
can you tell us?" he asked in a surprisingly deep baritone voice.

"We think Victor's former employer holds the key to his whereabouts," Sara answered.

"We never knew who that was," Renee replied. "Vic said he was
bound by a confidentiality agreement and couldn't discuss anything
about his boss or the ranch."

"Who was his boss?" Ed demanded.

"Let's back up a little bit," Clayton said. "When was the last time
you heard from Vic?"

"It's been three and a half years." Renee jumped to her feet. "He sent
a note that he was quitting his job. Let me get it." She rushed upstairs.

"You're not here with good news, are you?" Ed asked quietly.

Sara smiled. "We don't have bad news for you, Mr. Gleason. We hope to find him."

"Well, for God's sake, if you can't do that, at least find a way to give my wife some peace of mind."

"We'll do our best," Sara said.

Renee returned, thrusting an envelope into Sara's hand. It was post-marked Glenwood, New Mexico, three and a half years ago. It read:

Dear Mom,

I've quit my job as of the end of the month and plan to go north to Canada and find work there on one of those big Alberta out-fits. I hear they're always looking for good hands. Saved up some money, so I'll probably make some sightseeing stops along the way. I'll write when the dust settles. Give my best to Ed.

    Love,
    Vic

"We haven't heard from him since," she said. "He'd never go off like that without visiting first. Another thing: His handwriting's all shaky. He didn't have the best penmanship, but he could write better than that."

"Is he a drinker?" Clayton asked.

"Not a heavy one," Ed replied. "He's a hardworking man who loved his work and enjoyed a drink or two."

Sara leaned toward Renee. "Did Vic ever talk to you about his job, or the ranch?"

"He said the man who owned it was rich and very eccentric, and lived there with his wife and his father. He said everybody had to check in when entering or leaving the property, and there were lots of high-tech security gadgets."

"Were there guards or security officers?" Clayton asked.

"No, just the gadgets," Ed replied. "It didn't bother Vic, because he was mostly out with the livestock or working with the ponies, and the pay was really good."

"That's very helpful," Sara said. "Did he ever tell you where it was?"

Renee shook her head. "No, but on his last visit, he said the ranch had an electronic gate with a speaker phone, keypad, and camera. The access code changed every month, and he was always getting into trouble for forgetting it and having to call in."

Clayton and Sara glanced at each other and stood up.

"Thank you for your time," Clayton said.

There were tears in Renee's eyes. "Nobody has come to talk to us about Vic since the day the deputy took the missing person report. Please find him."

Sara took Renee's hand. "We'll let you know what we learn."

Ed Gleason stood. "I'm sorry, you never told us what agency you're with."

"We're with army CID," Sara answered. "Because of national security, I can't tell you more."

Ed nodded soberly. "We understand."

In the car, Clayton shook his head. "That's got to be hard, having a son missing for over three years."

"Awful," Sara agreed.

"Are you thinking foul play?" Clayton asked.

Sara shrugged. "I don't have a clue. Maybe."

Clayton drove to the end of the block and made a U-turn. "Army CID agents, are we?"

"It was the first thing I could think of."

As they crossed Highway 70, Clayton saw a black Ford Explorer with U.S. government plates turn onto Main Street.

CHAPTER 31

It was after dark when Paul Avery got back to his rented cabin in Glenwood, bone-weary from his search for the cell tower, which he'd finally located on a distant foothill. Disguised as a pine tree, it stood on posted private land he'd yet to access, stymied by jeep trails that petered out far from his destination. His unmarked unit took a beating, the undercarriage scraping against rocks, the springs and struts stretched to the limit, and the body scratched and scraped from over-hanging tree branches.

He'd better return with something tangible to show Mondragon, otherwise he'd be chewed out big-time for the damage to the unit. He sat in the vehicle and pulled up the computer search results on the three DEA agents who'd stayed at the cabins. All were out of the El Paso office. He couldn't guess who they were looking for in the backwoods.

The diner across the highway was closed, as was the office for the rental cabins. Two nearby cabins had been rented while he was gone, both to drivers of newer-model SUVs with New Mexico plates. He

could see thin ribbons of light and movement behind closed window curtains.

Hungry, but unwilling to drive miles out of his way for a meal,
he settled on packaged junk food from the snack machine outside the
manager's office, washed it down with the complimentary bottle of
water in his cabin, fell into bed, and woke up in the morning hungry.

Fortunately, the village diner opened early to accommodate local
farmers and ranchers in need of coffee and conversation before continuing their daily chores. Avery showered, dressed, and stepped outside
into the cool, clean air. The two SUVs from last night were still there
and the curtains in the front windows of the cabins were open, but no
one was visible inside.

He crossed the highway to the diner, where a line of parked trucks
testified to a good breakfast crowd. Inside, the clatter of dishes, the
din of conversation among the locals, the cook in the kitchen clanging
about, and a skinny young waitress with a toothy smile whisking by
with plates of food momentarily occupied his attention. A glance at the
back of the room, across tables filled with customers busily chowing
down, made him freeze. Clayton Istee was staring hard at him from a
corner table he shared with Gary Dalquist and Kerney's wife.

Clayton was the last person Avery wanted to see. As he approached,
Clayton stood, a challenging look on his face. For a second, Avery
thought he was going to get punched.

"Join us," Dalquist said congenially, gesturing at the empty chair.
"We're just having our first cup of coffee."

Avery forced a smile and sat.

Clayton returned to his chair, his expression unchanged. "I heard
you got booted off the investigation."

Avery nodded. "Yeah, I was following in your footsteps. But I still
have a job, and you don't."

Clayton's back stiffened.

Dalquist interceded with a broad smile. "No time for quibbling, gentlemen. I'm glad you're here, Mr. Avery. You've met Sara Brannon, haven't you?"

"No, I haven't." Avery smiled thinly at Kerney's wife. "My pleasure, ma'am." He'd been told she was attractive, and that was true enough. But she also looked like she could handle herself.

Sara nodded. "Are you here to keep an eye on us?"

"No," he replied, pausing to order coffee from the waitress. "But I wouldn't mind knowing what you're up to."

"You first," Clayton said.

Avery considered telling the truth, but decided against it. "It has nothing to do with any of you."

Clayton looked doubtful. "I don't believe that."

Avery shrugged. "Like you said, I'm off the case. Why are you here?"

"Stop playing games, Paul," Clayton snapped.

"Don't get in my way, Clayton."

"Or what? You'll arrest me?"

Avery smiled. "Why don't you pay another visit to Bud Elkins at the veterans center? Maybe there was something he forgot to tell you while you were pretending to be a cop."

The waitress approached with Avery's coffee and asked if everyone was ready to order. Hungry as he was, Avery stood and put several dollar bills on the table.

"Give us a few more minutes," Dalquist said. She retreated, and he turned to Avery. "Before you go, let me explain our purpose here. A man who owns a nearby ranch and goes by the name Louis Page is really Earl Page, a former DEA agent who stole five million dollars from a drug cartel many years ago. The woman who lives with him is Loretta Page, Kim Ward's cousin. We think Loretta can help clear Kerney's name."

"Why should I believe this?"

Clayton gave him a frosty look. "We have no reason to lie."

"Have you spotted an electronically controlled ranch gate any-where nearby?" Sara asked.

Avery blinked. Yesterday he'd passed it twice. "No."

Dalquist's phone rang.

Avery used the distraction to head for the door.

Clayton watched him weave his way around the tables. "He's lying."

"I agree," Sara said. "We should tail him."

"Yeah."

Dalquist ended his phone conversation. "Sheriff Root can't join us. He's detained investigating an overnight burglary. Now, what's the best way to get to the Page ranch?"

Clayton stood. "Sara and I will follow Avery. See if you can find the local fire chief. I bet he knows where the gate is and even has the access code. The station is just down the road."

"I'll go there now," Dalquist said.

The waitress reappeared just as they were leaving. Sara left a large tip to cover inconveniencing her as they hurried out.

———

The night before in his Duncan hotel room, Muniz had studied high-definition NSA satellite photographs of ranches in and around Alma. He zeroed in on one that had CCTV cameras at various locations, a cell tower, satellite dishes, a large solar array, an electronic gate with a camera and speakerphone, and a backup generator for emergency power.

It smacked of somebody who paid attention to details and was pre-pared for either an incursion or a siege.

Convinced he'd found Earl, he used latitude and longitude coordi-nates from the satellite images and emailed a completed criminal com-plaint to Hodges, requesting she get an arrest warrant for Earl Matson Page as soon as possible. She promised to get right on it.

He left Duncan two hours before dawn without hearing back from her. As soon as he entered the Apache National Forest, his phone service went dead. With the rising sun in his eyes, he drove on an empty, twisting highway through high-country forests and meadows, glancing impatiently every now and then at his phone. It didn't show any signal strength until he crossed into New Mexico. There were no waiting messages.

He pulled off the pavement and speed-dialed Sam's number. It rang once and went dead. He tried several more times before giving up and driving on. He stopped in front of the post office in the tiny ranching settlement of Mule Creek and reached for his phone just as it rang.

"The warrant has been signed," Sam said. "You should have it on your tablet."

"Thanks," Muniz said, checking. The warrant was there. He resisted the impulse to ask what had taken her so long.

"Want me to ask for local law enforcement assistance?"

"No, I want to look around first."

"Ten-four, and congratulations."

"Not yet, Sam. Not yet." He disconnected. When he got to Glenwood, he topped off the tank at the gas station, and watched a man leave the diner, cross to the cabins, and drive away in an unmarked police unit with New Mexico plates. Curious, he found the owner, Darryl Wheatley, in the office and asked who he was.

"Cop, same as you," Wheatley replied sullenly.

"Don't leave me breathless, waiting for more," Muniz snapped. "What else can you tell me?"

Wheatley's attitude wilted. "Okay, okay. His name is Avery and he's with the state police. Checked in yesterday. Asked me if I knew of anybody with a cell tower on their property. The wife said he asked her the same thing."

"Well, do you?" Muniz demanded.

Wheatley ran a finger over his mustache. "Can't say that I do."

Muniz wondered how many locals were being paid for their silence. Security and fences kept people out, but money passed around to the locals might give Page an early warning system for a fast getaway.

Through the office front window, he saw two men and a woman cross the highway to the cabins. He didn't recognize the men, but something about the woman clicked. It was the accused ex-cop's wife, Sara Brannon.

Apparently it was about to become open season on his old buddy. Muniz watched the younger man and Brannon drive away in an SUV. The older man left in another SUV, headed in the opposite direction.

Wheatley stared at Muniz with wary eyes.

"How much does Page pay you to keep people away from his ranch?"

Wheatley blinked. "What do you mean?"

Muniz reached across the counter, grabbed Wheatley by the shirt, and pulled him close. "You're going to tell me where the Page ranch road is, or I'm going to have federal and state tax agents climbing up and down your backside tomorrow."

Wheatley shook his head. "I'll tell you."

Muniz released his grip. "Talk."

Wheatley talked. Muniz was out the door before Wheatley stopped blathering.

———

Sheriff Merlin Root had called Page the day before about Dalquist's request for a morning meeting in Glenwood, so he knew the wolves were circling. Late into the evening, after attending to final details, he spent hours with Loretta, holding her hand, reminiscing when she was awake, listening to her labored breathing while she slept. She was almost gone now, her once-sparkling eyes a thing of the past.

After breakfast, Jack refused to stay at the house, even when Page told him he'd be leaving the gate open.

"Makes me no never-mind," Jack said. "I'll put a shot over their bow, or into their keel, when they come sailing past."

"Don't be foolish," Page said. Jack shuffled behind his walker out the front door to his truck, beeped his horn, and drove away.

Page stacked dishes in the sink and was about to look for Alice when she appeared. "I've been thinking we should move Loretta into the safe room with you," he suggested.

"There's no need," she replied, with tears in her eyes.

Page dropped the pan he was holding and took the stairs two at a time, his heart pounding. Last night he'd promised her to be there when the time came. An empty prescription bottle stood on the bedside table. She'd deliberately left the world without him.

Did he have time to bury her? He kissed her and covered her face with a sheet. His phone rang. The screen displayed Jack's number. Before he could tell him about Loretta, Jack told him that Merlin Root was at the gate.

"Says he needs to see you right away," he added.

Page decided it was better not to tell Jack his daughter was dead. "I'll let him in. Hold him at your place for a few minutes, if you can."

"Okay," Jack said, disconnecting.

Page turned to find Alice, her face tear-stained, standing behind him, a suitcase in hand. "I won't stay in the safe room. I can't. I want to leave now."

"Okay, but do it quick and don't stop for anybody."

"She made a video on her phone for the police."

"She told me."

"I have a copy. Who should I give it to?"

"I don't care, but do as she asked. And thank you, for all you've done."

Alice nodded, turned, and left, her heels clicking down the staircase.

Page watched her car speed down the ranch road and glanced at his phone screen. Root was in his patrol vehicle at the gate. He waited until Alice left the property and Root passed through, then hit the code to keep the gate open.

There was no time to bury Loretta. He'd put her in the fireproof safe room. It would be her tomb, and he'd burn the damn house down around her.

He picked Loretta up, carried her gently downstairs, and arranged her on the bed. She'd dressed for the occasion, wearing a lovely gown he'd bought her in London. On a sleeve she'd pinned an envelope addressed "To whom it may concern." The contents had to be about Kim Ward's murder.

He sealed the safe room door wondering who would bury her. Maybe it didn't matter.

In the library, he stuck a fifteen-round semiautomatic Beretta in his waistband at the small of his back, went to the kitchen, and opened all the gas valves on the stove. He did the same at the boiler and water heater in the garage and the barbecue grill on the back deck. He closed all the doors and windows and set his phone to the app icon that would ignite the kitchen stove burners.

Finished, he stood and waited at the top of the driveway, wondering what made Merlin Root think he could kill him, and who would be next in line.

———

A blowout on the highway a quarter mile before the county road turnoff that led to the ranch gate slowed Avery down. As he threw the shredded tire and jack into the trunk of his unit, a black Explorer with U.S. government plates flew past, its left turn signal flashing. Avery got a partial look at the license plate. It matched one of the DEA units that had been registered at the cabins.

He cranked the engine and followed. On the washboard county road, the Explorer kicked dust and small pebbles that gouged his windshield. Up ahead, it turned off and barreled through an open gate. Avery stayed with him. Behind, he could see a faint dust cloud and wondered if he had a tail.

———

Merlin Root had one simple goal: kill Page before any cops could talk to him. After he'd lied to Dalquist about being unable to meet, his secretary had barged in with a fax printout of a new DEA fugitive warrant advisory on Earl Matson Page from the U.S. attorney in El Paso. Within minutes he was on the twisting mountain highway running silent code three to Alma.

He'd been on Page's payroll for seven years, pulling in enough money to cover his son's drug rehabilitation and put a large chunk aside. He wasn't about to let his life go down the tubes.

As Root sped past, Jack Page was out in front of his house trying to wave him down. He needed Page dead first, then he'd come back for Jack.

———

A mile in, dirt coating his cracked windshield, Avery saw a timber-frame house close to the road, and an old man standing outside behind a walker firing shotgun rounds at the Explorer. Up ahead, out of range, a sheriff's unit, lights flashing, accelerated.

The old man swung the shotgun on Avery, and he ducked low behind the wheel. A round shattered the right passenger-door window. He drove faster, waiting for another round, trying to close on the Explorer. In his rearview, he saw the old man pushing his walker toward a pickup truck, the shotgun resting on the handrails.

———

Merlin Root heard gunfire. In his rearview mirror he saw a swerving black Explorer followed by an unmarked state police cruiser. Behind it was Jack Page's pickup truck. Cursing, Root punched the accelerator.

———

Sara had followed Avery on the winding county road, staying as far back as possible, following the dust kicked up by his vehicle. She barreled through the open gate to the ranch, with the sound of gunfire echoing up ahead in the distance.

Clayton retrieved his Glock 9mm and Sara's SIG Sauer 9mm from the glove box. They were locked and loaded. "What are we in for?"

Sara shook her head. "Nothing good."

———

Page watched the approaching vehicles. Merlin Root in his SO unit was barely in the lead, a black Explorer on his heels, followed by what surely had to be an unmarked state police vehicle. Jack, in his truck, was back a ways, but gaining ground, firing an occasional .45 round out the open driver's-side window. That old boy just never quit. Behind him, dust from the ranch road signaled more company.

Page smiled. It was turning into a perfect recipe for a great exit.

Root screeched his unit to a stop ten feet away, emergency lights flashing, and ran toward Page, grabbing for his holstered weapon, shouting at him to surrender.

Page shot him in the head.

The black Explorer ground to a halt next to the SO vehicle, and

Muniz stepped out, standing behind the vehicle door, handgun at the ready through the open window.

Page put the Beretta back in his waistband. "Oliver, what a surprise," he said genially.

"Don't move," Muniz ordered. "Keep your hands where I can see them."

"Of course."

A car door to the unmarked unit slammed shut.

"Who's behind me?" Muniz demanded.

"A man with a gun," Page answered.

"State police," Avery yelled, his weapon trained on Muniz's back. "Drop the weapon."

"DEA," Muniz shouted. He pulled his badge case and held it up. "Either assist me or stay the fuck out of my way."

Jack arrived before the state cop could respond, firing .45 rounds from his truck in the general direction of the state cop. His handgun empty, Jack threw it away and reached for his shotgun.

The cop shot him through the windshield. Jack's head snapped back, blood splattering the rear window.

Muniz looked away long enough for Page to find cover at the SO unit. He bent low and squeezed off two rounds that dropped the state cop like a rock.

"That wasn't smart, Earl," Muniz said.

"He shouldn't have killed Jack," Page replied.

"Tough shit," Muniz replied.

An SUV rolled to a stop ten yards from the downed cop. A woman and man took cover behind their vehicle.

"Identify yourself," Sara demanded.

"Special Agent Oliver Muniz, DEA."

"Who else is here?" Sara yelled. "Speak up."

Page stood, the Beretta discarded where Muniz couldn't see it, cell phone tucked in his back pocket. "The old man in the truck was Jack Page. Sheriff Root came here to kill me, so you wouldn't find out I'd been bribing him for years. I shot him for being stupid. The state cop got his for killing Jack. You've already met the man with his gun pointed at me. I'm Earl Page. Oliver, do you know those people?"

"The woman is Sara Brannon, and I'm guessing the man with her is the ex–police chief's Apache son. Didn't Jack get a big government check after you were declared legally dead?" Muniz asked.

"Yeah, and I felt so bad about it, I almost asked him to send it back."

"I recently discovered he never cashed it," Muniz replied. "Isn't it interesting how little things like that slip through the cracks? If a clerk had reported the check had never cleared, I would have been looking for you years ago."

"Well, here you are now."

"Quite the place."

"You like it? I put a conservation easement on the ranch, so it can't be subdivided. That should give the government fits when they try to seize it as unlawfully gotten gains."

"You've always been inventive. I'll pass that information along to our lawyers."

"Do that," Page said.

"We need to speak to Loretta Page," Sara called out.

Since exiting the vehicle, Clayton hadn't moved from behind the rear of the SUV, his semiautomatic pointed at Page's chest.

"Is she inside?" she asked.

"Yes, she is." Page reached for the phone.

"Keep your hands where I can see them," Muniz ordered.

"It's just my phone." Page turned sideways so Muniz could see it protruding from his back pocket. "I'll call her."

Page hit the icon on his phone and the house blew up behind

him, flames blowing out windows, crawling up exterior walls to the roofline.

He ducked, retrieved the Beretta, stood, and, just as he'd planned, let Muniz kill him neat and quick.

Frozen by the action, Sara watched flames engulf the structure. Clayton had moved to Paul Avery's side, checking for a pulse. He looked up, shook his head, and reached for his friend's lifeless hand.

Sara called it in, police and fire, code three, wondering how in the hell they were ever going to clear Kerney's name.

CHAPTER 32

The video left at the Grant County Sheriff's Office showed a thin old woman in a hospital bed, claiming to be Loretta Page, and swearing Kim Ward had been with her the day after Kevin Kerney reported her missing. By evening, it was all over YouTube, posted by an anonymous source, getting thousands of views.

It wasn't enough to convince NMSP Deputy Chief Robert Serrano to ask the DA to dismiss the murder charge against Kerney.

First, there was no proof the woman on the recording was who she said she was. Second, there was no way to know if she was telling the truth. Last, an unidentified person dropping off a video to the police that conveniently exonerated Kerney and posting it on YouTube might be nothing more than a well-played ruse dreamed up by a lawyer given to dramatics. Gary Dalquist fit that profile perfectly.

Serrano's reasoning vaporized when the female corpse recovered from the intact safe room at the destroyed ranch house was positively identified as Loretta Page. In an envelope found with the body was a handwritten note from Kim Ward, thanking Loretta for the loan of thirty dollars and a ride to the Deming bus station. Handwriting experts confirmed the note was authentic, corroborating Page's video statement.

Serrano received the findings before leaving to attend Paul Avery's funeral in Las Cruces. It soured his already dampened mood. Despite his recent unhappiness with Avery's performance, he'd been one of his agents, doing the job. He imagined Luis Mondragon felt the same.

At the church service for Avery, members of the state police honor guard stood solemn watch over the closed casket in the center of the transept, U.S. and New Mexico flags bracketing the officers. Family members, including Avery's ex-wife, his two children, his parents, and his three siblings sat in the reserved front row. Directly behind them, Serrano joined his chief and other high-ranking officials. Mondragon, with his officers and staff, filled the third and fourth rows. Over a hundred and fifty men and women in uniform from police and sheriff departments across the state and nation crowded into the nave.

When the eulogies ended, Serrano stood with the congregation as the casket was carried slowly down the aisle. He turned in time to spot Clayton Istee in the vestibule slipping out the front entrance. He'd heard Avery had been Istee's friend. He wondered what pain gnawed at his gut.

Outside, as the congregation dispersed for the drive to the cemetery, Chief Deputy DA Henry Larkin approached.

"Sad day," Larkin said.

Serrano nodded his assent.

"I've deposed Kerney, his wife, and Clayton. Even Dalquist gave a voluntary statement." Larkin paused to look at the crowd that had waited outside during the standing-room-only service. "We're dropping the charges against Kerney. I'll release a statement to the news media tomorrow."

"Thanks for letting me know," Serrano said. On the street in front of the church, TV satellite news teams were uploading live feeds. Little did they realize today's news would be nothing compared to tomorrow's headlines.

He spotted Mondragon on the curb and walked over.

———

The shoot-out at the Page ranch had all the ingredients to make the national television news outlets send their A-team reporters to cover the event. The drama of a DEA agent who'd disappeared into the Colombian jungle decades ago with stolen drug millions, the ex-partner who tracked him down and shot him dead, the murder of a corrupt county sheriff, and the killing of a relentless state police officer searching for the truth, were good enough. But wrap it around the shocking exposé of incest, and an astonishing deathbed revelation that cleared a retired New Mexico police chief of a forty-five-year-old murder, and it became the stuff news editors dream about.

And it was all recorded at the crime scene by reporters in front of the burned-out ranch house where the smoke-stained safe room stood like an ancient crypt amid the charred rubble and debris of a once-magnificent home.

The public couldn't get enough. Documentary TV specials were being pitched to broadcast executives. Hollywood screenwriters had scripts in development, and major national magazines had cover stories in the works.

Harassed by endless phone calls and requests for interviews, Kerney and his family, including his in-laws, fled to Mescalero, where they unplugged from the outside world. Isabel had arranged for them to stay at a lodge owned by the tribe that was tucked away near the village. Used primarily for tribal functions and ceremonies, it occasionally served as temporary lodging for family members who lived off the rez.

Soon they'd be joined by Clayton and his family, who would be staying with Isabel.

Kerney was feeling stronger every day, but he still needed additional surgery and long-term physical therapy. The muscle damage to his chest had healed nicely, as had the small puncture wound to his head. Today, none of that mattered. He had his family intact and together, his reputation restored, and a whole lot of unexciting days ahead to enjoy.

On the afternoon of their arrival, Sara, her mother, and Isabel made a grocery run to town. Dean strolled down to see the famous church that overlooked the village, while Kerney and Patrick took a hike to a decades-old burn area, now a lovely meadow reseeded and brought back to life with young, healthy trees and native grasses.

"I'm glad you're not a criminal anymore," Patrick said.

Kerney laughed. "I've been a lot of things, but never that."

"You know what I mean. Now that you're better, what are you going to do?"

Kerney stopped in his tracks. "I thought we made a deal to ranch together, at least until you go to college."

Patrick grinned. "Just checking."

Kerney wrapped his good arm over his son's shoulder. "Come on, partner, I'm good for at least another half mile before we turn around. We've got some serious thinking to do about what kind of critters to raise and what kind of puppy to get."

Later that evening, after a good meal and relaxed conversation, Dean and Barbara retired, Patrick retreated to read, and Isabel went home to wait for Clayton and the family. Wrapped in blankets, Kerney and Sara sat on the porch, listening to a coyote chorus.

"Are you doing okay?" he asked her.

Sara took his hand. "I'm getting there. I thought civilian life was supposed to be serene and mellow. Big joke."

Kerney knew if Sara needed to talk about the ranch shoot-out or the plane crash, she would. "Didn't you once say you married me because I made life interesting?"

Sara laughed. "I did, but you can dial it back a couple of notches now, cowboy."

Kerney chuckled. "Gladly."

"Will we ever conclusively know if Todd Marks killed Kim Ward?" she asked.

"Probably not, but the circumstances point firmly at him. But why bury her at Erma's to make me the suspect?"

"Jealousy?" Sara proposed. "Perhaps she told him about sleeping with you to punish him for beating her and cheating with other women."

"That's possible."

"In the end, it was a destructive, drug-fueled relationship," Sara said. "When it finally disintegrated, Todd Marks killed her."

"And wound up living with the mother of the woman he murdered."

"How could they do that?" Sara shivered and snuggled in the blanket. "Do you think it was sexual?"

"We'll never know," Kerney replied.

"I need to reach out to Renee Gleason in Duncan," Sara said. "Her son, Vic, worked for Earl Page and went missing over three years ago."

"What are you going to say to her?" Kerney asked.

"I don't know. Life isn't very tidy, is it?"

"I'll settle for a long stretch of uneventful," Kerney replied.

"Me, too." Sara sighed. "Three good men died."

"Yeah."

"Not our fault."

"Still."

Sara reached for Kerney's hand. "I know."

———

Clayton and his family showed up at the lodge the next morning. What-ever uneasiness there had been in the past between the two families seemed to have evaporated. Wendell, Hannah, and Patrick appeared perfectly comfortable with each other, Grace and Sara chatted like best friends, and Isabel whisked Dean and Barbara off for a private tour of the Mescalero Apache Cultural Center & Museum.

In some ways, Isabel remained a marvel to Kerney. Seeing her always reminded him why he'd fallen in love with her long ago in col-lege. He delighted in her friendship.

Clayton, in good spirits, with his police officer certification intact, had two possible job offers. In the kitchen, he talked to Kerney about them. A tribal conservation law enforcement officer position was vacant, and the Doña Ana County sheriff had approached him about signing on as an investigator.

He was still mulling it over with the family, but Kerney could clearly see his first choice was the rez job. But the reality of a Las Cruces house hours away, a wife with a career, and two kids in college could easily cancel out that option.

"You and Grace will make the right decision," Kerney predicted. "You always have."

Clayton shook his head. "I never want to go through what you did."

"I wouldn't have made it without you."

"Not at first."

Kerney smiled. "We can forget that part."

"You sure?"

"You're my son, we're family, and that's what really counts."

"*Guzhuguja,*" Clayton said in Apache. "Then all is in balance between us."

Kerney nodded. "I like that notion a lot."

———

Late that night when everyone was asleep, Clayton left Isabel's home and drove to a ceremonial mesa with a clear view of the Tularosa Basin and the San Andres Mountains. Once before, he'd come here to help a fallen comrade move from the Shadow World of life into the Real World beyond. Tonight, he'd do the same for Paul Avery. He placed one large rock to mark north, and a second to mark west, the direction the dead took when beginning their passage. Between the rocks, Clayton buried a photograph of Paul, surrounding it with stones to separate the image from the living world, and covered it with handfuls of dirt. In four days, when Paul was safely in the Real World, he'd return and remove all traces.

ACKNOWLEDGMENTS

During a time of sudden transition in my writing career, Marcy Posner, of Folio Literary Management, gave me support, guidance, and, most importantly, her friendship, for which I am truly grateful. My editor, Amy Cherry, brought me back home to W. W. Norton, and with her enthusiasm, attention to detail, and considerable skills, made *Residue* a better book.

How lucky can you get?